**A.C. Arthur** was born and raised in Baltimore, Maryland where she currently resides with her husband and three children. Determined to bring a new edge to romance, she continues to develop intriguing plots, sensual love scenes, racy characters and fresh dialogue; thus keeping the readers on their toes! Arthur loves to hear from her readers and can be reached through her contact form or via email at acarthur22@yahoo.com

**Marion Lennox** is a country girl, born on an Australian dairy farm. She moved on, because the cows just weren't interested in her stories! Married to a 'very special doctor', she has also written under the name Trisha David. She's now stepped back from her 'other' career teaching statistics. Finally, she's figured what's important and discovered the joys of baths, romance and chocolate. Preferably all at the same time! Marion is an international award winning author.

**Susan Meier** spent most of her twenties thinking she was a job-hopper – until she began to write and realised everything that had come before was only research! One of eleven children, with twenty-four nieces and nephews and three kids of her own, Susan lives in Western Pennsylvania with her wonderful husband, Mike, her children, and two over-fed, well-cuddled cats, Sophie and Fluffy. You can visit Susan's website at susanmeier.com

# Second Chance for Christmas

A.C. ARTHUR

MARION LENNOX

SUSAN MEIER

MILLS & BOON

First Published in Great Britain 2024
by Mills & Boon, an imprint of HarperCollins*Publishers* Ltd,
1 London Bridge Street, London, SE1 9GF

www.harpercollins.co.uk

HarperCollins*Publishers*
Macken House, 39/40 Mayor Street Upper,
Dublin 1, D01 C9W8, Ireland

# ONE MISTLETOE WISH

## A.C. ARTHUR

To those who watch Christmas movies and listen to Christmas music all year long. You rock!

# Chapter 1

"Bah, hamburger!" Ethan Malloy shouted. His skinny arms were wrapped around his chest, lips poked out and still red from the punch he'd had during the break.

Morgan Hill rubbed her temples and held back a sigh.

"It's humbug, Ethan. Say it slower this time and remember the word is *humbug.*"

He wouldn't remember. Or rather, he did know the correct pronunciation, but Ethan thought he was a five-year-old Kevin Hart, minus the cursing. So everything he said or did was in search of a chuckle or a laugh from those around him—his audience, so to speak. His personality worked Morgan's last nerve. She'd chastised herself more than once about feeling this way about a little boy. She was trained to deal with children, as she'd gone to the University of Maryland and received her bachelor's degree in elementary education. Unfortunately, there were no classes that would have prepared her for Ethan Malloy.

He was the only child of Rayford Malloy, the sixty-three-year-old president of the Temptation town council, and Ivonne Danner-Malloy, his twenty-five-year-old video-dance-queen wife. Between his father being too busy and too tired to discipline him and his mother being too young, too conceited and too everything else to be bothered, Ethan never had a chance. Those were the reasons Morgan used a good portion of her patience with the child. Morgan's granny always said—whenever Ida Mae Bonet had the displeasure of being in the presence of her brother's children—"we don't get to choose who our parents are."

That was certainly the truth, Morgan thought as she watched Ethan continue with his rendition of the scene where Ebenezer Scrooge continued to refuse heat or any other comfort for his only employee, Bob Cratchit, played by seven-year-old Wesley Walker. Wesley, unlike Ethan, knew his lines and probably the lines of everyone else in the play. He was a perfectionist and determined to prove himself to everyone in this small town, despite the fact that his father had run off and left his mother with four kids, a broken-down old Nissan and a mountain of debt. It was a shame, Morgan thought as she watched the young fella on stage, walking around and holding his head up high—even though Bob Cratchit wasn't such a proud man. But a boy at such a tender age shouldn't be faced with the gossip and cruelty that could be dished out in a small town.

They lived in Temptation, Virginia, population 14,364 as of the last census, two years ago. Temptation had a rich history and struggled to catch up with the modern world. With its ten-member town council—the majority of whom were descendants from families that had been around since the town's inception in the 1800s—and the newly elected mayor, Cinda Pullum, going toe-to-toe in battles over everything from revitalizing Mountainview Park to the weekly trash pickup, Temptation could be as lively as any of the reality shows that littered today's television channels.

The town could also be as traditional and heartwarming as an old black-and-white movie with things such as the annual Christmas Eve celebration, which included the play that Morgan and her crew of youngsters were now painstakingly rehearsing. There were two things Morgan loved about living in Temptation—the traditions and the resilience of the citizens. No matter what the people of this town had gone through—from the Civil War to the dark days of the Great Depression and the hostile times of the Civil Rights movement—they'd always bounced back and they never stopped doing the things that made the town so special in the first place. The families were the heart of Temptation, as they were determined to live in harmony in their little part of the world. More recent and localized catastrophes had hit Temptation and now, sadly, Morgan found herself living through her own test as a citizen of the town.

"You should put him out, Mama."

The soft voice of Morgan's five-year-old daughter, Lily, interrupted her thoughts.

"What?" Morgan asked.

Lily looked up from where she was sitting cross-legged on the floor with an unruly stack of twinkle lights in her lap. Her little hands had been moving over the strands in an attempt to separate the tangled mass for the last half hour. There hadn't been much progress but Lily was much more patient than Morgan would ever claim to be. She was also the prettiest little girl Morgan had seen in all her twenty-eight years.

Her daughter shook her head, two long ponytails swaying with the motion.

"He's a mess," she told Morgan. "A hot mess, like Aunt Wendy says all the time."

Morgan couldn't help it, she smiled. Wendy, her older sister by barely a year, talked a mile a minute and Lily always seemed to be around soaking up each and every word that fell out of Wendy's mouth, good or bad.

"He's trying," Morgan told her, knowing without any doubt who her daughter thought was a hot mess. "We have to give him a chance."

Lily shook her head again. "No, we don't. You're in charge."

She was, Morgan thought, even if she didn't feel that way. She hadn't wanted Ethan for the lead in the play in the first place. But Rayford had stopped by her house the Monday before Thanksgiving and told her in no uncertain terms that he expected his "boy" to have a prominent part in the play this year. Especially since this was most likely the last year the community center would be open to house the play and the Christmas celebration. Morgan and a good majority of the town had been worried about this hundred-year-old building and two others—the Plympton House, which had been converted into a hospital during the war, then restored, expanded and renamed All Saints Hospital in the sixties, and the Taylor House, a now almost dilapidated Victorian that had once been the home of the town's biggest financial benefactor. She'd been so concerned with the possible loss of three of the town's historic buildings that she hadn't had the energy to fight with Rayford about something as trivial as his son's part in a play. Now, however, she wished she'd mustered up some resistance because Lily was right, Ethan was a hot mess.

"I wanna load the presents," another child's voice called from behind Morgan and before she could move a hand, there was tugging on the hem of her shirt.

"Didn't you say it was my turn to load the presents in the sleigh, Mama? You told me last night, 'cause I'm tall enough to do it."

Morgan turned around ready to reply to her son with his dark brown eyes—slanted slightly in the corners as a result of his father's half Korean, half African American heritage—and butter-toned complexion, courtesy of Morgan's mother and grandmother, who were descendants of the Creole-born Bonets of Louisiana. His twin sister had the same features. Jack and Lily were different, not only by their gender, but they also had opposite personalities. Where Lily was quiet and somewhat serious, Jack was boisterous and playful. They were sometimes like night and day, but always the very best of Morgan and her late husband, James. Each day she looked into their precious little faces she was reminded of that fact and, at the same time, overwhelmed with love and grief.

James Stuart Hill had been a wonderful man. Kind, loving, compassionate and totally committed to his young wife and family. Morgan had met him in Baltimore, during her senior year of college. He'd been on leave from the army to finalize the sale of his late mother's convenience store and her house. An American-born Korean, Mary Kim had raised her only child alone, after his African American father had been shot to death in an attempted robbery. Although Morgan had never met Mary, she felt she'd known the woman through the great man she'd raised.

Their courtship had been fast and passionate and by the time Morgan graduated from college, she'd learned that she was pregnant. James was leaving for a year-long tour in Hawaii two weeks later. So they married quickly in Granny's backyard and then traveled to Honolulu, where she gave birth to her two precious jewels. A year later James received a temporary assignment in Virginia and Morgan came home to Temptation with her twins, where the four of them had lived a happy, normal life. Until James was shipped off to Afghanistan. He was killed a week before the twins' second birthday. Three years later, the pain of that day still had the power to take Morgan's breath away.

"Some people are only in your life for a season," Granny had said as she'd stood leaning on her cane.

They'd been at the cemetery then, the one in Maryland right next to where James had buried his mother. Hours later they were back in Temptation and Morgan was tasked with raising her two young children alone. With the love and support from her grandmother and her sister, she'd managed to make it through those first tough weeks. She'd taken a job as a first-grade teacher at the elementary school, went to church on Sundays and played all day with her babies on Saturdays. Her life had managed to move on even though there were still some days when all she wanted to do was cry for all the possibilities that had been lost.

"Marley's coming! Marley's coming!" Alana, a six-year-old playing one of Bob Cratchit's children, yelled from where she was sitting at the end of the stage.

"It's not time yet," Ethan complained. "I'm not finished saying 'bah, hamburger.'"

"He needs to shut up," Lily said with a sigh.

"You're not adding the chains this time, Mama," Jack stated loudly. As if the noisier he said it, the faster she would start doing it.

Usually, when it was time for Jacob Marley—played by Malcolm Washington, who was missing one of his front teeth—to make his ghostly appearance, Wendy, who was her part-time assistant whenever she wasn't on duty at the hospital, would knock on the desk to make the footstep sounds and rattle the bike chains in her bag. But Ethan was right, it wasn't time for Jacob's appearance quite yet.

Still, Morgan could not deny the sound of footsteps coming fast and almost furiously down the hallway toward the hall where they were rehearsing.

"Hush, children," she said as she stood.

Morgan was walking toward the door, or rather tiptoeing like she actually expected to see the ghost of Jacob Marley come through that doorway, just like she knew the now-quiet children were. The footsteps continued and so did Morgan. She was wearing her bright orange-and-fuchsia tennis shoes today, along with her black running suit, which Wendy said made her look more like a teenage track star than a grown woman. Morgan tended to ignore her older sister when it came to dressing because Wendy was a proud member of the single, sexy and seriously looking club. Whereas Morgan was a mother and a teacher and she was perfectly content with that.

"Oh!" she yelled.

"Sorry," a voice said as he reached out to grab her shoulders and keep her upright.

She'd bumped into what felt like a concrete wall and was embarrassed to discover it was simply a man's chest. Well, there was really nothing simple about this man or his chest, which she figured out the moment she stepped back and looked up at him.

He was tall with a honey-brown complexion, a strong jaw, a precisely cut goatee and seductive dark brown eyes. His shoulders were broad, the suit he wore expertly cut. His hair was wavy and black, his lips of medium thickness.

Morgan almost sighed. If this was the ghost of Jacob Marley, then she was seriously going to consider crossing over to the land of the walking dead, because standing before her was one fine-ass black man.

Gray removed his hands from her instantly. He had no choice. The warmth that had immediately spread up his arms and to his chest was so intense he thought of the heart attack that had killed his father two months ago. Sure, Gray visited his internist once a year for a physical, so he knew that he was in perfect health, but the feeling had shocked him.

*She* had shocked him.

"Are you all right?" he asked. She'd taken a step back from him, looking as if she'd seen a ghost.

A number of children had almost instantly flocked around her, as if offering their juvenile protection, should he be there for some nefarious reason. He wasn't, or at least he didn't think of it that way. Still, they were all glaring at him. Something else that made Gray uncomfortable.

"I'm fine," she answered, clearing her throat. "Can I help you with something?"

Gray didn't need anyone's help. He hadn't for a very long time, but that was not his response. At thirty years old, Gray had been running his own company for fifteen years, supervising billion-dollar deals and working with brilliant tech minds to create the most innovative products in the world. He could certainly travel back to the small, dilapidated town that had torn his family apart and take care of the sale of three measly buildings without anyone's help. Hence the reason he had secured a limited power-of-attorney document from each of his siblings. There was no need for all of them to come back to the place they all hated. He was the oldest and, as usual, he'd decided to bear the brunt of an unpleasant task.

"My name is Grayson Taylor," he told her. "I own this building."

"Oh," she'd said, taking another step back as if she was afraid he'd reach out and touch her again.

Gray frowned.

"I'm just stopping by to take a look around as I'll be selling the building hopefully in the next couple of months."

"Christmas is next month," the little girl holding tightly to the woman's hand told him matter-of-factly.

He nodded. "Yes. It is."

She was a cute little girl, with an intense stare that shouldn't have unnerved him, but just like touching the woman had, it did.

"Even though the sales probably won't be official until after the first of the year, I need to do a walk-through before then. I'll send my lawyers a report and they'll get started with the listing. If you don't mind, could you show me around?" he asked, returning his gaze to the woman.

His question was met with immediate silence and after a few seconds she shook her head. "I'm rehearsing with the children. We're just getting started with regularly scheduled rehearsals and the play is in four weeks. They have school during the day. We only have the weekends and an hour and a half in the evenings to rehearse."

Gray presumed she was telling him "no." That wasn't a word women usually used with him, but his ego wasn't bruised. This was business after all.

"Fine. I'll wait until the rehearsal is finished," he said. "Can I sit over here?"

There were chairs scattered about the spacious room, some lined directly in front of the small stage, where he suspected they were rehearsing their little play.

"You can watch me be Scrooge," a boy wearing a frizzy white wig and an oversize black tuxedo jacket with tails told him.

He'd stepped away from the woman and her entourage and motioned for Gray to follow him. Admiring the child's initiative, Gray walked behind him, leaving the still-leery gaze of the woman behind.

She didn't say another word, but moved across the room and gave instructions for the children to resume their places and continue. The little girl who had been holding her hand still stood right beside her, but the child peeked back at Gray more than once. She had questions, he thought. Who was he? Why was he here and what did that possibly mean for them? He'd stared into her pensive eyes and felt the urge to answer all her questions in a way that would make her stop looking at him with such sincere inquisitiveness. It was the strangest thought he'd ever had, especially since Gray wasn't known to get caught up in anyone's emotions about anything.

He was the strongest of the Taylor sextuplets, the first one to be born on that humid July evening thirty years ago. His brothers and sisters all shared his birthday, but none of them had ever shared the weight of being the first baby born of the first set of multiples in the town of Temptation. That had been his title for the first seven years of his life—"the first born of the first Temptation sextuplets." *The Taylors of Temptation* was what they'd named the reality show that featured his parents as they brought home their six bundles of joy and lived in the huge blue-and-white Victorian with the river at its back. As Gray recalled, the show would have been more aptly named if it had been called *Terror of the Taylors* instead.

"Do you like Christmas?"

He was yanked from his thoughts by the soft voice of the little girl who had been sneaking glances at him. Her hair was dark and long, brushing past her shoulders with red bows at the end of each ponytail. She wore jeans and a red-and-white striped sweater. Her boots had black-and-white polka dots.

"I don't know," he replied. "Do you like Christmas?"

She nodded and said, "Yes. I do. So does my mother."

As she said those words Gray nodded. "Is your mother up there directing the play?"

"Yes. Her name is Morgan Hill. She's a teacher, too."

"You're not supposed to talk to strangers," a little boy said as he came up beside the girl and pulled on her arm.

She jerked away. "He's not a stranger. His name is Grayson Taylor and he owns this building."

Gray didn't like the stoic way in which she'd mimicked his previous words.

"We don't know him, so he's a stranger," the boy, who looked a little like the girl, said. "I'm gonna tell Mama."

Gray almost smiled, but he felt his forehead drawing into a frown instead. Twins?

"No need to tell," he declared. "How about we all go up front and sit with your mother? That way she'll know where you both are."

It would also give Gray a chance to ask a few questions about the building. From the looks of the outside, he didn't think he'd get much for the building itself, but the land might be worth something. Between the sale of this building, the hospital and the house, the total should be a good chunk to split between the six of them. Not that Gray needed the money. His vision and the talented people he'd hired to work at Gray Technologies had made him a rich man years ago. No, any money that came from the properties would be what the Taylor sextuplets thought of as their father's payment for destroying their lives all those years ago.

"Mama, he wants to sit with you," the little girl said when they'd come to a stop next to the chair where her mother sat.

Morgan looked up from her clipboard and then hastily stood. "Oh, I apologize," she said. "I hope they weren't bothering you."

Now it was Gray's turn to simply stare. She was very pretty, he thought, as if he hadn't noticed that before. Her skin was smooth and unmarred by any cosmetics. Gray was used to seeing more glamorous women, from the ones he worked with to the ones trying to get into his bed. High heels, tight dresses, heavily made-up faces and beaming smiles—that's what he was used to.

Morgan was looking at him like she couldn't decide

whether to curse him out or be cordial to him. The look, coupled with the stubborn lift of her chin and the set of her shoulders, tugged at something deep inside him. Glancing away was not an option.

"He doesn't know if he likes Christmas, Mama," the little girl said.

"She's always telling," the boy added with a shake of his head.

"Hush," Morgan told them.

"Ms. Hill! Ms. Hill! Ethan forgot what to say," another child's voice exclaimed.

"I did not! I'm imposizing. That's what actors do," the boy in the white wig—who Gray now knew was named Ethan—argued.

"The word is *improvising*, Ethan, and I'd prefer if you just repeated what's written in the script," Morgan replied.

She'd moved quickly, heading to the stage where the two arguing children stood. She spoke in a voice that was much calmer than he suspected she was feeling. She guided the children to where she wanted them to stand on the stage and spoke the lines she wanted them to repeat, all while Ethan looked as if he had other, more exciting things to do.

"He thinks he knows everything," the little girl told Gray.

She'd scooted onto one of the chairs by then.

"Be quiet, Lily. Mama's gonna show Ethan who's the boss," the boy told her.

"I think he's the boss," Lily said to her brother and they both looked up to Gray.

He was just about to speak—to say what, Gray wasn't totally sure—when the lights suddenly went out. Screams were immediate and should have been expected since Gray didn't think there was anyone in this room over the age of six or seven, besides him and Morgan.

"Stay calm," he heard Morgan say over the growing

chaos of children's voices. "It's probably just a blown fuse again. I'll take care of it."

Gray slipped his phone from his jacket pocket and turned on the flashlight app, but when he attempted to take a step toward the stage, he found his moves hampered. Gray was six-two and he weighed two hundred and thirty-five pounds, which consisted of mostly muscle thanks to the ten to twelve hours a week he spent at the gym. Last year he'd run in the 5K marathon to fight diabetes and finished in under fifteen minutes, so there should have been no problem with him walking across this room to assist Morgan in whatever was going on. Except for the two sets of arms that had wrapped tightly around each of his thighs, holding him down like weights.

# Chapter 2

"Here's the fuse box," Morgan stated about two seconds before Gray's hands brushed over hers.

"I'll take care of it," he said, moving her hand to the side.

"You don't know anything about this building," she snapped. Her hand was still warm from where he'd touched her and Morgan rubbed it against her thigh as if she thought that would erase her reaction to his touch.

He was holding his phone, with its glaring light, pointed toward the fuse box, but Morgan could see the shadow of his face as he turned to look at her.

"I own this building," he replied.

Morgan huffed. "That doesn't mean you know your way around it, or how much it means to the people of this town," she quipped.

It was really hot in here. They were in the basement and Morgan tried to take a step back, but there was only a wall behind her. To her right was a door that led to the crawl space. To her left, the wall with the fuse box. Directly in front of her, the man with the flashlight and delicious-smelling cologne.

"But I do know how to turn on," he began, still watching her and, if she wasn't mistaken, moving a step closer.

Morgan tried to shift to the side, but she stumbled on some cords that were lying on the floor and ended up against his chest, again. The light from the phone wavered as his hands dropped to her shoulders, sliding down slowly as he kept her from falling. Embarrassed and irritated by the heat that had spread quickly from the hand that he'd touched moments ago to the rest of her body, Morgan tried to pull away from him. She slammed her back into the wall.

He shone the light in her face at that point, then looked at her as if he was going to…no, he wasn't, Morgan thought quickly. He wouldn't dare.

"It's the last circuit breaker," she said, hastily pointing over his shoulder. "That's the one that usually blows. It's been doing that for the past couple of months. Harry said he was going to look at it, but he hasn't had a chance."

Harry Reed owned the hardware store and worked part-time at his family's B and B. He also did handiwork around the town in his spare time, for which Morgan knew a lot of people were very grateful.

Now Grayson looked confused, which was just fine because that's exactly how Morgan was feeling.

"You just open the box and—"

He backed away from her and said, "I know how to flip the circuit breakers and turn on the lights."

The phone's flashlight moved and she could see him opening the box now.

"You're right," he told her as he began flipping the first breaker off and then on. "I don't know about this building, but I do know about fuse boxes. Turn everything off and hopefully, when you turn it back on…" He let his voice trail off as that last fuse clicked off and then…

"All power is restored," he said the moment the tight hallway they'd been standing in was once again illuminated.

Behind him, the kids who they couldn't leave in the dark room alone cheered.

"Great," Morgan replied. "Thank you."

She let out a whoosh of breath as she hurriedly slipped past him. It was a weird move, she knew, as she flattened against one wall and shimmied around the spot where he still stood, but Morgan didn't care. She simply needed to get out of that corner with him.

"That was fun," Ethan said immediately as she approached. "Can we do it again?"

"I'm hungry, Ms. Hill," Daisy Lynn added with a baleful look.

Morgan had a headache.

She looked at her watch and let out a sigh. "It's almost time for your parents to pick you up anyway. So let's get back upstairs and clean up our props. We'll rehearse again tomorrow after Sunday services," she told them.

She led the group up the basement steps and through the double doors. When they'd come down moments ago Morgan had instructed them to hold hands and onto the railing. This time, since the lights were on and probably because Morgan's thoughts were somewhere else, she hadn't instructed them to do the same. The lights were brighter in the upstairs hallways and the children ran to the main hall, where they'd been rehearsing. She was walking and thinking about him, but somehow completely forgetting that she'd left Grayson Taylor down in the basement.

"Considering running away before giving me the tour of the place?" he said from behind her.

"What?" Morgan said as she spun around to face him.

Her feet almost twisted as she did, but luckily she was able to right herself. Why had she become so clumsy around this man? "I'm not running anywhere. I have to tend to the children first," she told him.

He nodded, but didn't seem to believe her. That irritated Morgan and her headache throbbed more insistently.

"Look," she said with a sigh, "I may not be the right person to give you this tour. I'm pretty attached to this building. And to the hospital, since I was born there. That means I'm going to be pretty irritated when you knock down the buildings or sell them off to some developer who'll knock them down to build a strip mall or some other big-city franchise that we don't need around here."

Damn. She hadn't meant to say all that, at least not to his face. He slipped his hands into the front pockets of his pants and watched as she wondered what to say next. Nothing about her personal feelings, she decided. Temptation was her home. These buildings, the landmarks and the people all meant something to her. She understood that it would be difficult for outsiders to understand that connection, but Grayson Taylor wasn't an outsider. At least, he shouldn't have been.

"Millie Randall works with the chamber of commerce. Her office is in city hall. She'll be the better person to show you around. They open Monday at nine," she said with finality and turned to walk away.

"It's not my intention to knock anything down," he told her. "I plan for a quick sale."

"That's your business, Mr. Taylor," she replied without turning to face him.

"I'm not your enemy," he said when he'd easily caught up with her.

"And you're not a friend," she replied. "Now, if you'll excuse me, I have to go."

She did have to go. The children were waiting for her.

Their parents would arrive soon and she needed to clean up the hall and then get Lily and Jack home to feed them dinner. She did not have time to hang around at the community center with the man who could single-handedly take the building away from them. She definitely did not have to like how he looked and smelled, and damn, how it felt whenever he touched her. No, she didn't and wouldn't like any of that. Morgan promised herself she would not.

Gray ran fast and hard across the field of crisp frost-tipped grass. The air was cool and the sky a dull gray. The scents of nearby animals and the sounds of early-morning farm life wafted all around. This wasn't the NordicTrack he used in his home gym, or the three-mile track that looped around the top level of the condo building where he lived. Gray ran on either of those on a daily basis. When he was out of town on business, the five-star hotels where he stayed always had state-of-the-art gyms with top-of-the-line equipment, including pools where he could indulge in slow leisurely laps to relax his muscles after a hard workout.

The brochure on the table in the room had called it the Owner's Suite, but to him, it looked like a top floor had been added to an old horse's stable.

Gray had been out for more than an hour and he was sure he'd run well over five miles by now and seen more grassy hills and fog-covered mountaintops than he had in all his life. It would have been a breathtaking view for someone who didn't prefer the city life of bright lights, fast cars and hot women.

The latter, Gray thought as he made his way back to the portion of the Haystack Farm & Resort he'd rented, was what had him up at the crack of dawn. A hot woman camouflaged in a baggy running suit and surrounded by a circus of kids. He'd thought about her all night long. To the point where what sounded to him like someone strangling a rooster woke him just before he'd embarrassed himself with only the second wet dream of his life.

His feet crunched over the graveled walkway that led to the stables and Gray slowed down to a brisk walk. Stretching his arms above his head as he continued to move, he inhaled deeply and exhaled quickly, hoping the immediate slaps of cool air would erase the memories. All of them.

It didn't work. As he approached the steps Gray stopped. He did a series of three quick squats, then lowered his back leg and began stretching. She wasn't tall, he thought as he switched legs, his hands resting on his thigh as he lunged. Five feet and two or three inches tall, tops. She wasn't built, either. Her clothes had been loose but Gray had always been able to spot a great female body. Hers was tight, compact, curvy in all the right places and trim in the others. She had intelligent eyes and a stubborn chin. Her hair was short, styled but not overdone. Her face was cute, not gorgeous, but stick-in-the-mind pretty.

Gray sighed and stood up straight. He put his hands on his hips and let his head fall back as he looked up to the sky. No clouds, no sun, just a blanket of slate. Only one day in this small town and he missed Miami already.

He ran up the steps and let himself into the loft suite that carried the faint smell of the air fresheners that were plugged into every electrical socket in the space, and the earthier scents of hay and horseflesh. There were no five-star hotels in Temptation. Only two bed-and-breakfasts and this fully functional farm, which also billed itself as a resort. There were no televisions, either. No internet connection and no phones. The signal on his cell was weak, but the electrical outlets worked well enough so at least they kept his phone and tablet charged.

The shower worked, he thought with a frown. Thank the heavens for that. Stripping as he made his way back to the bathroom, Gray reminded himself why he was here.

To inspect the buildings and put them on the market. That was all.

When he stepped beneath the spray of hot water, he whispered again, "That is all."

But the moment he closed his eyes and tipped his head beneath the water, he saw her face. Big hazel eyes, a pert nose and small, very kissable lips. He'd wanted to kiss her as they'd been standing in that dark hallway. When he'd stepped closer to her it had been his intention to lean in and touch his lips to hers. It wasn't going to be gentle, rather demanding, hungry and needy. Gray dropped his head at the thought. He didn't need anyone. He never had.

If it was for sex, which his body was telling him with no uncertainty that it was, then he could call any number of women the moment he arrived back in Miami. He did not need to acknowledge his arousal around some small-town woman with a chip on her shoulder. Except that when she'd brushed up against him, his erection had come quick and hard, both times. Just that brush of her soft body against his had made him want her. Gray cursed. It had been a very long time since he'd wanted anything, or anyone.

He picked up the bar of soap and used the cloth he'd grabbed before entering the shower. Building a thick lather, he placed the soap back into the vintage silver tray and began to wash the sweat from his body. Only each stroke of that warm and sudsy cloth over his skin had him aching more with need. After the first few seconds Gray wanted to drop that cloth and wrap his hands around his burgeoning length. He wanted to stroke and stroke until there was a blessed release. His eyes opened quickly with that thought as he gritted his teeth and fought like hell to keep his hands on any other part of his body aside from his throbbing arousal.

When she'd looked up at him he'd wanted to whisper her name.

*Morgan.*

Morgan Hill.

She was just a woman.

Just a woman that he wanted to sink so deep inside of that everything about this dismal small town and what it had done to his family would be washed from his mind, once and for all. Gray had no idea if that would work, or if he even wanted to bother. Morgan had children, which meant there was most likely a father to those children in the picture somewhere. That was another entanglement Gray did not have the time or the inclination to manage.

With jerking movements he continued to wash and then rinsed beneath the steamy water. Once his shower was complete he dressed and sat at the little desk that faced the window. The view was breathtaking, if one liked such a thing. Gray did not. A country setting, simple living— neither was for him. He reached into his leather bag and pulled out the files he'd brought with him. Without internet access in this room, he would have uninterrupted time to go over his most recent sales projections and R&D reports. There was no doubt that once he logged into his email there would be numerous issues for him to address. Even on a Sunday morning.

His mother used to love Sundays, Gray thought as he stared down at the papers, then up to the window. She loved walking in the sand and watching the tide roll in just outside the house they'd lived in on Pensacola Beach. That was the only time Olivia Taylor had looked peaceful, Gray recalled. The only time after his father had left them.

"Hello?" Gray answered his cell phone, which had begun to ring loudly, snatching him out of his thoughts.

"Hi. How's it going?"

It was his sister Gemma. She was the oldest of the girls and the one Gray had been closest to since the two of them had taken care of the others when their mother began to get sick.

"Slowly" was his tired reply. "Apparently, the chamber of commerce doesn't open on Sundays. Nothing in this sleepy little town does."

"Weekends as a means of relaxation should be a crime," Gemma replied with her ready humor. "This is the only day of the week that I have all to myself so I don't want to hear one negative thing about it."

Gemma was a hair stylist. She owned one of the largest and most reputable salons in Washington, DC.

"I'm not complaining," Gray told her. "But I won't lie, if I could get this taken care of sooner, rather than later, I'd be much happier."

"I don't know that I've ever seen you happy, Gray," his sister said softly.

Oh, no, Gray thought with a shake of his head. They were not about to have this conversation. Gemma was the only one of his siblings who believed in the fairy tale of love, even though she'd yet to find her knight in shining armor. The fact that their mother had nursed a broken heart until her dying day didn't seem to matter to his sister. Gemma staunchly believed that love would always find a way. Gray usually allowed his sister her dream, but today he wasn't in the mood to humor her.

"First thing tomorrow morning I plan to march into city hall and speak with the rep at the chamber of commerce. It'll be good to get an idea of what the buildings are currently being used for."

"Why? I thought we were just going to sell them," Gemma replied. "You don't need that type of information to put them on the market."

Gray had thought of that last night as he'd left the community center. He hadn't needed to personally come back to Temptation, nor did he need an escort to show him around the buildings, either. It would have been much simpler to call his attorney and let him deal with the Realtors and the sale, an action he could have easily taken from his desk in his Miami office. There was just one thing stopping Gray from handling this the way he would any other business deal.

His mother.

"She would have wanted to know," he admitted quietly.

Gemma remained silent for a few seconds.

"She would have," she eventually agreed. "She'd always wanted to know about the town and how it was doing after we'd left. One of her greatest heartbreaks was that the loss of the money from our show and how the scandal that had followed our departure would have a negative effect on the town. She would have been happy to know the buildings were being used for something good, and she might not want us to sell them if they are."

Gray rubbed a hand over his forehead. "I've thought about all that, too. Garrek and Gen were on the fence about selling when I spoke to them," he said.

"Gia's trying to open another restaurant, so she says the money from the sale would come in handy," Gemma added.

"And Gage," Gray said before sighing as he thought about the youngest brother.

Gemma made a sound that mimicked his frustration with their brother. "He's so busy putting in hours at the hospital that he barely had time to sign that paper you had me take to him," she said and then sighed again. "It would have been a lot better if all of us could have gotten together and talked this through. Mama would not be happy knowing that it's been years since we were all in the same place, at the same time."

"We were born in the same place, at the same time," Gray stated drily.

"Now you sound like Gen, hating the way we came into this world."

Gray shook his head at that remark. "No, I don't hate that we were born. I just don't like all the attention that came afterward and the way this town that supposedly loved the Taylors of Temptation weren't there for us when everything came crashing down."

It didn't matter, Gray told himself immediately. When his mother decided to leave Temptation, her grandfather offered his vacation home in Pensacola Beach for her and the children to live in. His father, in a rare moment of generosity, hadn't contested the divorce or the spousal support and alimony payments. Eventually, years later, their family began to feel the benefit of Theodor's successful business endeavors through higher monthly payments. It was apparently much easier to write a check to his wife and six children than it was to live in the same house with them. The bottom line was that they hadn't needed anyone from this town back then and Gray definitely didn't owe them anything now.

"Look, I plan to have this wrapped up in the next day or so. I'll send a group email when the listings are up and then keep everyone posted on the sales."

"Right," Gemma said. "Business as usual. That's fine, Gray. I'll be sending out my gifts in the next couple of weeks, so be sure to check the mail at your condo."

Gray resisted the urge to sigh again. Instead, he squeezed the bridge of his nose. "You send us all Christmas gifts every year like you're our secret Santa. We're not kids anymore, Gemma."

"No," she said adamantly. "We're not. But Mama loved Christmas. She always had gifts for us under that tree no matter the circumstances. It's the least I can do to keep her alive in my heart, Gray. I know all of you have your way of dealing with the hand we were dealt in life, but this is mine so don't try to take it away from me."

After a few seconds of silence Gray replied, "I wouldn't think of it."

Gemma was right—she needed to deal with her life, in her way, just as the rest of his siblings did. Just as he did.

Gray ended the call with his sister and he was able to get lots of work done as the hours passed. Now, at close to six in the evening, he realized he hadn't eaten all day. Grabbing his jacket, Gray left the room and headed into town. He had driven to Virginia from Miami, deciding that he might enjoy the peace and quiet of the fifteen-hour drive. It was a drastic change from using his private jet to travel the globe and hiring drivers for the shorter distances when he traveled for business. This time it was personal, and Gray was certain he could handle maneuvering the streets of the small town.

That thought was short-lived. Almost an hour later, after going up and down street after street looking for a restaurant of his liking, Gray finally parked his car in front of Pearl's Diner on the corner of Sunset Drive and Evergreen Way. The first thing he noticed when he stepped out of his Porsche Panamera Turbo—besides the fact that the *i* and the *e* in *diner* were out on the lighted sign hanging in front of the establishment—was all the Christmas decorations. Thanksgiving had only been two days ago, but the holiday season was clearly in full swing in Temptation. Black lampposts positioned about six to eight feet apart had wreaths around the lighted tops and huge red ribbons in the center. Strung above the wires holding the street lights were large snowflakes formed from stencils and cheerful white lights. Funny, when he'd driven into town yesterday he hadn't seen any of this, or perhaps he hadn't wanted to see it. Could Gemma's earlier reference to how much his mother had loved Christmas be the cause of his revelation now?

Another reason he may not have noticed the decorations before—the more logical one that Gray preferred to consider—was that he'd avoided driving through the main streets of town when he arrived. Instead, he'd made a wrong turn the moment he entered the town from the highway, forcing his GPS to reconfigure the directions to the community center. That had worked just as Gray planned and he'd ended up traveling through narrow streets lined with houses before pulling up on Century Road, where the old planked structure of the community center sat on a corner. Gray hadn't wanted anyone to see him driving his fancy car through the old town. He recalled from his mother's stories how quickly news—good or bad—traveled in Temptation and how much the townsfolk enjoyed spreading such news.

Gray was still standing in front of the diner, looking at the holiday decorations, when he was approached by the first person in Temptation to lend credence to his mother's words.

"Well, aren't you a sight for these sore old eyes," a woman said. "You and that spicy little car you're driving."

She'd walked right up to him and now had a hand resting on his arm. Her perfectly coiffed dark brown hair was streaked with what looked like bronze in the front. Wrapped around her shoulders was some sort of black cape and she wore a festive red scarf.

"Good evening," Gray finally said, remembering once again how everyone in small towns thought they knew everybody else.

They'd all thought they knew how good a father and husband Theodor Taylor was, until the day he'd up and left his family in that big old house on Peach Tree Lane. So had Gray's mother, Olivia, and his siblings. That had been the moment of truth for Gray, one he would never forget, no matter how many years had passed, or how far away he managed to get from this town.

"You look awfully familiar," she said, squinting her eyes and moving in closer.

Her perfume was strong and her fingers clenched his arm a little tighter as if she thought the contact might jog her memory. For as much as Gray would like to have gone unnoticed a little while longer, he knew his presence would be made known eventually. Especially after he'd already introduced himself to the pretty woman at the community center last night.

"I'm Grayson Taylor and I'm just heading into the diner to have dinner," he told her.

"My word, Grayson Taylor," she said, a smile spreading instantly across her face. "The last time I saw you I don't think you came past here."

*Here* was the level near her thigh that she'd shown with a motion of her hand.

"How old were you then? Six or seven? That's when Olivia packed up and shuffled you poor children out of your home in the dark of night." She was shaking her head as she talked. "Shame the way she did that. You should have been allowed to grow up in your home, around the people that loved and cared about you all."

What she really meant was the people that loved all the revenue that the reality show his family had starred in brought to the town. The birth of the sextuplets had come at a time when Temptation was struggling to use its historic background to bring tourists and, subsequently, money into the town. The show had been a savior for the town, but a death sentence to his parents' marriage.

"I was seven years old back then, ma'am, and I really am hungry, so if you'll please excuse me," he said and attempted to walk away.

"Oh, don't go in there. Pearl doesn't work on Sundays.

Her daughter, Gail, does, but she's not as good a cook as her mama. You come on over to the hospital with me. They're having their annual charity ball and that food will be catered. Hopefully, it'll be better than Gail's since I know they paid this fancy new chef a ton of money."

She looped her arm around his and had started walking them across the street before Gray could accept or decline her offer.

"Ma'am, I'd rather not intrude," he began after a couple of steps.

"You can drop the *ma'am* and call me Millie. Millie Randall, that's what everybody around here calls me. And you're not intruding. We heard your daddy died a couple months back, poor fella. And with a young lady in his bed. At least that's what we heard." Millie whispered those last sentences.

She shook her head and continued before Gray could interject.

"So I suspect you're here about his properties. The hospital is one of them, so you might as well come on inside and see what you own."

First, Gray wasn't certain why the whispering was necessary, since they were the only two people outside at the moment. Second, her assumptions about his father's death were wrong and totally inappropriate, but still, he tried to keep his irritation under control.

"It's a pleasure to meet you, Mrs. Randall," he said because he'd already noted the gigantic diamond on her ring finger and he recalled Morgan mentioning her name last night. "I really don't think this is a good idea. I have other business to take care of."

"Always in a rush," Millie said with a shake of her head. She took two steps away from Gray and then turned back. "You get that from your mother. Olivia was always trying to move faster than she should have. Running to those fancy doctors and using all that money to produce that ungodly pregnancy."

"Wait a minute," Gray said, finally fed up with this woman and her comments.

He didn't give a damn who she was or where she worked. As he'd told Gemma earlier, he didn't need anyone in this town to show him the buildings he owned. He was simply trying to honor his mother's memory by coming back here and doing business as civilly as he could. That didn't mean he had to deal with any of this petty, small-town BS in the process.

"I'm here to handle current business, not to rehash the past," he told her curtly.

It was the best he could do, especially since instinct and habit were telling him to defend his mother and put this busybody in her place.

"Well, that's fine," she snapped and continued walking toward the building. "But we don't rush around in Temptation. It's not our way, so you'll just have to get used to that."

Gray frowned as he reluctantly walked behind her. He didn't want to get used to anything in Temptation.

# Chapter 3

"You're just not used to being close to men anymore," Wendy said as she zipped the back of Morgan's dress.

Morgan turned away from the full-length mirror and closed the closet door it hung on. "I don't have a problem being around men, I just don't like arrogant and snobbish men," she replied.

After stewing about the issue all night she'd finally broken down and told Wendy about meeting Grayson Taylor last night. Lily and Jack were staying with her grandmother tonight, while she attended the annual holiday charity banquet at the hospital with Wendy. The event was to benefit the Widows and Orphans Fund, which had been started years ago by an anonymous mother who at one point had lost everything, but then came into a huge sum of money and wanted to give back. No one in town had ever seen this woman in person, but they'd accepted the money and agreed to continue the efforts, using each year's proceeds to help support single mothers with young children.

Wendy had worked at the hospital for the past five years. So Morgan had been attending this event before becoming a widow herself. She'd always believed in its purpose, and now, being a single parent, she knew firsthand how important it was to have assistance. In her corner were Granny and Wendy. Her parents had been gone since Morgan was a sophomore in high school, when her father received a job offer in Australia.

"I hear he's sexy as hell," Wendy continued.

She was standing near Morgan's dresser now, fluffing her loose curls. Her older sister was gorgeous, from her five-seven height to the generous curves she'd been blessed with and the bubbly personality that had landed her as captain of the cheerleading squad in high school. They shared the same creamy brown complexion and wide, expressive eyes, but that's where the similarities ended. Where Morgan loved the fall and Christmas carols, Wendy wanted to swim in the lake every day of the summer and detested the cold.

"All of them," she continued. "There are three boys and three girls. I don't think any of them signed over the rights for the show to go into syndication or onto DVD, but Granny told me just the other day how good-looking they all had grown up to be."

"And how would she know?" Morgan asked after she'd slipped her feet into the four-inch-heel platform red shoes that she'd treated herself to. "You know she hates the internet. That computer we bought her two years ago would have inches of dust on it if she wasn't such a neat freak."

Wendy shook her head. "And you know that's the truth," her sister agreed while laughing. "But you know her and Ms. Dessa love reading the tabloids down at the supermarket. She said there was a story about them a few months back when the father died."

Morgan pulled at the hem of the dress that she'd already

deemed too short. Wendy thought it was perfect—red, festive and flirty, she'd said. Morgan figured she was either going to freeze her buns off tonight trying to be cute, or fall flat on her face the moment she walked into the Olivia Taylor Hall at the hospital.

Olivia Taylor had been the equivalent of the Virgin Mary in Temptation. Thirty years ago, when she and her husband had been bold enough to travel to Maryland so that she could be artificially inseminated with multiple eggs, she'd shown every women in Temptation that it was okay to take their fate in their own hands. Morgan, and just about everyone who lived in Temptation, knew the story.

"They both need to find something else better to do during the day," Morgan said, grabbing her shawl from the bed and heading for the door.

Wendy laughed as she followed her out. "They need a man! Two of them, or maybe one and they can share."

Morgan shook her head. "You're ridiculous," she said.

The shawl would be for when she was inside the hospital. As for right now, her long wool coat was warranted as the temperature was expected to drop below freezing later that evening. While Morgan loved the season and the crisp cold winter air, she did not like shivering and shaking from the deep freeze that Temptation was known to receive this time of year.

"Not ridiculous, just practical," Wendy said while slipping into her short leather jacket. "What woman wouldn't want a nice handsome hunk of man to keep her warm on a night like this?"

Morgan stepped out into the evening air, recalling immediately how warm she'd felt each time Grayson had touched her. She continued walking to the car, feeling the cold breeze as it whipped through the air.

"I don't have any problem keeping myself warm," she

told her sister as she climbed into the passenger side of Wendy's SUV.

Still, she was shivering when she finally pulled the door closed, her traitorous body begging to differ.

"This wing of the hospital was named after your mother," Millie told Gray.

Her voice had begun to grate on him, like nails sliding over a chalkboard. She'd been talking, mixing historical facts about the town with quick jabs of gossip and innuendo, like they were part of some insider tour. If they were, Gray didn't want to partake—not a second longer.

"I think I've seen enough," he told her. He was certain that the twenty minutes that she'd taken to walk him around the hospital had been nineteen minutes too long in her company.

Based on this tour alone, he knew exactly what he would do once he finally found a spot with internet access. Gray would tell his attorney to sell, sell, sell! This town was just as bland and behind the times as he'd recalled and he would be glad to leave first thing tomorrow morning. Actually, he thought as Millie touched her jeweled fingers to his arm for about the billionth time, he would be more than glad.

"So you see, it makes sense for you to be here tonight at the charity event," she told him, blinking those unnaturally long lashes at him.

She'd been doing that as if she thought the action was somehow coercing him. It wasn't. Instead, that action and Millie's comments were beginning to irritate the hell out of him.

"I'm really not up for attending any type of event," he began. "Besides, I'm not dressed for anything formal."

"Oh, we rarely do formal here in Temptation. You should remember that," she chided, slipping her hand right through his arm again and turning him toward glass double doors at the end of the hallway.

The tiled floor was old here, just as Gray had noticed throughout the rest of the facility. There were a number of areas that could be refreshed and updated, he'd thought as he walked through. Windows could have better coverings, computers at the main desk on all of the floors looked to be at least ten years old, which in any field these days was not good. A hospital especially should have the most up-to-date equipment possible.

"You see we kept your mother's name right over the doors, just the way they were when we put them there years ago. She never did come back to see it, though. Her cousin, BJ, never understood that. She always thought Olivia was ungrateful, but you know how family can be," Millie continued as she walked him closer to those doors.

"It was very nice of the town to dedicate this portion of the hospital to my mother. I'm sure she was very grateful," Gray told her.

"Not enough to come back, though," Millie continued with a shake of her head. "But tonight's about new beginnings. We all start afresh with the New Year, so this charity dinner gives us a head start. You know, moneywise."

Gray nodded because that was another point Millie had made sure to hit home. The town needed money.

"Really," Gray said, coming almost to a stop before they could get closer to the doors. "I should get going. I have emails to send and calls to make."

Millie shook her head. "Always got something better to do. Just like your father. It's just a dinner, Grayson. And you said you were hungry, so come in, sit down and have a bite to eat. Then you can rush on and do what you have to do. But I'll tell you, if you're thinking of selling these buildings and running out on this town again, I beg you to think again. Whether you like it or not this is your heritage. It's where you were born and where your children should have a chance to grow up and experience all the things you never did."

"I don't plan on having children," Gray replied immediately.

He had no idea why he'd told her that, just felt the words slipping out without his permission.

Millie's smile spread slowly. "You never know what this world's got in store for you. Despite what your mother thought at first, she soon found out that everything doesn't always go as planned."

Gray was just about to tell her he was totally different from both his parents. He was going to assure her that she was wrong and that he would definitely not be getting married or having any children. Ever.

Then she approached. He'd heard the clicking of heels across the floor but hadn't bothered to look away from Millie until the other woman was standing right there behind the older one. He'd glimpsed at the bright red of her dress first, then realized how little material there actually was as his gaze soon rested on her stocking-clad legs. Then moved slowly to the swell of her pert breasts over the bodice. Her hair was tapered on the sides and curly on top, her makeup light, but alluring.

There was another woman with her, Gray noticed when he figured staring was probably just as rude as it was embarrassing on his part.

"Hi, Millie. You trying to keep all the handsome men out here with you tonight?" the third woman asked, her smile wide and her eyes cheerful as she looked at Gray.

She was a couple inches taller than Morgan, who he had noticed was wearing some pretty sexy heels tonight. The other woman also had on heels. Her hair was longer, curls relaxing on her shoulders as long, icicle-like earrings dangled and glowed. *Pretty* wasn't a bold enough word for this one and the tight black dress she wore, with a festive red choker that had small jingle bells dangling from it, was definitely something to stare at. Still, Gray's gaze went right back to Morgan.

"Not at all," Millie said, her smile faltering. "This is Grayson Taylor. You know, he's one of *the* Taylors of Temptation."

Gray didn't like that title any more than he liked the way Millie had said it—as if he was *the* Dracula of Transylvania.

"Hello, Grayson Taylor," the woman said as she extended her hand to him. "I'm Wendy Langston. I'm one of the Langstons of Temptation. We've been here forever, too, but most of us have done the smart thing and escaped as well." She chuckled and so did Gray, liking her instantly.

"Please," he said, taking her hand and shaking it. "Call me Gray."

"Well, Gray, you should come on in and join the fun. You can sit with me and my sister, Morgan. I hear Magnolia Daniels was this year's caterer. She just graduated from some fancy culinary college in New York, so she was anxious to come back home and show us all her skills," Wendy told him.

"My sister attended a culinary school in New York as well," he said. "She owns her own restaurant now and teaches at the college. I wonder if it's the same school Magnolia attended."

"There's only one way for us to find out," Wendy said as she easily stepped in front of Millie to snag Gray's arm.

This time, Gray wasn't as irritated. In fact, he thought, he could appreciate Wendy's cheerful demeanor. He could also like the fact that Morgan had looked a bit chagrined at the way her sister so easily stepped up to him.

They walked through the double doors that Gray had sworn he hadn't wanted to enter and he was pleasantly surprised, at least for a few moments. The lights were dim and there were tables all around the floor, covered in festive red cloths with what looked like little gingerbread houses in the center. Holiday music played softly in the background as fifty or so people walked around or hovered over the punch table.

"I'm going to get something to drink," he heard Morgan say and then looked up in enough time to see her walking hastily away from the table where Wendy had led him.

"I believe you've met my younger sister already," Wendy said as she took a seat in one of the folding chairs.

Gray sat in a chair beside her after he'd forced himself to look away from Morgan's retreating body.

"Yes. We met last night at the community center," he replied.

Wendy nodded. "You interrupted Jacob Marley's grand entrance in Mountainview Elementary's first-grade-class presentation of *A Christmas Carol.*"

"Is that what they were doing?" he asked, then recalled the little boy named Ethan saying something about "bah, hamburger" when he'd taken his place on the stage after Gray first arrived.

"Yes. It's one of Morgan's favorites, so she begged the town council to let her class present the play, as opposed to the older members of the theater club, who had wanted to perform *The Sound of Music*. I think we're better off with the kids and that has nothing to do with my sister being the director," Wendy continued, chuckling again.

"I hope it turns out well," Gray responded.

He'd been wondering how long it was going to take Morgan to return. Not that he didn't like talking to her sister. Well, actually, Gray wasn't really in the mood to talk any more tonight. He did, however, want to be near Morgan Hill once again. That thought hadn't occurred to him earlier when he'd been busily immersed in his work. Yet,

the moment he saw her, he was unable—or unwilling...
he couldn't figure out which one just yet—to think about
anything else.

"It's going to be fun. You should think about sticking
around town to see the finished product."

This sister liked to talk. Gray was certain he hadn't gotten this many words out of Morgan the night before and
they'd been together longer. He looked at Wendy now, and
asked, "When is the production taking place?"

"Christmas Eve," she told him. "You weren't planning
on selling the community center before then, were you?"

Gray didn't immediately respond. Christmas was weeks
away. There was no way he planned on staying in town
for that long, and while he was immediately going to put
the buildings on the market, he wasn't optimistic that they
would sell so quickly. Who would want to buy run-down
buildings in this small town? There was no market value
to the purchases, only sentimental value, which he'd figured out from his talk with Millie, and Morgan's immediate reaction to finding out who he was.

"I don't think they'll be sold before Christmas," he answered. "Maybe I'll go help Morgan with the drinks."

Wendy had seemed to look at him knowingly as she replied, "Sure. You go right ahead and do that."

Regardless of what she said or thought about Gray as he
walked away, he kept moving. Too many people wanted to
chitchat with him in this town and he didn't want any of
that. What he wanted... Gray wasn't quite certain. Sure,
he'd thought he knew, just last night when he'd driven
into town, and earlier, when he talked to Gemma, but at
this moment...

Morgan turned away from the punch table just as he
walked up behind her. Quick footwork had him moving
just before she could turn with her outstretched hands,
which held two glasses filled with red punch. The red

punch that Gray had no doubt would have splashed all over his white shirt had they collided in the way they'd seemed destined to do.

"Let me help you with that," Gray offered and reached for one of the glasses.

She opened her mouth as if she was about to speak, then clapped her lips closed and allowed him to take the glass from her hand.

"Why don't we enjoy this over there near the tree," he said.

"That one is for my sister," she said, nodding toward the glass in his hand.

He shook his head and did not hesitate to lie. "She said she'd get something later."

"Why do you want to go over there? We can go back to our table," she said before lifting her glass to her lips and taking a sip.

"I want to be alone with you," he said, again without any hesitation.

Or any thought to what he was doing. All Gray could admit to with any sort of definitiveness was that he wanted to be with Morgan. His salacious thoughts from last night were at the forefront of his mind as he stood close to her, the light scent of her perfume wafting through the air.

"And I like Christmas trees," he continued when she only glared at him, one brow lifted in silent question.

"Lily said you didn't like Christmas," she replied after another few moments of silence.

"Your daughter," he said when he remembered the solemn-faced little girl from last night. "She and your son are twins, correct?"

Morgan nodded. "They're the loves of my life," she replied, then looked up quickly as if she hadn't meant to say that.

Gray decided to let it slide because there was another

pressing question he wanted an answer to. "And their father? Is he also the love of your life?"

For the first time ever Gray held his breath as he waited for the answer.

Her fingers seemed to tighten around the glass she held before she replied, "My husband died in Afghanistan."

It was a simple statement and yet it held as much power as if she'd reached out and socked him herself.

"I'm sorry to hear that," he said.

Gray moved beside her then, taking her elbow lightly, and began to walk toward the tree. "Do you like Christmas?"

"What?" she asked as they moved.

"Do you like Christmas? That's what Lily asked me last night. Now I want to know your answer."

"Yes, I love Christmas," she said before taking another sip of her punch.

Gray hadn't bothered to sip his.

"It's a wonderful time of year. A time for family and fellowship, miracles and happiness."

"You sound like one of those greeting-card commercials," he replied.

"And you sound like the star of my play, Ebenezer Scrooge," she snapped back.

They'd come to a stop near the huge Christmas tree that was nestled in a far corner of the room. It had to be at least ten feet tall and was decorated with what looked like every sort of bulb, bell, ribbon and light ever created for this season.

"I don't have anything in particular against the holiday," Gray confided. He'd walked farther around the tree toward the side that was facing two large windows.

The old window shades were tattered at the edges and if anyone attempted to pull them down farther, they'd surely crumple into pieces. So more than half the window was bare, leaving a view of the side street, where only two cars were parked and the sidewalk was clear. At this time of evening on a Sunday night, if Gray had looked out the window of his penthouse in Miami he was sure to see lines of traffic and people headed toward the clubs or the beach. There was always something going on in the city, some party or meeting, a huge wedding, or a celebrity sighting. Never a dull moment, and never a quiet street like this.

"Do you normally spend the holiday with the rest of your family?"

Gray lifted his head to see Morgan standing right beside him. She'd put her glass down on the windowsill and he did the same before thinking about an answer to her question. He hadn't thought of his siblings in the traditional sense of the word *family*. The fact that they each lived in different states could be the reason for that. They'd been born together and had lived together for eighteen years. They were the closest thing to friends Gray had ever had, and the only ones who shared the same dark disappointments of the past with him.

"No. My sisters and brothers have their own lives," he replied.

"There are six of you—surely you find time to spend with each other at some point. I only have one sister and it seems like we're never apart," she told him.

She looked across the room and Gray followed her gaze. More people had come in, filling up the tables. The sound of numerous voices had grown a bit louder. The instrumental holiday music still sounded over the guests' voices and Gray found himself thankful for the partial privacy of this corner. He didn't want to talk to any of the people out there, but here, on this side of the tree with all its twinkling lights reflecting off the window, he was content to stand with this woman.

"Yes, there are six of us. I'm the oldest. Born almost

immediately after me were Garrek, Gemma, Genevieve, Gage and Gia. Once we turned eighteen we all went our separate ways."

"And you don't keep in touch? That's not good. I mean, it's kind of sad. I would think that you would be closer," she said, then clamped her lips shut again.

Gray shook his head. "It's not a problem. A lot of people think a lot of things about the Taylor sextuplets. They have since the first airing of that damn television show. None of them know the truth."

"You sound as if the truth is sad," she replied quietly.

Gray shrugged. "It is what it is."

She nodded. "Just like you selling the buildings, I guess."

Her back was to the window and Gray moved to stand in front of her. He rubbed the backs of his fingers lightly over her cheek.

"Those buildings mean something to you, don't they?" he asked her.

She shrugged this time, shifting from one foot to the other as if his proximity was making her nervous. Being this close to her was making him hot and aroused. He wondered if that's what she was really feeling as well.

"This town means something to me. There are good people here and we're trying to do good things."

"That's what my mother used to say," Gray continued, loving the feel of her smooth skin beneath his touch. "Temptation was a good place. Love, family, loyalty. They meant something to the town. Always. That's what she used to tell us when we were young. But that was after the show, after my father found something better outside of this precious town of Temptation."

Gray could hear the sting to his tone, felt the tensing of his muscles that came each time he thought about Theodor Taylor and all that he'd done to his family. Yes, Gray had buried his father two months ago. He'd followed the old man's wishes right down to the ornate gold handles on the slate-gray casket, but Gray still hated him. He still despised any man who could walk away from his family without ever looking back.

"Show me something better," he said as he stared down into Morgan's light brown eyes. "Show me what this town is really about and maybe I'll reconsider selling."

"Are you making a bargain with me?" she asked. "Because if you are, I don't know what to say. I'm not used to wheeling-and-dealing big businessmen like you."

"I'm asking you to give me a reason why I shouldn't sell those buildings. Just one will do. If you can convince me—"

She was already shaking her head. "I won't sleep with you, if that's what you mean by *convince* you."

Gray blinked. That wasn't what he'd meant and the vehement way in which she'd made that declaration had scraped his ego raw.

"I didn't ask you to sleep with me," he told her and took a step closer. "But if I did..." He purposely let his words trail off, the tip of his finger sliding closer to the edge of her lips.

"I'd still say no. I don't sleep with uptight businessmen," she told him, that stubborn chin of hers jutting forward.

If she could have, Gray was certain she would have backed all the way out of that window to get away from him. That wasn't going to happen, especially not when he snaked an arm around her waist and pulled her closer to him, until she was flush against his chest the same way she had been last night when she'd bumped into him. He liked her right there, liked the heat that immediately spread throughout his body with her in this position.

"Don't worry," he whispered. "I won't ask you. I don't

sleep with small-town women with chips on their shoulders."

"I'm not—" she began but Gray quieted her words by touching his lips immediately to hers.

White-hot heat seared through him at the touch. His tongue swooped inside, taking her by surprise. A warm and delicious surprise that had him wrapping his other arm around her and holding her tight. Her hands came around to his back, clenching the material of his suit jacket as she opened her mouth wider to his assault. They were consuming each other, right here in the corner of this room at the hospital where Gray and his siblings had been born.

He wanted to turn her just a little, to press her back against the wall and take her right here, just like this. He could feel how hot she was and could imagine that same heat pouring over him as she came. She would wrap her legs around him, her short but strong legs would hold him tightly, keeping him securely embedded inside her. They would be short of breath, but love every second of their joining. It would be the best sex…no, it would be really good sex, for Gray, something he hadn't indulged in often enough.

It would be… Something moved at his side. It made a noise and moved again. She stilled in his arms, then abruptly pulled back. Gray was cursing as he realized what was moving was his vibrating cell phone. With a frown Gray pulled it out of his pocket and looked down at the text on the lighted screen. He would have never considered that Morgan might look down as well.

"I'll let you go tend to Kym," she said icily, before stepping around him and making a hasty exit.

# *Chapter 4*

The Sunnydale Bed-and-Breakfast was a stately white colonial with black shutters nestled in the center of a cul-de-sac and surrounded by a number of beautifully mature trees. Gray admitted the next afternoon as he approached the dwelling that it looked as if it should be featured on a postcard boasting the simplicity of small-town living. The American flag flying high above the black double doors and brick walkway slammed home the patriotic angle, while chubby shrubs lined the perimeter with the precise planning of a *Better Homes and Gardens* portrait. Once inside, the historic charm continued with scuffed wood-planked floors, emerald-green-and-white textured wallpaper stretching throughout the front foyer and along the wall next to a winding glossed cherry-wood railing.

There was just enough of the new world interspersed with the old, as the front desk clerk had spoken to Gray after hanging up the telephone and was taking an inordinately long time to type a reservation into a computer.

"I'm here to see Kym Hutchins. I believe she has a room here," Gray told the clerk, who was staring at him over gold wire-rimmed glasses.

"Well, I'll be damned," the older gentleman began. "Millie wasn't lying after all."

"Pardon me?" Gray asked even though he had a hunch what was about to take place.

The man shook his head before coming around the desk to stand right in front of Gray. He wore tan pants that were at least three sizes too big, held up by black suspenders, which again, didn't really fit him well, but were drawn so tight they looked almost painful on his shoulders. His short-sleeved dress shirt was a lighter shade of tan, and a wrinkled handkerchief poked out of his breast pocket. His skin was a very weathered almond color, while his hair—what was left of it—was short, gray and curled close to his scalp.

"You're one of the Taylors, all right. Tall and broad just like your daddy was," the man said as he continued to look Gray up and down. "Got some fancy clothes on, too. I know because no stores in Temptation even carry dress pants with studs at the bottom, or shirts with those fancy gold cuffs you're wearing. Nowhere to go in town where you gotta be that sharp, unless it's in your own casket."

Gray frowned. People in this town said whatever came to their mind, whenever they saw fit. It was a good thing Temptation was still somewhat thriving because its people wouldn't make it in the big city.

"Sir, if you'll be so kind as to let Ms. Hutchins know that I'm here," Gray said, again employing all his patience to deal with the older members of this town.

"Oh, she's already waiting in the parlor. Came down in her fancy dress and par-r-r-fume," he said, mispronouncing and dragging the word out until it sounded totally ridiculous.

Ridiculous and just a little bit funny, as the man's face

had contorted in a way that Gray presumed was his rendition of being upper class.

"Then I'll just go on in and see her," Gray said and turned to the right to go through a walkway.

"The parlor's this way," the man told Gray.

He'd turned and walked, his posture a little bent over, toward double pocket doors to the left.

"Guess you two got someplace to go all dressed up like you are," he continued. "I don't reckon any man around here wears suits and ties on a daily basis. And the women, they don't wear skirts with matching jackets unless they're going to church. Me, I don't go anywhere I need to put on shiny suit jacket and shave. Used to tell my Ethel that all the time. If I go to church I put on pants and a shirt. I brush my teeth and my hair and I'm done. She never understood, but she never left me, either."

He was chuckling so hard, Gray thought he might actually tip over from the effort. He stood close just in case that did happen. Instead, the man began to wheeze just as they stepped into the parlor, which had a plush burgundy carpet.

"Ma'am, you got a beau come to see you," he told Kym.

"Thank you, Otis," Kym said when she stood from the spot where she'd been sitting.

"You're quite welcome, ma'am," Otis replied and turned to leave.

Gray glanced at the man once more, trying to figure out if he was really blushing or if there was some other health condition going on.

"She's a looker," Otis whispered, his bushy eyebrows dancing up and down as he grinned.

Gray couldn't help but smile—the man might be old in years, but he hadn't lost a step when it came to women.

Kym Hutchins was indeed a good-looking woman. She was tall at five foot nine and a half inches, with a slim figure, a light golden complexion and long black hair that was always perfectly styled. Her makeup was flawless, as usual, her legs long in the knee-length navy blue skirt with the matching jacket, which perfectly accented her sophisticated and professional demeanor. She was a very intelligent woman and she was his executive assistant. None of which explained why she was here in Temptation.

"Hello, Grayson," Kym said when Otis had meandered away, leaving them alone in the cozy parlor.

There were heavy-looking drapes hanging almost from floor to ceiling in a strange mustard color and four round mahogany tables with matching chairs around them. In the center of each table was a bouquet of roses, in the exact shade that was on Kym's lips as she gave him a brilliant smile.

"Hello," he replied. "I'm not sure how you knew I was here. I didn't put anything on my calendar."

With a flick of her hand, the large curls that had been draped over her shoulders were pushed back as her chin tilted slightly.

"I came by your place to drop off the Miago contracts but you weren't there. When I spoke to your doorman he indicated that you'd taken the Porsche and said you would return in a week. I know you've been handling your father's estate so I took an educated guess," she told him.

"And you showed up without me inviting you? Without letting me know your intentions?" Gray wasn't certain how he should feel about that.

"Why don't we have a seat, Grayson. Otis is going to bring us a beverage. I asked for wine spritzers but he politely informed me that this establishment does not sell or serve alcoholic beverages. Can you imagine?" she asked with a shake of her head.

Kym was already taking a seat, crossing her long, bare legs as she did. Gray figured it made sense to sit and talk to her, even though he was still trying to figure out why she'd come all this way in the first place.

"Did you know they don't have any hotels in this town?" With that said, Kym let out a short sigh. "I don't know what they do with the tourists, whenever they get them."

"They have two B and Bs and a resort," he told her, keeping it to himself that the resort was actually a farm.

"No four-star hotels, no wine. It's a wonder they're still functioning at all," she replied.

Gray didn't speak, but let his hands rest on his thighs as he continued to stare at her. "Did you bring the contracts with you?"

"My briefcase is in my room. Since you sent a text indicating that we would meet later, rather than first thing this morning as I'd presumed, I thought we'd have a drink and catch up first." She talked as she pulled her tablet from a large designer bag that she had sitting in a chair next to her.

Gray had taken his time getting over there, part of the reason being he still wasn't certain why she'd come.

"There's a phone conference with Tokyo on Thursday. Are you still going to make that? Should I have them call you at…wait, where are you staying?"

Kym looked up at him just as Gray was staring at a painting hanging on the wall between the two large windows. It was of an African American couple, perhaps taken in the early 1900s as evidenced by the style of dress the woman was wearing and the bowler hat worn by the man, who was sitting down. Trees and grass covered the background of the piece. The couple looked anything but happy and Gray found himself wondering who they were and what their story was. Normally, such a thing would not have intrigued him—the emotional state of people not being high on his list of priorities. He'd learned long ago that a person could go for years and years hiding their true feelings. Still, this couple piqued his interest. Enough so

that Kym had reached over the table and was now pulling
on his jacket sleeve as she called his name.

"Yes?" he replied curtly to her and then had to take a
deep breath and start over. "What were you saying?"

She blinked several times as if he'd spoken a foreign
language and then Gray could actually see her pulling herself together. It was in the straightening of her shoulders,
the slow setting of her hands on the sides of her tablet and
the careful way in which she spoke.

"I asked where you're staying. They said there was only
one room left here when I checked in last night, but when
I asked if you were here they said no. Actually, the woman
who had been on duty just about laughed at my question,"
Kym said.

"I have a room at the resort," he told her curtly. "I can
sign the contracts today and you can head back to Miami.
What time is your flight out?"

Temptation did not have an airport so she had to have
driven here, or taken a taxi from Dulles International Airport. It would have been a town car, he thought, and she
would have charged it to her expense account because
that's how Kym rolled. No way was she driving—even
though she owned a Mercedes S550, she never went farther
than from her apartment to the office on any given day.

"I didn't book a return flight," she replied. "I figured
we'd return together and since I didn't know your plans I
waited. Are you finished wrapping up your father's estate?
I told Philip to be on standby in case you needed him."

Philip Stansfield had been Grayson's personal and business attorney for more than ten years.

"No. I'm not finished and I'll contact Philip if I need
him," he told her.

She reached across the table once more, touching Gray's
arm again. His gaze fell to her hand this time as she spoke
quietly.

"You do not have to go through this alone, Grayson. I've been with you for six years and I've never heard you mention your father. So I know this might not be the easiest task for you."

Gray was just about to respond. He was trying to figure out a cordial way to ask her to stop touching him. She'd never touched him this much in the past. Before he could speak another hand appeared. A smaller one, with light pink painted fingernails. She wrapped those little fingers around two of Gray's and said, "Hello."

He looked over to see Lily standing there, her hair pulled back into one ponytail today, with a green-and-white ribbon at the top. When she looked at Gray she smiled. He couldn't help it—he smiled, too.

"Hello, Lily," he said, moving his arm so that Kym's hand slipped away and his grip tightened on Lily's hand.

"Are you having tea?" she asked.

"No. I don't think so," Gray replied.

"This is the room where people have tea. That's what Nana Lou said."

"Nana Lou?"

Lily nodded. "Uh-huh, she's in the kitchen. I was helping her make dough, but my hands were tired."

"I see. Where is your mother?" Gray asked.

"At work," Lily replied and then turned to Kym and asked, "Who are you?"

Gray turned to his assistant to see her staring down at Lily as if she was some type of anomaly. Kym's pert nose had crinkled, her dislike apparent until she caught Gray looking at her.

"Ah, hello, little one," she said before clearing her throat. "My name is Ms. Hutchins and I'm with Mr. Taylor."

Now he was Mr. Taylor. Gray tried not to show his confusion. "She works with me, Lily. How about I take you back out to the kitchen with Nana Lou."

Lily shook her head. "I want to stay here and have tea with you and her."

"My name is Kym Hutchins and we're not having tea. We're talking. You know, adult talk, so you can run along now," Kym told Lily with a wave of her hand as if the little girl needed the direction.

Gray stood then, lifting Lily into his arms. Behind him he thought he heard Kym gasp, but he didn't turn around.

"Sure, we can have tea together. Let's see if Nana Lou will make it for us," he said as he began walking out of the parlor, only to be stopped when Lily greeted Morgan loudly.

Morgan didn't know what to say.

Gray was holding Lily in his arms.

They looked, well, for lack of a better word, happy.

"Hi, baby," she said after another second of silence. "What are you doing out here with Mr. Taylor?"

She lifted her arms and welcomed her daughter into her embrace. She smelled like cinnamon rolls and icing, Morgan thought as Lily held her tightly around the neck. Lily was always glad to see Morgan when they'd been apart, as if she thought there was a chance she might not see her again. The twins had barely been two when James died, but sometimes Morgan thought they remembered that exact day he'd left them, the same way that she did.

"I'm taking a break," Lily told Morgan. "We're gonna have some tea. Me, Ms. Kym and, Mr. Gray?"

"He's Mr. Taylor," Morgan said, correcting her daughter.

"She can call me Mr. Gray," he said with a smile.

He still stood very close to Morgan, one hand slipped into the pocket of the crisply pleated black pants of his suit.

His shirt was bright white, just as it had been last night, but today's tie was an icy-blue color. There was no question that this man looked phenomenal in a suit. Nor was there any question that the kiss they'd shared last night had kept Morgan up into the early-morning hours. She silently chastised herself. It was just a kiss. That was all.

Then why was Gray looking at her as if he knew exactly what she was thinking and that he begged to differ—that their kiss was... definitely *something*?

"Hello," a woman said.

Morgan shook her head and looked away from Gray. Coming to stand beside him was a gorgeous woman with a frosty smile and assessing eyes. Morgan instinctively tightened her grip on Lily as she cordially said, "Hello."

"You have a lovely daughter," the woman volunteered. "Grayson and I work together. We were taking care of some business when this little one showed up."

Morgan had to blink to keep the words running through her mind from spilling out. Was this woman serious? Did she have an attitude about Lily being there?

"Lily and I were going to get some tea," Gray added, without looking at the woman at his side.

Wait, did Lily say Ms. Kym? Morgan held back her frown, along with the smart remark she'd already been trying to keep to herself. So this was the Kym who had sent Gray that text message last night. The one who had said simply, "I'm here in town. Call me."

"That's fine, you get back to your business. I'll take Lily out of your way," Morgan told Gray.

She hadn't bothered to look at Kym again, either, until the woman spoke one more time.

"That would be wonderful. Please let the staff know that we'd like some privacy. Thank you."

As if it was that simple to command someone to do her bidding, Kym turned away and pulled out a chair to have a seat at one of the tables. Morgan stared at Gray, who she thought looked like he wanted to say something to this Kym person. If that was the case, he was taking too long.

"Oh, you must be mistaken," Morgan said to her. "I don't work here, nor do I work for Mr. Taylor. My daughter and I will be going now."

She was out of the parlor and had just dropped a kiss on Lily's forehead when Gray touched her arm.

"You keep running from me," he said in an irritated tone.

Not wanting to make Lily think that something was wrong, Morgan slowly eased away from Gray, until his hand was dropping away from her arm.

"Not running, leaving. You're busy with work and I have to get Jack," she told him.

"You ran out on me last night," he said, his brow furrowing as if he was still trying to figure out why.

Well, he didn't have to try any longer—Morgan planned to tell him, but then Lily moved and she remembered that her daughter would hear everything she said, so she bit her tongue once more.

"We were finished last night. You're the one who chose not to stay for dinner," she replied. "Or rather, you're the one who had someplace else to be."

Gray's lips thinned into a straight line as he, too, looked down at Lily.

"What about what we were discussing last night?" he asked her finally.

Morgan had thought about that during the night as well. He'd said if she could give him a reason that he shouldn't sell the buildings, he wouldn't. Which was the exact reason why she'd been grateful when Harry asked to pick up the children after school today. She'd gone to the chamber of commerce to meet with Millie. Armed with all she needed to know about the buildings that Gray owned and a bit more, she felt like she was more than ready to show him why he should leave Temptation and those buildings alone forever.

"Whenever you're ready for me to present my case, let me know," she said.

"I'm ready right now," Gray responded.

Morgan shook her head, then looked to the doorway of the parlor to see Kym standing there.

"I have to get to the community center for rehearsal and then home to bed because we have school tomorrow. On Tuesdays and Wednesdays the theater club has the center for their rehearsals, so we won't rehearse tomorrow. I can meet you at your parents' house at six."

He frowned and Morgan realized it was probably because she'd called the old Victorian "his parents' house." After what Millie had told her—the parts that Morgan had deemed true, despite all the rest that Millie had thrown in—she could sort of understand why Gray didn't hold much love for that house, or this town for that matter. Still, she had enough love for Temptation to try and save what they were already starting to build.

"Is that time all right with you, or will you still be working?" she asked and refused to look at Kym, who she knew was listening to every word they said.

Gray took a deep breath then let it out slowly, so that his broad shoulders moved slightly. A part of Morgan wanted to hear his side of the story. She wanted to know why his father had really left his family and why Gray's mother thought her only recourse was to leave the town that had been her home. More importantly, Morgan found herself wondering about Gray and the man he had become. Feeling a quick spurt of guilt, she looked away from him.

"It's fine," he said immediately, as if he thought she might be ready to renege on her offer.

She nodded and turned away, alarmed at the fact that

she had been about to tell him to forget it. How could she continue to be in this man's company when every time they were together he switched on something inside her that she'd thought she'd buried years ago with her husband? Every. Damn. Time.

## Chapter 5

"Hi, Morgan. Why didn't you call me? I would have brought the children over to the community center," Harry said the second Morgan entered the front foyer.

She hadn't seen him standing there on the other side of the steps and was just about to walk past him when he spoke.

"Oh, hi, Harry. That's okay. You've done enough. I really appreciate you picking them up and watching them for me," Morgan said.

Morgan had known Harry since they were little kids. He'd grown into a tall man, broadly built with a dark-chocolate complexion, bald head and warm smile. He was the oldest of three children born to Louisa and Clyde Reed and one of the most reliable people that Morgan knew. He also had a crush on Morgan, at least that's what Wendy had said for years. Morgan had always considered Harry a friend. That's all. Besides, she hadn't thought about another man romantically since James's passing. Until Gray. She shook her head again to clear the wayward thoughts that had been plaguing her these last couple of days.

"You know it's no problem," Harry said. "Where'd you run off to, little lady?" he asked Lily.

She still clung tightly to Morgan.

"I heard voices and then I saw Mr. Gray. I wanted to have tea with him," Lily announced as if that was as normal as saying she wanted to watch *Doc McStuffins* on television.

Morgan wished she hadn't said it and Harry looked confused.

"She's talking about Grayson Taylor," Morgan told him. "He's in the parlor with his, um…a woman he works with. He's been in town for a couple of days. Lily met him when he stopped by the community center a couple of nights ago."

Harry had only nodded while she spoke, his brow creasing. "So the rumors are true. He's gonna sell those buildings and add to the millions he's already got."

"He may not sell them," Morgan said, then wished she hadn't.

Harry frowned down at her. "How do you know what he's going to do?"

She shrugged. "I'm going to try to talk him out of it."

"What? You don't know him. You don't know men like him at all, Morgan. You should just steer clear and let him do what he needs to do and be gone."

"I can't do that," Morgan said.

Jack came running into the room at that moment and Morgan hastily grabbed his hand.

"Thanks again, Harry," she said. "I've got to get going."

Morgan walked through the front doors and down the walkway to her car. She didn't look back, as she was sure to find Harry staring at her.

* * *

The next afternoon, when Gray climbed out of his car to flashing lights and questions being hurled at him from at least three reporters, he wanted to reach out and punch somebody in the face. Of course, he resisted that urge, especially since two of the reporters were women.

They'd been following him around town since he'd walked out of the coffee shop where he'd met Kym for coffee and bagels that morning.

"I can talk to them if you want," Kym had offered when they'd walked to his car.

"I don't have anything to say to them and that means you don't, either," he told her.

"But they're here to see what you plan to do for your hometown this time. Your family was so instrumental in helping to revitalize the town thirty years ago, the people here are hoping you'll do the same. The press is eating all this up, which you know is going to be great for the launch in a couple of months."

Gray Technologies was launching a new cell-phone-and-tablet combo that was small and slim enough to fit into a wallet. Its battery life and network range was triple that of the strongest and most popular product on the market. It was one of the biggest and brightest inventions yet, so yes, Gray had to admit it was a huge deal. But not big enough to sell his soul to the devil that was the press. He'd hated them all his life and avoided them like the plague, relying solely on his PR department to deal with all media coverage. He didn't plan to stop now.

"I don't know how they knew I was here," he said.

"Does it matter? They're here and so are you. This is free advertising, Grayson. No matter what you decide to do here, it's a win-win for us," Kym had insisted.

Gray had only shaken his head and climbed into his car

just as one of the reporters had skirted around Kym and pressed a microphone in his face.

"Tell us how it feels to be back in your hometown, Grayson?" the reporter had asked just before Gray slammed his car door shut.

He spent the rest of the day closed in his room at the resort, reading more of his reports and thinking steadily about his meeting with Morgan later that day.

It would be the first time he walked into the house where it had all begun. There'd been happiness and excitement as his parents had waited for the birth of the sextuplets. The town had shared in the anxiety of watching Olivia waddle to church, to the grocery store, to visit with her family and then back to the big house to wait a little more. When the babies finally came, so had the press. Then came the cable television station that had offered the Taylors more money than they'd ever dreamed of to let cameras follow them around day in and day out.

The money was for the medical bills and to put into college funds for each of the children. That's what his mother had told him one day when Gray was a teenager. It was a wonderful plan to ensure their children had the very best of everything, she'd said as her gaze had lingered on the rolling waves. She loved the water at the beach, but Gray knew that his mother had loved this little town much more.

The hours had passed quickly enough and Gray, without the help of his PR people, had called the front desk of the resort to ask about a back way out of their property. Netta Coolridge, the owner's sixteen-year-old daughter, had come to his room carrying a tray of covered dishes, which gave the impression of him having a large meal. Instead, she'd smiled as she lifted one of the domed covers to reveal a thick length of rope.

"What's that?" Gray asked as he looked from the rope back to Netta's smiling face.

"It's how I get out of the house without my parents knowing," she replied with a brilliant, braced-teeth smile.

She was a cute girl with high cheekbones and long, straight honey-gold hair on one side. The other side was shaved like a man's, with a row of four curving lines that showed her scalp. She wore jeans and a hooded sweatshirt with the logo of a popular teen clothing store etched across the front.

"This window will lead you down to the back of the stalls. Your car is parked right on the side. It's already getting dark so if you stay close to the wall in the shadows those nosy reporters won't see you."

Netta talked as she walked across the room to open one of the windows. She'd taken the rope with her and tied a knot as she wrapped it around the leg of the massive armoire lodged in the corner.

"Mama insists on feeding those rude vultures and she's just about finished with the spaghetti and meatballs she prepared. She offered to let them come inside and eat, but they already told her they needed to keep watch. So I'll go back down and start bringing the fixings out to them, while you sneak out."

"Wait a minute," Gray asked, confusion giving way to incredulity at this point. "You expect me to climb down a window and sneak to my car? I've never done such a thing in my life," he told her.

When she'd dropped the other end of the rope out the window, Netta turned to him and shrugged. "Well, there's a first time for everything," she quipped.

Gray had discarded his suit jacket and slipped a sweater over his dress shirt this time. He grabbed his leather bomber jacket and was pushing his arms into it as he shook his head. "I'm not ducking and hiding from these people," he declared.

Netta shook her head and made a tsking sound with her

teeth. "Suit yourself," she told him. "But I counted five news vans and two cars when I came over. They're not in the driveway because Daddy threatened to shoot any of them that parked on our land, but they're right down there by the front gate. If you want to, you can drive right on out that way and see how far you get. Me, I'd get to shimmying out that window and take the back road along the creek to avoid them."

She was walking past Gray now, and stopped to clap a hand on his shoulder. "But you handle it your way, city slicker, and let me know how that works out for you."

The knowing grin that spread across her face as she turned for the door both amused and annoyed Gray. He was frowning by the time he grabbed his phone and keys and headed toward the window.

Now, forty minutes later, he was getting out of his car when the reporters flanked him once more. A threat to sue their newspaper and a reminder that he was about to be on private property had them quickly backing up.

Gray was about to walk up the broken bricked pathway to the house where he'd spent the first seven years of his life. There was a tear at the bottom of his left pant leg from jumping down after climbing out the window and down the rope. He'd gotten caught on one of the bushes that Netta neglected to tell him were circling the building. She had been right about him making a quiet getaway using that back road—as far as Gray could tell, none of the reporters had followed him back into town.

It was chilly tonight and this part of Peach Tree Lane was untouched by the Christmas decorations and holiday cheer. Gray didn't know how he felt about that, just as he wasn't sure how this meeting was going to go. The place looked the same, he thought as he came closer to the front steps. He couldn't see all the details of the house. It sat in the shadows of early evening almost like one of those haunted houses used for horror movies. With his hands thrust into the pockets of his jacket, he gazed up, not yet ready to take the stairs and walk along the wood-planked porch.

Yes, it was the same, he thought. The feeling that he'd always had when he was there. Warmth spread throughout his chest without his permission. Sounds of little boys rolling toy trucks up and down that porch while little girls took turns on the tire swing that used to hang from that huge oak tree to his left echoed in his mind. Food would be cooking by now because it was close to dinnertime. On the grill in the backyard, because that's where Dad liked to stand and show the cameras how he prepared a BBQ supper for his family. That was only one of the falsehoods that Theodor Taylor perpetuated.

"Sorry to keep you waiting," Morgan said as she came up to stand beside him. "I've got a key if you don't have one. Millie gave it to me yesterday when I met with her."

It took a moment for Gray to remind himself of the present. His quick look into the past left a bitter taste in his mouth.

"Does the head of your chamber of commerce always give citizens keys to properties that don't belong to them?" he asked and bristled at the chill in his tone.

Morgan pursed her lips and replied, "Millie's husband, Fred, owns the property management company that's been keeping this place from falling down over the years. When I told her I planned to show you around town, she was the one who suggested I start here. Fred agreed and offered me the key."

Disappointed in the fact that he seemed to be taking his bad mood out on her, Gray only nodded at first. He looked up to the house again—even in the growing darkness he could see the loose shingles on the roof.

"I don't have a key, so I suppose their foresight works out," he said.

"I suppose it does" was Morgan's response as she moved past him and started up the steps.

She wore jeans tonight, dark ones that fit quite nicely over the curve of her backside, and a white puffy coat that made her look like a snowball at the top. Gray followed behind her and only hesitated slightly before walking through one of the two red doors. He'd never liked that stark and bold color against the pale blue of the house, but ignored it now as he stepped inside, the old wood floors squeaking beneath his weight.

"They keep the power on," Morgan said as she switched on the lights. "Fred said they'd been in contact with someone from your father's legal team last year. They were talking about converting the house into a museum."

Gray was busy looking around. On either side there were archways leading into separate rooms. The room to the right served as their playroom, while the space on the left was the formal living room. Large area rugs had covered the majority of the wood floors—which at that time still gleamed from his mother's care.

"What? A museum? Are you serious?" he asked as her words finally registered.

She unzipped her coat while skirting around him to close the door that he'd left open behind them.

"Yes," she said. "Apparently, your father wanted to commemorate all that he and your mother had gone through to get pregnant. There was supposed to be a new wing at the hospital dedicated to the study of obstetrics, employing doctors who specialized in fertility options and multiple births."

"My brother Gage specializes in that area," Gray said, still frowning as he tried to understand exactly what she was telling him.

Morgan began walking ahead of him. She moved farther through the foyer, passing the stairs that were still lined in the forest green carpet. As children they'd always wanted to slide down the railings, but since the steps turned sharply to the left, it had been out of the question.

"In addition to the new wing at the hospital, your father's plan was to have this house show all the milestones you and your siblings made while you were here. Apparently, there'd been a deal in the works with another television network, to do a sort of where-are-they-now segment."

"Why didn't I know about this?" Gray asked as they made their way toward the back of the house. "How can they do something like this, using our name and likeness, without consulting any of us?"

They were in the dining room now and Gray had moved to stand near the fireplace. Dark oak columns stretched to the ceiling, guarding the old brick that surrounded the actual fire pit. The mantel was still there, even though it looked as if it had seen better days. Above hung a huge mirror, now marred with dust.

"I would think your father or someone from the network would have reached out to you and your siblings at some point," Morgan said, reminding him that he wasn't on this tour alone.

"Before his death, I hadn't spoken to my father since my high school graduation," Gray confessed.

He lifted a hand to run his fingers lightly along the dusty mantel. His thoughts traveled back to that day. They'd all gone to the same school, a public school because his mother hadn't wanted them to feel separated from the other children in town. Olivia never wanted her children to feel segregated or ostracized as she'd suspected they'd begun to feel while on the television show. The last time they'd seen their father before then was at their tenth birthday party, when Theodor also had business in the area. He'd dropped by their house just in time to sing "Happy Birthday" and drop off his gifts. Then he was gone. At the graduation he'd been there for the entire ceremony, telling each one of them how proud he was at the end, and then leaving again. That time he'd had a woman with him. Gray believed that was the moment his mother had truly become ill, even though she would live another four years before dying from complications of pneumonia.

"He didn't come around much after he left us," he continued.

"Why did he leave?"

Her voice was quiet, but close, as if she was standing right behind him. Gray didn't turn around to see, he simply took a deep breath before speaking words he'd never spoken before in his life.

"My father had an affair," he said solemnly. "It was with one of the production assistants on the show. My mother didn't find out, the way most clichéd cheating husbands meet their fate. No, my mother was oblivious. My sister Gemma used to say she was in love with her husband and her children, as if that was an excuse."

He paused, hearing the edge to his tone. "I don't blame her. In fact, I admire her for accepting and moving on the way she did. My father wanted to build a new life with this woman who had made her name from filming him and his family. So one night he told my mother he was leaving. The next morning, before my mother could even figure out what to do or say, he was gone. News spread like wildfire and many of the townspeople turned on my mom, blaming her for forcing the pregnancy and then having so many babies.

"It was a terrible time, that week following my dad's departure. My mother cried a lot. We stayed in the house with all the doors locked, the shades pulled down tight on the windows, as if we were being held hostage. There were lots of phone calls and arguments with the network executives. My mother didn't want to continue with the show. She hadn't wanted to do it after the first year anyway. The original plan had been to make enough money to start college funds for her children. But the demands of being in front of a camera nonstop and the subsequent promotion of the show were more than she wanted for herself or us. So she wanted out of the contract. If my father could get out of the marriage, then she felt like she could walk away from everything else. And she did."

"How old were you then?"

"Seven."

But Gray remembered feeling like he was a grown man with the amount of information he'd retained in that week alone. He'd heard the one-sided arguments as his mother spoke on the phone and stood outside the door of the sunroom while she'd talked to her grandfather. "She always sounded so strong when she talked of the plans for our new life. But I knew she cried at night. I heard her. We all did."

"That's so sad," Morgan whispered.

Gray turned then and saw that she was, in fact, standing right behind him. She hadn't turned on any lights in the room, but the old curtains were open at the windows and the lampposts right outside provided a hazy glow of illumination. She looked ethereal as she stood there, her gaze trained on his. Her hands were clasped in front of her and Gray knew that she was feeling the same disappointment he'd experienced as a young child.

"What makes you sad, Morgan?" Gray asked, even though he wasn't totally sure why.

Whenever he looked at her that happened. He found himself wanting to know more about her, needing to touch her, or to taste her once more. There was this tugging between him and her that had been there since that very first night and he was damned if he could explain it.

She licked her lips quickly and shook her head. "I try not to think of sad things," she replied.

"But it's inevitable, isn't it? Life happens and more often than not it brings sadness. I want to know what hurts you, so that I can never do those things."

Those words could not have sounded any more foreign to Gray than if he'd spoken them in another language. But he couldn't take them back now, nor did he want to.

"I—" she began and then paused. Her hands unclasped, arms coming up to cross over her chest. "I was sad when my parents moved away to Australia." She took a deep breath and let it out quickly. "I know it was a good opportunity for my father, and my mother, too—she'd never been anywhere but Temptation. But I wanted them to stay here with me. I was only in the tenth grade when they left me and Wendy with my grandmother. It hurt."

"But you got over it," Gray concluded for her. "Then you fell in love. Was that a feeling that made you happy? Did it make you forget the pain you'd felt when your parents left?"

He wanted—no, needed—to hear her answers to those questions. Maybe it was because he'd been going through his entire life trying to figure out if there was an ever after to the pain he'd felt and witnessed. His mother's heartbreak had been real and had lasted until she'd taken her last breath. One man had done that to her and Gray swore he'd never forgive his father for it.

"James was like a breath of fresh air," she said and Gray noted the light that entered her eyes.

"He was everything that every guy I'd ever met in Temptation was not. Worldly and ambitious and at the same time a gentleman. I didn't think about him romantically at first because I was just so amazed at the things he knew and the places he'd been. But then slowly that changed and just when I thought I couldn't love any one person any more, I had the twins."

She shook her head and looked out the window, then back to Gray. "There are no words to describe how I felt after giving birth. The only word to accurately depict how I felt with two-year-old babies, and the announcement that my husband was dead, would be *devastated*. That pain was just all consuming."

Just like Gray's mother had experienced when his father left. He gritted his teeth and turned away from her again. Placing his hands on the mantel, he dropped his head and tried to let those thoughts go. He was too old for this. All of the things that had happened to hurt him in the past were over and done with. He couldn't change them even if he'd tried. This was the present, he continued to tell himself. This was the house that needed to be sold so that he and his siblings could get on with their lives.

There was no other choice—no matter what Morgan did or said, Gray knew what he had to do.

## Chapter 6

"The first Christmas after James's death, Wendy and I drove to the outlet mall. There was a Santa village there and Wendy thought the twins were old enough to see Santa in person for the first time and not be afraid. So we walked through the small village and I remember there were trellises covered with artificial snow-tipped garland. There were four or five of them that stretched the length of the walkway until they reached Santa's chair and the elves' station. At the center of each of the trellises was a bundle of mistletoe. Wendy had been the one to remind me of something our grandmother had always insisted we do during the holiday season. So I wished upon the mistletoe. Just one wish under each bunch that I repeated every time I stood beneath it. Then the babies saw Santa and they laughed happily, taking the most adorable picture ever. It was the most perfect day," Morgan said before sighing.

"Santa doesn't always bring you what you want," Gray said quietly.

Morgan nodded, trying to keep her fingers from fidgeting, they wanted to reach up and touch him so badly. He'd sounded so depleted when he talked of his family and what had happened to them. Since the moment she'd met him Morgan had been convinced he was an arrogant, narrowminded rich guy, but as she got to know about his past, she'd seen there was more to him. Deep inside there was an agony that he struggled with, a past that he was both embarrassed and hurt by. She could relate to the pain, but only in the basic sense of loss. No way could she imagine what it was like for a seven-year-old to watch his family fall apart and to witness his mother's heart breaking until she died. It was one of the saddest stories she'd ever heard, which probably made her all kinds of naive and overly sensitive, but she didn't care at the moment.

"That's mostly true," she replied. "But that's when you grow up and learn that what you want is not always what's best for you. I wished that I could get over James and move on with my life, that I could not hurt anymore, not for another minute. It didn't happen. But I learned to live with it."

"Really?" he asked.

He then moved quicker than she'd anticipated and before she could stop him, he'd wrapped his arms around her waist and pushed her back against the wall. She gasped. The motion was so fast and so shocking. Not because his touch had sent instant heat soaring throughout her body and the proximity of his face to hers made her want more than she ever had in her life. At least, she was really trying to convince herself that wasn't the reason.

"What if I said I want you?" he asked, his breath fanning warmly over her face.

"For—for Christmas?" she asked and felt like a colossal idiot.

He didn't smile, but shook his head, his hands slipping

under her coat to rub along her back. "No. Right now. I want you, Morgan."

He moved again and Morgan saw his arm lifting. He was going to touch her. No, wait, he was already touching her. She should move. She should put lots of distance between them to keep whatever was about to happen from happening. But she didn't. She couldn't. His fingers grazed her jaw, came over her chin, then up to tap her bottom lip.

"You can't want me," she said, her body beginning to tremble even though it was the last thing she wanted to do.

"I can and I do," he told her, his other hand falling softly to her hip. "I want to take you right here against this wall. What does wishing on mistletoe tell you about that?"

She wanted to moan, but that wasn't an answer. Dammit, she couldn't think of any words and she certainly wasn't thinking about mistletoe at a time like this. Morgan tried to breathe in deeply and exhale slowly—a known relaxation technique that usually worked…but not this time. His scent permeated every pore of her body and she actually felt dizzy with arousal.

"Gray," she whispered and the tip of his finger touched her tongue.

His other hand went lower, gripping the curve of her bottom and pulling her up close to his arousal. He was thick and hard and she licked his finger, because what else was she supposed to do?

"Don't," he said. "Please, just don't deny this. There are so many things going on, I just need for this to be real. Whatever this is between us needs to be real and not some wish."

If a huge sprig of mistletoe was dangling over their heads right at this moment, Morgan knew exactly what she'd wish for. Now, whether or not that wish would come true…she didn't have another second to contemplate.

Gray's lips took the place of his finger as he kissed

her deeply. Her hands went to his shoulders, grabbing the leather of his jacket in a tight grip. He pressed closer as his tongue delved deeper into her mouth. The kiss was a scorcher, burning her from the tip of her tongue to the heels of her feet. She came up on tiptoes to meet him, and his hand continued to knead her bottom, until she finally lifted her leg and he wrapped it around his waist. Morgan finally gave in to the moan as he devoured her mouth and she accepted every delicious stroke of his tongue. The room was spinning, a kaleidoscope of lights pouring into the dark space. Heat surrounded them even though the furnace in the house was not lit.

Gray thrust his hips into her and Morgan trembled in his arms. The feel of his arousal pressed against her center had her quaking with need, even though the connection was hampered by their clothes.

"Now," he whispered. "I need you now."

Her body screamed yes. Her nipples were so hard pressing against his chest it was almost painful. How long had it been? Morgan had actually forgotten. The need was so great, her hunger so potent it almost choked her. Yes. Just say it, she told herself. Say it and let go.

"Stop," she whispered. "Please stop."

He did, immediately.

Morgan pulled away from him, breathing heavily as she made her way out of the dining room and back through the house the way they'd come. She was running, she knew, but didn't give a damn. He'd scared her. The need that was so great inside her for him was terrifying. It had surpassed anything Morgan had ever felt before, for anyone. Even James.

Digging into her jacket pocket, she fumbled for her keys as she ran down the front steps of the house and over the lawn until she reached the spot where she'd parked her car. Finally unlocking the door, without looking back or caring where Gray was, she jumped inside and put the key in the ignition. Turning it, she called herself every type of idiot in the book, but prayed just to get home. She would get her kids, put them to bed and then find herself a glass... no, a bottle of wine to drink. Completely. It was going to be that kind of night, she thought as she turned the key in the ignition again, and waited.

Nothing.

The engine didn't turn over. In fact, it didn't make a sound. Cursing, Morgan tried again, and then once more, before she finally slapped her palms on the steering wheel.

She jumped at the knock on her window and closed her eyes to the sight of Gray standing there.

"Is there a mechanic's shop around here?" Gray asked after they'd driven in silence for more than five minutes.

She hadn't wanted to get into his car. In fact, she'd gone as far as pulling out her cell phone and attempting to call her sister to come and pick her up. But her sister did not answer, which had only irritated her more as the children were supposed to be with Wendy at their grandmother's house. She'd said as much in between ranting about her car being undependable. When he'd finally heard enough, Gray had simply led her to his car, opened the door and had been about to ease her inside when she looked at him with a serious glare.

"I can take care of myself," she'd stated.

"But can you fix your car?" he'd asked.

When she didn't reply, but simply slipped inside the car and stared straight ahead, Gray had counted it as a victory. She could have replied yes and he would have been more defeated than shocked. He absolutely believed that this woman could do anything she put her mind to. Still, there was no doubt that Morgan Hill was one stubborn woman.

"Yes," she finally said in response to his current question.

Gray noticed how far she'd moved in her seat. It was a good thing he'd made sure the passenger side door was locked, or she may have fallen out as he drove.

"If you know the name of the place I can call them while you run in and get your kids," he told her when he turned down the street where her grandmother lived.

"That's not necessary," she told him. "I can call in the morning."

Gray nodded, having momentarily forgotten where he was. In Miami and most major cities, he guessed, leaving a car abandoned was like an invitation for vandals, the car to be stolen or towed. But this was Temptation, and while she was parked in front of an empty house and people would definitely notice her car there in the morning, Gray doubted anyone would bother it. They were probably more likely to call her and ask her why she'd left it parked there, or worse, come up with their own reason and spread it throughout the town. Just as someone had obviously done when he'd returned.

"I was just thinking about your car possibly being stolen, but I guess that's not an issue here," he told her.

"No," she said when he pulled into the driveway. "We don't do that here."

As soon as he stopped the car, she pushed the button to unlock her door and opened it to get out. Gray reached out and touched her arm.

"I'm just trying to help, Morgan. I'm sorry if what happened back there made you uncomfortable."

She pulled her arm slowly from his grasp. "I'm not uncomfortable," she said. "At least not the way you think. I mean…" She sighed and then turned to face him.

"I'll get Wendy to take me home."

"That's ridiculous. I'm here, just go get your kids and I'll drive you home."

"I don't want to impose and I don't want…whatever

this is…or what you think you might be doing with me. It's just not going to work and I don't want to give you the wrong idea," she told him.

Gray was just about to tell her that it wasn't her. It was totally him. He couldn't take back the kiss, nor did he want to. Still, he knew the moment she'd pulled away from him that she'd regretted it.

"Who's that?" an older woman's voice asked outside the car, just before she began tapping on the windshield.

"Who is this coming to my house unannounced? You better not be selling anything!" the woman continued.

Gray could see her using a cane to tap on the window again. She either didn't know the act could break the glass, or simply didn't care.

"I'll call the sheriff and…wait a minute, Morgan? Is that you?" the woman asked.

Morgan simply shook her head and stepped out of the car. "Yes, it's me, Granny."

*This* was her grandmother.

Gray opened his door gingerly. The older woman was leaning over his side of the car. She backed up a little, still holding her cane out in front of her like a weapon. She was a little taller than Morgan, with a slimmer frame. It was dark, but the motion lights affixed to the top of the garage had come on so Gray could see the woman's very light complexion. Her glasses were large framed and black, her gray hair pulled back from her face.

"Ida Mae Bonet, meet Grayson Taylor," Morgan said as she'd come to stand beside the woman. "Gray, this is my grandmother."

Gray immediately stepped forward and extended his hand. "It's a pleasure to meet you, ma'am," he said.

She grabbed his hand, pulling him closer as she looked up at him. That must not have been good enough because then she hooked her cane on her other arm and used her free hand to pull her glasses down her nose so she could look over them.

"Hot damn! You sure are Grayson. The oldest boy. You used to wet the bed, too. Olivia didn't know what to do about that. I told her to put a hand to your bottom and you'd stop that nonsense," she said before laughing like she'd told the best joke ever.

If she wasn't still holding tight to Gray's arm, he may have tried to leave at that moment. Embarrassment didn't even seem to describe what he was feeling at this moment.

"Granny, where are the children?" Morgan asked as if she sensed Gray's discomfort.

"Oh, they're in the house fast asleep. I made my famous beef stew tonight. Let them run around and play until the bread finished baking, then I fed 'em. Before I could get the dishes washed they were asleep," Ida Mae said.

"It's not quite their bedtime, but I guess that's okay. I'll just go on inside and Wendy can take us home."

"Oh, she's not here," Ida Mae said quickly, stopping Morgan from walking away.

"What do you mean she's not here? She said they were going to get pizza and watch movies while I was meeting with Gray at the Taylor house," Morgan insisted.

Ida Mae shook her head, looking up to Gray once more. "You went back home, did ya? How'd you like that?"

"Granny, where's Wendy?" Morgan interrupted, clearly not interested in Gray's feelings on his family home at the moment.

That was just fine with Gray.

"Oh, she had to go in to work," Ida Mae said, waving a hand at her granddaughter. "Let's all go in and you both can get the babies. I'll bet Grayson has room in this shiny little car to fit them. He can take you home. That's what a gentleman would do after a date," she said and hooked her arm in Gray's.

He smiled. It came naturally to him, without having to think or wonder if it was the right thing to do. In the last two days, two women had linked their arm in his. In his entire life he had lost count of how many other women had done this. But none of them compared one bit to these women in Temptation.

Gray tried not to pay attention to the look of frustration on Morgan's face as he and Ida Mae moved into the house.

Old colonial was the style of Ida Mae's house, and Gray got a homey and welcoming feeling the second he was inside. The floors were covered in dark brown carpet and the walls had pictures of family members, no doubt. Some were old, in black and white, while others were in color and most likely more recent. There was furniture everywhere, which was a contrast to his more minimal decor back in Miami. A sofa, love seat and two recliners filled the living room. There was a coffee table with magazines neatly stacked, end tables with lamps, ashtrays and pictures in frames. Across the back of the sofa was a colorful quilt that looked old and precious. When he inhaled, he smelled the faint scent of Ida Mae's beef stew and homemade bread.

"They're lying back here in the den," Ida Mae said as she continued walking through the living room and into a smaller room. In the adjoining room there was a big-screen television that looked totally out of place with another old sofa and rocking chair across from it.

"Little darlins, aren't they?" Ida Mae asked Gray when he entered the room behind her.

"Yes," he replied because he wasn't certain what else to say.

Gray also wasn't sure what was going on. How did he end up in this house, which distinctly reminded him of his grandfather's house—the one he'd had here in Temptation before he'd died? And why was he thinking of the Sunday dinners his mother used to cook for them, the ones that she made them get dressed up for and had used her best dishes to set the table?

"They won't have their booster seats in your car, but I guess it'll be okay this one time. If you could just take Jack to the car, I'll get Lily," Morgan said as she moved past him. "I really appreciate your offer to take us home, Gray."

She did appreciate it, Gray thought. But she definitely did not like it.

He picked up Jack and the little boy instantly wrapped his arms around Gray's neck.

"Kids know," Ida Mae said, looking at Gray with a smile. "They know before grown folk do."

Gray didn't wait to hear an explanation and instead said a quick good-night as Morgan headed for the door. She'd yelled back to her grandmother that she'd call her in the morning, but Ida Mae was still talking to Gray as she walked with him to the door.

"Your mother was a strong woman. She did what was best for her children. That's what a good woman does. And a good man, well, he walks his own path," she said.

Gray turned to her then and said what came first to his mind. "I'm not like my father."

Ida Mae stared at him for a few moments before nodding. "You know, I don't think you are. Nope, I sure don't think you are."

He thought about Ida's words as he drove down more quiet streets. The houses were not equally spread apart and did not look the same, but all had a quaintness that Gray didn't see in Miami. He tried to ignore that, too. Morgan was quiet. Gray suspected she was trying to ignore him. He figured that made them two of a kind.

Her house was long, almost like a trailer, but Gray knew it was one of those prefab homes. He'd seen a few in Miami and had once entertained the idea of investing in a company that specialized in them. He had thought that the dwellings didn't feel like real houses. But when he walked into Morgan's, he felt differently. This was her home.

It was neat, with a homey feel. There was a corner full of the children's toys in the small living room. Going back farther there was a neat table that seated four and beyond that was a kitchen with cheery yellow paint. The bedrooms were past a bathroom and what Gray thought might be a closet. There were only two. The one to the left belonged to the children. The one to the right, he deduced, was Morgan's bedroom.

"Jack's bed is over there," she told him as she entered the room.

She hadn't turned on the light but the one in the hallway partially lit the room. Gray moved to the bed and laid Jack down easily. He looked over his shoulder and saw that Morgan was slipping off Lily's shoes. He did the same with Jack.

Gray stared down at the sleeping boy and felt something shift inside. Jack was a good-looking kid. His complexion was just a shade lighter than his mother's creamy brown. His hair was darker, his eyebrows thick, lips partially open as he slept.

"Thank you," he heard Morgan say from behind.

Gray turned to her. "You're welcome."

They stood there, staring at each other for what felt like a lifetime, before Morgan moved.

"I'll walk you out," she said after closing the bedroom door.

Yes, he should leave, Gray thought as he followed her. He should leave this house because he couldn't stop himself from wanting to ask how she liked living there alone with her kids. When he was at her grandmother's he'd wanted to know if they had Sunday dinners there. Morgan, the twins, her sister and Ida Mae. Did they spend Christmas Eve together and wake up on Christmas morning to a huge tree and lots of gifts? How did the children react? Did they try to defy sleep and wait for Santa? What was on their Christmas list this year?

No, he shook his head as he came closer to her front door. Those weren't questions he needed answers to. That wasn't why he was here.

"About earlier," Morgan began.

Her back was to him as she let one hand rest on the doorknob.

Gray cleared his throat and tried to do the same with his mind. She'd taken off her jacket and he could now see that the shirt she wore was fitted to her compact body. His hands itched to touch her pert breasts, his body heating with each breath he took because it was full of her scent.

What the hell was wrong with him?

"What about it?" he asked gruffly.

"I don't know why it happened," she told him as she turned to face him. "I—I mean, not since my husband." She cleared her throat this time. "I'm not that type of woman. I don't sleep with guys I've just met. I don't sleep around. Sex is not casual for me. I just—"

"You just want me as badly as I want you, that's all," he said and removed his jacket.

"If you're asking yourself why, I don't know the answer." Gray tossed his coat to the floor and immediately began undoing the buttons of his shirt. Her gaze followed his movements but she did not speak.

"I didn't come here for this," he said, a part of him still feeling totally confused.

Her children weren't that far away. Sure they were asleep and they'd closed the bedroom door, but she had children. That fact alone should have curtailed his actions, but they did not. He undid the belt and buckle of his pants.

"But just like in business I know when to act and when to retreat," he told her, his hand resting over his erection.

She licked her lips and Gray thought he would come right then and there.

"This isn't business," she whispered.

"No," he told her before lifting a hand to crook a finger at her, beckoning her to come closer. "This is definitely not business."

## Chapter 7

She wasn't going to stop him.

Even though her children weren't that far away. They were asleep in their bedroom and rarely ever woke during the night.

No, she wasn't going to stop him, or this.

It was an impulsive decision and that was not her style. This was more like something Wendy would do. Taking a chance, walking on the wild side. When had her normally cautious demeanor changed? Maybe it was when she'd taken that first step toward him. Or, perhaps it was the second his strong hands grabbed hold of her shirt, yanking it out of her pants, up and over her head without saying a word. It could have been the moment his gaze dropped to her breasts and rested there.

It didn't really matter because the sigh she'd just released was one of total surrender.

He'd carried her over to the couch, lifting her right off her feet in one swift motion. When he laid her down it was with a gentleness that she hadn't expected. Her body hummed with desire, her hands shaking with the urge to reach out and touch him. His shirt hung on his shoulders, the white tank he wore beneath melded to his chest and abs. She wanted him naked. That was the first thought she had as she lay back on the couch.

She'd turned on a lamp across the room when they had come in, so there was a soft golden glow around them. He looked like a bronzed god as he seemed to read her mind and stripped off his shirt and tank top. He looked like a bodybuilder, she thought. Or a professional athlete of some sort. Morgan knew Gray looked good in a suit. That's all she'd ever seen him in. But she had no idea that without clothes he would be this...gorgeous.

When she sat up and lifted a hand to him, he stepped closer and allowed her to push his pants over his hips. She was shaking, Morgan thought as her hands clumsily moved over the bulge in his boxers. It had been so long. He cupped her face in his hands then, tilting her head until she looked up at him. He didn't speak and Morgan didn't really think he needed to. She knew what he wanted, because it was what she wanted, too.

She let her hands fall from him and slipped them behind her back to unclasp her bra. He took off his shoes. She unbuttoned her jeans and pushed them down her legs until she realized they weren't going to move past her ankle boots. He unzipped the boots and slipped them from her feet. She then pushed her pants off completely. He had already stepped out of his pants and was now rubbing one hand from her ankle up to her thigh. His touch was soft and tantalizing. It was a simple one and yet undeniably sexy as tendrils of desire shot through her body. He stroked her other leg, spreading them apart slightly, and Morgan gasped. He cupped a hand over her juncture and she felt her arousal seeping through the cotton material of her panties. For a second she thought that perhaps she should be embarrassed that she wasn't wearing something sexier. The look of pure pleasure on Gray's face when his gaze locked on hers had that feeling dissipating. Her panties were removed next before Gray came over her, his lips immediately finding hers.

Again his kiss was hungry, hot and everything she'd come to expect from him. Her hands rubbed along his strong back, her legs wrapping around his waist. The first touch of his hot length against her damp center sent another spike of lust vibrating through her. She jumped and gasped and he whispered in her ear, "I've got you, baby."

Morgan liked the sound of his voice. He'd called her *baby* and she'd shivered. He kissed along the line of her jaw and she trembled.

"You don't understand," she said, but he didn't stop kissing her.

She was drowning in his kiss, her hardened nipples rubbing against his broad chest.

"It's been a while," she whispered and flattened her hands against his chest. "I mean, um, not since…"

Gray touched a finger to her lips to silence her.

"I understand," he said softly. "Are you sure you want to do this?"

His gaze seemed a bit softer, although his eyes were still darkened by desire. His jaw was strong as she lifted shaking fingers to touch him. There were so many reasons for her to answer no and only one for her to say yes. Morgan had suspected that it had been hard for a man like Grayson Taylor to refrain from anything he wanted. His wants and needs were always met, probably without him ever having to voice them. Yet he had with her.

"I want you," she told him without wavering another moment. "I want you, Gray."

She was the one to lift up at that moment, at the same

time guiding his head down so that their mouths could meet for a kiss. Their tongues dueled, moans mingled, and Gray slowly slipped inside of her. There was a rush of heat, a slight tensing, and then Morgan was falling. She matched Gray's thrusts, her eyes closing involuntarily as she held tight to him for fear of falling off the cliff to a bottomless abyss.

Every stroke, every whisper, every time he kissed her shoulder, her chin, her closed lids and her lips—it was all intoxicating. Morgan forgot everything and everyone. There was only Gray. Only this moment and he filled it and her with complete satisfaction.

So complete that she didn't want it to end.

Yet, she knew that it would. It had to, and then where would she be?

He held her when she trembled in his arms, her release taking her completely by surprise. It was a wave of pleasure that she couldn't resist but wanted to hold on to for dear life. Gray fell right behind her, holding her so tightly she could barely breathe. It was a wonderful feeling, a safe and cherished feeling, which, of course, Morgan knew would end and probably too soon.

"What are you doing here?"

"I'm picking you up for work. You do have to teach today, right?" Gray said the next morning when he showed up at her door.

Morgan didn't understand. Well, she did, but she hadn't anticipated that he'd be there. She'd already talked to Wendy—who was apologetic about last night—this morning. Her sister was supposed to roll out of bed and bring Morgan her car to use today. When she got to work she planned to call Otis to see if he could tow her car over to Smitty's, Temptation's only official auto-mechanic shop. She had not expected to see Gray at all.

"There's no need to inconvenience your sister. I'm here and I can take you," he insisted.

"You were here last night," Jack said.

Morgan had left Jack and Lily at the kitchen table with orders to finish their cereal while she answered the door. Apparently, Jack was finished. Morgan doubted that, but here he was.

"Yes, I was, and you were sound asleep," Gray replied.

"Not all the way. Your car has cold seats," Jack continued and Morgan froze.

She wondered if Jack remembered anything else about last night besides riding in Gray's car. Her son hadn't mentioned anything about Gray this morning, so the fact that he knew he'd been here was news to her. Yet another thing for her to think carefully about today.

Gray gave a nod as he moved past Morgan and into the living room. "I have seat warmers. We can turn those on this morning. I think it's colder today."

"It's gonna snow," Jack told him.

Morgan closed and locked the door behind her, turning in time to see Gray and Jack walking back toward the kitchen like they were old friends. They weren't, however. Gray was just passing through town. He would be gone as soon as he decided what to do with his buildings. Then they would never see him again. He'd made it perfectly clear that he did not like being back in Temptation. The pain, for him, was too great, and Morgan could understand that. No matter how her body wanted something totally different.

"Mr. Gray!" she heard Lily chime just before she entered the kitchen.

By the time she entered, she saw Lily once again in Gray's arms. Jack, who was standing close to his leg, looked up as he asked, "Do you know how to build a snowman?"

Gray had been touching the ends of Lily's hair. Her

daughter had wanted to have the ends of her ponytails left loose today. No twists or bows at the end, she'd instructed Morgan. Normally, Morgan didn't like for Lily's long and sometimes untamable hair to be worn loose while she was in school. It made for a distraction that the ABCs could not compete with. This morning, however, the conflict over just how wrong Morgan had been to have sex with a guy she hardly knew, on the couch in her living room, while her children were in the other room fast asleep, had made her a little more relaxed on the rules.

"I haven't seen snow in a very long time," Gray told Jack.

"How can you not see snow? It comes every year," Jack insisted, his little brow furrowed in confusion.

"We have fifteen minutes, you two. Finish your breakfast," Morgan interjected. "Would you like a cup of coffee?" she offered Gray, since he was there.

"Sure," he replied, sitting Lily down in her chair.

Jack slipped into his seat and scooped another spoon of cereal into his mouth, drops of milk dripping down his chin. Morgan looked up after taking another mug down from the cabinet to see Gray leaning in to wipe Jack's face with one of the napkins from the center of the table.

"How do you like it?" she asked, her voice unusually loud.

Gray and the children looked her way.

"Your coffee, I mean," she clarified, feeling uncomfortable.

The scene before her was extremely domestic and she didn't know how to digest it. Just like in her dining room, there was just a small table in the center of the kitchen floor where, normally, only three people sat. None of those people had been a man, because there had been no male in her life since James.

"Black," Gray replied.

James liked lots of cream and sugar in his coffee, just like Morgan did. Her husband hadn't been a millionaire, either. He'd driven a Jeep and not a Porsche. He was exactly six feet tall, not an inch over. Gray was much taller and more muscular than James. She wouldn't say Gray was stronger or more handsome, though. She just couldn't. It would be disrespectful to James's memory. Hell, everything she'd done and thought since meeting Grayson Taylor had been like spitting on all the love and memories she'd shared with James Hill and Morgan hated that thought.

"I live in Miami," Gray informed the children. "We don't get snow to build snowmen."

"No snowmen?" Lily asked. "That's sad. I want it to snow on Christmas. Just like the song Mama listens to on the radio."

"She listens to those songs all the time," Jack quipped.

"All right you two, less talking and more eating," Morgan chided lightly as she brought Gray's coffee to the table.

There was nothing else for her to do but take a seat across from Gray while the children continued to eat.

"Mr. Taylor's going to give us a ride this morning," she announced when there had been a few moments of silence while the children finally did what she'd told them to do. Her cell phone was sitting on the table and she picked it up to send Wendy a text to let her know.

"Where's your car?" Lily asked.

"It died." Jack shook his head. "Just like our dad. Did you know that our dad died, Mr. Taylor?"

Morgan almost dropped the mug she'd just been bringing to her lips. Her gaze shot to Gray's, but he only looked mildly taken aback. He probably wasn't used to the candor of children. Morgan was, but she had to admit that she hadn't anticipated Jack bringing up his father. The children rarely said anything about James, because they had no real memories of him, aside from the things that Morgan had told them.

Gray had just taken a sip from his coffee and now he slowly lowered his mug to the table as he looked from Morgan to Jack.

"My father died, too. Just over two months ago," Gray told him.

"Did he get shot?" Lily asked.

"Maybe we shouldn't be talking about this right now," Morgan said trying to intercede.

Gray shook his head as he looked over to her and said, "It's fine."

It wasn't, Morgan wanted to yell, but she didn't want to argue in front of the children.

"No. He wasn't shot," Gray said to Lily. "He had a heart attack."

"Oh," Lily said, her eyes wide now. "Our dad was in the army."

"He was a soldier," Jack offered. "He was fighting wars to help people but he got shot instead."

Morgan's chest constricted at the words and her hands shook so she pulled them away from the mug completely. Her mind was whirling with guilty thoughts about James and having this man sitting here at the table with James's children. A part of her knew how silly that was. James would never have expected her to remain a widow for the rest of her life. He would have wished for her to find happiness again, even if that happiness was in the arms of another man.

But Gray wasn't that man. There was no happiness to be found with him because he had no plans to stay in Temptation. Not to mention the fact that Morgan wasn't the type of woman that landed a man like Grayson Taylor. She knew that each time she let herself recall meeting Kym Hutchins. That woman—as much as Morgan instinctively did not like her—was exactly the type that would be on Gray's arm.

"It's time to go," Morgan said as she immediately stood. "Grab your coats while I clear the table."

The children were glad to be finished with their breakfast and hurriedly pushed away from the table. They were on their way out of the room when Jack turned back and asked Gray, "Are you going to heat up the seats now?"

Gray nodded. "Sure will. By the time you come outside they'll be all warm for you."

Jack smiled. "Okay, I'll hurry."

Now alone, Morgan struggled for the right words. She would text Wendy and cancel, then she would accept Gray's ride to work this morning, only because he was already here and they were in danger of being late. But then she wanted him to stay away from her children.

"You look like there's a battle going on inside your head," she heard him say.

"What?" she asked and picked up the two bowls from the table, then carried them to the sink.

"Your brow's all wrinkled and you were rubbing the back of your neck like you were trying to push some difficult thoughts out of your mind," he told her.

Morgan put the bowls in the sink and tried to relax. He was right, but he didn't need to know that. "I'd like my car to be fixed and I'm hoping that Otis can get to it today."

"Otis? He's the guy at the B and B?"

"Yes," she answered. "He does a lot of odd jobs around town since his wife died. Before that he'd worked at the train station for thirty-five years and then retired. Granny says he used to drive Ms. Ethel crazy when he was sitting in that house all day doing nothing. Now he spends his days helping out at the B and B and wandering around town giving people rides, dropping off packages, fixing broken bikes or raking up the leaves. Anything to keep him from sitting still too long because then he'd miss Ethel too much."

She'd said the last quietly, her hands clenching the side of the sink.

"Like you miss your husband?" Gray asked softly.

Morgan turned quickly and was shocked to see that he'd gotten up from the table and now stood just a couple feet away from her.

"I—I didn't say anything about that. About him, I mean," she said and then paused. Taking a deep breath, Morgan let it out slowly. "I apologize for the children bringing him up. I don't know where that conversation came from."

Gray looked as if he was going to say something, then he stopped and simply waited.

"I can't do this," she admitted. "I don't know how to do this casual sleep-together thing that I'm sure you're used to. I'm not as worldly as you or Kym and I don't want to be. All I ever wanted was to have a family and to live right here in Temptation, just like my parents did. I never expected my husband to die so quickly and now I can only focus on my kids. I hope you don't sell those buildings because they mean a lot to us. Your father even had plans for them. Although I'm not sure they were the best plans. Still, the town's counting on you continuing with your father's ideas so that we can reap the revenue and hopefully draw in more tourists. There are lots of updates we need here in Temptation. We could be such a rich and prosperous town for future generations, but if you sell, outsiders will come in and do what they want."

She stopped because she'd been babbling. All the things that had been rolling through her mind for many nights just came tumbling out and now her heart pounded and her hands shook.

Gray took a step toward her. He reached out, cupping

a hand at the nape of her neck. He didn't rub the spot, but simply held his hand still there. The heat and comfort spread instantaneously and she almost leaned into him with relief.

"I'm not trying to make you forget your husband," he said quietly. "I don't know what a love that deep feels like, but I have to say it's admirable. As for the town, I don't know what I'm going to do about that yet."

It was an honest answer, she figured. Honest and conflicted. Was Gray having as hard a time dealing with his dead father as she was with the strong memory of her dead husband?

"Now, let's get you to work," he said, pulling his hand slowly away from her. "You don't want to be late."

He'd walked out of the kitchen then, leaving Morgan alone with her thoughts. The ones that did not want to obey her declarations. She did feel guilty about James and she did want what was best for the town. But she also wanted Grayson Taylor. Damn, how she wanted him.

# Chapter 8

"I want all of his files delivered here. No later than to-morrow, Phil," Gray said into his cell phone. "And see if you can locate my brother Garrek."

After hanging up with his lawyer, Gray sat back in the chair at the coffee shop where he'd been for the last hour. The manager of the shop, a very lovely lady in her mid-forties named Clarice, had given him permission to use the back two tables as his makeshift office.

"I don't know why Jim and Darlene won't get with the times and have Wi-Fi installed out at the farm. I swear some people are so resistant to change," Clarice had told him as she'd brought him coffee and the whole wheat bagel he'd ordered.

"It's all right," he'd told her. "I kind of like the solitude, for small stretches of time, that is."

Gray smiled and for the first time since he'd been in Temptation, he felt totally relaxed.

After dropping Morgan and the children off at school

he'd come straight to the coffee shop with his tablet, cell phone and a small file he'd begun to compile late last night. He'd spent hours thinking about the time he'd spent at the old house. The feelings he'd felt while walking through the rooms, the memories that continued to push further and further to the forefront of his mind. They all swirled through his head until he'd spent most of the night and early morning sitting up staring out the window to the dark outline of the mountaintop. After finally getting a couple hours' sleep, he'd showered and headed straight to Morgan's house. There'd been no question that he'd drive her to work that morning.

With that done, now Gray had a lot of research he wanted to get done.

Theodor Taylor had been up to something before he'd died and Gray wanted to know what.

The man who he and his siblings had all developed a love-hate relationship with over the years had secrets. Gray had never doubted that. One of the things his mother had always said about their father was that he had an uncanny ability to keep things to himself, whereas she was an open book. Olivia had always blamed herself for that flaw. Gray had actually found it refreshing that all he'd ever had to do was ask his mother a question to get an honest answer.

Where his father was concerned, well, there weren't many times Gray had even attempted to ask the man anything of substance. During his childhood there had only been a couple of visits from his father and sporadic phone calls. Theodor just sent money. That was all he'd been able to do for his family after they left Temptation. Gray considered that enough since the man's presence never failed to upset his mother. Had he been left to make the choice about leaving town, he would have chosen to see his mother with some semblance of happiness every time.

Some of his other siblings didn't agree, but Gray couldn't carry their burdens as well as his own.

Morgan had told him that just about a year ago his father had been in touch with Fred Randall, the real estate agent and property manager. He was also Millie's husband. Gray had written all these names down last night. Now he typed the agent's name into the computer to see what he'd come up with. There wasn't much, but the agency did have a website with Fred and his wife smiling on the front page. They stood in front of a sparkling white colonial that Gray figured was their house. He went to the contacts page on the site and wrote down the address and phone number. He would pay Fred Randall a visit today.

"There you are," a female voice said as she approached the table. "I've been looking all over for you. Those people at that so-called resort you're staying at are rude and unprofessional. I guess I shouldn't expect too much considering where we are."

Gray looked up from his tablet to see Kym. "Good morning," he said to hopefully stop her from talking.

She sighed in return. "It will be when I get a decent cup of coffee. I swear, one of the first things I'm going to do when I get back to the office is write a letter to Starbucks and tell them they need to open up a shop in this ho-hum town."

"Ms. Clarice makes a wonderful latte," Gray told her as he resumed shutting down all the windows he'd opened on his screen. He'd closed the document he'd been writing the moment Kym sat down.

"I don't want a latte," she told him. "I want an extra-hot grande caramel macchiato with extra caramel and I don't need anybody asking me if I'm going caroling tonight, either."

Caroling was tonight, Gray thought as he sat back in his chair. Clarice had told him about it when he'd first come in. She said they'd start at city hall and walk down Main Street so that all the shoppers could hear them as they mulled about in the local stores.

"Joya and Martina will have hot cocoa and hot soups at the church afterward," Clarice had added with a wide grin. "You ain't had nothing 'til you've tasted Joya's Maryland crab soup."

Gray had nodded and thanked her for telling him, but until this moment when Kym mentioned it, he hadn't given much thought to attending. Now, he found himself wondering if Morgan would want to go with the children. Not as disturbed by that thought as he should have been, Gray reluctantly returned his attention to Kym.

"Did you bring the contracts for me to sign?" he asked her, already knowing what her answer would be.

She shook her head, then frowned as the young waitress—instead of Clarice—brought Kym her cup of coffee. When the woman walked away, Kym leaned over to sniff the beverage and rolled her eyes.

"No. I don't have the contracts and obviously I don't have a good cup of coffee, either," she snapped.

"I'd really like to get those contracts signed, Kym, since you've come all this way. Then you can make arrangements to head back to the office," he told her.

"When are you coming back to the office?" she asked.

She was wearing beige pants and a jacket with a peach turtleneck today. Her hair was pulled back neatly, gold earrings at her ears. She looked crisp and efficient, a bit rigid and way too attitudinal. Gray had never made that assessment of her before.

"There's more to work here than I originally thought," he told her. "So I'm going to stay a little longer."

Last night, before he'd put Jack to bed, and before he'd had sex with Jack's mother on their couch, Gray only thought he'd stay in Temptation for a few more days while he figured out what exactly his father had planned. This morning when he'd heard the children speak of their father and saw the pain of losing her husband still so clear in Morgan's eyes, he'd decided to work through his business a little quicker. He figured he'd need another day or two just to get all the facts straight in his mind. That's how Gray liked to make decisions—with all the facts and a thorough list of pros and cons before him. There had never been memories or emotions in the mix. Hence the reason he hadn't been able to give Kym the exact timeline of his return.

"Then I'll stay and help you," she immediately offered. "What do you need? I can pull the numbers on property taxes and values in this area. We can also do a study on the town's viability as a tourist destination and historical landmark. While I was wandering around with nothing to do last night, I heard from many of the townspeople about all the battles fought in Temptation. Some of them were also talking about an outlet mall possibly being built here to help bolster their economy. There were two women in particular who had more details than the others. I told them that would be a wonderful idea. That's exactly what they need here, a blast of the twenty-first century."

"A mall? Where would they put an outlet mall?" Gray asked, his attention now firmly back on the town and what his father's plans were.

"The first woman said something about the land behind the community center was the prime location. I don't know where a community center is here, but she seemed hopeful. The other woman—I didn't get either of their names, but she was the loud and bossy one, with a bad highlight job—interrupted, declaring the community center was vital to the town and should stay where it is." Kym shook her head. "Old people hate progress."

"Progress shouldn't always entail forgetting the past," he said thoughtfully.

Gray wasn't totally sure where those words had come from, or why he'd felt the need to say them. The look Kym gave him said she couldn't believe he'd said them, either.

"You do know our business is about future innovation," she said, her brows lifted in question. "I mean, that's what we do at Gray Technologies. We're constantly trying to stay three steps ahead of anyone else. Developing the most high-tech and revolutionary ideas around. If you have the chance, why wouldn't you wish the same for the town where you were born?"

He didn't have an immediate answer. That did not deter Kym. In fact, Gray thought as he watched her lean forward, a familiar gleam appearing in her eyes, she already had something specific in mind.

"What we should do is find out who the developer is for the outlet mall. We can meet with him and secure its biggest lot for the Gray Café. Think of all the publicity behind Grayson Taylor returning to his hometown to open the first brick-and-mortar Gray Technologies store. It would be phenomenal! And most of the publicity would be free. The town would probably foot the bill since this will definitely increase their revenue," she said, her excitement evident.

Gray frowned. Maybe because Millie Randall and Otis had just walked through the front door and the first thing Otis said was his name.

"Damned if I didn't talk the city slicker up," Otis said as he begin making his way back to where Gray and Kym were sitting.

"Mornin', ma'am. You're looking pretty as a picture today," Otis said, pulling a worn herringbone cap from his head as he made a mock bow in front of Kym.

She didn't scowl, but the smile she gave him was less than enthusiastic. "Good morning," she said.

"Mornin' to you, son," Otis said when he was once again standing as straight as he could and looking over to Gray. "You keeping this woman busy with all your work and stuff? She needs time to get out and see the sights. Maybe she wants to go caroling tonight? If not, couple of us grown folk will be down at Pat's Bar. Nothing like hot chocolate with a dash of tequila."

Gray almost chuckled. He totally believed this man would have a bottle of tequila sitting right beside his mug of hot chocolate.

"I don't think we'll be stopping by the bar tonight," Gray told him.

"But you should come out for the caroling," Millie added as she joined them.

"Hello, Ms. Millie," Gray said. "Let me introduce you to my assistant, Kym."

Millie was already shaking her head, heavy gold-and-orange earrings moving at her ears. "We already met last night," Millie informed Gray without giving Kym a glance.

"You were out with Morgan last night, right? How did you like seeing your old home? Olivia and Theodor were so happy there," she continued.

Gray gritted his teeth at that presumption, then decided it was better to be cordial to Millie, especially since he would need to speak with her husband regarding his father's dealings in the last year. Besides, it wasn't her fault that his father had fooled the citizens of this town.

He was just about to respond when he noticed Kym staring at him. It was a look that he wondered if he should address. He didn't, of course. There were too many ears around. He did, however, try to reroute the conversation.

"Ms. Millie, if you could let your husband know that I'd like to stop by his office this afternoon to speak to him about the properties and my father, I would really appreciate it," he told her.

Millie smiled and nodded. "Of course, I'll give him a call right now." She began fumbling through a purse that looked more like a piece of carry-on luggage.

"You going down to the real estate office?" Otis asked.

"Yes. I have a few calls to make right now so I'm going to head back to my room. But I'll be back in town a little later this afternoon so I can see Mr. Randall then."

Otis began scratching his head. He looked as if he was trying to figure something out, but Gray had no idea what.

"Oh, I just thought you'd be heading over to the school this afternoon. You know, to pick up Morgan and the kids. Heard you dropped them off this morning," Otis said.

Kym put down the cup she was sipping from with a loud clanking sound. Not only did Gray look her way, but Otis and Millie did also.

"I thought her car would be fixed by now," Gray replied when he turned back to face Otis. "She said she was going to have it towed."

Otis nodded. "Yep. I got right over there this morning after she called me. Got it all hitched up to the back of my truck and took it down to Smitty's. He owns the garage, you know. But Smitty said he's got to order some part, seeing as the car's so old it might be a while before it comes in."

"Oh, it's going to be brisk this afternoon," Millie chimed in, obviously putting off the phone call to her husband. "I told Georgia down at the church to make sure there was plenty of blankets and hot chocolate for tonight because people are going to be downright chilled to the bone when they come in. Those kids shouldn't be walking home in this weather," she said with a knowing nod to Gray.

"No," he said. "They shouldn't."

"We were going to meet with the real estate man this afternoon, correct, Gray? Are you going to call your husband and confirm his availability?" Kym asked Millie.

Millie not only ignored Kym's question, but she also turned so that her back was now facing Kym as she looked directly at Gray.

"I think Fred's only available after four today. That'll give you plenty of time to pick up Morgan and the kids," she said.

If he wasn't sitting in the middle of this very odd scenario, Gray might find it funny. It was obvious what Millie and Otis were trying to do. When in actuality, all Morgan had to do was call him and let him know she'd need a ride. He would have immediately told her he'd be there. He then realized she didn't have his phone number and he did not have hers, either. He'd had sex with this woman and had no way of communicating with her afterward. On any other day, when he was back in Miami, that might have been the ideal situation for Gray. Today, not so much.

"Tell your husband I'll be at his office at four," Gray told Millie. "After I pick up Morgan and the kids."

Kym huffed and then let out a little yelp as Otis traded places with Millie and now stood close enough that he could've lean over and sniffed Kym's hair.

Gray smiled then. This was definitely not a scenario that would have taken place back in Miami.

Morgan's first-grade classroom was located on the first floor of the old schoolhouse building. The structure had been renovated ten years ago, when there was an increase in enrollment—which came as a direct result of a blizzard six years prior that dropped three and a half feet of snow onto their tiny town. Prefab or modular structures, as some people called them, similar to the one Morgan lived in, had been situated in a *U* formation around the original building to add additional classroom space. The same had happened to the middle and high schools, which were originally two old mills that had been converted.

On Wednesdays, the last hour of her class time was normally quiet as her students were in the music room with Mrs. Ellersby. Earlier she'd found her holiday music playlist on her phone and was now playing it as she graded homework. The hope was that the music and the work would numb her mind to the nagging thoughts of Gray and last night—and having what was easily the best sex of her life on a couch, no less!

Her cheeks warmed and her stomach clenched each time the thought surfaced in her mind. How could she have been so careless? Lily had nightmares sometimes and Jack didn't always go to the bathroom before he got into bed. Either of them could have come out of their room and wandered into the living room, where they would have undoubtedly seen the light. Of course, they would have also seen something else. She cringed at the thought.

Gray was everything she'd thought he would be, taking into consideration that most of what she knew about him had come through secondhand stories from numerous people in town. The first time she'd seen him—well, actually, she'd bumped into him and felt every hard and tantalizing muscle of his chest—she'd known he would be a good lover. Not that she was all that experienced in the area. James hadn't been her first, but there had been only a couple before him. So, no, she would never consider herself to be a sex expert. Still, she could tell by the way he stood, with his legs partially spread and the strength in his arm as it had circled her waist. Morgan wasn't even going to add into the equation the moment she'd first felt his thick erection the night of the charity event. Yes, she'd been thinking about sleeping with him ever since that night. So what happened last night should not have come as any surprise.

Yet it did. She'd loved James with all her heart. How could she now so easily fall into bed—or wherever—with another man? Okay, she told herself with a heavy sigh,

James died three years ago. She had not been with any other man since then, had not even thought of dating, let alone sleeping with someone else. Until Gray. So logically, there was no reason why she shouldn't have jumped that fine-ass man's bones. None at all.

Then why did she feel like she'd made a colossal mistake?

"Hey there. You're much too pretty to be in such deep thought about anything," Harry said as he entered the room.

Morgan looked up from her desk to see his familiar face. He was wearing dark pants and a button-front shirt with the hardware store's logo on the front pocket. His boots made a dull sound as he crossed the tile floor, his face sporting the smile he almost always carried.

"Grading papers on who has the neatest coloring techniques is not as easy as you may think," she joked with him.

It was easy to joke with Harry because she'd known him forever. They talked as easily as brother and sister, but got along much better, she figured. Harry had taught her how to drive a stick shift. He'd given her and James a two-hundred-dollar gift voucher to his store. He'd also brought over the famous lasagna and tuna-mac casserole his mother made the day after James was buried. There wasn't a time in her life that Harry Reed had not been there and Morgan truly appreciated his friendship. But today, he was the last person she wanted to see.

"Well, you should stop grading those papers," he said as he came closer to the desk and looked down at her. "We can get the kids and head on over to the B and B, where my mom's cooked up her famous barbecue spare ribs, collard greens, and mac and cheese. Have dinner and then go out caroling. I know Lily's been looking forward to that. She couldn't stop talking about it the other day."

Yes, Lily loved to sing. The fact that Harry knew that made Morgan feel just a bit sadder. She was beginning to think that Wendy was right after all. Remembering the way that Harry had looked at Gray the other night when she'd picked up the kids had opened her eyes to something she felt guilty about not noticing before.

"That sounds wonderful," she told him. "But Granny's been making salads and sandwiches all day for the church. She has chicken salad and homemade bread. She called me earlier to tell me to stop by and get some leftovers."

Granny had made sandwiches for most of the celebrations in Temptation because everyone loved her chicken salad. The one time she'd tried to switch it up and brought tuna salad instead, there'd almost been a revolt.

Harry's smile didn't falter. "That sounds just as good. Nothing like Ms. Ida Mae's chicken salad on fresh white bread. I can take you over there and then we can head down to the town square. I had asked Otis about your car when he came into the store today and he said it wasn't ready yet."

"Ah, actually, I already have a ride," she told him.

Now Harry frowned. "I hope it's not with that Taylor guy. I heard you let him drive you in this morning. Look, you really need to be careful around him, Morgan. He's not who you think he is."

Morgan sat back in her chair then and simply looked up at Harry. This was the second time he'd warned her against Gray. The first time she'd brushed it off as him being another citizen who didn't want Gray interrupting their flow in Temptation. Now, she wasn't so sure that was all Harry was trying to say.

"Well, who is he then?" she asked out of curiosity. Maybe he knew something she didn't. Perhaps someone had told him something that was so ridiculously untrue that Morgan would have no choice but to set him straight.

Harry sighed, wiping a hand down his bald head. "I don't mean like that," he told her. "I'm just saying that he's not the type of person you're used to dealing with."

"Right. Because I have absolutely no experience dealing with grown men." She hadn't been offended when he'd said something similar the day before, but now she was. Did Harry really think she was some bubblehead who didn't know how to handle herself?

"Not that," he continued. "You do just fine around men. I mean, you know, you do just fine around town with all the people you've known forever. But nobody knows a thing about this guy. He left Temptation when he was just a kid and now he's back. Just like that. And we're all supposed to go around kissing his ass and making sure we suck up to him just so he won't sell some old run-down buildings. That's just bull!"

Now she was angry. How could Harry, of all people, act as if losing those buildings was no big deal to this town? One was actually the hospital, which they desperately needed since it was the only one in town.

"Well, I don't know about you, Harry, but I'd like to see those run-down buildings stay right here in this town. They're a part of our history and even if he's just returning to town, they're a part of Gray's history as well," she insisted.

"'Gray,' as you call him, doesn't give a crap about this town or those buildings. He's just worried about how much money they can make him," Harry quickly retorted.

Morgan wanted to yell. She wanted to tell him that Gray did care and that's why he was still here, giving her time to prove that the buildings should stay. But she couldn't because she really didn't know that what Harry just said wasn't true. Instead, she stood and shook her head.

"Somebody has to try and convince him to do otherwise. But since people in this town would rather sit back and talk a situation to death instead of getting up off their butts and doing something, I guess that someone has to be me," she said.

"He doesn't give a damn about you or anyone else in this town. The only use he has for a pretty woman is to get her in his bed."

Morgan's cheeks were on fire now. Her hands clenched at her sides as she tried valiantly to remain calm. Harry had no idea that she'd been with Gray in that way. He couldn't possibly know.

"I'm sorry," he said quickly. "I don't mean to upset you."

She was already shaking her head. "No. I'm not upset."

Morgan lied. She was upset and embarrassed and she wanted Harry to leave so that at least some of her emotions would subside.

"But I do have a ride home. Thank you so much for the offer, though. I guess I'll see you later at the caroling," she said when Harry made a motion to walk around the desk to where she was standing.

"Who's taking you home? I saw Wendy going to the hospital. She's working the night shift."

Okay, she hadn't secured a ride home, but Morgan would walk if she had to. It wasn't that far, even though she'd probably end up carrying Lily at some point. It didn't matter—she was not getting in Harry's truck.

"I am." Gray's deep voice sounded from the back of the classroom.

Harry turned and Morgan looked back to see Gray—dressed in another custom-fit and too-damn-sexy suit—walking toward them.

"She doesn't need to take rides from you in that fancy car," Harry said the moment Gray stood in front of him. "I can drive her around just fine."

That might be true, but Morgan didn't want him to. If she was still not completely convinced that Harry's feelings for her were much more than she wanted to reciprocate, she was positive now.

"That's okay, Harry. You don't have to spend your time worrying about me and my kids. Gray can drive us home," she said.

On one hand, she was still feeling too embarrassed and confused to be around Gray again. On the other, being with Harry was only going to feed his belief that there was something more between them. Morgan figured she was choosing the lesser of two evils.

He turned so fast and stared at her with such hurt and anger that Morgan almost faltered. Harry just continued to look at her as if waiting for her to say something different. She didn't and when he took a step toward her, Morgan saw Gray move. He was standing beside her in the next second.

"I'm ready whenever you are," Gray said, more to Harry than to her, she thought.

"I, um, just need to grab my things and go get the children. The bell should be ringing in a few minutes and the music class is near the back door," she said and moved to the side, away from both men.

"You don't get to come here and start barking orders," Harry told Gray.

Morgan looked up at him, still shocked that he was acting this way. "He's not giving anyone orders, Harry. He offered me a ride and I accepted. That's all."

"He's using you!" Harry shot back.

Morgan was angrier now than she'd thought she'd ever been before. "Using me? I'm a grown woman, Harry. And I'm pretty sure I'm capable of deciding who can give me a ride home. How that equates to him using me, I'm not sure."

"He's cozying up to you so that he can get you to give in about those damn buildings. That's what his type does to women. You don't see him coming to town to talk to any of the men about the buildings, do you? Hell, he should be dealing with Fred Randall, not you. You're just a teacher."

"That's enough," Gray said solemnly and once again moved closer to Morgan.

"Don't talk to me like that," Harry said, his voice booming in the room as he stepped closer to Gray.

"Stop it!" Morgan said, squeezing between the two men. "Harry, you're acting like an ass. I'm taking the ride home with Gray and since you think I'm nothing but a fluff-head female that can't tell when someone is using me or not, why don't you run along and find yourself someone else to insult!"

She didn't move and wouldn't look away when Harry stared down at her. It was a standoff, which she never would've imagined herself in, between two men who looked like they could probably do each other bodily harm. And her own adrenaline was drumming through her veins as if she might want to physically do some damage herself.

How dare Harry stand here and say all the crap he'd just said to her?

"You should leave," she heard Gray say from behind her.

"You," Harry said, pointing a finger at him. "Don't tell me what to do!"

"Go, Harry!" Morgan said. "I have a ride so there's no need for you to be here right now."

She felt a little like crap speaking to Harry—her long-time friend—that way, but hell, he deserved it after insulting her the way he just did.

Harry huffed and looked like he was going to actually take a punch at Gray, but he didn't. Instead, he stormed out of the classroom looking like a petulant child.

# Chapter 9

*Have a holly jolly Christmas! Have a holly jolly Christmas!*

Gray rolled over, dropping an arm over his still-closed eyes, and grinned. Three days after they'd gone caroling, he could still hear Lily singing. She'd sung all that night, even as she ate chicken salad sandwiches and slurped chicken soup at the church. Every song they'd sung as they walked through the streets of Temptation, plus a few she'd added because she said she'd heard them on the radio earlier that day. Gray took that to mean two things—that she loved Christmas as much as her mother and that she also loved to sing.

Jack, on the other hand, wanted his sister to stop the minute she'd begun.

"She sings so loud," he'd complained as he walked beside Gray, holding his hand.

Lily, once again, was in Gray's arms. He never really knew how she ended up there, just that whenever he came near her, his arms seemed to itch to hold her. She was light as a feather, her cherublike cheeks soft as she nuzzled against him when she hugged him close. Was there ever anything that had felt this good? Gray had wondered as they'd moved through the streets.

"It's cold enough to snow," Jack had said after two or three songs.

He'd only sung the parts to the songs he knew, and usually only after Morgan had given him a questioning look because he was too quiet. Gray could totally relate. He wasn't a singer, either. Still, there were some lyrics he knew and when they came to a stop across from a row of homes where he was told the town's oldest living couple lived, they sang "O Come, All Ye Faithful" and Gray sang along. His mother had liked this song. She had sung it every holiday as they decorated their Christmas tree.

When he opened his eyes it was to a dim room and Gray immediately turned to look at the clock on the nightstand. It was after eight in the morning. He'd stayed up late last night going through the boxes of documents that Phil had sent from his father's house and his office. There'd been so many interesting things inside that Gray hadn't wanted to stop until he'd gone through each one.

One box had been full of Theodor's papers, copies of his divorce decree and all their birth certificates, which had been clipped together. Gray had frowned when he'd found those, then quickly put them to the side. His mother had the originals. Gray knew because he and Gemma had been the ones to go through Olivia's things after she'd died. Another box had large brown envelopes inside. On each envelope was one of the Taylor children's names. Gray shuffled through until he found the one with his name. He didn't realize how long he held that envelope in his hands until finally he decided to put that on the side, too.

There were also notes on what Theodor had planned

for the properties in Temptation. He'd wanted the hospital to undergo another renovation, one that would include an addition to the building. This would be called the Taylor Generational Wing and would feature a state-of-the art facility focusing specifically on infertility and the management and care of multiple pregnancies through multiple births. Theodor planned to put twenty-two million dollars into the project.

Gray had been stunned.

The money from Theodor's estate had been equally divided between him and his siblings. There was nothing else. So where was Theodor getting this type of money from?

Gray continued going through the other boxes, finding pictures of them when they were young, many more than he'd ever thought his father would have kept. There were also bonds for each of them that probably should have been kept in a safe-deposit box. Gray doubted they were worth very much, but he'd put them on the table with the envelopes that he would have delivered to his siblings. The last thing Gray had found before he'd headed to bed was a picture of his mother and father. It immediately reminded him of the portrait he'd seen that day at the B and B, because his mother was seated and his father stood behind her with a hand on her shoulder. Theodor did not wear a hat, as the man did in that portrait, but his facial expression was stoic, almost to the point of being worried. His mother's expression was complacent, a look he'd seen her with much too often. Still, his gaze had rested on his mother's wedding ring and the gold band his father wore also. They were committed to each other, regardless of what was going on at that moment in time. Gray had wondered what had happened to that commitment.

Sleep had taken a while to come that night. He'd been plagued by thoughts that he was more like his father than he'd wanted to realize. The only thing that Gray had ever committed fully to was his company. He kept tabs on his siblings and communicated with them, because he knew his mother would have wanted them to stay together. But if there was something that needed to be done on the work front, he'd been known to put his family on the back burner. What did that say about the type of man he was?

With a sigh Gray climbed out of bed and went to the window. He looked out to see the farm blanketed in snow. The weatherman had predicted winter weather the night they'd gone caroling and Jack had been more than ready for it, but it never came. Now, days later, it looked like a world of white out there.

Gray went to take a quick shower. Once he was dressed he tried to bring some semblance of order to the papers and things from the boxes. He didn't want to repack them just yet because he was still taking notes on the buildings and Theodor's plans for them. He also wasn't ready to put away the envelopes with their names on them—something inside warned him that they were important. So important that looking at them right away was almost terrifying.

Gray made a call to Phil, instructing him to go back over all of his father's financials to see if he had some hidden stash of money that even Theodor's lawyers didn't know about.

"I want to know about every penny and every account with his name on it," Gray told his lawyer. Then he had a thought.

Turning with his cell phone in hand, Gray looked at the six brown envelopes still lying on the table where he'd put them last night.

"Check for bank accounts in our names," he told Phil. "Use each of the children's names and search the banks in and around the area of Temptation. Also, offshore accounts."

Phil probably had no idea what Gray was talking about—it was barely ten in the morning on a Saturday. Gray was positive that his thirty-year-old attorney, who liked to spend his nights in hot clubs and his days in the courtroom, was still rebounding from his Friday-night antics. Gray didn't care, he needed to find out if Theodor had been hiding money and why. His father had studied engineering while in college, only to return to Temptation, where he worked in the town council's office supervising and approving any road work and handing out permits for renovations to citizens. Once he'd left the town and his family, Theodor had opened the first Taylor Manufacturing Company in Syracuse, New York. There, the different engines he designed began being sold to various toy and clock companies.

Over the years Theodor made good money and then he'd been contracted by a Japanese auto company to build engines for their entire new lineup of cars and trucks. After that, Gray had watched the stock in Taylor Manufacturing soar and his father become a billionaire before he turned fifty. To an extent, Gray knew that was part of what drove him. He'd always wanted to be better than Theodor Taylor.

When the call was finished, Gray grabbed his coat and a change of clothes. What he had planned for the day was bound to get messy, he thought with a smile as he left his room and ventured out into the blustery cold morning.

His car was not made to be driven in a foot of snow, but with the help of Jim Coolridge, who was already up and out shoveling his walkway so that he could get out and tend to his animals, Gray's car was finally on the road. He drove slowly, as there'd been no plow coming down these streets. He marveled at the fluffy white substance that hung on trees and covered the landscape because it had been so long since he'd last seen it. When the weatherman had called for snow and Gray knew he'd still be in town, he'd ordered some things online. Luckily, they'd arrived yesterday morning. He wiggled his toes in the insulated boots he was now wearing. They were oddly comfortable, even if the puffy ski jacket he wore was beginning to make him sweat in the heated interior of the car.

When he pulled up in front of Morgan's house, Gray couldn't wait to go inside. He felt like a kid again as he slumped through the snow, only to frown as he saw that the snow had once again started to fall and that Morgan's sidewalk was covered with it.

"Got a shovel?" he asked the moment she answered the door.

"What?" she asked with a confused expression, obviously not used to men showing up at her door on Saturday mornings.

"So I can shovel the sidewalk," he told her.

While she was standing there looking perplexed, Gray smiled. He liked seeing her hair matted to one side and her thick purple robe belted tightly around her slim waist. He knew that as cold as it was out there, the last thing he should be thinking about was how sexy she looked, but he couldn't help it. He wanted to grab her up in his arms and swing her around. He'd nuzzle her neck the same way Lily did his and enjoy the softness of her.

"Yay! Mr. Gray's here! We're gonna make snowmen!" Jack yelled from where he now stood behind his mother.

"Can we, Mama? Can we go out and make snowmen now?" Jack asked.

"It's cold and it's still snowing and—" Morgan stammered.

"I know I'm from Miami, but I'm thinking these are the best conditions to make snowmen," Gray told her.

"Uh-huh. Uh-huh. It is. Best conditions, Mama. The best!" Jack continued, this time pulling on the belt of Morgan's robe.

"Mr. Gray's here in the snow! He's not wearing a suit, Mama," Lily noted when she peeked her head around Morgan's other side.

Gray shrugged. "You might as well toss me the shovel and get them dressed. They're never going to give you any peace if you don't."

Her frown said she'd deal with him later. The children's excited laughter as she backed away and closed the door meant she was going to take his suggestion. The shovel was tossed outside moments later, followed by the door slamming.

Two hours later it was still snowing. Morgan had never seen such huge flakes as they fell all around them. She'd bundled up the kids and dressed herself warmly and had come outside to see Gray moving the snow with ease. He'd been almost finished shoveling the walkway at that point and she'd gone over to help him, while Jack and Lily had instantly fallen onto the ground to make snow angels.

"You make one, Mama," Lily insisted, coming over to grab Morgan's hand.

"Let me finish this first," Morgan said.

Lily pouted and seconds later, Morgan felt herself being lifted from the spot where she stood. With a yelp she wrapped her arms around Gray's neck as he'd easily scooped her up into his arms. "You wouldn't," she warned just seconds before he'd grinned down at her and then dropped her into the snow.

Stunned, embarrassed, irritated. None of those words meant a thing in comparison to Lily's and Jack's immediate giggles. They both jumped happily on her as she lay there and Morgan hugged them close. She loved when they were happy. That was the reason she'd hustled them to the side, got up and then fell back in the snow on her own, spreading her legs and arms to make an angel.

Gray was standing beside her when she got up.

"Beautiful," he said, and used his gloved hands to wipe flecks of snow from her face.

"I've always been good at making snow angels," she told him.

He shook his head and whispered, "Not the angel."

Jack's snowman took priority after that and the four of them worked long and hard to build the biggest and friendliest one they could. Morgan tracked snow through the house to find a scarf, an old thick Magic Marker for its nose and spare buttons for the eyes.

"He doesn't look like Frosty," Lily proclaimed as they stood back and admired their handiwork.

"That's because his name is George," Gray said. "George the snowman."

"That sounds silly," Jack proclaimed and then laughed. "That's our snowman, George. Take a picture so we can send it to Aunt Wendy and Granny!"

Gray dug his phone out of his coat pocket and snapped a picture of George.

"All of you go stand beside him," Gray instructed and they followed.

Morgan stood beside George while Jack and Lily kneeled down in front of him. When the kids scrambled out of the way, tossing more snow at each other, Morgan thought she saw another flash. She looked around and then back at Gray, who snapped another picture of her.

"What are you doing?"

"Making a memory," he replied instantly.

Later that afternoon, once Morgan had gotten the kids and herself out of their wet clothing and fixed grilled cheese sandwiches and tomato soup for everyone, she and Gray sat in the living room alone.

"They'll sleep for a couple hours they're so worn out," she told him.

He'd taken off his wet clothes and slipped on a pair of sweatpants that should have definitely been banned for any man built like Gray to wear. His T-shirt was fitted, his feet covered in white socks as he sat on her couch, looking as if he belonged there. With a resigned sigh to not entertain any more guilty thoughts about James, she'd taken a seat on the other end of the couch. The only other furniture in her living room besides the couch was an old recliner, which had a tendency to recline on its own. She usually steered clear of it while the kids loved to play on it. Which was probably the reason it was broken.

"They had fun," Gray said. He was holding a mug of hot chocolate she'd just made for the two of them. His big hands wrapped tightly around the Scooby-Doo mug. "I'd forgotten how much fun it could be to play in the snow."

"I'll bet you and your siblings had a great time in that big yard. The property surrounding that house is so spacious and totally conducive to a big family," she said before hurrying to sip from her cup in fear she had said too much.

Gray sat with his elbows on his knees and stared down into his cup.

"We played all day in the summer. After breakfast we'd head right outside. Me, Garrek and Gage, we liked to build forts and keep the girls out." He chuckled. "Gemma and Gia were always plotting ways to get inside. But Gen, that's what we call Genevieve, she didn't care. She was always the more serious one out of all of us. She learned how to read first and never let any of us forget that she could do it best."

"Wendy did most everything better than me. She ran faster, did better splits and cartwheels. She even sounded better yelling cheers than I did," Morgan said and then shrugged. "But I had kids first and she hates that."

"My mother always said she was glad she decided to keep all her babies. She'd wanted a big family and she'd gotten it in a one-shot deal," he said.

Morgan couldn't help but feel admiration for Olivia Taylor. Having twins had been quite a task for her, so there was no way she could imagine giving birth to sextuplets.

"I imagine it was hard for her, the pregnancy and everything."

"The press was the hardest part," Gray said. "She never liked them being around all the time. I guess that's why I don't, either."

Morgan sighed. "Granny said they've been driving all around town talking to people and speculating about what you're going to do."

He shook his head. "It shouldn't matter to them. I mean, it's just a story they get to tell. Just like they told the story about my family before, only they got that one all wrong."

"No," Morgan admitted. "It probably doesn't really matter to them. But it does to me. Especially because after I lost James, this town and the people here were all I had left. They took me and my kids in and they showered us with their love and generosity. It's my home and it just matters," she told him with a quiet shrug.

Gray sat back on the couch then and looked over at her. She didn't turn away, although his gaze was intense. It was also needy and Morgan couldn't bear not to be there for him. She suspected that nobody had been there for Gray all these years. He was a fixer and so he fixed things, but he didn't share and he didn't grieve. She thought that was very sad.

"I know it matters to you," he told her. "I'm trying to do the right thing here, Morgan. I just need to figure out what that is."

She nodded. "I understand."

She did and then she didn't. What she thought was so

simple, she imagined was much harder for someone with the feelings Gray was harboring.

"My father had plans for those buildings. I want to know exactly what those plans were and how he was going to implement them."

"And then what? Will you carry out his plans even though you still hold so much resentment toward him?"

He frowned and then took a sip from his cup. "I'm going to do what I think is best for everyone involved. I'll ask my siblings when I make a decision and then I'll go from there."

"The community center has been the hub for our theater program. Kids in the town over have taken school trips out here to see plays. It doesn't bring in a lot of money, but I was thinking that we could invite other theater groups here, larger ones to put on plays maybe around the holidays. We have lots of great shops here so tourists could not only pay to see really great professional plays, but also shop around and purchase unique gifts," she offered.

"And what about the hospital?" he asked.

Morgan leaned forward to set her mug on the coffee table. Then she turned, lifting one leg to rest on the couch as she faced Gray. "Well, for starters, it's the only full-service medical facility we have. Doc Silbey still has his clinic down on River Street, but he's getting older and mostly only tends to minor bumps and bruises. Besides, my sister works at the hospital and so do a lot of other people. Where will they find work? What will happen when Granny finally cracks someone over the head with that cane of hers because they ticked her off?"

He laughed at that. Morgan liked his laugh, the deep rumble that came bursting out of his chest. She was liking way too much about this man.

"I can actually see that happening," he told her when he'd regained a bit of his composure.

"Me, too," she said, and had to chuckle herself because he'd started laughing again.

Then she sobered a bit, propped her arm on the back of the couch and leaned her head on her hand. "What I'm saying is that we have a use for the buildings here. Sure, they may need to be renovated, but they also need to stay. If you sell them to someone, who knows what they'll want to do with them. They might even think it's best to just tear them down. So I hope you'll consider all this when you make your final decision."

"I will," he said. "I'm going to consider something else, too."

"What's that?" she asked casually. Throughout the day she'd grown more and more comfortable with Gray being there. Though that wasn't totally true, she admitted to herself. The comfort had been growing in the last week as he'd picked her up for work and brought her home after work, as if it was their daily routine. When he showed up the second morning, Morgan decided not to argue the transportation issue anymore. The kids loved riding in the fancy car with the heated seats and Morgan kind of liked not having to hear Wendy complain about getting up too early in the morning to come and get her while her car was still in the shop.

"How much I like kissing you," he answered.

No matter how comfortable she thought she felt, his words still caught her off guard.

She cleared her throat. "I'm, ah, I'm not sure we should go down this road again."

Gray moved closer to her. "I'm not sure we can avoid it."

He was right and Morgan couldn't figure out anything to say to rebut his statement. That was all Gray needed to react. If she gave him the smallest opening, he'd fill it, quickly and completely. His hand cupped her face in a motion so soft and endearing she sighed.

"I never imagined a man like you coming into my life," she admitted. "And I'm sure I'm not the type of woman you usually spend your time with."

His thumb rubbed along her cheek as a smile slowly spread across his face. "That just means that neither of us were thinking enough of ourselves."

"Gray," she sighed again, her eyes fluttering as she saw him moving closer.

"Yes?" he answered, his lips just a whisper away from hers.

"I like kissing you, too."

# Chapter 10

He wanted to see all of her this time and he didn't want her on a damn couch. So Gray took Morgan by the hand and they both stood. She stepped close to him and wrapped her free arm around his waist.

"This won't end well," she said softly, resting her forehead against his chest.

He leaned forward and kissed the top of her head. "I don't want to talk about the end," he told her. "I don't want to talk at all."

In the next instant he was lifting her into his arms, cradling her small frame against his chest as he walked back toward her bedroom. She lay her head on his shoulder and Gray looked down at her as he stepped into her room. Using his foot, he closed the door behind them and moved closer to her bed. The room was small. She'd taken the smaller one and had given her children the larger room. Her queen-size bed barely fit, leaving room for only one nightstand on that side of the room. There was a window and right next to the door was her dresser.

Standing at the foot of her bed, Gray let her down slowly, loving the way her body felt moving along his. She kept her palms flat on his chest and looked up at him. Gray leaned down, taking her lips in a soft and slow kiss that only stoked the fire already brimming inside him.

What was it about this woman? She was absolutely right when she had said she was not the type of woman he dated. He could count on one hand how many female bedrooms he'd seen over the years, preferring a hotel room to the personal space of him or the woman he was with. Had he ever known any of their family members? No. He was certain of that fact.

Gray knew that Morgan liked lots of sugar and a little cream in her coffee and that she drank that coffee from a Tinker Bell mug every morning. He knew that her shoe size was an eight and a half—he'd learned that when he'd helped the kids pull her boots off earlier when they'd come inside. She laughed a lot when her children were around. Her eyes danced with the action and her cheeks lifted high on her face.

When her arms came up to wrap around his neck, Gray wrapped his tighter around her petite body. He now held her so close to him that he felt the moment she came up on tiptoe to meet his demands. Pulling away from the kiss, he set her slowly on the bed. She'd changed into thin pants that left absolutely nothing to the imagination. Her full bottom had enticed him terribly as she'd moved throughout the kitchen fixing their lunch. Now, he pulled those pants down her legs slowly. They trembled slightly and he touched one thigh, while dropping a soft kiss on the other.

He removed her shirt, his fingers brushing against the pale green lace of her bra. When he'd tossed the shirt to the side, Gray couldn't help himself—he leaned in, dragging his tongue over the hill of cleavage. She sucked in a breath and he moved to the other breast to lick the smooth skin there as well. When her hand went to the back of his head, his erection throbbed, pressing against the restraint of his boxers and his sweatpants.

Her hands were fast and before he could take another breath, Morgan was reaching down the fabric of his pants, grasping his length in her palm. The breath didn't come and he almost choked, pleasure spiking through his blood. Gray hurriedly unsnapped her bra so he could get his mouth on her pert nipples. Morgan moved just as quickly, as she pushed at his pants and boxers, until she could wrap her bare hands around his length, stroking him from the base to the tip. Gray moaned, closing his eyes and suckling her breast with more urgency than ever. He thrust his hips into her strokes, loving the warmth and the desire that continued to spread like wildfire at her touch.

"Off!" she moaned and tried to push at his pants once more.

With Herculean strength he pulled away from her, her breast leaving his mouth with a popping sound. Gray pulled at his clothes, tossing them wherever they fell in her room. He'd clean up later, he told himself. All that mattered now was her.

She slid back farther on the bed until her head rested on the pillows. Then she let her legs open wide, her arms lifting to him. Had he ever seen anything as beautiful as Morgan lying naked on a bright rainbow-colored bedspread? Gray didn't think so. He did think, however, that he was going to make a fool of himself and come right then at the sight of her tender folds open and damp with her arousal for him.

"You were right," he said, his voice gruff as he climbed on the bed, moving slowly toward her. "You're not like any other woman I've ever met."

When he thought he saw her tense, Gray touched the inside of her thighs, pushing them farther apart until he leaned forward and dragged his tongue through her moist center. "You're so much more," he whispered before touching his tongue to her soft, wet flesh once more.

She gasped and then moaned as he continued, lifting her hips as if she wanted to feed him. That was just fine with Gray because he was hungry, so damn hungry for her. She was delicious, soft, hot, sweet. He couldn't get enough as he delved deeper, his fingers clenching her thighs. He was intoxicated—that's the only way Gray could think to describe the woozy feeling he had each time he inhaled the scent of desire and tasted her thick nectar. The more she moved against his mouth, the hungrier he became. He didn't think he would ever get his fill of her.

"Gray!" she moaned and he knew she was trying her best to be quiet.

He wanted to help her with that, but he couldn't stop. Each time he told himself that he'd had enough and tried to pull back, he opened his eyes and look down at her plump flesh so moist and delectable, and all for him. Yes, he told himself, she was for him. All of her.

When her body trembled beneath him and she clenched the back of his head until the waves of pleasure had finally abated, Gray moved over her. He slipped inside of her in one thrust, filling her completely and loving every inch of his length she'd sucked into her waiting abyss.

It was heaven. No, for Gray this was so much more. It was a place he'd never imagined, a feeling he'd never conceived. Buried to the hilt inside of Morgan, he closed his eyes to the onslaught of feelings. On the one hand he wanted to hold her tightly to him. On the other, he wanted her in every position he could visualize, taking every bit of this desire he had for her. He wanted her release, again and again. He wanted her moans against his mouth, her softness against his skin. If he could hear her voice...

"Gray," she moaned when he thrust deep into her once more, as if on cue.

"Say it again," he told her. "Please say it again."

Because if she did he'd know without a doubt this was where he belonged. This place, right here, right now, was made just for him.

"Yes, Gray," she whispered. "Yes!"

"Yes," he said, echoing her. "Yes!"

This was where he was supposed to be. He moved in and out of her, dropping kisses over her forehead, down her nose and onto her waiting lips. She wrapped her arms around his shoulders, her legs around his waist and held on tight. He stopped thinking—hell, he may have even stopped breathing, she felt so good.

When she pushed against him and he rolled over onto his back, Gray thought he'd never seen anything so beautiful. He'd been wrong. She looked like a sex goddess rising over him with her hair slightly mussed, her high pert breasts staring down at him. When she opened her legs and straddled him, Gray moaned. He grabbed her hips, guiding her. She didn't need the help, he thought as she grabbed his erection with ease, positioning him so that she could lower herself onto his shaft. It was hot and exciting, the connection striking him like ten thousand bolts of lightning.

She lowered herself slowly and Gray watched with intense pleasure as his length disappeared inside of her. When she was completely impaled he squeezed her hips, reached his hands up to cup her breasts and whispered her name this time.

"Morgan," he said. "My sweet and hot Morgan."

She rode him then, letting her head fall back as she arched over him, driving him crazy with desire. When they finally laced their fingers together, holding their arms above them, Gray pumped wild and fast inside her, loving the sight of her keeping up with his pace, her breasts moving and her mouth open as she moaned her pleasure. They came together this time, squeezing each other's fingers and trying like hell not to yell out as the intense feelings of desire completely washed over them.

Dinner was homemade pizzas.

The reason why there was now red sauce splashed over the counters and on the table. The mozzarella-and-Romano-cheese mix was sprinkled across the floor in almost a direct path from where Lily and Jack had carried their handfuls from the counter to the table, where their individual pizzas were being prepared. It had only taken two trips for Morgan to realize it was smarter to move the bowl of cheese to the table with the rest of the ingredients. The table was small so she'd been trying to leave plenty of room for the two of them to work, but that had only created more of an issue as they bumped into each other as they moved back and forth.

As for Gray, well, his white T-shirt had red splashes all over it. Then while Jack was trying to carry the tray with his pizza to the oven, he'd even dropped a huge glob of pepperoni soaked in sauce and cheese on Gray's foot. To say it had been an adventure in the kitchen was definitely an understatement.

While the pizzas cooked, Gray had volunteered to take the twins into the living room to watch *Frosty the Snowman*. After about two minutes of feeling grateful, Morgan realized he'd done it to get out of cleaning the kitchen. She smiled and shook her head as she went to the side of the refrigerator to retrieve the broom.

Her cell phone, which had been charging all day on the counter by the blender, rang just as she began sweeping.

"Hey," she said after seeing Wendy's name on the caller ID.

"Hi," Wendy replied. "How are you guys holding up in this storm? Need me to come over with anything?"

"No, we're good. How are you and Granny fairing?" Morgan asked.

They were probably at each other's throats, which was their norm. Two years ago the doctor had told Granny she needed that cane and glasses. She hated both. Wendy and Morgan had decided that their grandmother probably needed more in the way of daily care, so since Wendy was still single and had no kids, she'd given up her apartment and moved in with Ida Mae. They'd been battling ever since.

"She's in the kitchen cooking. You know that's the only thing that keeps her quiet. That and *Jeopardy*," Wendy added with a chuckle. "What are you guys doing? Been out in the snow yet? I know Jack's been worrying you to death about it," Wendy continued.

Morgan moved around the kitchen sweeping up everything that had fallen onto the floor, which was a lot. "We went out this morning when Gray came over."

The moment she said the words, Morgan knew they were a mistake.

"Gray came over in a snowstorm?" Wendy asked with more than a little suspicion laced in her tone. "Wait, is he still there?"

Morgan couldn't lie, not to her sister.

"Yes, he is," she said simply and prayed that would be the end of it.

No such luck.

"And just what is he doing now? Or maybe I should ask what are you doing? That might be the better question," Wendy said. Morgan could hear the grin in Wendy's voice. "Is my little sister having a sordid affair with the new guy in town?"

Morgan really hated how that sounded, but she couldn't deny it. She was, and actually, she was really liking it.

"Okay, I am," she told Wendy. "But it's not as sordid and scandalous as the way you make it sound."

"Oh, really? Then tell me what it is. Because from where I'm sitting, you had sex with him just a few days after you met him and if you haven't already, I bet you'll have sex with him again tonight."

"What makes you say that?" Morgan asked, unable to really sound surprised by Wendy's statement, considering she and Gray had not too long ago done exactly what her sister was suggesting.

"Hello, we're in the middle of a snowstorm. What do people do in snowstorms besides shovel snow? Make love," Wendy quipped. "You remember how the school became overcrowded in the first place. In another five years we'll be building another extension to those buildings."

"Stop it," Morgan insisted. "It's not like that."

"Mmm-hmm," Wendy said and began to laugh.

"I'm hanging up now," Morgan told her.

"Okay, okay, look, I know my sister so I think I know that you're serious when you say it's not some scandalous affair. So what is it? Are you two falling in love or something? Oh, that would be awesome. I saw him coming out of the school the other day with the twins and he's great with them. Wouldn't it be wonderful if you did fall in love and get married? The twins would have a father and you'd have someone to share your life with. Plus he's rich so you'd definitely get to move out of Temptation into some big ol' house with fabulous furniture and jewelry."

Wendy loved jewelry and shoes. She also enjoyed dying her hair different colors and eating coconuts and fancy chocolates.

Morgan sighed.

"No, definitely not all that. And I don't care about

Gray's money. I'm—I'm just enjoying this for right now. That's all. Can't I do that?" she asked.

"You definitely can," her sister replied. "You deserve to enjoy whatever moments you can find. You were a widow at a young age, a mother, too—of course you deserve some happiness. I'm just jealous, that's all. Gray's hot and loaded." Wendy laughed.

Morgan shook her head, but couldn't help but smile. "Yeah. He is."

He was also spending the night with her, which Morgan realized hours later, after dinner and the many holiday movies they watched.

Last night had been the most fun Gray had at Christmastime since he was a young boy. That giddy feeling in the pit of his stomach that started around the first of December when he was a kid had made a home there now. He'd already planned to go into the coffee shop at his earliest convenience so he could go online and buy all the things Jack and Lily had told him they were expecting Santa to bring.

Sometime in the middle of the night, he'd realized he wanted to see their faces when they opened their gifts. He wanted to hear their laughter and experience their joy. He wanted a family.

Several hours had passed after this morning's pancake-and-scrambled-egg breakfast that Gray had tried to help Morgan prepare. He was a horrible cook, but he'd figured cracking eggs wouldn't be too difficult. He was so wrong and thus they'd had a few crunchy moments when eating their eggs.

Gray had been in the living room playing a board game that the twins were definitely winning when he realized Morgan had been gone for quite a bit of time. She'd excused herself when her phone rang. It had taken a few minutes, about ten he recalled, as he looked at his watch again and moved toward the bedroom, where he suspected Morgan had gone. He told himself he wasn't the jealous type. He'd never had a reason to be. Yet, something had nagged at him about her being gone on a call for this long. Something he wasn't too keen on acknowledging.

"Everything all right?" he asked when he saw her staring out the window in her bedroom.

She jumped at the sound of his voice.

"Ah, yeah. Everything's fine. I'll be out in a minute," she told him.

That was meant to dismiss him, but Gray didn't leave the room.

"Who were you talking to?" he asked her.

The look she gave him was nothing short of pissed off. "I don't think that's any of your business, Gray. I mean, we haven't known each other long enough for you to question me."

Gray knew then that whomever she'd spoken to on the phone had upset her and he was lucky enough to be the one standing in the room with her at the moment. He was the one that was undoubtedly going to take the brunt of her anger.

He crossed the room, coming to stop right in front of her. Yet Gray was careful to remain far enough away. If she wanted to take a swing, she'd miss, but he was close enough if she needed a shoulder to lean on instead.

"I'm not questioning you," he told her. "I'm concerned."

"Concerned about what? Your precious buildings?" she snapped and then shook her head. "I'm sorry. That's not fair."

"What's going on, Morgan? Who upset you?"

She clenched the phone in her hand, then brought it up to her forehead, tapping it there while she waited. "I should have known better," she began. "I've lived here all my life so I should know how they are by now."

"You should know how who is?" Gray asked, getting a sinking suspicion he wasn't going to like where their conversation was going.

Sighing heavily, Morgan tossed the phone onto her bed and looked at him. "That was my grandmother on the phone. She was calling to tell me that it doesn't look good for a single mother to have a man spending the night at her house."

Gray could only stare at her in disbelief, even though he was familiar with the rumor mill in Temptation.

"Somebody apparently rode by and saw your car here. They couldn't wait to get on the phone to start spreading it around. Granny said that Martina from the church just called her to ask what was going on between us," Morgan told him.

"Wow." It was all Gray could say at first. "I've heard the saying 'word travels fast' but I never knew that meant it traveled through a snowstorm," he told her. "Who the hell was out last night or yesterday in the storm to know that I was here? And why were they driving down this road again today to see if I was still here?"

"My first guess is Otis," she said. "He has a plow that he hitches to the front of his truck and uses to clean the main streets. The town council hires a professional but sometimes they take a while to get here."

"So Otis ran back and told who? Because I don't see him picking up the phone and passing along this news," Gray said, like it even mattered.

"He probably would have stayed at the B and B to help out Mr. Reed with the guests and getting their vehicles shoveled out," Morgan said and then she paused.

"What?" Gray asked.

"Your assistant is staying at the B and B," she told him.

"Kym? She wouldn't call anyone in this town to tell them a damn thing. She barely likes speaking to the people around here." That was certainly true, as was the fact that Kym was still in town. Each day that Gray had spoken to her she'd had another reason to stay. He'd decided that he had other things to focus on besides Kym. He wondered briefly if that had been a mistake.

"Yeah, I heard that about her," Morgan added. "But if Otis mentioned your name and Kym was around, I'm sure her diamond-stud ear would have perked right up."

She was probably right about that, Gray thought.

"What about Harry?"

"What about him?" she asked.

"Would he call around and tell people?"

She seemed to think about it for a moment. At the same time Gray heard something outside. He looked out the window to see a local news truck pulling up and cursed.

"I guess it doesn't matter who called who, the reporters know now so the whole world is about to find out," he said.

Morgan came up behind him, a hand going quickly over her mouth. "Why would they care?" she asked.

"Because I'm a Taylor and I'm back in Temptation. It's news for them. We've always been just news to them."

They stood there for a few moments in silence, watching as the cameramen set up just a few feet away from Morgan's house. The snow had stopped sometime in the middle of the night and now the sun was shining brightly. Gray had gone out again last night to shovel the walkway. If he'd known it would have just make things easier for the reporters to get closer to the house, he wouldn't have. But there was nothing he could do about it now.

"Let's give them something to report," Morgan said from beside him.

"What?" he asked.

She looked up to him. "If they're here it's because

somebody already told them that this is where you were. They obviously want something to report, so let's give it to them."

Gray couldn't believe she was saying that. "What did you have in mind?"

# Chapter 11

It had been over two weeks since Gray, Morgan and the twins made national headlines as they'd decorated Morgan's Christmas tree in front of an open window and an entire news crew.

Now, just five days before Christmas, Morgan was at the community center practicing the play with her kids again. The town was abuzz with festivities. All up and down Main Street, holiday music played through the speakers that had been hung outside the buildings. Storefronts were decorated with everything from Santa and his reindeer, to snow villages and huge decorative gift boxes. It looked like a scene out of an old movie and Morgan loved walking through the street to get to the community center.

She'd told Gray that she had a ride because Wendy was off work that night and could help her with the rehearsal. He'd seemed a little distant when she'd spoken to him, but Morgan had forced herself not to think about it. Wendy was meeting her at the community center, so she and the kids had walked from the school. It was a chilly day, but Jack and Lily loved playing in the new snow that had fallen just yesterday.

"Granny says with all the snow we've had so far, we probably won't get any now on Christmas Day. It would have been nice to have a white Christmas," Lily stated as Morgan worked on the last of the props for the play.

"She might be right," Morgan replied, looking up quickly at Lily.

Her daughter had been laughing so much lately that the return of her usual solemn tone caused Morgan to worry.

"We haven't had a white Christmas in Temptation since I was a little baby," Morgan told her. "But it'll still be Christmas."

Lily pouted. "Will it still be Christmas if Mr. Gray leaves?"

Morgan didn't know how to answer that question. In the past few weeks, Gray had been with them almost every day. If he wasn't driving them somewhere, he was stopping by her house. He played with the kids while Morgan caught up on housework or worked on lesson plans. Last night, he'd even taken them to Sal's Italian Bistro for dinner. Jack had so many cannoli he'd had a stomach ache by the time they had arrived home.

"Christmas always comes, regardless of who's here or who's not," Morgan finally answered.

"Like it came all those times while Daddy was gone," Lily added for clarification.

The words tugged at Morgan's heart.

"Yes, baby, just like that," she answered.

Lily shook her head. "But Mr. Gray's not dead. He can be here for Christmas, can't he, Mama?"

Morgan sighed. She was in big trouble now. Her mind had warned against getting involved with Gray from the very start. She'd known that he had no plans of staying in Temptation, and yet she hadn't cared. Everything that had happened between Morgan and Gray had been for her pleasure only. How her children would bond with him and how they were going to feel in turn when he left town had not been a big enough priority for her. Dammit.

"Of course he's staying for Christmas," Jack said when he came over to join them. "You heard him say we were gonna put that train set that Santa's going to bring me together. I'm gonna be the conductor and Mr. Gray's gonna work for me."

Her son spoke so proudly. He was poking out his chest and looking as serious as an adult as he talked to his sister.

"There's no need to worry. We're gonna have the best Christmas ever!" Jack continued.

Morgan didn't know if that was true or not, just as she didn't know if Ethan was going to recite the lines they'd rehearsed for the past few weeks, or make up his own on Christmas Eve. What she did know, and probably the only thing Morgan thought she could control, was that she needed to draw a line between her, Gray and her kids before it was really too late.

A few minutes before rehearsal was over, Morgan jumped at a tap on her shoulder. This was the fifth time they'd gone over the Jacob Marley scene. Even though she knew the ghost was really Cabe Dabney's voice and Lily and Wendy rattling the chains, Morgan was starting to feel a little edgy.

"Sorry," Harry said. "Didn't mean to frighten you."

"Oh, no," Morgan told him, shaking her head. "I'm fine. How are you, Harry?"

She hadn't seen much of him in the past couple of weeks, not since the blowup they'd had in her classroom that day.

"I'm good. How've you been?" he asked, thrusting his hands in the pockets of his work pants.

Morgan tried to smile, but she was really tired and had a headache. A big part of her wished the twenty-fourth would hurry up and get here so she could be finished with this play. Wendy, of course, had thought what she said was hilarious when Morgan had said it out loud about half an hour ago.

"I'm hanging in there," she admitted with a sigh. "The kids are really excited, though. It's going to be a nice production." Lord, she hoped so, she thought as she closed her eyes.

"That's good. You know my mom's spearheading the potluck that's going to be held in the kitchen here that night," he told her.

Morgan nodded. "Yes, I heard. That's so generous of her. Granny said she's not making chicken salad again. She's baking cakes instead. I think she said a Kentucky butter cake, a rum cake and a pineapple upside-down cake."

Harry pulled a hand out of his pocket to rub over his stomach. "Then I'm definitely coming to see the play."

Morgan chuckled and for a moment it felt like old times between them. The easy rapport they'd always had was back and she was glad. She really hadn't wanted any hard feelings over what had happened between them.

"I can't wait until it gets here," she said. "Is that why you stopped by, to drop off some things for your mother?"

"Oh, no. Smitty finished with your car so I told him I'd drive it over," Harry told her.

"That's fantastic! You don't know what it's like to be at someone else's beck and call until your car breaks down. Thanks so much, Harry," she said and on impulse gave him a hug.

Harry hugged her back. Tightly.

"What's the special occasion?" Wendy asked when she walked up to where Morgan and Harry stood. Morgan pushed away from Harry to turn to her sister.

"Harry brought my car over. It's fixed," she told Wendy. "Now you don't have to drive me home."

Wendy was looking at Harry, one hand on her hip. "Oh, did he now? That sure was nice of you, Harry."

"No big deal. I just wanted to make sure she got it as quickly as possible," he said.

"Uh-huh," Wendy commented and nodded.

Morgan's cell phone vibrated in her back pocket and she pulled it free to read the text message. It was from Gray. He wanted to know if she needed a ride home. She hurriedly typed that she wouldn't because her car was now fixed. He replied instantly, saying that was great, and then asked if she would mind coming by the resort. There was something he wanted to tell her.

"She can just drop me off at the B and B once she leaves here," Harry was saying when Morgan looked up to see that he and Wendy were still standing there.

"Ah, actually," Morgan said, "I was going to ask Wendy to take the kids home with her. Granny wants them to help her wrap presents."

"Sure," Wendy said with a slow nod toward Harry. "And since your parents' B and B is right around the corner, I can drop you off, too."

Harry immediately looked to Morgan.

"That's great," Morgan said. "I have to just get the kids together so they'll be ready when their parents show up. Thanks again, Harry."

Morgan replied to Gray's text as she walked away. Tomorrow she'd have to buy Wendy some of those chocolate-covered raisins she loved so much from Mr. Edison's candy shop. Not only was her sister taking her kids, but she'd also thwarted Harry's plan to be alone with Morgan.

\* \* \*

It had been a while since Morgan had been out to the Coolridge farm. Two years ago, with revenue from the farm tight, the Coolridges decided to use the space where the family used to breed horses to hopefully make ends meet. As far as Morgan knew, they were still barely scraping by as there didn't seem to be that many tourists who wanted to come stay on a farm without the basic amenities of the real world.

She walked up the steps to the Owner's Suite, where Netta had informed her Gray was staying. For a moment Morgan had thought about texting Gray and asking where his room at the farm was instead of alerting someone else to her presence there. Then she decided *what the hell*. The entire town already knew she and Gray were involved ever since she'd had the brilliant idea for them to decorate her Christmas tree in front of the news cameras.

"Hi," she said when he opened the door.

"Hey. Come on in," Gray said before walking away.

The first thing Morgan realized as she stepped inside and took off her coat was that she'd never seen Gray like this before. He was disheveled. He wore jeans, which she'd gotten used to over the past couple of weeks. There was no doubt that this man could wear the hell out of a suit, but the jeans gave him an even more dangerous and rugged look that she found enticing as well. Closing the door behind her, Morgan also noted that he wasn't wearing any shoes and his T-shirt, which he would normally have neatly tucked into his pants, was out and wrinkled.

There were boxes and papers all over the place. A tablet sat on the table amidst more papers and files. On the bed were his cell phone and briefcase. Something was definitely going on with him and despite her resolve to draw the line between them, Morgan wanted to know what it was. She wanted to help, if she could.

"What's going on, Gray?" she asked.

"I found it," he said.

He ran a hand down the back of his head and sighed heavily. "I found it," Gray repeated.

"You found what?" she asked. It looked like he could easily *lose* something in this room.

"The money," he told her, a slow grin creeping onto his face.

"What money?"

Gray was a multimillionaire, Morgan knew that. So watching him look excited and relieved over money left her baffled.

"My father's money. I mean, the money he put aside for the town," Gray continued.

He moved quickly to the table, picked up a folder and thrust it toward Morgan as he continued to talk.

"It was Fred," he began. "He's the one that told Millie about my dad's plans for the hospital. Remember you told me about that?"

Morgan looked up from the bank statements she was reading and nodded. "Yes, I remember."

"Well, I found the plans. They're right here," Gray said, picking up another file. "He outlined everything here. When I first saw them I read them over and over again, wondering why he would go through all the trouble to write this down if he didn't really have intentions to see it through."

"Okay, wait a minute, slow down. I don't understand," Morgan told him.

"After my father's attorney read his will, me and my siblings split the money and sold his house in Syracuse. None of us wanted it. I had everything from the house put into storage until one of us felt like dealing with it. There were two cars, a truck and a sedan. His will said he wanted them donated to the Pediatric Cancer Foundation in Richmond. He was born there and he had a twin brother who died from leukemia when they were three. Then I came here to sell the last properties he owned. We just wanted to be done with everything that concerned him as quickly as we could."

"Okay," she said, trying to follow the conversation and relate it to the huge sums of money she read on the statements she held. "So if you already split the money, sold the properties, put his belongings in storage, what is this?"

Gray smiled then. A huge smile that touched his eyes and squeezed Morgan's heart.

"My father was a simple man. One of the things I remember about him was that he didn't like flashy cars or clothes. When we were on television there were lots of offers for endorsements. Companies would send boxes and boxes of clothes and toys and things. Dad sent them all back. The paycheck from the show was all we needed. That's what my mother told us. That's one of the reasons she couldn't understand why my dad had suddenly fallen for the glamorous producer and walked away from his family."

He shook his head.

"After he was gone and they divorced, Dad started doing something he'd always loved—building things. He built engines and he turned that into a profitable business. My mother never had to fight him about child support because he always paid and sent gifts on our birthday and Christmas. He also sent us clothes at the beginning of the school year. He had bought a house in Syracuse—a modest house—and the two cars. Everything else, every other dime he made, he'd put into seven accounts in a bank on Grand Cayman Island."

Morgan was beginning to understand now.

"He saved money for each of us and for this town," Gray told her. "It was his intention to give back to the town that had given him his family."

She looked down at the statements again and shook her

head the same way Gray had just done. It was incredible and astonishing, and it made Gray extremely happy. For Morgan, surprisingly, that was enough. She stepped over the papers on the floor and went to him, wrapping her arms around him and hugging him tight.

Gray hugged her even tighter, burying his face in the crook of her neck.

"All these years," he said, "I wanted to hate him. He left us and we didn't know why. We thought he didn't love my mother, or us, enough to stay. As I grew older I just thought he was an ass and I didn't want anything to do with him. But while I wanted nothing to do with him, all he thought about was us the entire time he was gone."

Morgan nodded. "Yes, he did. He was determined to take care of you and your brothers and sisters, even when he was gone."

Gray pulled back. "And this town. He loved Temptation and all that the town had brought him."

"It seems he did," Morgan said, still holding the folder. "He loved the town a lot." A nervous giggle escaped as she recalled the 6.8 million-dollar sum in the account marked The Taylors of Temptation, LLC.

"He did," Gray said with a nod. "He absolutely did love this town, and you know what?"

"What?" she asked as Gray slipped the file from her hand and dropped it to the floor.

"I can see why he did. I can see why this small town of Temptation was so alluring to him."

"You can—" Her words were cut short when Gray grasped the nape of her neck, pulling her lips to his for a scorching-hot kiss.

He was devouring her and she loved it, loved the feel of his fingers scraping over her scalp as he tilted her head for deeper access. The other hand, strong, gripped her bottom, pressing her closer to his already thick arousal.

"Since day one," he murmured against her lips, "it's been you. Not this town, but you."

Morgan heard his words, even over the wild beating of her heart. She wrapped her arms tightly around his neck in an effort to hold him as close to her as she possibly could. Gray apparently wanted the same thing. As he turned, he lifted her up so that her legs wrapped quickly around his waist.

"Now you're all I think about," Gray said before thrusting his tongue deep into her mouth once more.

Morgan accepted his kiss and luxuriated in the heated sensations moving swiftly throughout her body. The sound of his voice, the touch of his hands, his mouth. Everything about him, about this moment was like a drug and she was deathly afraid that she was addicted. So much for drawing a line between them.

He walked them over to the bed then, keeping her in his arms as he reached behind him to push everything on top of the comforter onto the floor. He lowered her to the bed, yanking her sweater over her head, then hastily undid her pants and pushed them down her legs. When they stopped at her boots, Gray pulled them off quickly, tossing them across the room. Morgan undressed him as well, as anxious to feel him completely as he was to feel her.

"Since day one," she said, repeating his words, "it's been this way since day one." And there was no denying that now.

"Yes," he murmured, now naked, as he came over her, lifting her legs to once again lock behind his back. "Just you," Gray said, sinking his rigid length slowly, but most deliciously, inside of her.

Morgan trembled, her blunt-tipped nails digging into the skin of his shoulder. "Just you."

He moved much slower than she'd anticipated, which made the moment that much more intense. This was the moment she knew she had fallen. She'd wondered in the past few days, thought it was a fantasy, that it could ever happen this way, this quickly. Hell, she'd been in love before so Morgan was certain she knew how it felt. She was so damn wrong.

They rolled over the bed, Gray holding her tightly as she came up over him, continuing their slow ride to pleasure. When he sat up, too, holding her closely and kissing her mouth eagerly, she whimpered. This emotion was so much stronger and gripped her heart until she thought she might choke.

"I don't do relationships," he whispered in her ear. "You don't want this."

Morgan shook her head. "No," she sighed. "I don't."

He moved and she moved, their bodies joined to the hilt. He was thick and hot inside of her, filling physical and mental places she'd never even known existed.

"Yes," he whispered again, his hands going from her back, down to cup her bottom. "Yes, Morgan. Yes!"

She was shaking her head, her legs and arms trembling. His voice echoed in her head. His laughter, his smile, his words.

"Yes," she said, repeating him. "Yes, Gray. Yes!"

This plunge was different than before. Not like she'd fallen off a cliff to bliss, but as if she'd decided in that moment to make the jump. "Gray!" she yelled as every part of her shivered and shook with the intense release that claimed her.

He was right behind her, holding her tightly as his erection throbbed deep inside of her. He kissed her then, swallowing her cries into his own, until they both went still, only their hearts beating.

"Sonofabitch!" Kym screeched the moment she stepped inside Gray's room.

He moved quickly, pushing Morgan away from him and

pulling the comforter over to cover her nakedness. As for the fact that he, too, was naked, Gray didn't really care. He was much more concerned with his assistant, who had just barged into his room without calling or knocking first.

"What are you doing?" he asked as he got off the bed and reached for his jeans.

"Apparently, not as much as you are," Kym quipped. "I heard the rumors flying around, but you know, it's a small town so you never know what to believe. Besides, I didn't think you would ever sink so low."

Kym gasped and pointed to where Morgan still sat on the bed. "Her? Really, Grayson? You're choosing her?"

"You're out of line," Gray told her once he had his pants buttoned. "You've been out of line for weeks. I want you to leave this town today and get back to the office."

"She's a small-town slut!" Kym continued. "Looking for a daddy to her bratty children."

"Now you wait a minute," Morgan said, climbing off the bed, the comforter still wrapped around her. "You are not going to talk to me or about my children like that."

"Shut up!" Kym yelled at her. "You're stupid, too. How can you be tasked with teaching children when you're so damn stupid? He's not in love with you. This isn't some rags-to-riches story, sweetie. He's a millionaire. He doesn't belong in this sorry town and he certainly won't stay here with you, no matter how much you put out."

Gray didn't see it coming. He would have never in his wildest dreams thought it would happen right in front of him, but it did. Morgan punched Kym so hard in the face that Kym fell flat on her ass, onto the pile of papers Gray had been reading just an hour ago.

"I'm pressing charges," Kym immediately squealed as she tried to get up.

Gray looked at Morgan to make sure she was all right.

She wasn't even breathing hard. He resisted the urge to smile and moved to help Kym up from the floor.

"I want her in jail, Grayson. She needs to be behind bars and then we'll get out of this dirty little town," she continued.

"No," he said simply. "You're going back to Miami. Today. And if I hear one word about you talking to the cops, you're going to be sorry you ever met me."

Now on her feet, Kym wrenched her arm free of his grasp and looked at him with pure anger bubbling in her eyes. "I already do," she told him before turning and walking out of the room.

"She's going to sue you for wrongful discharge," Morgan said from behind him.

He'd been watching the open doorway, feeling the brisk cold of the evening against his bare chest and wondering how he'd come to be here in this place and in this predicament. Six months ago he was in Dubai brokering yet another lucrative business deal. He was sleeping in penthouse suites and sipping fifty-thousand-dollar bottles of champagne. Now, he was staying on a horse farm, wearing jeans and freezing his ass off.

"She can't," he said as he moved to close the door. "She's an at-will employee. Meaning she's there at my will. I have the sole authority to fire her without cause or notice. My employee handbook is clear and airtight, as per my attorney, who is on a monthly retainer."

She'd pulled on her jeans by then, and her sweater, alerting Gray to the fact that she'd thrown that punch while wrapped only in a comforter. How was that for sexy?

Morgan ran her fingers through the top of her hair.

Gray moved closer to her, taking her hand and kissing her slightly bruised knuckles.

# Chapter 12

*Christmas Eve*

Today was going to be a busy day. Not that the last couple of days hadn't been, Morgan thought as she sipped on her second cup of coffee. Wendy had already picked up the children and they were doing what her sister called the best type of shopping—the last-minute kind. They were all going to meet at the community center at four o'clock this afternoon. Before then, Morgan needed to wrap her own gifts, clean her house and make sure everything was in line for the play that night. That meant she needed to go to the center and check on all the props, the programs and the lights, and had to call Mrs. Reed to see if she required any assistance with the food.

Yes, Morgan thought, she needed this second cup of coffee, and possibly a clone to get through this day. That thought had her smiling and shaking her head. She realized she wouldn't want her life any other way. She loved the tasks she was responsible for in Temptation, and loved the thought of all the pleased faces once the play was finally being performed. Tomorrow would be Christmas, the first Christmas where the children would have her and Gray…and the barrage of toys he'd purchased for them.

Morgan still couldn't believe all the stuff that was delivered to Gray's room at the farm. The train set that Jack had been begging her for all year long and the baby doll that looked like a real child that Lily insisted she needed to complete her five-year-old life. Plus so much more. He'd also bought clothes, shoes and coats for them. It was too much, Morgan knew, and she'd attempted to tell him the same.

"Nothing is too much for them," he'd told her. "This is the only time in their entire lives that the most important thing will be the promise Santa keeps. It's a magical time of wishes and expectations, cheer and excitement. I want that for them. The same way I had it, I want Jack and Lily to have the same."

She'd stopped the argument then because the mere fact that this man wanted so much for her children left her speechless. There was a lot about Gray that had left her without words or explanations lately. She'd enjoyed thinking about him about as much as she enjoyed being with him, which was part of the reason she almost didn't hear the knock on her door.

Morgan put down her cup and made her way to the door, then pulled it open without looking through the peephole to see who it was. A part of her had thought—hoped—it was Gray. That part was sadly mistaken.

"Happy Christmas Eve," Harry said, a huge grin on his face.

Morgan heard his voice but it took her a moment to realize he was down on his knees.

"Happy Christmas Eve, Harry. What are you doing?" she asked, pulling her robe closed tighter around her.

Harry reached for her hand, holding it tightly in his. "I wanted to do this right now before things got too hectic today," he told her.

"Harry," she began, hating the sick feeling creeping in the pit of her stomach.

"No. Please don't interrupt me," he said. "I've been practicing this for years but I'm still as nervous as a schoolboy."

Harry chuckled and Morgan shook her head. "But Harry, I don't think—"

"Right," he said, reaching into his coat pocket. "I don't want you to think. Not just yet anyway. Let me just get this out."

"But—" Morgan tried again to stop him.

"Morgan Ann Langston Hill," he began loudly. "I swear I've been in love with you since the sixth-grade dance when you brought me that cup of water after I choked on those dry, stale crackers."

She remembered that day and now she couldn't help but think it might have been easier to simply let him choke. Surely, someone else would have saved him. Maybe Patsy Glenn would have done the honors. Then Harry would be at Patsy's doorstep right now making a fool out of himself, instead of at Morgan's.

"I can't think of any other woman but you. I didn't have anything to offer you when we were young. You went away to college and I vowed that I'd have my own place and my own business started by the time you returned. That way I could take care of you, of us and our family. Then you came back and got married before I could even get over here to see you." Harry sighed.

"I watched you all those years with him and then you had his babies and I just wanted to die. But I didn't and he did and I thought, 'Thank You, Lord. Thank You. Thank You. Thank You.' I knew it was my time. But I had to let you grieve. I've always been slow. My daddy says that all the time. Anyway, I'm not moving slow anymore. Morgan, I'm asking you to be my wife."

With one hand Harry popped open the little black box. There was a diamond staring back at her, like an eye judging her for allowing him to get this far when she already knew what her answer was.

"Harry..." she began.

He shook his head. "No. I want you to take a few minutes. Inhale the crisp Christmas Eve air and think about all that we've been through and all that we can be to each other. I can adopt the twins. You can move into my place or I can move in here until we find something bigger. We can be a family, Morgan, just like we've both always wanted."

She had wanted a family and for a while Morgan had thought it would be with a man from Temptation. That notion had been dispelled when she'd married James. Now, she had this guy who had been born and raised here. Harry had roots here, he loved this town and he wasn't going anywhere. That's exactly what Morgan always thought she wanted. Until Gray.

"No, Harry. I'm sorry, but I cannot marry you," she told him.

The words seemed cold, or was it the breeze that had decided to blow at just that moment?

Harry shot to his feet instantly.

"You didn't think about it long enough," he said. "Let's go inside. Maybe you're too cold to think."

"No, it's not that," Morgan said even as Harry stepped toward her.

She stepped back, letting him into her house.

"Harry, I've always thought of you as a good friend," Morgan began. This had to be done and it had to be done right now. Harry needed to know that he should move on without her.

"I'm not in love with you," she said simply.

"But we're good friends," Harry said, looking at her as if he was really trying to understand her words. "A husband and wife should be good friends."

"We are," she told him. "And I know that a married couple should have a friendship. But that's not enough, Harry. Not for me or for you. There should be love. You should love your wife above all else and cherish her."

"I've cherished you for so long, Morgan. And I shouldn't have waited. I'm so sorry, I shouldn't have waited."

He moved closer and Morgan took another step back. She didn't like how Harry was looking at her.

"I won't wait any longer, Morgan. I won't let you make us wait," he said as he reached out and grabbed her by the arms.

"Let go of me," she said, trying to remain calm.

"No," Harry insisted. "Not this time."

"I'm serious, Harry, let me go!"

Instead, Harry grasped her arms tightly and lifted her right off her feet before pushing her back until she slammed into the wall. "I'm not going to let you go. Not. Again!" he screamed into her face.

Then Morgan felt like she was sliding. Harry's grip on her was quickly released and before she could speak she was sliding down the wall to her knees.

"I believe the lady answered your question," Gray yelled at Harry.

Harry was now on the floor beside Morgan's broken coffee table, where Gray had tossed him across the room.

"You!" Harry blurted, quickly coming to his feet.

Morgan stood as well. She had déjà vu, only with a different cast of characters. Knowing how the previous incident had ended, she hurried over to stand in front of Gray.

"Harry, I want you out of my house before I call Sheriff Duncan over here and have you arrested for assault. That would ruin your mother's Christmas, now wouldn't it?" she shouted at him.

"He doesn't love you!" Harry yelled. "He's just using you! I know it, half the town knows it! Hell, his assistant, who's known him forever, knows it. You're the only one too blind to see it."

"I want you to go," Morgan said, trying valiantly to ignore his words.

"You heard her," Gray insisted. "Get out and don't come back."

"I'll do whatever I damn well please," Harry shouted back, but he moved toward the door.

"Not to her and not anymore," Gray continued. He moved toward the door as well. "This is the last time I'll see you here."

"Oh, yeah?" Harry asked as he stepped to Gray.

"Yes," Gray answered without hesitation as he stepped toward Harry. "Don't let the suit fool you," Gray warned. "I'll break your jaw before you can throw the first punch and that'll only be the beginning."

There was something sexy about those words, spoken so icily and coming from a man dressed in a designer black suit. He looked formidable, almost like those gangsters in mob stories. His tone sounded deadly enough that it wouldn't have surprised Morgan one bit if he'd reached behind his back and pulled a gun from the band of his pants.

Harry must have thought the same thing, or something in that neighborhood, because he backed away so quickly he almost fell through the door.

"You're gonna be sorry," Harry continued, still yelling as he walked to his truck. "When he breaks your heart, Morgan, you're gonna be so sorry you let me walk away.

And I'm not gonna let you back in. Even when you're crying and sorry, I won't!"

Harry pulled off with a screech of tires and Morgan slammed the door. She leaned into it, letting her head fall as she wondered how the hell she'd missed Harry's true feelings for her. If she'd cut him off earlier, years ago, this would have never happened.

"Hey," Gray said, touching a finger to her chin and lifting her head until she was staring up at him. "He's a fool."

She began shaking her head. "No. He's not. He was just in love with me."

"No," Gray told her simply. "If he was truly in love with you he would beg, steal, tear down walls and climb mountains to keep you."

Morgan didn't know what to say to that. She didn't know what had made Gray say it and she was too afraid to ask. Instead, she accepted his hug and the warmth of his sweet kiss. She did not, however, contemplate the words that Harry said about Gray using her, or the fact that Kym had basically said the same thing. She wouldn't think about what might possibly happen between her and Gray in the future. Not right now.

"Let it be Christmas every day!" Ethan shouted, a huge grin spread across his face.

Arielle Beaumont, who played Tiny Tim, simply shook her head. They'd spent three hours yesterday going over this part. Morgan had corrected Ethan at least four times, telling him the line was "I will keep Christmas in my heart," but Ethan, true to form, did his own thing.

"God bless us, every one," Arielle stated, her voice loud and clear over the chuckles that had begun.

The stagehands, Lenny and John Petrie, pulled on the curtains until they closed completely and the crowd continued to clap. Morgan let out a deep breath. It felt like she'd been holding it in for the last four hours, when final preparations for this evening's event had kicked off.

Mayor Pullum took the stage then, with Rayford Malloy standing proudly beside her. Rayford's chest remained poked out—he was proud of his son for making a mockery of the play with his original lines and gestures.

"We want to give a hearty thanks to Morgan Hill and her first-grade class for bringing Charles Dickens's timeless classic to a whole new life here in Temptation. It was truly a wonderful time," Mayor Pullum enthused.

More applause and Morgan smiled as she hurried to the back, where Wendy and Granny were helping to get the children undressed. There would be mingling and refreshments for probably another half hour. Nana Lou and her daughter, Pam, were in the front hall of the community center, where they'd cleaned up after the potluck dinner and now had cake, cider and coffee prepared.

As for Morgan's part in Temptation's annual holiday extravaganza, it was done. Now she was looking forward to a hot bath and quiet Christmas Eve with her twins. Tomorrow would be breakfast after the children enjoyed their gifts and then dinner at Granny's. She was due at her grandmother's house at noon to help with the cooking and preparations and Morgan was really looking forward to spending that time with her family. These were the people she knew and was sure of, unlike Harry. And Gray.

All day long Morgan had attempted to put the memories of what had happened at her place with Harry and Gray out of her mind. Just five days ago she'd been seen naked by Gray's assistant, the woman she'd ultimately had to punch in the face for running her mouth about Morgan's children. Then the confrontation with Harry that Morgan was sure could have gotten more out of hand if Harry hadn't come to his last bit of sense and left her house when Gray told him to.

Morgan didn't know what was going on. When did her quiet and routine life get turned upside down by rude and delusional people? The moment Gray Taylor waltzed back into town was the undeniable answer.

"He's making a statement." Wendy tugged on Morgan's arm. "Come on, we gotta get up front so we can hear him."

Morgan had just arrived in the back room, only to see that the children were already dressed in their regular clothes and headed toward the foyer with their happy chatter.

"Come on!" Wendy insisted.

Morgan followed her sister with tired feet and a headache she'd been praying would stay tamped down until she got home. That probably wasn't going to happen, Morgan thought as she stepped into the auditorium once more to see Gray standing on the stage where Mayor Pullum had been.

"I know that some of you have wondered why I've been here for just about a month now," he said.

He looked really good, as always, wearing gray slacks, a gray shirt and cheerful red tie. Morgan had gotten used to seeing him in his casual clothes these last couple of weeks, but nothing beat the sight of this man in dress clothes. He took her breath away every time. Tonight, she couldn't resist the small smile as she noticed he was wearing the tie that Jack and Lily had insisted Morgan buy when they were out gift shopping earlier in the week. It was all red, but at the bottom there was a wintry scene with two snowmen having a snowball fight.

"It's just like when we played in the snow and built George," Jack had said as he stood in the store holding it up proudly.

"Yup, it is. It's a memory!" Lily had added with her own excitement at having participated in finding the perfect gift for Gray.

To Morgan's surprise and relief, Gray had been elated to receive the early gift from the children and had promised to wear it tonight. Morgan wasn't sure how she felt about him making promises to her children, even if he did keep them. No, that wasn't totally true. She was sure it made her feel wonderfully warm on the inside, her heart near to bursting with joy. She just didn't know if it was safe to like that feeling so much.

"I decided that to make an informed decision about whether or not to sell this building and the hospital that I needed to get to know the town of Temptation once more," Gray continued. "When I left this town I was only a child. This used to be home, only it wasn't as happy and wonderful as some of you may have thought. In these past weeks, however, I've experienced more change than I think I have in my entire adult life. I owe that to some pretty special people."

Morgan's cheeks burned with embarrassment as some of the adults looked to her. Wendy did a quiet hand clap in Morgan's direction because she was all for giving people in town something to talk about.

"Let them gossip, girl," she'd told Morgan after Morgan had shared what happened with Kym in Gray's room. "That's what they do around here. No sense in you or anybody else trying to change that. At least they're gossiping about you and a good man, instead of some deadbeat."

As usual Morgan hadn't thought of things that way, but leave it to Wendy to put her own slant on a situation. Morgan added that to all the things her big sister did better than her.

"I'm not sure how all of you collectively will feel about my decision, but I've decided that tonight would be the best night to announce my plans," Gray said.

The room went completely quiet at that moment and Morgan touched a hand to her stomach, which immediately had butterflies flipping and flopping around. She was just clearing her throat when she saw Jack and Lily run up on the stage with Gray.

"What are they doing?" she whispered and then made a motion to go and get them.

"Let them be," Granny said, touching a hand to Morgan's arm. "They wanted to be with him and I let 'em."

"But it's rude, Granny. He's up there talking and look at them," Morgan stated as she looked back at her grandmother and then up to the stage, where Gray had already picked up Lily, planting her on his side. Lily dutifully lay her head on his shoulder, while Jack stood right beside Gray as if he was attached to his leg.

There were a few chuckles as Gray said, "Thanks for the help you two," and grinned wildly.

"My father had plans to return to Temptation," Gray continued. "He wanted to come back and finish helping the town that had given him his family. So in that vein, I will not be selling the hospital. I will be renovating it and adding on The Taylor Generational Wing, which will focus on obstetrics and fertility studies."

There was immediate applause and Granny laced her fingers with Morgan's. But she didn't look to her grandmother—her gaze was trained on Gray.

"In addition to the hospital," he said over the low murmurs, "I will also be renovating the community center. This facility can serve such a bigger function here in Temptation and I'd like to see it flourish. One of the main updates to the center will be a separate theater center, where professional plays can be put on for the public."

If Morgan had been blushing before, she was about to full-on gush now, as Gray stated the idea she'd given him for the community center's use.

"It took a while to figure this out, but Temptation will always be home to the Taylors, and a family should always take care of home," Gray said. "I wish the town of Temptation and all of you a very merry Christmas and a happy start to the New Year."

He walked off the stage with Jack and Lily in tow, just as Millie hurried over to where Granny, Wendy and Morgan were standing.

"You did it!" Millie said to Morgan. "Hot damn, Ida Mae, she did it!"

Millie pulled Morgan to her for a quick hug. Behind her, Fred grinned.

"Yes, I must say we're in for some big changes here in town and we owe that all to you, Morgan," Fred said.

Morgan was already shaking her head. "No. You're mistaken. This was Gray's decision, I had nothing to do with it."

"Oh, Ida Mae, this girl here is something," Millie told Granny. "She doesn't know a thing about a woman's power, does she? But I knew it all along. Ever since I saw you two together at the charity ball. I knew you would be the one to turn him around. That's why Fred and I gave you all that information. We knew you would help save our town."

"But I didn't," Morgan responded.

"Just smile and say it's wonderful, Morgan," Granny said.

Wendy agreed with their grandmother's declarations as she leaned in to whisper in Morgan's ear. "That's right, just smile. This town's going to be kissing your ass for years to come for this."

Morgan didn't want anybody kissing her ass and she didn't want to take credit for something she didn't do, but just about an hour and a half later, as she walked into her house, she heard Gray say the same thing.

"None of this would have been possible without you," he stated.

Jack and Lily had gone into their bedroom to change

into their pajamas. The Christmas tree was lit in the living room, presents underneath. The house still smelled like the cookies Morgan and the kids had baked yesterday and the pine candle that Granny had given her when she'd complained about Morgan not having a real tree.

"You made the decision that was right for you and your family, Gray. Your father had those plans long before I came along. I won't take responsibility for a conclusion you came to on your own," she told him.

He shook his head. "If you hadn't insisted I look at those buildings, I wouldn't have. Then I would have never found out about what my father had planned all these years. I wouldn't have learned more about a man I thought I never wanted to know."

Morgan took a deep breath and let it out slowly. "I don't know what's going on anymore," she admitted. "Things have just been going so fast. One minute I'm going along with life as usual and the next you're here and I'm showing you buildings like I'm some real estate agent and you're making snowmen with my kids."

He'd come to stand close to her then. "You forgot the part about the great sex," he said with that grin that never failed to warm her.

She shook her head. "I don't think either one of us can forget that."

"Not on your life," he said, reaching out to touch a finger to her chin. "It's good, Morgan. All of this feels right. I didn't expect it, either. It's not something I planned or would have even believed if somebody had told me this was where I'd be one year ago."

"No," Morgan told him with a tilt of her head. "You thought you'd be in Miami, maybe going to a corporate holiday party, or perhaps you would have taken a trip for the holidays. You'd lie on some beach all Christmas Eve and then spend a very quiet Christmas with room service."

The thought sounded lonely to her, but it was exactly how she pictured Gray's holiday celebrations.

He shrugged. "Sometimes I think you know me better than I know myself."

She didn't know what to say to that.

"But this is so much better, Morgan. This is more of what my mother would have wanted for me, for all of her children. I'm a little tired after helping Fred, Lenny and John with the final setup for tonight. Discovering that half the chairs in the hall were broken and having to transport ones from the hospital in the Porsche was a little grueling. But I loved every second of it," he told her.

"Yeah, Nana Lou was pissed that Harry didn't show up like he'd promised," she said and then frowned.

"Don't do that," he told her with a shake of his head. "That's not your fault. Harry Reed is a grown man. Grown men get rejected by women every day. It's been happening since the beginning of time. There's no excuse to act like a jealous ass."

Morgan knew that but it didn't mean she couldn't feel bad about how things had turned out. "I'm too tired to argue," she said with a little chuckle.

Jack and Lily came running out at that moment.

"Can we open one gift tonight?" Jack asked.

"Yes, Mama, can we?" Lily begged.

Morgan shook her head. "Now, you know we open gifts on Christmas morning after Santa comes."

"That's the old way, though," Lily continued. "Can't we do something new?"

"Yeah, like we built a snowman and named him George. We didn't do that last year. So this should be the year of new stuff," Jack added.

"That's right, we should. Right, Mr. Gray?" Lily asked.

Then her daughter leaned over to whisper—which was very loud because at five years old, Lily had not perfected her inside voice. "We asked the right way, didn't we? That's what you told us to say, right?"

Morgan looked at Gray, who instantly looked away from Lily and then grinned. "You did it perfectly. Both of you should have had bigger parts in the play, instead of just being the children playing in the street."

"So this was an audition for them to be in next year's play?" Morgan asked skeptically.

Gray shook his head and moved over to the tree. He reached down and retrieved a slim box.

"No. I just had this idea that since I was doing something new this year, that maybe we all should," he said before reaching out to hand her the box. "Merry Christmas, Morgan."

She didn't take the box. In fact, Morgan had slipped her arms behind her back, where her hands were now clenched together.

"Open it, Mama," Jack told her. "Open it so we can see what he got for you!"

Her son was bouncing from one foot to the other, always the impatient one, she thought as she tried to ignore the rapid beating of her heart. When Morgan realized that Gray intended to stay for Christmas she'd known she had to get him a gift, from the kids, of course. They'd picked out socks and a Temptation T-shirt so that he'd remember them when he returned to Miami. It was a simple gift, one that she would have purchased for any friend. Only there hadn't been a male friend in Morgan's life to buy gifts for in a very long time.

"Take it, Mama. It's rude to give a gift back," Lily said, interrupting her thoughts.

Morgan had told her daughter this same thing when Bert Valley had given Lily a live frog for her birthday last year.

"Take it, Morgan," Gray said. "I want you to have this."

With hands that betrayed her, as they shook and showed

how nervous she was feeling, Morgan took the box. She saw her kids watching her expectantly, so she shook it and they laughed, as she knew they would.

"You can't guess what it is like that. You gotta open it," Jack told her with another giggle.

"Well, maybe I should sit down first," Morgan said, trying to buy time and to get off her feet because her knees felt wobbly.

"Come on," Gray said as he helped her over to the couch.

"You're loving this, aren't you?" she said, looking up at him, unable to keep her own grin at bay.

"It's great," he told her. "Just like you."

Her stomach did another flip-flop and Morgan dropped onto the couch. She hurriedly opened the box because having three sets of eyes on her in anticipation was more pressure than worrying about whether or not she should be taking gifts from Gray. That worry was magnified when she finally lifted the top of the box to see the sparkle of blue sapphires glinting in the lights from the Christmas tree.

"Gray," she whispered. "This is way too much."

"It was in the envelope," he told her. "The one my father left with my name on it. He'd planned to give it to my mother that year for their anniversary. The year he left."

Morgan shook her head and pushed the box back toward him. "I can't take this. It belongs to you and your family. I can't."

"You can because I'm giving it to you," he told her, reaching down to take the necklace out of the box.

"It's so pretty," Lily exclaimed. "Shiny and pretty and your favorite color is blue, Mama."

"You should have gotten her a deck of cards," Jack said with an unimpressed look on his face. "She likes to play solitaire more than she wears fancy stuff."

Jack was right—Morgan never went anywhere that she

could wear something like this. She was about to use that as her excuse for giving it back to Gray when her house phone rang. Saved by the bell, she thought as she hurriedly moved away from Gray, who had been waiting to put the necklace on her.

"Hello?" she answered. "What? When? How?" she asked, her heart thumping wildly. "...Right...Fine. Get here fast!"

"What is it?" Gray asked the moment she turned around.

"That was Wendy," she said, still clutching the phone. "The community center is on fire."

# *Chapter 13*

It was gone.

As Gray stepped out of his car and raced across the street to follow Morgan, he knew the moment they were stopped by police officers. Morgan gasped, covering her mouth with her hands, her head shaking as tears filled her eyes. Inside Gray raged, but he put a steady arm around Morgan and held her close.

The sight was unlike anything he'd ever seen before. Black smoke billowing up into the night sky, bright and angry flames licking over what was left of the building's structure, destroying everything in their wake.

"It's too hot to put out right now, Mr. Taylor," a man dressed in a fireman's uniform said as he came to stand beside Gray.

"Call me Gray," he said to the man, who nodded.

"I'm Chief Alderson. But call me Dave."

"I want to know what caused this fire as soon as you know, Dave," Gray told him.

Dave nodded once more, his solemn gaze focused on the fire, just as Gray's remained.

"It's damn hot in there. I pulled my men out after about ten minutes. We couldn't get past the first thirty feet inside. Offhand, I'd say some sort of accelerant," Dave reported.

The man had said the last sentence in a hushed tone and he'd leaned in a little closer to Gray as he spoke. Morgan was on Gray's other side and with the noise of the fire and the people still coming onto the scene, Gray hoped she hadn't heard what Dave had said. Gray, however, clenched his teeth in anger.

"Oh, my lord, it's burning," Millie said as she came running over to them. "What could have happened?"

Morgan had shifted so that she now faced Millie and Fred, who were standing close.

"You turned off everything when you left, didn't you?" Millie instantly questioned Morgan.

"Of course I did," Morgan replied with much irritation, rightfully so.

Gray looked at Millie with only partial disbelief. He'd been around town for weeks and in that time he'd watched Millie talk friendly with some townspeople and in the next instant cut them close with her sharp tongue. She was a force to be reckoned with, someone that most citizens of the town did their best to steer clear of. Gray had no intention of being like the majority.

"We checked everything before we left, Millie. Even that faulty fuse box in the basement. Fred, you're paid a monthly fee to manage this property. When was the last time you had the electrical wiring checked?" Gray asked.

"Now look here, you can't come here and start accusing my husband. We take our jobs and life in this town seriously, Gray," Millie insisted.

Fred was nodding beside his wife. "I got some reports

that there was a problem. Harry told me he'd been over to fix it a couple of times so I thought it was fine."

As if hearing his name had conjured his presence, Harry walked up. Gray wasn't thrilled to see the guy, but he definitely was not prepared to see Kym walking right beside him. Gray hadn't seen her in days and had presumed she'd left town like he'd told her to do.

"I did check out the fuse box and like I told you last month, it was fine," Harry said, his angry glare toward Gray evident.

"The power went out again a month ago," Morgan said, more to Gray than to anyone else.

He nodded. "I remember. The first night I was in town I had to go down and flip the fuse for the power to switch back on," Gray said.

"I can't fix a problem I didn't know about," Harry insisted. "Maybe if you'd called me instead of letting this suit-and-tie guy try to meddle in things that weren't his business, this could have been prevented."

"Hold on, everyone," Dave interjected. "I haven't given a cause for this fire yet. So let's put a cap on all this blame you're tossing around. Now, I'm gonna have to ask that you all go home, or get across the street because the building's frame is gonna start breaking off any minute now."

Morgan looked over to the building, shaking her head once more. "I can't believe this," she said. "After all the worrying and contemplating what you were going to do with this building and now it's just gone."

"When one building goes, you build another," Kym quipped. "I know of two developers who would love this spot. You know them, too, don't you, Millie?"

At Kym's words both Gray and Morgan looked to Millie to see what her response would be.

"You ten-cent whore!" Millie spat. "I warned you not to come to my town with your drama. Yet you're still here and now you have the nerve to push this in my direction."

Within the next second, Millie was lunging for Kym. Fred and Gray both held her back while Kym stood with a sickening smirk on her face.

"Just tell them that you've been in touch with the developers trying to see how much money the town could make off the strip mall they want to build. Tell them how you were against the idea at first, but when one of the developers suggested that maybe Fred would be interested in managing the rental and maintenance of the outlet mall they proposed, your eyes turned from shifty brown to greedy green."

Millie tried to go after her again and this time, Morgan stepped closer to Kym.

"Why don't you just leave town. You don't like it here and you obviously don't like the people. So it would make all the sense in the world for you to go back where you came from," Morgan told her.

"It would make all the sense in the world for you to grow a brain," Kym stated.

Harry stood right beside her, looking as if he agreed with every ridiculous word that Kym said. For the first time in his life Gray wanted to physically harm someone.

"Let's go," he said, touching a hand to Morgan's arm.

When she readily moved to stand beside him Gray could almost hear his mother's words echoing in his mind. *Jealousy and hatred are two emotions you can neither predict nor cure. Let the ones who suffer with it be, live your life in spite of.*

With a shake of his head and a last look at both of them, Gray walked Morgan to his car and helped her inside.

* * *

Morgan held on to Wendy as she cried when they returned to Morgan's house.

"It's going to be all right," Wendy told her. "Gray's going to rebuild, aren't you?"

He hadn't given it a second thought. "Definitely. We were planning to add an additional building onto the back side anyway. This way we'll do a completely new design. I know a wonderful and innovative architect that I can call as soon as the holiday is over. It's going to be bigger and better, without any doubt."

"See, it's all going to work out," Wendy said, pulling away from Morgan and giving Gray a grateful look. "As for that tramp and Harry's punk ass, they're going to get what's coming to them. You know Granny wholeheartedly believes in karma."

Morgan chuckled then as she wiped her eyes and Gray wanted nothing more than to hold her in his arms and tell her just what her sister had just told her. Everything was going to work out. He was going to make sure that it did.

When Wendy was gone, Morgan turned to Gray and said, "You know Granny also believes wholeheartedly in voodoo hexes and curses. I wouldn't put it past her to be in her house now mixing up some concoction to make sure Harry and Kym got just what they deserved for being spiteful."

"I'm not going to say that's a bad idea," Gray joked.

Morgan shook her head. Her stance was still tense, but a little smile came through. A very tired and weary one.

"Look, the children are asleep. It's late and you're tired. How about I run you a hot bath and put you to bed?"

She leaned against the closed door and sighed. "That sounds heavenly."

"Then it shall be done," Gray said immediately.

He went to the door, moved her gently to the side while he checked the locks and then walked her back toward the bathroom. While they walked he massaged her shoulders, hating all the tightness he felt there.

"Dave is going to find out how the fire started and we're going to rebuild. I don't want you to worry about any of that," he told her.

She remained silent while they moved into the bathroom. He turned on the water and waited until the temperature was right, then said, "Now, let's get you bathed and ready for bed."

She'd been staring at him, her arms folded over her chest. "I'm not one of the children, Gray. And I'm not one of your business deals that you're fixing."

He moved to stand in front of her. "Never mistook you for either," he said.

"This was exactly what I was afraid of all along," she said with a sigh. "I don't like this feeling and I know it sounds silly and probably unrealistic, but I don't like loss. It's just too heavy for me to deal with. My kids are at the community center all the time. When it wasn't this play it was arts-and-crafts night, or story time. There was always something there for them to do and now it's gone."

He cupped her cheek and shook his head. "That old building is gone," Gray told her. "There will be a new building and all those activities and many more will resume. Remember, you planned some of the things that will take place there. We can plan even more."

She was still shaking her head and when she looked up at him there were tears in her eyes once again. "The only thing that was here for me after James died was this town. That community center and the people there saved me plenty of nights when I thought I would go crazy with loneliness and the kids would hate me for being such a boring mother. This is exactly what I was afraid of when you first came to town. And I know that you said you're going to rebuild, I just still feel this sense of loss."

"Stop it," he said sternly, but not angrily. "I know about loss, too, Morgan. I lost my mother when all I ever knew was to count on her. I lost my father long before that and I still don't think I ever understood why. So I know all about that lonely feeling that grows so big and so heavy inside of you until you think there's no way you can take another breath. I know about not being sure what you'll do the next day and the day after that, because you've lost someone." He cupped both hands to her face now and stared intently into her eyes.

"But what I also know right now, standing in this space with you so close to me, is that I've never felt more complete in my life. The here and now is what's important. Nothing else. And I'm right here with you, right now. Jack and Lily are sleeping soundly in their beds waiting for Santa to drop off all their goodies and that tub is about to overflow with the hot bath you requested."

She smiled just as one tear slipped down her cheek. Gray caught it, wiping it away with his thumb, and smiled down at her.

"We're going to have a fabulous Christmas, something new and exciting for us all. We're not going to think about this mess with the fire or anything else that doesn't make us feel happy and content. Just for one day, we're going to do that."

He looked up at the ceiling and then back down to her. "I wish there was some mistletoe up there right now."

"Why? So you could kiss me and then get lucky? Taking advantage of an emotionally drained woman doesn't seem like your style, Mr. Gray," she told him jokingly.

Gray smiled. "I'm going to put you into this bathtub

and I'll take advantage of you later," he said before kissing her lips.

She kissed him back, wrapping her arms immediately around his neck and making Gray want to get into that tub with her. In fact, Gray thought in that moment that he wanted to do everything with this woman. Eat, talk, plan, pray every day—he wanted it all.

## Chapter 14

Gray carried Lily into her grandmother's house, while Jack walked beside Morgan holding tight to the Spider-Man super car Gray had given him this morning.

"Merry Christmas!" Granny shouted the moment she walked into the hallway to see everyone taking off their coats.

"Merry Christmas!" the children replied as they ran and hugged her.

Gray turned to hand Morgan their coats, as she was standing near the closet and had just hung up her own.

"Merry Christmas," he said, and she turned just in time to see him locked in a tight hug with Granny.

Wendy came out next, an apron around her waist and an already exasperated look on her face.

"Merry Christmas, y'all," she said, bending down to hug the kids as they ran to her.

Granny pulled Morgan close for a hug after she'd hung

up the coats, which he'd finally given to her after his embrace with Granny.

"Stop looking so sad," Granny whispered in Morgan's ear. "It's Christmas, remember. Only happiness today."

Morgan nodded as she released her grandmother, but seeing Gray also hugging Wendy and laughing made her pause once more. They'd slept together again last night—no sex, just sleep. Gray held her all through the night, his arms wrapped tightly around her while Morgan had tried to fall asleep. She'd stared into the dark for longer than she cared to remember, thinking about all that had happened in just one month's time.

"Hey there, sis, you hanging in there?" Wendy asked as she came to stand in front of Morgan once Granny had returned to get Lily and Jack.

She was carting the children off into the living room, to open the gifts she'd bought for them, no doubt.

Shaking her head and taking a deep breath, then releasing it slowly, Morgan stared at her sister.

"I'm okay, I guess," she said.

"We're all going to be okay around here. It's about time Temptation stepped into the twenty-first century. I was thinking last night that Gray is just the person to propel us in that direction," Wendy told her.

Gray had gone into the living room, too, probably sensing that Morgan needed to be alone with her sister for a few minutes. He was like that, she thought, always knowing what she needed before she even verbalized her wishes. It was different having someone around to do that when for so long it seemed like she was the only one supplying needs in her household, putting her own on the back burner.

"But will he stay here to do that?" she asked Wendy. "Or will he go back to Miami, where his home, his business and his life is?"

"Wait," Wendy said, grabbing Morgan by the shoulders. "You're not asking just for the sake of the town, are you? You're thinking about you and him? Oh, my goodness, you're in love with him, aren't you?" Wendy squealed.

"Be quiet," Morgan said, waving a hand at her sister and looking toward the living room. "What's the point in waiting until we're alone to have a conversation if you're just going to shout out what we're talking about?"

"Oh my, oh my!" Wendy said, stepping from one foot to the other like an excited child. "Morgan's in love. She's really in love!"

Wendy had spoken in a more hushed tone this time. Morgan frowned.

"I was in love before, with my husband, remember?" she said to Wendy. Even though, to be quite honest, Morgan hadn't thought about her marriage or her relationship with James in the last couple of weeks.

In the beginning, when Gray was here and after the first time they'd had sex, she had thought about James a lot. Reconciling with herself over the fact that there was now another man in her life, she figured. But since then, her only thoughts of James had been regarding the children and what it would mean to them to have a man around who wasn't their biological father. Which brought her right back to the question she'd asked Wendy—was Gray going to stay in Temptation with them?

Wendy nodded. "I'm not saying you weren't. But for so long you've been acting like your life only revolves around the kids. I mean, hell, you haven't even been dressing like you used to."

Morgan immediately looked down at her black jeans, leather knee-length boots and red-and-white holiday sweater.

"I think I look just fine," she replied.

"Yeah, but before you met James, you looked fabulous.

All the time. I mean, you wore dresses and sexy blouses. You had longer hair and did your makeup."

"I like my hair short, it's easier to manage. And makeup in Temptation is like snow in July—absolutely out of place," Morgan quipped.

Wendy shook her head. "Not true. I put on my face every day, no matter what. And there are dozens of other women living here that do the same. You just adopted all these new rules once you became a widow. But now you're in love again and you and the kids can have a complete family. I think it's fantastic."

"Ah, excuse me, but your grandmother sent me out here to collect you two. She said it's time to open gifts," Gray said.

Morgan instantly froze at the sight of him, praying he hadn't heard their conversation, especially the parts from Wendy because apparently her inside voice was still disabled.

"We're coming," Wendy said happily and started walking toward the living room.

Gray looked at Morgan. "Everything all right?" he asked.

Morgan fixed a smile on her face and replied, "Everything's fine." She headed into the living room, hoping and praying that things would be fine in the end. Although she still wasn't quite sure.

Gray was overwhelmed.

"Go on and open it, stop being so silly," Granny told him after the second box had been set in front of him.

At Morgan's place this morning, the children had presented him with another gift. Leather slippers because Jack said his mother insisted everyone wear slippers in the house and each time Gray had stayed over, he'd only walked around in his socks. Morgan had also given him a gift—a book on vintage cars because he'd told her about his hobby of looking at the cars, but had never bought one.

"You should have a hobby," she'd told him. "Something to occupy your mind other than work."

Gray almost told her that there was *someone* who had been occupying his mind more than work lately.

Now, her grandmother and sister were presenting him with gifts. It was a good thing he'd thought ahead and ordered gift cards online when he'd been picking out the gifts for the children. When he'd entered the hallway to get Wendy and Morgan for their grandmother, he'd gone into the closet to reach into his coat pocket, where he'd slipped the envelopes with the gift cards inside.

"I don't know what to say," Gray said as he was tearing open the box.

When he lifted the top and pulled back the tissue paper he was shocked to see the gift was a newspaper article in a nice oak picture frame. The title of the article was The Taylors of Temptation.

"I clipped that thirty years ago," Granny revealed. She was sitting in her recliner, legs crossed at the ankles, her long charcoal-gray-and-white skirt giving way to bright red slipper socks that she had pulled all the way up.

"Your parents were so proud when they brought all y'all babies home. And you know what? The town was proud, too," Granny told him. "There were so many news people here. Way more than there are now. Everybody wanted to see not only the first set of multiple births in Temptation, but the first African American sextuplets in this town. It was monumental."

Gray held the picture in his hand, staring down at his mother's and father's smiling faces. They were sitting on the top step of the porch of the house where they'd lived, six baby seats with little bundles of life inside each one. It was the happiness in his parents' eyes that grabbed on to him and held tight. Gray never remembered seeing that look on either of their faces when he was growing up.

"Wow, you kept that all this time," Wendy said.

"I sure did," Granny continued. "That's what pride is. You believe in something forever and you stand by it."

"It's a wonderful gift," Gray said to her finally. "I really appreciate it."

Granny leaned forward, the recliner snapping upward with her motion. She didn't miss a beat, but rested one elbow on her knee and pointed a finger from the other hand at him.

"I don't want you to appreciate me giving you that picture. I want you to do something with your legacy. It's your duty and your parents expected it. They worked hard, saved and borrowed money to make it possible for the six of you to be here on this earth. It's shameful that none of you live in this town, or even bother to visit. I don't care how Olivia and Theodor's relationship ended, there was once love between them and you children are the product of that. Don't let it be in vain, you hear me? Don't disappoint them like that."

Once more Ida Mae Bonet's words echoed in Gray's mind, long after she'd spoken them. So much so that after the dinner at her house and after he'd dropped off Morgan and the children at their house, Gray returned to his room at the resort and called his sister.

"Merry Christmas," he said to Gemma the moment she answered.

"Well, merry Christmas to you, too, Grayson," his sister replied happily. "I thought you were going to be the only one I didn't speak to today."

"You talked to Garrek?" Gray asked.

"I sure did. Only for a minute, though, because he said something about needing to catch a flight, but it was good to hear his voice," she told him.

Gray nodded. "It's good to hear your voice."

She was quiet for a moment.

"Are you all right, Gray? Did something happen?"

He sighed heavily, rubbing his eyes as he'd also allowed himself to really think about what had happened last night.

"The community center burned down last night," he told her. "It's completely destroyed."

"Oh, no. How did that happen?" Gemma asked him.

Gray shook his head, then remembered he was on the phone with his sister and not having a face-to-face conversation with her. How long had it been since that had happened?

"Oh, no, Gray. That's such a shame. What's going to happen now?" she asked after a few moments of silence.

Gray sat back in the chair, the phone to his ear, his other hand pushing the curtains back so he could see out the small window in his room. He liked the view out of Morgan's bedroom window better because George was still standing, even though his bottom layer was partially melted, and his nose and one of his eyes were gone. It had snowed twice since the big storm, but there hadn't been much in the way of accumulation.

"I'm going to build a new one," he said simply.

The decision had been just that, simple and unquestionable.

"The town needs the community center and the hospital and we need to keep the house. It's what Mom and Dad would have wanted," he said for the first time out loud.

Gemma went quiet.

"Are you sure?" she asked finally.

Gray nodded again. "I'm positive. So listen, there's something else going on here. I went through Dad's papers and things and he left an envelope for each of us. I'm going to send them out tomorrow, so you'll have yours by the end of the week. He was doing some things that we didn't know and I'm still trying to figure them all out. But I've decided to keep all the buildings and see some of his intentions to fruition. I typed up a memo with a summary for all of you to look over, but I really think it would be a good idea if you all came to Temptation. Just to see how you feel about everything."

This idea had come to Gray while he sat at the cherry oak table in Ida Mae's house earlier that night. There was talk about the Valentine's Day dance coming up and then the Spring Fling, which they were all hoping that Millie did not plan the way she had last year. The children were excited about summer break and going swimming at the lake. All things that he and his siblings had done at one time in this town.

"Wait a minute, are you asking us to move to Temptation?" Gemma asked him.

"No," he replied quickly. "Not at all. I'm just thinking that we all owe it to Mom and Dad to do more. They cared about this place and since we were born here, maybe we should, too."

"Gray," Gemma said, "is there someone in that place that you care about now?"

He pinched the bridge of his nose. He had felt as if he had no one to talk to about all these new emotions brewing inside of him.

"She's a single mother. Multibirth, just like Mom. She teaches and she directs children's plays. No bigger than a fairy, but stubborn and resilient as hell. And the kids, they're adorable. Jack has a quick mind while Lily is the thinker—she contemplates and then decides. She's as sweet as candy, but serious and no-nonsense like her mother," he said before sighing heavily. "What am I going to do without them when I head back to Miami?" he asked, more to himself than his sister.

"Hmm, maybe you should be asking yourself what you want to do with them there in Temptation" was Gemma's reply.

# Chapter 15

"Arson," Dave said solemnly as he sat across from Gray at Pearl's Diner, three days after Christmas.

"Used paint thinner and lots of it," he continued. "Started with it down in the basement, right near that fuse box you were talking about, and poured it all the way up to the top floor. The origin was in the basement, though, right by the back door, so they could escape quickly."

Gray rubbed a hand over his chin as he took in each word that Dave had said.

"Burned quick and fast, it did. Still hot over there, too, so don't you go poking around. I'll have a written report by the end of the day so you can send that to your insurance company," he told Gray.

"Thanks for that," Gray said. He'd just finished eating the best tuna and lettuce on whole wheat he'd ever had in his life and now he had to attempt to digest this news on top of that.

Dave shrugged and finished his coffee. "Just doing my job, nothing special."

"Would contacting the sheriff about your findings be part of your job?" Gray asked.

Dave nodded. "Sure would. And I've already done it. Sheriff Duncan and his deputy, Harlow, are going to meet me there in about an hour and I'm going to show them where I found everything."

"You mean the origin of the fire?"

"No. I mean where I found the earring and the bucket that points to who started the fire."

Gray sat straight up then, staring Dave directly in the eye.

"You know who set the fire?"

Dave Alderson was a stout man with an olive complexion, a center bald spot and bushy eyebrows. He wore a wedding ring on his chubby finger and a gold hoop earring in his left ear. Right now, he was rubbing that bald spot and staring at Gray as if he was torn between telling him the truth and waiting until someone else could take on that task.

"If you know, Dave, I want to know. I'd rather not wait until there's an arrest or the sheriff does whatever he's going to do. It was my building and I want to know," Gray told him.

"I don't have any obligations to tell you this. Hell, you ain't even a citizen of this town so I don't believe I owe you any allegiance," Dave told him.

Gray nodded his agreement to the man's words, all the while contemplating how it would look when he jacked him up by his collar and shook the admission out of him.

Dave leaned back against the seat and let his hands drop to the table. "But my mother was a good friend of your mother's, back when she lived here. I was about six and I can remember them two sitting on our back porch talking while I played with my dog, Loppy. Best damn golden retriever you'd ever want to meet. When he died it almost killed me."

Dave waved a hand as if telling himself to stop his speech. "Anyway, your mother had a kind smile and always gave me lollipops."

Gray didn't move a muscle, simply looked at the man expectantly.

"There was an earring left at the scene, just a few feet away from the back door. Got a little charcoaled but near as I can tell it's real gold, got some diamonds on the side of it, too."

"So the person who set the fire was a woman," Gray said, trying to connect Dave's imaginary dots.

"There was also a glove and a bucket," Dave continued. "The bucket was farther away—somebody dropped it behind the bushes down at the end of the block in the back of the building. It wasn't burned at all and it had a price sticker on the bottom of it."

"I don't know where you're going with any of this," Gray admitted, his patience with Dave growing very thin.

"Your little assistant friend, she was there getting sassy with Morgan and you that night," Dave told him. "She was only wearing one earring."

Gray frowned. "Kym? You think Kym did this?"

Dave shook his head. "Not by herself. You see that price sticker on the bucket—it's from Harry's Hardware down on Sycamore Street. The glove's a big one, large or extra large, I suspect for someone with big hands. Harry used to wrestle when he was back in high school. Was good at it, too."

The waitress came over then and Dave ordered another coffee. "Now, what do you think about that?" he asked Gray when they were alone again.

Gray sighed. "I have no idea what I think about everything you've just told me. None, except if we can prove this, I want their asses in jail for a very long time!"

"You're not supposed to be here," Sheriff Kevin Duncan said when Morgan walked up the path toward the stairwell leading to Harry's apartment.

Kevin was a fourth-generation officer in Temptation, having just taken over from his father in the last four years. He was taller than his father had been at just about six feet, with close-cropped hair and a full beard. His second-in-command was Harlow Biggins, who was the complete opposite of Kevin, with his short, round build, pale skin and scraggly stubble at his chin.

"It's a free country, Sheriff," Morgan said as she came to a stop right beside Gray.

She was spitting mad, had been since receiving Gray's call less than an hour ago.

"I just had lunch with the fire chief," he'd said solemnly over the phone.

Morgan had been cleaning up her living room, throwing away wrapping paper and boxes and those annoying plastic ties that came in the boxes with dolls and action heroes. She loved Christmas, but the days that followed always kept her moving as she tried to keep some semblance of order in a house where her kids could think about nothing but opening the next toy.

"What did he have to say?" she'd asked with the phone clutched between her ear and her shoulder, both hands full of trash that she stuffed into the recycle trash can.

"It was arson. Someone intentionally set the community center on fire. Well, not just *someone*." Gray had sighed then, but before Morgan could ask another question, he continued, "There's evidence to support that it may have been Harry and Kym."

"What? Are you serious?" she'd yelled so loud the kids

had actually stopped what they were doing to look at her. Morgan had made a conscious effort to calm the ripples of shock filtering through her at that moment.

"Tell me what's going on, Gray," she'd said in a slower, much more relaxed tone. A small smile had even crept along her face as she nodded toward the kids so that they could resume their play.

She'd listened to him talk, all the while walking back to her bedroom, where she slipped on her boots. "I told the sheriff that since I'm the building owner I wanted to be there when they questioned Harry," he'd informed her. "He didn't like it, but I didn't give a damn. We're headed there now."

"I'll meet you," she'd said in response before disconnecting the call. If he'd wanted to tell her not to come, it was pointless because she'd been in her car, dropping the kids off at Granny's in less than ten minutes, and now she was there.

"This is not how it works," Sheriff Duncan said, his brow furrowed as he stared at both Morgan and Gray. "My deputy is here to assist with this questioning. Civilians stay in their homes or at the station until I decide to brief them on what's going on."

"Except when it's my building that was burned to a crisp," Gray said sternly.

"And in my town, where some outsider and someone that I thought was a friend decided to burn that building to a crisp," Morgan added.

Harlow scratched the top of his head as he looked questioningly toward the sheriff. "You guys really think Harry could do something like this? He's lived here all his life. Hell, I used to play down at the lake with him and his sister when we were eight years old. His parents are as honest as they come."

"And paint thinner from his store was found at the scene," Gray said.

"Anybody could have bought that and left it there," Harlow quickly retorted. "Including that mean-spirited vixen that rolled into town behind you."

"And we're not going to know which one of them did it for sure if we keep standing out here freezing our butts off," Morgan added as she wasn't really in the mood for another male pissing match.

On the drive over she'd thought about her last interactions with Harry. The ones that included her trying her damnedest to keep Gray and Harry from coming to blows. No, the next time two men wanted to puff up and act like teenagers, she was going to let them. Especially since the memory of punching Kym in the face was still very fresh in her mind.

When the guys still stood there looking at one another she moved past them and headed for the steps. Harry lived in the upstairs apartment over top his hardware store. The entrance to his place was in the back and faced a thick copse of trees, with the lake running on the other side. She was just about to take the stairs when the sheriff grabbed her arm to stop her.

"I'll go in first," he told her, his grip on her arm light, but insistent.

Gray stepped up to him then, pushing the sheriff's hand away from Morgan's arm. "That's fine. We'll be right behind you."

The sheriff frowned and nodded toward Harlow. "Keep them at a distance while I do the talking," he said before walking up the stairs.

Harlow stayed behind Gray and Morgan, so close behind that when they'd come to a stop in a single-file line at the top of the landing, Harlow had bumped right into Gray's back.

Gray had stared at the deputy with irritation, while Harlow brushed down the front of his jacket as if it was somehow soiled at the connection. The sheriff shook his head in exasperation.

*Knock. Knock. Knock.*

Sheriff Duncan let his arm fall to his side and waited a few seconds.

"He's home," Harlow said from the end of their little convoy. "There's his truck over there."

Sure enough, Harry's older model beige 4x4 was parked at the end of the long grassy yard.

*Knock. Knock. Knock!*

They waited again, this time with the sheriff's frown growing almost as deep as Gray's.

"Open up, Harry Reed! I know you're in there. Don't make me call your momma over here with her key," the sheriff finally yelled.

A few seconds later the clicking of the locks could be heard and the door opened slowly. Harry peeked through the crack and said, "Yeah? What's up, Kevin?"

"This is official business, Harry," the sheriff told him. "I need to come inside and talk to you."

"Oh? What…" Harry began then looked around the sheriff to see Morgan and Gray standing there.

"What's going on?" Harry asked.

The sheriff sighed. "Let me in and I'll tell you what it's all about."

"No. I'm not letting all of you in my house," Harry insisted. "Especially not them, get the hell off my property!"

That order was directed to Morgan and Gray, of course.

"Don't mind them," the sheriff insisted. "The quicker we can get in and ask these questions, the quicker we'll be out of your hair. Is that smoke I smell, Harry?"

The sheriff was sniffing the air now, leaning in closer to Harry and the partially opened door. "You burning something in there?" he asked Harry, whose eyes had grown larger. "Let's just take a look."

Kevin Duncan was a lot stronger than his slim frame suggested. He'd gone into the marines right out of high school and had once entertained the idea of becoming an FBI agent. So he'd taken lots of classes at Quantico and still worked out feverishly to keep himself in shape. It was nothing to see him jogging through the streets of town in the early morning hours, or on the back porch of his house lifting weights.

Catching Harry off guard also made it easier for the sheriff to push his way inside Harry's home. Morgan followed him immediately, even while Harry cursed and swore to have some other authority come and throw her and Gray out. Harlow came bustling inside, positioning himself between Harry and Morgan and Gray, even going as far as holding a hand up at Gray to keep him from saying or doing anything untoward. Gray, of course, hadn't even acted as if that was what he was going to do. Instead, he held tight to Morgan's hand.

"Somebody's been in here smoking," the sheriff said as he looked down into an ashtray. "You don't smoke, Harry. Got company?"

Harry shook his head, his face angry and his hands fisted at his sides. "You got no right to be in here like this."

The sheriff nodded. "Okay, let me just ask you this straight out, then. Did you happen to sell somebody about a hundred gallons of paint thinner on Christmas Eve?"

Harry's lips trembled, his brow so furrowed it looked like all the excess skin from his head was rolled up there. "You got no right!" he yelled this time.

"Just answer the question, Harry. And then we can get going," Harlow insisted.

"Paint thinner is what caused that fire at the community

center," Kevin continued as he walked casually around the living and dining room area of Harry's open-concept place.

"A bucket of it was found behind the building. You know, after it burned to the ground," the sheriff continued.

"I don't have to say a word. I have rights," Harry insisted.

"You do," the sheriff said with a nod as he walked across the room, getting closer to one of two closed doors. "But I'll just keep on asking questions. Do you know a woman that would wear a diamond-and-gold earring? A big ol' hoop thing like the movie stars wear?"

Harry's gaze shot to Gray.

"I don't need you two here gloating. You got her all brainwashed and I lost. So what?"

"It doesn't have to be this way, Harry," Morgan told him.

She'd never seen him like this before. In fact, she wondered if this was even the same Harry she'd grown up with.

"Oh, yeah, it does. You made it that way. You went out and picked another outsider over me. He doesn't give a crap about this town or you! But that's for you to find out now. I'm done."

"So done that you burned down the community center?" the sheriff asked. "Did you have help or did you operate on your own?"

Harry looked over to the sheriff. "I want you to go now, too. You want something else from me, you get a warrant."

Harry moved toward the door, where Morgan guessed he was finally going to insist that they all leave without answering any questions. That's when she noticed he was only wearing his boxer shorts. Before Harry could say another word, another door opened. The sheriff stood expectantly as Morgan figured he'd just noticed Harry's state of dress, or rather undress, as well.

When Kym came through the door wearing leggings

and knee-length black leather boots, flipping her hair up from the inside of the sweater in a motion that told them she was just putting the garment on, there was total silence. Until Harry spoke.

"It was all her idea!" he blurted out. "She came here and stayed in my parents' place. Every night telling me about how her and Grayson were going to get married and make so much money. She said he was going to sell these buildings here and then they were going to elope. But that was all lies. That night she caught Gray and Morgan in bed together she was mad as a hellcat! Came banging on my door here saying I had to do something. That I needed to get Morgan away from Gray before something bad happened to her and the kids. So I proposed but you turned me down! You let that bastard toss me out of your place like he'd been the one to paint your kitchen and help plant that garden in the back.

"I was spittin' mad when I left your place and when I got back here she was sitting on my steps, legs crossed wearing those high heels that'll drive a man crazy," Harry continued. "She said she had the best way to take care of this once and for all. That the fire would wake Gray up and let him see that nothing in this town was worth his time and effort. He'd sell the other buildings real quick and head back to Miami. I didn't want to do it, my sister had her wedding reception at that community center. But I figured she knew Gray well enough that she'd know what his next step would be. She told me to go down to my store and get the paint thinner and then we waited until the play was over and everybody was out of the building. 'Cause I'd never hurt anyone. Not anyone in this town. We poured the thinner and—"

"Oh, for god's sake, shut up!" Kym yelled at him. "Don't

you know you have the right to remain silent, you dumb country idiot!"

"You are officially fired," Gray said to Kym through clenched teeth.

"Who gives a damn?" Kym spat. "I'm sick of this town and trying to convince you that the grass is definitely greener on the upscale side. You want to be here and play in the mud with them, have at it! I'm out of here."

She took a couple steps but was pulled back by the sheriff, who slapped handcuffs onto her wrists. "Not so fast, Ms. Upscale," he said to her. "You are under arrest for arson. You now officially have the right to remain silent."

"I'll let you get some clothes on first, Harry," Harlow said quietly. "Then I gotta arrest you, too."

"You did this!" Harry yelled at Morgan. "It was all your fault. We could have been happy, before he came here. You let him change everything, and for what? What's he promising you? Nothing, right? He's not offering to marry you, adopt your kids or even move here permanently." Harry shook his head. "It's all your fault!"

Harry kept talking even as Harlow ushered him into the bedroom to get his clothes. The sheriff walked out the door with a very angry, but now silent Kym, leaving Morgan and Gray alone.

"You do know that he's crazy," Gray said when Morgan had walked away from him to look out the window. "Nothing you or I did or said made them act the way they did. Absolutely nothing."

Morgan watched as the sheriff held a hand to the top of Kym's head as he lowered her into the back of his cruiser.

"I know that," Morgan said and then turned back to face Gray. "But what I don't know, Gray, is if everything that Harry and Kym said was totally wrong."

She didn't know what Gray's plans were in regard to

her and her family. She had no idea if his decision to keep the buildings in Temptation meant he wanted to keep her and the twins as well. Sure, she could simply ask the question, but right at this moment, Morgan wasn't so sure she wanted to know the answer.

# Chapter 16

*Second week of January*

"I think this has run its course," Morgan said on a Friday evening when Gray had returned to Temptation.

The morning after Kym and Harry had been arrested, Gray had told her he needed to go back to Miami.

"I left a lot of things in limbo when I came here a month ago and I need to get back to my office. Especially now that Kym's gone. I'll need to see my attorney to confirm that all those ties are severed and I need to also work on obtaining legal ownership of the LLC account in the Grand Caymans," he'd said as he stood outside her house.

He'd called her and asked her to come out, to avoid seeing the children, Morgan had assumed. It was very early and since they were still on Christmas vacation, the children had been still asleep, so there was really no need for them to meet outside like sneaky teenagers. But Morgan hadn't bothered to say that.

"I understand," she'd replied instead.

"An architect and construction manager will be here by the end of the week. I want the new community center up and running by the spring," he'd continued.

"That's a good idea," Morgan had said.

"The hospital's renovations and new programs are going to take a little more planning. But I'll hire someone to spearhead that as soon as I get back to Miami," he'd said.

His hands were in the pockets of his leather jacket. He wore black wingtips, the cuff of his navy blue pants falling perfectly over them. Gray was wearing a suit again. He was officially *the* Grayson Taylor once more.

"I'm sure everything will work out just the way your father had planned," she'd told him.

"I'll call you" was the last thing Gray had said to her.

Morgan had only nodded because she hadn't believed him for one minute. And she'd been right to not believe him.

In the ten days that he'd been gone Morgan had not received one call. After the second day she'd stopped checking. Now, she was convinced it had all been for the best.

"Why don't we sit down and talk about this," Gray said.

Today, he wore his puffy coat and khakis. On his feet were black boots. His goatee had grown a little thicker, his complexion looked a little healthier. Or maybe that was simply because she hadn't seen him in a while. She didn't know, nor did she allow herself to care—too much.

Reluctantly, she let him into her house and walked to the dining room, where she sat at the table. Tonight was Disney movie night and since the community center was gone, the church board had approved hosting this monthly event in their fellowship hall. Granny had taken the twins, telling Morgan—in that not so polite but honest way that only Granny possessed—that Morgan looked like she needed some rest.

"There are some things I want to tell you," he began once he removed his coat and sat down. "Things that it has taken me some time to get a grip on myself."

Morgan immediately shook her head. "I'm not sure that's necessary, Gray. And really, it's not a big deal. We're both adults and we knew all the facts before walking into this…um, affair," she said and then had to clear her throat.

Morgan had never had an affair before and while this one had been fun while it lasted, she was positive that she never wanted to experience another one.

"Really?" he asked as he sat back in the chair, letting one arm rest on the table. "Why don't you tell me what those facts are."

This entire conversation was pointless. They'd slept together a handful of times, had dinner at the diner and played in the snow. Her kids adored him, but they were young and would soon find something else to fall in love with. He'd been gone for ten days with no communication whatsoever and now he was back looking as handsome as ever, but still not as if he belonged here. There was no changing any of that.

"Temptation is a small town, Gray. There are no high-rise buildings, no nightclubs or fancy garages to park your equally fancy car. We're simple people here, living a simple life. I've never seen as many numbers on a bank statement as I did on that one that belonged to your father. And I do just fine buying my children's Christmas presents, but this living room has never been so full of gifts that I had to make a path to walk around them."

He nodded.

"And what exactly does all of that mean?"

He was eerily calm as he continued to study her. Morgan figured that may have been the way he studied a new car or a new pair of shoes before he purchased them, but no, his eyes were much too intense for that.

She sighed heavily. "It means that we were a mixed match from the beginning. I'm a widowed teacher with two children. You're an internationally known business-man with your own life and goals that I could never begin to compete with." She shrugged. "We were doomed from the start."

Gray rubbed a hand over his chin as he continued to look at her. Then he reached into his pocket and pulled out a red pouch. He set it on the table and they both stared at it for a few moments. He finally pulled the drawstrings and opened the pouch, pulling out a ring and sitting it on top of velour fabric. Morgan resisted the urge to gasp, but couldn't stop staring down at the huge sapphire ring with a circle of diamonds surrounding it. This looked just like the sapphire necklace he'd given her for Christmas, the one that she still had in a box in her underwear drawer.

"Along with the account my father had in each of his children's names, there was a safe-deposit box. This was in mine," Gray told her. "He was going to give this to my mother for her birthday. It was three months after their wedding anniversary when he planned to give her the necklace. Those dates were nine months from the day he walked out on his family."

Gray took a deep breath and then let it out slowly. He looked over to Morgan, his gaze softer now. "He never stopped loving her or us. I figured that out once I went through everything that was in his house, the pictures he kept, all the gifts my mother had ever given him, our first toys. None of that stuff was dusty or uncared for because he kept them out, he took care of them. Just as he always planned to take care of us. I have to believe that there was another reason for them breaking up, a reason that neither of them ever spoke of. If it was just an affair, why keep all those memories of the past?"

With his fingers, Gray brushed down his goatee, closing his eyes for a few moments before opening them again. "In the last weeks I've learned that life is not always what it seems, Morgan, and that sometimes people aren't, either. I thought I knew what I wanted and where I wanted to be, but I was wrong. The moment I left Temptation for the second time I realized that I wanted to be here with you and the children. But we're apparently too mixed matched for that."

She should have felt like a jerk for the things she'd said to him, but Morgan could feel only sorrow.

"Neither of us knew the things we know now when we first met," she said instead. "I've heard everything you've said about your parents and I'm so happy that you're finding out things that you didn't know before. But Gray, that doesn't change the differences between us."

"The social differences that don't mean a damned thing. Is that what you're referring to?" he asked.

Morgan clasped her hands together. "After you left, all people in town could talk about was how shocked they were that Harry had gotten involved in this situation. They couldn't figure out why he would do such a thing when before you came to town Harry had seemed so happy. It was easy enough to accept Kym's involvement because they didn't know her and didn't care to. But then that left me. I became the connection between Harry and you, to the fire and to the Reeds' utter embarrassment that their son was going to jail. All of that rested on my shoulders."

"It shouldn't have and you know that."

She nodded. "I do. But if I'd never gone to visit that house with you, if I had just stayed in my lane and let you go about your business, then maybe Harry's life wouldn't be ruined and the Reeds' reputation wouldn't be in shambles. Maybe a woman who only did her job and fell in love with a handsome man wouldn't have found herself in what she thought was dire circumstances and wouldn't be facing prison time. We can't undo the past," she told him. "But it's probably smart if we start to think about other people besides ourselves when we start working toward the future."

Again, Gray was silent. He looked at her and then down at the ring. After a few moments he put the ring back into the pouch and stuffed it into the pocket of his suit jacket once more.

"You seem to know how you feel on this subject," he said as he stood up and grabbed his coat. "I'll leave you alone with that decision."

And that was that, Morgan thought, as she got up from her seat and walked Gray to the door. Not nearly as hard as she'd thought it would be and certainly not as exhausting as the scene with Harry. Except, she spoke too soon.

When Morgan opened the door to let Gray out the twins came rushing inside.

"Mr. Gray! Mr. Gray!" they yelled in unison, both of them wrapping their arms around each of Gray's legs to hug him.

Morgan felt like a weight had been dropped on her chest as she watched Gray go to his knees to hug them both.

"You went away and we missed you!" Lily told him as she kissed his cheek.

"Yeah. I didn't have anybody to play with my train with me. Mom and Lily are girls and they don't understand," Jack complained when he kept an arm around Gray's neck and leaned in to him.

"I'll have to come around and play with you some other time," Gray told him. "Right now, I've got to go."

"No," Lily pleaded, her little face crumbling instantly. "Don't go away again, Mr. Gray. Please don't."

"We want you to stay here with us," Jack said. "We even wished on the mistletoe like Mama does."

"Right," Lily continued. "We wished for you to be our new daddy since our other one died."

Morgan swallowed and tried desperately to keep her composure. In the days that Gray had been gone the children had asked about him every day and Morgan had given them a very generic he-had-to-go-back-to-his-home reply. She'd hoped that in time the questions would stop, but apparently her children were missing him much more than she initially thought. Her stomach churned and she thought she might actually cry or faint, one or the other, or possibly both.

"There's magic in those wishes," Granny said.

Morgan hadn't even noticed her grandmother come into her house and take off her coat, but Granny was now standing right beside her.

"I'll be back," Gray told them. "I promise I'll come back and play with you sometime. And Lily, we can have another tea party."

Lily's bottom lip quivered, while Jack's remained poked out as Gray stood. He looked at Granny. "Nice seeing you again, Ms. Ida Mae."

"Good to have you back, Grayson," Granny replied.

Gray nodded and then looked at Morgan. He didn't say anything but turned to walk out of the house.

The moment the door was closed Morgan held up a hand to stop whatever words were about to come out of the mouths of her grandmother and her children. "Not right now," she told them. "Just, not right now."

She ran from the room at that moment, emotions swirling quickly and potently throughout her body, causing her to be sick.

Three days later Morgan lay facedown on her bed when Wendy came into the bedroom.

"Well, you missed a very lively MLK Day parade. Millie tried to ride one of the Coolridge horses instead of getting in the car with Mayor Pullum. You know she hates that woman with a passion."

Wendy talked as she moved around the room, pushed open the curtains, and then plopped down on the bed as she took off her boots and dropped them to the floor.

"Then Fred ran over to try and help her up, but the horse bucked and when it came down it was in a puddle of muddy water that splattered all over Millie's snow-white suit and Fred's suede jacket. And that's not all," Wendy continued. "Jerline Bertrum ate three huge bags of Mr. Edison's rainbow sherbet cotton candy and when it came time for her solo she barfed over the microphone and a good portion of the flower-lined float she was riding on. The kids all tried to laugh at first, but then there was a gust of wind and the smell hit everyone. There was barfing and crying and screaming. Girl, it was a mess."

Morgan groaned.

"You been laying here the entire time?" Wendy asked.

Morgan opened one eye to see her sister looking down at her. "Uh-huh," she murmured.

"Why? Are you sick?" Wendy flattened her palm on Morgan's forehead. "You're clammy but not feverish. You think it's the flu?"

"No," Morgan said quietly.

"Maybe it's that stomach virus that's been going around. Have you been vomiting or having diarrhea?"

Morgan did not want to think about either, but she was pretty sure she didn't have a stomach virus.

"I'm pregnant," she said, maybe even more quietly than she had the previous answer.

Wendy waited a beat and then said, "Excuse me?"

With a heavy sigh Morgan turned over onto her back, tossing the white stick she'd been holding in her hand for the last hour at her sister.

"What? Oh. My. Oh. My," Wendy said over and over again. "You're pregnant!"

"Give that girl a prize," Morgan sighed.

"It's Gray's baby. You're pregnant by Grayson Taylor," Wendy said as she bounced up and down as if it was the happiest day in her life. "Oh, just wait until Granny hears this. She's been talking about you and Gray for days now, saying how that mistletoe wish was bound to come true for the twins, no matter how you tried to stop it."

Morgan dropped an arm over her face and groaned. "I didn't try to stop it. I wanted to protect me and my kids."

"Whatever," Wendy said, thankfully getting up off the bed.

Morgan's stomach was not on solid ground, hadn't been for days now.

"There's no protecting people from falling in love. I don't know why anyone ever tries that stunt in the first place. And those children, they're too young to know about games and hiding from their feelings. They knew what they wanted all along," Wendy said.

"But he wasn't theirs to want," Morgan argued. "He wasn't mine. He didn't even want to be here."

"Well, he's certainly here now," Wendy told her.

Morgan sat up on the bed to see her sister with her cell phone in hand. "What do you mean he's here now? And who are you texting?"

"I'm telling Granny. You know she doesn't carry that phone around that we got her so I'm guessing it'll take her about an hour before she sees it. That gives you more than enough time to shower and pretty yourself up so you can go and tell Gray about the baby."

Morgan narrowed her eyes at her sister. "What? Wait. I don't know if we should be telling Granny yet. And it's my news so I should really be the one to tell her. And how am I going to go and tell Gray anything? He's back in Miami."

Wendy shook her head. "Nope. He never left Temptation. He's been staying at his parents' house. The one where construction trucks have been parked out front since yesterday. He's got work going on at the community center, the hospital and the Taylor house. So you can just go on over there and tell that man you're having his baby."

"I can't," Morgan said as she remembered all the things she'd said to him just days ago. All the things that she'd thought at the time were the right thing to say.

"You can and you will," Wendy said, now finished with her text message. She came over and grabbed Morgan by the hand.

"Stop thinking of reasons not to do it and just go. You can't keep his baby from him and you're certainly not the type to even consider any other option," Wendy continued.

"He probably thinks I'm some idiotic fluff head," Morgan complained as she entered the bathroom.

"Well, you've certainly been acting like one. But we can easily blame that on the pregnancy. Now, here, I'll run your water and when you get out I want you to put on the clothes I pick out for you. No fussing. Just get dressed and go," her sister ordered her.

"Wendy," Morgan said when she was standing near the shower stall, the water that her sister had turned on already sprinkling her arm. "What if he tells me to go away?"

Wendy shook her head as she smiled at her sister. "If he wanted you to go away, Morgan, he would have never come back to Temptation."

# *Chapter 17*

The red doors were gone.

That was the first thing Morgan noticed when she stepped out of her car and walked across the street toward the Taylor house on Peach Tree Lane. As Wendy had already told her there was a large dump truck and a smaller white pickup parked on the front lawn. The dilapidated white picket fence that surrounded the entire corner property was gone and there were workmen moving in and out of the house.

"Is Mr. Taylor here?" Morgan asked one of the men as she stepped gingerly onto the front porch.

"Straight back, in the kitchen with the site manager," he said, barely looking at her while ripping another long slab of wood from the railing.

She walked into the house, seeing even more activity. There were holes in some of the walls, electrical wiring pulled out, several men standing around it talking about what they saw, she guessed. All the drapes had been removed from the windows and rugs had been taken up from the scuffed wood floors. Dust tickled her nose as she continued toward the back of the house. Nobody even asked why she was there—they all simply continued to work as if they didn't see her in the midst of their workday.

She stepped into the kitchen to see even more people, including Gray. He was standing in a corner, a bank of huge windows that went from one side of the wall to halfway around the other. The view of the backyard was stunning, but it was the tiny peak of the mountaintop that had Morgan moving closer without speaking a word. This was a gorgeous view and as she stared out to the cloudy January day, she had a quick flash of children playing in this yard. First, it was of multiple children, six to be exact, three boys and three girls, running and laughing, tossing a bright red ball between them. In an instant the scene remained the same, but the children were different—there were two of them, a boy and a girl. The red ball still rolled around the yard, with laughter and cheering loud in the air. On the porch, just a short distance away, was a cradle with a baby wrapped tightly in a blanket inside.

"Good afternoon," he said from directly behind her, his voice deep and warm.

Morgan spun around quickly, her back hitting against the windows as she faced Gray. He looked even better than he had a few days ago, she thought as she swallowed, trying to calm her jittering stomach. This wasn't morning sickness, although Morgan had been having her time with that. Hence the reason she'd finally purchased the pregnancy test.

"Hi," she said, her hands behind her, clasping the windowsill.

They were silent the next few minutes, both of them looking at each other as if searching for the right words to say. He wore a long-sleeved shirt today that melded against every muscle of his upper body. His jeans were dark denim, his boots black. If she didn't know better Morgan might have mistaken him for one of the crew. But she did know better. She knew that there was a three-inch scar under his right knee where he'd fallen off his bike and into a ditch when he was thirteen. She also knew that his favorite ice cream was chocolate and that he'd never been to Walt Disney World. Another thing she knew, without a doubt, in that instant that she saw him standing in this old kitchen where his family once lived was that she loved this man.

"I thought you were leaving," she said.

"I left your house because you told me to go," he replied, stuffing his hands into his front pockets.

Morgan nodded. "I know."

She'd told him that because she was afraid of hearing him say he didn't want to stay. It had all boiled down to that. Well, whether or not Gray stayed in Temptation he deserved to know that she was carrying his child. Regardless of how she felt about him—even though she'd been too silly and too cowardly to just tell him that she loved him—he was free to go wherever he pleased. She wasn't going to try and guilt him into staying with her. She was already a single mother, there was no reason why she couldn't continue on that way. After all, thousands of women did every day.

Morgan took a deep breath and decided it was simply best to say it and get it over with.

"I'm pregnant."

The words fell into the room that was bustling with activity around them. Still, they had the impact of a gigantic pink elephant stepping immediately between them.

One of his brows arched and Gray opened his mouth to speak. He closed it and then tried again. Nothing.

"Just about six weeks," Morgan continued. "So it must

have been that first time. When we were at my place. Um, I counted back and that had to be the night. I haven't been with anyone since James died, so I'm positive it's yours. I wouldn't be standing here if I wasn't absolutely certain."

She began shaking her head as he continued to stare at her. "But you don't have to do anything. I'll be all right. I mean, we'll be all right. I totally understand that you have a life in Miami and business and all that."

He slowly placed a finger to her lips. "Shush."

Morgan's heart was beating so fast that, coupled with the noise of something that had fallen in the other room, she had to ask, "What did you just say?"

Gray took a step closer to her. "I said to shush."

This time it was Morgan who opened her mouth to speak, just to have the words cut short when Gray grabbed her at the waist, pulled her up against him and kissed her.

It was what great chick flicks were made of. The slow and poignant hold, his gaze trained on her as he came in closer. Their lips parting slightly and then touching hotly. Morgan fell completely into the act the moment his tongue touched hers. She held him tightly, loving the feel of his strong arms doing the same to her. This was safe, she thought suddenly. It was safe and solid and…home.

"I thought you were leaving," she whispered against his lips when they'd had to choose between continuing the kiss or breathing. "I haven't seen or talked to you in weeks."

Gray shook his head. "I was giving you space," he told her and cupped her face in his hands.

"Space? I don't understand," she said, leaning into his touch, not wanting it to go away. "That day with Harry, you said if he truly loved me he would beg, steal, tear down walls and climb mountains to keep me. But you just came over here and started doing…what are you doing exactly?"

He smiled. "I meant exactly what I said that day. When a man truly loves a woman he'll do anything to keep her. So when you told me that you wanted me to leave, even after I told you that I wanted to be here with you and the children, I did exactly that. I also moved into this house and starting mapping out the plan to our future. It starts with renovating."

"Renovations? Our future? Gray, I'm sorry. I don't know if it's the noise or the dust, or the flip-flopping of my stomach that's making me a bit nauseous, but I don't get what you're saying."

He kissed her lips quickly, letting one of his hands fall to cup her still-flat stomach. "I'm saying that I was just waiting for you to come to the conclusion I'd already reached. All my life I've wondered about my purpose and my place in this world. I didn't think it could be that I belonged in the same town where I started out, or that I could possibly want what my parents had, but I do. I want the home and the family. I want a wife and children that will run and play in this yard and grow up in this small crazy town."

Gray shook his head as if he couldn't believe his own words. "You're the one that I've been waiting for all this time, Morgan. You're the one that made me see what it was I truly wanted and love you so very much for being too stubborn to just let me come into this town with my business-as-usual attitude. I love you for being strong enough to walk away if I couldn't truly commit to you. And I love you for this," he said, looking down at his hand on her stomach. "So very much, Morgan. I just love you."

Her eyes were full of tears, her heart beating so fast she thought it could be seen through her shirt.

"You're the one I've wished for," Morgan said, blinking furiously to keep her tears from falling. "All those wishes under the mistletoe, for all those years. And then you showed up. It was you all along, Gray. I love you."

"We're going to be so great together," he told her. "You, me, Lily, Jack and this one." He patted her stomach then. "We're going to be a family. The new Taylors of Temptation."

\* \* \* \* \*

# CHRISTMAS WHERE THEY BELONG

## MARION LENNOX

This book is dedicated to Lorna May Dickins.

Her kindness, her humour and her love are
an inspiration for always.

# CHAPTER ONE

'DIDN'T YOU ONCE own a house in the Blue Mountains?'

'Um…yes.'

'Crikey, Jules, you wouldn't want to be there now. The whole range looks about to burn.'

It was two days before Christmas. The Australian world of finance shut down between Christmas and New Year, but the deal Julie McDowell was working on was international. The legal issues were urgent.

But the Blue Mountains… Fire.

She dumped her armload of contracts and headed for Chris's desk. At thirty-two, Chris was the same age as Julie, but her colleague's work ethic was as different from hers as it was possible to be. Chris worked from nine to five and not a moment more before he was off home to his wife and kids in the suburbs. Sometimes he even surfed the Web during business hours.

Sure enough, his computer was open at the Web browser now. She came up behind him and saw a fire map. The Blue Mountains. A line of red asterisks.

Her focus went straight to Mount Bundoon, a tiny hamlet right in the centre of the asterisks. The hamlet she'd once lived in.

'Is it on fire?' she gasped. She'd been so busy she hadn't been near a news broadcast for hours. Days?

'Not yet.' Chris zoomed in on a few of the asterisks. 'These are alerts, not evacuation orders. A storm came through last night, with lighting strikes but not much rain. The bush is tinder dry after the drought, and most of these asterisks show spot fires in inaccessible bushland. But strong winds and high temperatures are forecast for to-morrow. They're already closing roads, saying she could be a killer.'

*A killer.*

The Blue Mountains.

*You wouldn't want to be there now.*

She went back to her desk and pulled up the next con-tract. This was important. She needed to concentrate, but the words blurred before her eyes. All she could see was a house—long, low, every detail architecturally designed, built to withstand the fiercest bush fires.

In her mind she walked through the empty house to a bedroom with two small beds in the shape of racing cars. Teddies sitting against the pillows. Toys. A wall-hanging of a steam train her mother had made.

She hadn't been there for four years. It should have been sold. Why hadn't it?

She fought to keep her mind on her work. This had to be dealt with before Christmas.

Teddies. A wardrobe full of small boys' clothes.

She closed her eyes and she was there again, tucking two little boys into bed, watching Rob read them their bedtime story.

It was history, long past, but she couldn't open her eyes. She couldn't.

'Julie? Are you okay?' Her boss was standing over her, sounding concerned. Bob Marsh was a financial wizard but he looked after his staff, especially those who brought as much business to the firm as Julie.

She forced herself to open her eyes and tried for a smile. It didn't work.

'What's up?'

'The fire.' She took a deep breath, knowing what she was facing. Knowing she had no choice.

'I *do* have a house in the Blue Mountains,' she managed. 'If it's going to burn there are things I need to save.' She gathered her pile of contracts and did what she'd never done in all her years working for Opal, Harbison and Marsh. She handed the pile to Bob. 'You'll need to deal with this,' she told him. 'I'm sorry, but...'

She couldn't finish the sentence. She grabbed her purse and went.

Rob McDowell was watching the fire's progress on his phone. He'd downloaded an app to track it by, and he'd been checking it on and off for hours.

He was in Adelaide, working. His clients had wanted to be in the house by Christmas and he'd bent over backwards to make it happen. Their house was brilliant and there were only a few decorative touches left to be made. Rob was no longer needed, but Sir Cliff and Lady Claudia had requested their architect to stay on until tomorrow.

He should. They were having a housewarming on Christmas Eve, and socialising at the end of a job was important. The *Who's Who* of Adelaide, maybe even the *Who's Who* of the entire country would be here. There weren't many people who could beckon the cream of society on Christmas Eve but Sir Cliff and Lady Claudia had that power. As the architect of their stunning home, Rob could expect scores of professional approaches afterwards.

But it wasn't just professional need that was driving him. For the last few years he'd flown overseas to the ski fields for Christmas but somehow this year they'd lost their appeal. Christmas had been a nightmare for years but finally he was beginning to accept that running away didn't help. He might as well stay for the party, he'd decided, but now he checked the phone app again and felt worse. The house he and Julie had built was right in the line of fire.

The house would be safe, he told himself. He'd designed it himself and it had been built with fires like this one in mind.

But no house could withstand the worst of Australia's bush fires. He knew that. To make its occupants safe he'd built a bunker into the hill behind the house, but the house itself could go up in flames.

It was insured. No one was living there. It shouldn't matter.

But the contents…

The contents.

He should have cleared it out by now, he thought savagely. He shouldn't have left everything there. The tricycles. The two red fire engines he'd chosen himself that last Christmas.

Julie might have taken them.

She hadn't. She would have told him.

Both of them had walked away from their house four years ago. It should have been on the market, but…but…

But he'd paid a housekeeping service to clean it once a month, and to clear the grounds. He was learning to move on, but selling the house, taking this last step, still seemed…too hard.

So what state was it in now? he wondered. Had the bushland encroached again? If there was bushland growing against the house…

It didn't matter. The house was insured, he told himself again. What did it matter if it burned? Wouldn't that just be the final step in moving on with his life?

But two fire engines...

This was ridiculous. He was thinking of forgoing the social event of the season, a career-building triumph, steps to the future, to save two toy fire engines?

But...

'Sarah...' He didn't know what he intended to say until the words were in his mouth, but the moment he said it he knew his decision was right.

'Yeah?' The interior decorator was balancing on a ladder, her arms full of crimson tulle. The enormous drawing room was going to look stunning. 'Could you hand me those ribbons?'

'I can't, Sarah,' he said, in a voice he scarcely recognised. 'I own a house in the Blue Mountains and they're saying the fire threat's getting worse. Could you make my excuses? I need to go...home.'

At the headquarters of the Blue Mountains Fire Service, things looked grim and were about to get worse. Every time a report came in, more asterisks appeared on the map. The fire chief had been staring at it for most of the day, watching spot fires erupt, while the weather forecast grew more and more forbidding.

'We won't be able to contain this,' he eventually said, heavily. 'It's going to break out.'

'Evacuate?' His second-in-command was looking even more worried than he was.

'If we get one worse report from the weather guys, yes. We'll put out a pre-evacuation warning tonight. Anyone not prepared to stay and firefight should leave now.' He looked again at the map and raked his thinning hair. 'Okay, people, let's put the next step of fire warnings into place. Like it or not, we're about to mess with a whole lot of people's Christmases.'

# CHAPTER TWO

THE HOUSE LOOKED just as she'd left it. The garden had
grown, of course. A couple of trees had grown up close to the
house. Rob wouldn't be pleased. He'd say it was a fire risk.

It was a fire risk.

She was sitting in the driveway in her little red coupé,
staring at the front door. Searching for the courage to go
inside.

It was three years, eleven months, ten days since she'd
been here.

Rob had brought her home from hospital. She'd wandered into the empty house; she'd looked around and it
was almost as if the walls were taunting her.

*You're here and they're not. What sort of parents are
you? What sort of parents were you?*

She hadn't even stayed the night. She couldn't. She'd
thrown what she most needed into a suitcase and told Rob
to take her to a hotel.

'Julie, we can do this.' She still heard Rob's voice; she
still saw his face. 'We can face this together.'

'It wasn't you who slept while they died.' She'd thrown
that at him, he hadn't answered and she'd known right then
that the final link had snapped.

She hadn't been back since.

*Go in,* she told herself now. *Get this over.*

She opened the car door and the heat hit her with such force that she gasped.

It was dusk. It shouldn't be this hot, this late.

The tiny hamlet of Mount Bundoon had looked almost deserted as she'd driven through. Low-lying smoke and the lack of wind was giving it a weird, eerie feeling. She'd stopped at the general store and bought milk and bread and butter, and the lady had been surprised to see her.

'We're about to close, love,' she said. 'Most people are packing to get out or have already left. You're not evacuating?'

'The latest warning is watch and wait.'

'They've upgraded it. Unless you plan on defending your home, they're advising you get out, if not now, then at least by nine in the morning. That's when the wind's due to rise, but most residents have chosen to leave straight away.'

Julie had hesitated at that. The road up here had been packed with laden cars, trailers, horse floats, all the accoutrements people treasured. That was why she was here. To take things she treasured.

But now she thought: *it wasn't*. She sat in the driveway and stared at the house where she'd once lived, and she thought, even though the house was full of the boys' belongings, it wasn't possessions she wanted.

Was it just to be here? One last time?

It wasn't going to burn, she told herself. It'd still be here…for ever. But that was a dumb thought. They'd have to sell eventually.

That'd mean contacting Rob.

*Don't go there.*

*Go in,* she told herself. *Hunker down. This house is fire-safe. In the morning you can walk away but just for tonight… Just for tonight you can let yourself remember.*

Even if it hurt so much it nearly killed her.

* * *

Eleven o'clock. The plane had been delayed, because of smoke haze surrounding Sydney. 'There's quite a fire down there, ladies and gentlemen,' the pilot had said as they skirted the Blue Mountains. 'Just be thankful you're up here and not down there.'

But he'd wanted to be down there. By the time he'd landed the fire warnings for Mount Bundoon had been upgraded. *Leave if safe to do so.* Still, the weather forecast was saying the winds weren't likely to pick up until early morning. Right now there was little wind. The house would be safe.

So he'd hired a car and driven into the mountains, along roads where most of the traffic was going in the other direction. When he'd reached the outskirts of Mount Bundoon he'd hit a road block.

'Your business, sir?' he was asked.

'I live here.' How true was that? He didn't live anywhere, he conceded, but maybe here was still…home. 'I just need to check all my fire prevention measures are in place and operational.'

'You're aware of the warnings?'

'I am, but my house is pretty much fire-safe and I'll be out first thing in the morning.'

'You're not planning on defending?'

'Not my style.'

'Not mine either,' the cop said. 'They're saying the wind'll be up by nine, turning to the north-west, bringing the fire straight down here. The smoke's already making the road hazardous. We're about to close it now, allowing no one else in. I shouldn't let you pass.'

'I'll be safe. I'm on my own and I'll be in and out in no time.'

'Be out by the time the wind changes, if not before,' he said grudgingly.

'I will be.'

'Goodnight, then, sir,' the cop said. 'Stay safe.'

'Same to you, in spades.'

He drove on. The smoke wasn't thick, just a haze like a winter fog. The house was on the other side of town, tucked into a valley overlooking the Bundoon Creek. The ridges would be the most dangerous places, Rob thought, not the valley. He and Julie had thought about bush fire when they'd built. If you were planning to build in the Australian bush, you were stupid if you didn't.

Maybe they'd been stupid anyway. Building so far out of town. Maybe that was why...

*No. Don't think why.* That was the way of madness.

*Nearly home.* That was a dumb thing to think, too, but he turned the last bend and thought of all the times he'd come home, with kids, noise, chaos, all the stuff associated with twins. Sometimes he and Julie would manage the trip back together and that was the best. *'Mummy, Daddy—you're both here...'*

*Cut it out,* he told himself fiercely. *You were dumb to come. Don't make it any worse by thinking of the past.*

But the past was all around him, even if it was shrouded in smoke.

'I'll take their toys and get out of here,' he told himself, and then he pulled into the driveway... and the lights were on.

She'd turned on all the lights to scare the ghosts.

No. If there were any ghosts here she'd welcome them with open arms—it wasn't ghosts she was scared of. It was the dark. It was trying to sleep in this house, and remembering.

She lay on the king-sized bed she and Rob had bought the week before their wedding and she knew sleep was out of the question. She should leave.

But leaving seemed wrong, too. Not when the kids were here.

The kids weren't here. Only memories of them.

This was crazy. She was a legal financier, a good one, specialising in international monetary negotiations. No one messed with her. No one questioned her sanity.

So why was she lying in bed hoping for ghosts?

She lay completely still, listening to the small sounds of the night. The scratching of a possum in the tree outside the window. A night owl calling.

This house had never been quiet. She found herself aching for noise, for voices, for…something.

She got something. She heard a car pull into the driveway. She saw the glimmer of headlights through the window.

The front door opened, and she knew part of her past had just returned. The ghost she was most afraid of.


'Julie?' He'd guessed it must be her before he even opened the door. Firstly the car. It was a single woman's car, expensive, a display of status.

Rob normally drove a Land Rover. Okay, maybe that was a status thing as well, he conceded. He liked the idea that he might spend a lot of time on rural properties but in truth most of his clients were city based. But still, he couldn't drive a car like the one in the driveway. No one here could. No one who commuted from here to the city. No one who taxied kids.

Every light was on in the house. Warning off ghosts?

It had to be Julie.

If she was here the last thing he wanted was to scare

her, so the moment he opened the door he called, 'Julie, are you here? It's Rob.'

And she emerged from their bedroom.

*Julie.*

The sight of her made him feel… No. He couldn't begin to define how he felt seeing her.

It had been nearly four years. She'd refused to see him since.

*'I slept while they died and I can't forgive myself. Ever. I can't even think about what I've lost. If I hadn't slept…'*

She'd thrown it at him the day he'd brought her home from hospital. He'd spent weeks sick with self-blame, sick with emptiness, not knowing how to cope with his own grief, much less hers. The thought that she blamed herself hadn't even occurred to him. It should have, but in those crucial seconds after she'd said it he hadn't had a response. He'd stared at her, numb with shock and grief, as she'd limped into the bedroom on her crutches, thrown things into a suitcase and demanded he take her to a hotel.

And that had pretty much been that. One marriage, one family, finished.

He'd written to her. Of course he had, and he'd tried to phone. *'Jules, it was no one's fault. That you were asleep didn't make any difference. I was awake and alert. The landslip came from nowhere. There's nothing anyone can do when the road gives way.'* Did he believe it himself? He tried to. Sometimes he had flashes when he almost did.

And apparently, Julie had shared his doubts. She'd written back, brief and harsh.

*I was asleep when my bab es died. I wasn't there for them, or for you. I can barely live with myself,*

*much less face you every day for the rest of my life.*
*I'm sorry, Rob, but however we manage to face the*
*future, we need to do it alone.*

And he couldn't help her to forgive herself. He was too busy living with his *own* guilt. The mountain road to the house had been eroded by heavy spring rains and the collapse was catastrophic. They'd spent the weeks before Christmas in the city apartment because there'd been so much on it had just been too hard to commute. They were exhausted but Julie had been desperate to get up to the mountains for the weekend before Christmas, to make everything perfect for the next week. To let the twins set up their Christmas tree. So Santa wouldn't find one speck of dust, one thing out of place.

He'd gone along with it. Maybe he'd also agreed. Perfection was in both their blood; they were driven personalities. They'd given their nanny the weekend off and they'd driven up here late.

But if they'd just relaxed… If they'd simply said there wasn't time, they could have spent that last weekend playing with the boys in the city, just stopping. But stopping wasn't in their vocabulary and the boys were dead because of it.

Enough. The past needed to be put aside. Julie was standing in their bedroom door.

She looked…beautiful.

He'd thought this woman was gorgeous the moment he'd met her. Tall, willow-slim, blonde hair with just a touch of curl, brown eyes a man could drown in, lips a man wanted to taste…

It was four years since he'd last seen her, and she was just the same but…tighter. It was like her skin was stretched to fit. She was thinner. Paler. She was wearing a simple cotton nightgown, her hair was tousled and her eyes were wide with…wariness.

Why should she be wary of him?

'Julie.' He repeated her name and she stopped dead.

She might have known he'd come.

Dear heaven, he was beautiful. He was tall—she'd forgotten how tall—and still boyish, even though he must be—what, thirty-six?—by now.

He had the same blond-brown hair that looked perpetually like he spent too much time in the sun. He had the same flop of cowlick that hung a bit too long—no hairdresser believed it wouldn't stay where it was put. He was wearing his casual clothes, clothes he might have worn four years ago: moleskins with a soft linen shirt, rolled up at the sleeves and open at the throat.

He was wearing the same smile, a smile which reached the caramel-brown eyes she remembered. He was smiling at her now. A bit hesitant. Not sure of his reception.

She hadn't seen him for four years and he was wary. What did he think she'd do, throw him out?

But she didn't know where to start. Where to begin after all this time.

Why not say it like it was?

'I don't think I am Julie,' she said slowly, feeling lost. 'At least, I'm not sure I'm the Julie you know.'

There was a moment's pause. He'd figure it out, or she hoped he would. She couldn't go straight back to the point where they'd left off. *How are you, Rob? How have you coped with the last four years?*

The void of four long years made her feel ill.

But he got it. There was a moment's silence and then his smile changed a little. She knew that smile. It reflected his intelligence, his appreciation of a problem. If there was a puzzle, Rob dived straight in. Somehow she'd set him one and he had it sorted.

'Then I'm probably not the guy you know, either,' he told her. 'So can we start from the beginning? Allow me to introduce myself. I'm Rob McDowell, architect, based in Adelaide. I have an interest in this house, ma'am, and the contents. I'm here to put the most…put a few things of special value in a secure place. And you?'

She could do this. She felt herself relax, just a little, and she even managed to smile back.

'Julie McDowell. Legal financier from Sydney. I, too, have an interest in this house.'

'McDowell?' He was caught. 'You still use…'

'It was too much trouble to change it back,' she said and he knew she was having trouble keeping her voice light.

'You're staying despite the fire warnings?'

'The wind's not due to get up until tomorrow morning. I'll be gone at dawn.'

'You've just arrived?'

'Yes.'

'You don't want to take what you want and go?'

'I don't know what I want.' She hesitated. 'I think… there's a wall-hanging… But it seems wrong to just…leave.'

'I had two fire engines in mind,' he admitted. 'But I feel the same.'

'So you'll stay until ordered out?'

'If it doesn't get any worse, maybe I can clear any debris, check the pumps and sprinkler system, fill the spouts, keep any stray spark from catching. At first light I'll go right round the house and eliminate every fire risk I can. I can't do it now. It's too dark. For the sake of a few hours, I'll stay. I don't want this place to burn.'

*Why?* she wanted to say. *What does this house mean to you?*

What did it mean to her? A time capsule? Maybe it was. This house was what it was like when…

But *when* was unthinkable. And if Rob was here, then surely she could go.

But she couldn't. The threat was still here, even if she wasn't quite sure what was being threatened.

'If you need to stay,' she ventured, 'there's a guest room.'

'Excellent.' They were like two wary dogs, circling each other, she thought. But they'd started this sort of game. She could do this.

'Would you like supper?'

'I don't want to keep you up.'

'I wasn't sleeping. The pantry's stocked and the freezer's full. Things may well be slightly out of date…'

'Slightly!'

'But I'm not dictated to by use-by dates,' she continued. 'I have fresh milk and bread. For anything else, I'm game if you are.'

His brown eyes creased a little, amused. 'A risk-taker, Jules?'

'No!'

'Sorry.' Jules was a nickname and that was against the rules. He realised it and backtracked. 'I meant: have you tried any of the food?'

'I haven't tried,' she conceded.

'You came and went straight to bed?'

'I…yes.'

'Then maybe we both need supper.' He checked his watch. 'It's almost too late for a midnight feast but I could eat two horses. Maybe we could get to know each other over a meal? If you dare, that is?'

And she gazed at him for a long moment and came to a decision.

'I dare,' she said. 'Why not?'

\* \* \*

He put the cars in the garage and then they checked the fire situation. 'We'd be fools not to,' Rob said as they headed out to the back veranda to see what they could see.

They could see nothing. The whole valley seemed to be shrouded in smoke. It blocked the moon and the stars. It seemed ominous but there was no glow from any fire. 'And the smoke would be thicker if it was closer,' Rob decreed. 'We're safe enough for now.'

'There are branches overhanging the house.'

'I saw them as I came in but there's no way I'm using a chainsaw in the dark.'

'There's no way you're using a chainsaw,' she snapped and he grinned.

'Don't you trust me?'

'Do I trust any man with a chainsaw? No.'

He grinned, that same smile... *Dear heaven, that smile...*

Play the game. For tonight, she did *not* know this man.

'We have neighbours,' Rob said, motioning to a light in the house next door.

'I saw a child in the window earlier, just as it was getting dark.'

'A child... They should have evacuated.'

'Maybe they still think there's time. There should still be time.'

'Let me check again.' He flicked to the fire app on his phone. 'Same warnings. Evacuate by nine if you haven't already done so. Unless you're planning on staying to defend.'

'Would you?' she asked diffidently. 'Stay and defend?'

'I'd have to be trustworthy with a chainsaw to do that.'

'And are you?' The Rob she knew couldn't be trusted within twenty paces of a power tool.

'No,' he admitted and she was forced to smile back. Same Rob, then. Same, but different? The Rob of *after*.

This was weird. She should be dressed, she decided, as she padded barefoot back to the kitchen behind him. If he really was a stranger...

*He really is a stranger*, she told herself. Power tool knowledge or not, four years was a lifetime.

'Right.' In the kitchen, he was all efficiency. 'Food.' He pushed his sleeves high over his elbows and looked as if he meant business. 'I'd kill for a steak. What do you suppose the freezer holds?'

'Who knows what's buried in there?'

'Want to help me find out?'

'Men do the hunting.'

'And women do the cooking?' He had the chest freezer open and was delving among the labelled packages. 'Julie, Julie, Julie. How out of the ark is that?'

'I can microwave a mean TV dinner.'

'Ugh.'

But Rob did cook. She remembered him enjoying cooking. Not often because they'd been far too busy for almost everything domestic but when she'd first met him he'd cooked her some awesome meals.

She'd tried to return the favour, but had only cooked disasters.

'What sort of people occupied this planet?' Rob was demanding answers from the depths of the freezer. 'Packets, packets and packets. Someone here likes Diet Cuisine. Liked,' he amended. 'Use-by dates of three years ago.'

She used to eat them when Rob was away. She'd cooked for the boys, or their nanny had, but Diet Cuisine was her go-to.

'There must be something more...' He was hauling out

packet after packet, tossing them onto the floor behind him. She was starting to feel mortified. Her fault again?

'You'll need to put that stuff back or it'll turn into stinking sog,' she warned.

'Of course.' His voice was muffled. 'So in a thousand years an archaeological dig can find Diet Cuisine and think we were all nuts. And stinking sog? For a stink it'd have to contain substance. Two servings of veggies and four freezer-burned cubes of diced meat do not substance make. But hey, here's a whole beef fillet.' He emerged, waving his find in triumph. 'This is seriously thick. I'm hoping freezer burn might only go halfway in or less. I can thaw it in the microwave, chop off the burn and produce steak fit for a king. I hope. Hang on a minute.'

Fascinated, she watched as he grabbed a torch from the pantry and headed for the back door. That was a flaw in this mock play; he shouldn't have known where a torch was. But in two minutes he was back, brandishing a handful of greens.

'Chives,' he said triumphantly and then glanced dubiously at the enormous green fronds. 'Or they might have been chives some time ago. These guys are mutant onions.'

Clarissa had planted vegetables, she remembered. Their last nanny…

But Rob was taking all her attention. The Rob of now. She'd expected…

Actually, she hadn't expected. She'd thought she'd never see this man again. She'd vaguely thought she'd be served with divorce papers at some stage, but she hadn't had the courage or the impetus to organise it herself. To have him here now, slicing steak, washing dirt from mutant chives, took a bit of getting used to.

'You do want some?' he asked and she thought *no*. And then she thought: *when did I last eat?*

If he had been a stranger she'd eat with him.

'Yes, please,' she said and was inordinately pleased with herself for getting the words out.

So they ate. The condiments in the pantry still seemed fine, though Rob dared to tackle the bottled horseradish and she wasn't game. He'd fried hunks of bread in the pan juices. They ate steak and chives and fried bread, washed down by mugs of milky tea. All were accompanied by Rob's small talk. He really did act as if they were strangers, thrust together by chance.

Wasn't that the truth?

'So, Julie,' he said finally, as he washed and she wiped. There was a dishwasher but, as neither intended sticking round past breakfast, it wasn't worth the effort. 'If you're planning on leaving at dawn, what would you like to do now? You were sleeping when I got here?'

'Trying to sleep.'

'It doesn't come on demand,' he said, and she caught an edge to his voice that said he lay awake, as she did. 'But you can try. I'll keep watch.'

'What—stand sentry in case the fire comes?'

'Something like that.'

'It won't come until morning.'

'I don't trust forecasts. I'll stay on the veranda with the radio. Snooze a little.'

'I won't sleep.'

'So…you want to join me on fire watch?'

'I…okay.'

'You might want to put something on besides your nightie.'

'What's wrong with the nightie? It's sensible.'

'It's not sensible.'

'It's light.'

'Jules,' he said, and suddenly there was strain in his voice. 'Julie. I know we don't know each other very well.

I know we're practically strangers, but there is only a set-tee on the veranda, and if you sit there looking like that…'

She caught her breath and the play-acting stopped, just like that. She stared at him in disbelief.

'You can't…want me.'

'I've never stopped wanting you,' he said simply. 'I've tried every way I know, but it's not working. Just because we destroyed ourselves… Just because we gave away the idea of family for the rest of our lives, it doesn't stop the wanting. Not everything ended the night our boys died, Julie, though sometimes…often…I wish it had.'

'You still feel…'

'I have no idea what I feel,' he told her. 'I've been try-ing my best to move on. My shrink says I need to put it all in the background, like a book I can open at leisure and close again when it gets too hard to read. But, for now, all I know is that your nightie is way too skimpy and your eyes are too big and your hair is too tousled and our bed is too close. So I suggest you either head to the bedroom and close the door or go get some clothes on. Because what I want has nothing to do with reality, and everything to do with ghosts. Shrink's advice or not, I can't close the book. Go and get dressed, Julie. Please.'

She stared at him for a long moment. Rob. Her husband.

Her ex-husband. Her ex-life.

She'd closed the door on him four years ago. If she was to survive, that door had to stay firmly closed. Behind that door were emotions she couldn't handle.

She turned away and headed inside. Away from him. Away from the way he tugged her heart.


He sat out on the veranda, thinking he might have scared her right off. She didn't emerge.

Well, what was new? He'd watched the way she'd closed

down after the boys' deaths. He was struggling to get free of those emotions but it seemed Julie was holding them close. Behind locked doors.

That was her right.

He sat for an hour and watched the night close in around him. The heat seemed to be getting more oppressive. The smoke hung low over everything, black and thick and stinking of burned forest, threatening enough all by itself, even without flames.

*It's because there's no wind,* he told himself. Without wind, smoke could hang around for weeks. There was no telling how close the fire was. There was no telling what the risks were if the wind got up.

He should leave. He should make Julie leave, but then… But then…

Her decision to come had been hers alone. She had the right to stay. He wasn't sure what he was protecting, but sitting out on the veranda, with Julie in the house behind him, felt okay. He wasn't sure why, but he did know that, at some level, the decision to come had been the right one.

Maybe it was stupid, he conceded, but maybe they both needed this night. Maybe they both needed to stand sentinel over a piece of their past that needed to be put aside.

And it really did need to be put aside. He'd watched Julie's face when he'd confessed that he wanted her and he'd seen the absolute denial. Even if she was ever to want him again, he'd known then that she wouldn't admit it.

Families were for the past.

He sat on. A light was still on next door. Once he saw a woman walk past the lighted window. Pregnant? Was she keeping the same vigil he was keeping?

If he had kids, he'd have them out of here by now. Hopefully, his neighbour had her car packed and would be gone at dawn, taking her family with her.

Just as he and Julie would be gone at dawn, too.

The moments ticked on. He checked the fire app again. No change.

There were sounds coming from indoors. Suddenly he was conscious of Christmas music. Carols, tinkling out on…a music box?

He remembered that box. It had belonged to one of his aunts. It was a box full of Santa and his elves. You wound the key, opened the box and they all danced.

That box…

Memories were all around him. Childhood Christmases. The day his aunt had given it to them—the Christmas Julie was pregnant. 'It needs a family,' his aunt had said. 'I'd love you to have it.'

His aunt was still going strong. He should give the box back to her, he thought, but meanwhile… Meanwhile, he headed in and Julie was sitting in the middle of the living room floor, attaching baubles to a Christmas tree. She was still dressed in the nightgown. She was totally intent on what she was doing.

*What…?*

'It's Christmas Eve tomorrow,' she said simply, as if this was a no-brainer. 'This should be up. And don't look at the nightgown, Rob McDowell. Get over it. It's hot, my nightie's cool and I'm working.'

She'd hauled the artificial tree from the storeroom. He stared at it, remembering the Christmas when they'd conceded getting a real tree was too much hassle. It'd take hours to buy it and set it up, and one thing neither of them had was hours.

That last Christmas, that last weekend, the tree was one of the reasons they'd come up here.

'We can decorate the tree for Christmas,' Julie had said. 'When we go up next week we can walk straight in and it'll be Santa-ready.'

Now Julie was sitting under the tree, sorting decorations as if she had all the time in the world. As if nothing had happened. As if time had simply skipped a few years.

'Remember this one?' She held up a very tubby angel with floppy, sparkly wings and a cute little halo. 'I bought this the year I was trying to diet. Every time I looked at a mince pie I was supposed to march in here and discuss it with my angel. It didn't work. She'd look straight back at me and say: "Look at me—I might be tubby but not only am I cute, I grew wings. Go ahead and eat."'

He grinned, recognising the cute little angel with affection.

'And these.' Smiling fondly, he knelt among the ornaments and produced three reindeer, one slightly chewed. 'We had six of these. Boris ate the other three.'

'And threw them up when your partners came for Christmas drinks.'

'Not a good moment. I miss Boris.' He'd had Boris the Bloodhound well before they were married. He'd died of old age just before the twins were born. Before memories had to be put aside.

They'd never had time for another dog. Maybe now they never would?

Forget it. Bauble therapy. Julie had obviously immersed herself in it and maybe he could, too. He started looping tinsel around the tree and found it oddly soothing.

They worked in silence but the silence wasn't strained. It was strangely okay. Come dawn they'd walk away from this house. Maybe it would burn, but somehow, however strange, the idea that it'd burn looking lived in was comforting.

'How long do Christmas puddings last?' Julie asked at last, as she hung odd little angels made of spray-painted macaroni. Carefully not mentioning who'd made them. The twins with their nanny. The twins...

Concentrate on pudding, he told himself. Concentrate on the practical. *How long do Christmas puddings last?* 'I have no idea,' he conceded. 'I know fruitcakes are supposed to last for ever. My great-grandma cooked them for her brothers during the War. Great-Uncle Henry once told me he used to chop 'em up and lob 'em over to the enemy side. Grandma Ethel's cakes were never great at the best of times but after a few months on the Western Front they could have been lethal.'

'Death by fruitcake…'

'Do you remember the Temperance song?' he asked, grinning at another memory. His great-aunt's singing. He raised his voice and tried it out. *'We never eat fruitcake because it has rum. And one little bite turns a man to a…'*

'Yeah, right.' She smiled back at him and he felt strangely triumphant.

Why did it feel so important to make this woman smile?

Because he'd lost her smile along with everything else? Because he'd loved her smile?

'Clarissa made one that's still in the fridge,' she told him. Nanny Clarissa had been so domestic she'd made up for both of them. Or almost. 'And it does contain rum. Half a bottle of over-proof, if I remember. She demanded I put it on the shopping list that last… Anyway, I'm thinking of frying slices for breakfast.'

'Breakfast is what…' he checked his watch '…three hours away? Four-year-old Christmas pudding. That'll be living on the edge.'

'A risk worth taking?' she said tightly and went back to bauble-hanging. 'What's to lose?'

'Pudding at dawn. Bring it on.'

They worked on. There were so many tensions zooming round the room. So many things unsaid. All they could do was concentrate on the tree.

Finished, it looked magnificent. They stood back, Rob
flicked the light switch and the tree flooded into colour.
He opened the curtains and the light streamed out into the
darkness. Almost every house in the valley was in darkness. Apart from a solitary light in the house next door they
were alone. Either everyone had evacuated or they were
all sleeping. Preparing for the danger which lay ahead.

Sleep. Bed.

It seemed a good idea. In theory.

Julie was standing beside him. She had her arms folded
in front of her, instinctive defence. She was still in that
dratted nightgown. Hadn't he asked her to take it off?
Hadn't he warned her?

But she never had been a woman who followed orders,
he thought. She'd always been self-contained, sure, confident of her place in the world. He'd fallen in love with that
containment, with her fierce intelligence, with the humour
that matched his, a biting wit that made him break into
laughter at the most inappropriate moments. He'd loved
her drive to be the best at her job. He'd understood and admired it because he was like that, too. It was only when the
twins arrived that they'd realised two parents with driving
ambition was a recipe for disaster.

Still they'd managed it. They'd juggled it. They'd
loved…

*Loved.* He looked at her now, shivering despite the oppressive heat. She looked younger, he thought suddenly.

Vulnerable.

She'd never been vulnerable and neither had he.

But they'd loved.

'Julie?'

'Yes?' She looked at him and she looked scared. And
he knew it was nothing to do with the fires.

'Mmm.'

'Let's go to bed,' he said, but she hugged her arms even tighter.

'I don't…know.'

'There's no one else?'

'No.'

'Nor for me,' he said gently. He was treading on egg-shells here. He should back off, go and sleep in the spare room, but there was something about this woman… This woman who was still his wife.

'We can't…at least…I can't move forward,' he told her, struggling to think things through as he spoke. 'Relation-ships are for other people now, not for me. But tonight… For me, tonight is all about goodbye and I suspect it's goodbye for you as well.'

'The house won't burn.'

'No,' he said, even more gently. 'It probably won't. At dawn I'll go out and cut down the overhanging branches— and even with my limited skill with power tools, I should get them cleared before the wind changes. Then we'll turn on every piece of fire-safe technology we built into this house. And after that, no matter what the outcome, we'll walk away. We must. It's time it was over, Jules, but for tonight…' He hesitated but he had to say it. It was a gut-deep need and it couldn't be put aside. 'Tonight, we need each other.'

'So much for being strangers,' she whispered. She was still hugging herself, still contained. Sort of.

'I guess we are,' he conceded. 'I guess the people we've turned into don't know each other. But for now…for this night I'd like to take to bed the woman who's still my wife.'

'In name only.' She was shivering.

'So you don't want me? Not tonight? Never again?'

And she looked up at him with those eyes he remembered so well, but with every bit of the confidence, humour, wit and courage blasted right out of them.

'I *do* want you,' she whispered. 'That's what terrifies me.'

'Same here.'

'Rob...'

'Mmm.'

'Do you have condoms? I mean, the last thing...'

'I have condoms.'

'So when you said relationships are for other people...'

'Hey, I'm a guy.' He was trying again to make her smile. 'I live in hope. Hope that one morning I'll wake up and find the old hormones rushing back. Hope that one evening I'll look across a crowded room and see a woman laughing at the same dumb thing I'm laughing at.'

That had been what happened that night, the first time they'd met. It had been a boring evening: a company she worked for announcing a major interest in a new dockland precinct; a bright young architect on the fringes; Julie with her arms full of contracts ready to be signed by investors. A boring speech, a stupid pun missed by everyone, including the guy making the speech, and then eyes meeting...

Contracts handed to a junior. Excuses made fast. Dinner. Then...

'So I'm prepared,' Rob said gently and tilted her chin. Gently, though. Forcing her gaze to meet his. 'One last time, my Jules?'

'I'm not...your Jules.'

'Can you pretend...for tonight?'

And, amazingly, she nodded. 'I think...maybe,' she managed, and at last her arms uncrossed. At last she abandoned the defensive. 'Maybe because I need to drive the ghosts away. And maybe because I want to.'

'I need more than *maybe*, Jules,' he said gently. 'I need you to want me as much as I want you.'

And there was the heart of what she was up against. She wanted him.

She always had.

Once upon a time she'd stood before an altar, the perfect bride. She remembered walking down the aisle on her father's arm, seeing Rob waiting for her, knowing it was right. She'd felt like the luckiest woman in the world. He'd held her heart in his hand, and she'd known that he'd treat it with care and love and honour.

She'd said I do, and she'd meant it.

Until death do us part...

Death had parted them, she thought and it would go on keeping them apart. There was no way they could pick up the pieces that had been their lives before the boys.

But somehow they'd been given tonight.

One night. A weird window of space and time. Tomorrow the echoes of their past could well disappear, and maybe it was right that they should.

But tonight he was here.

Tonight he was gazing at her with a tenderness that told her he needed this night as well. He wanted that sliver of the past as much as she did.

For tonight he wanted her and she ached for him back. But he wasn't pushing. It had to be her decision.

*Maybe I can do this,* she thought. *Maybe, just for tonight, I can put my armour aside...*

Her everyday life was now orchestrated, rigidly contained. It held no room for emotional attachment. Even coming here was an aberration. Once the fire was over, she'd return to her job, return to her life, return to her containment.

But for now…that ache… The way Rob talked to her… That he asked her to his bed…

It was like a siren call, she thought helplessly. She'd loved this man; she'd loved everything about him. Love had almost destroyed her and she couldn't go there again, but for tonight… Tonight was an anomaly—time out of frame.

For tonight, she was in her home with her husband. He wasn't pushing. He never had. He was simply waiting for her to make her decision.

Lie with her husband…or not?

Have one night as the Julie of old…or not?

'Because once we loved,' he said lightly, as if this wasn't a major leap, and maybe it wasn't. Maybe she could love again—just for the night. One night of Rob and then she'd get on with her life. One night…

'But not if you see it as scary.'

His gaze was locked on hers. 'It's for pleasure only, my Jules,' he said softly. 'No threats. No promises. No future. Just for this night. Just for us. Just for now. Maybe or yes? I need a yes, Jules. You have to be sure.'

And suddenly she was. 'Yes,' she said, because there was nothing else to say. 'Yes, please, Rob. For tonight, there's no maybe about it. Crazy or not, scary or not, I want you.'

'Hey, what's scary about me?' And he was laughing down at her, his lovely eyes dancing. Teasing. Just as he once had.

'That's just the problem,' she whispered. 'There's nothing crazy about the way I feel about you. *That's* what makes it so scary. But, scary or not, for tonight, Rob, for the last time, I want to be your wife.'

For those tense few minutes when they'd first seen each other, when they'd come together in the house for the first time in years, they'd made believe it was the first time. They were strangers. They'd relived that first connection.

Now…it was as if they'd pressed the fast forward on the replay button, Rob thought, and suddenly it was the first time he was to take her to bed.

But this was no make-believe, and it wasn't the first time. He knew everything there was to know about this woman. His wife.

But maybe that was wrong. Yes, he knew everything there was to know about the Julie of years ago, the Julie who'd married him, but there was a gaping hole of years. How had she filled it? He didn't know. He hardly knew how he'd filled it himself.

But for now, by mutual and unspoken consent, those four years didn't exist. Only the fierce magnetic attraction existed—the attraction that had him wanting her the moment he'd set eyes on her.

They hadn't ended up in bed on their first date, but it had nearly killed them not to. They'd lasted half an hour into their second date. He'd gone to her apartment to pick her up…they hadn't even reached the bedroom.

And now, here, the desire was the same. He'd seen her in her flimsy nightgown and he wanted her with every fibre of his being. And even if it was with caveats—*for the last time*—he tugged her into his arms and she melted.

Fused.

'You're sure?' he asked and she nodded and the sound she made was almost a purr. Memories had been set aside—the hurtful ones had, anyway.

'I'm sure,' she whispered and tugged his face close and her whisper was a breath on his mouth.

He lifted her and she curled against him. She looped her arms around his neck and twisted, so she could kiss him.

Somehow he made it to the bedroom door. The bed lay,

invitingly, not ten feet away, but he had to stop and let himself be kissed. And kiss back.

Their mouths fused. It was like electricity, a fierce jolt on touching, then a force so great that neither could pull away. Neither could think of pulling away.

He had his wife in his arms. He couldn't think past that. He had his Julie and his mind blocked out everything else.

His wife. His love.

She'd forgotten how her body melted. She'd forgotten how her body merged into his. How the outside world disappeared. How every sense centred on him. Or on *them*, for that was how it was. Years ago, the moment he'd first touched her, she'd known what marriage was. She'd felt married the first time they'd kissed.

She'd abandoned herself to him then, as simple as that. She'd surrendered and he'd done the same. His lovely strong body, virile, heavy with the scent of aroused male, wanting her, taking her, demanding everything, but in such a way that she knew that if she pulled away he'd let her go.

Only she knew she'd never pull away. She couldn't and neither could he.

Their bodies were made for each other.

And now…now her mouth was plundering his, and his hers, and the sensations of years ago were flooding back. Oh, the taste of him. The feel… Her body was on fire with wanting, with the knowledge that somehow he was hers again, for however long…

Until morning?

No. She wasn't thinking that. It didn't matter how long. All that mattered was now.

Somehow, some way, they reached the bed, but even before they were on top of it she was fighting with the buttons of his shirt. She wanted this man's body. She wanted to feel the strength of him, the hardness of his ribs, the tightness of his chest. She wanted to taste the salt of him.

Oh, his body… It was hers; it still felt like hers.

Four years ago…

No. Forget four years. Just think about now.

His kiss deepened. Her nightgown was slipping away and suddenly it was easy. Memories were gone. All she could think of was him. All she wanted was him.

Oh, the feel of him. The taste of him.

*Rob.*

The years had gone. Everything had gone. There was only this man, this body, this moment.

'Welcome home, my love,' he whispered as their clothes disappeared, as skin met skin, as the night disappeared in a haze of heat and desire.

Home… There was so much unsaid in that word. It was a word of longing, a word of hope, a word of peace.

It meant nothing, she thought. It couldn't.

But her arms held him. Her mouth held him. Her whole body held him.

For this moment he was hers.

For this moment he was right. She was home.


He'd forgotten a woman could feel this good.

He'd forgotten…Julie?

But of course he hadn't. He'd simply put her in a place in his mind that was inaccessible. But now she was here, his, welcoming him, loving him.

She tasted fabulous. She still smelled like…like… He didn't know what she smelled like.

Had he ever asked her what perfume she wore? Maybe it was only soap. Fresh, citrus, it was in her hair.

He'd forgotten how erotic it was, to lie with his face in her tumbled hair, to feel the wisps around his face, to finger and twist and feel her body shudder as she responded to his touch.

The room was in darkness and that was good. If he could see her...her eyes might get that dead look, the look that said there was nothing left, for her or for him.

It was a look that had almost killed him.

But he wouldn't think of that. He couldn't, for her fingers were curved around his thighs, tugging him closer, closer...

His wife. His Julie. His own.

They loved and loved again. They melted into each other as if they'd never parted.

They loved.

He loved.

She was *his*.

The possessive word resonated in his mind, primeval as time itself. She was crying. He felt her tears, slipping from her face to his shoulder.

He gathered her to him and held, simply held, and he thought that at this moment if any man tried to take her his response would be primitive.

*His.*

Tomorrow he'd walk away. He'd accepted by now that their marriage was over, that Julie could never emerge from the thick armour she'd shielded herself with. In order to survive he needed to move on. He knew it. His shrink had said it. He knew it for the truth.

So he would walk away. But first...here was a gift he'd long stopped hoping for. Here was a crack in that appalling armour. For tonight she'd shed it.

'For tonight I'm loving you,' he whispered and she kissed him, fiercely, possessively, as if those vows they'd made so long ago still held.

And they did hold—for tonight—and that was all he was focusing on. There was no tomorrow. There was nothing but now.

He kissed her back. He loved her back.

'For tonight I'm loving you, too,' she whispered and she held him closer, and there was nothing in the world but his wife.

# CHAPTER THREE

*Note: if a bush fire's heading your way, maybe you should set the alarm.*

He woke and filtered sunlight was streaming through the east windows. Filtered? That'd be smoke. It registered but only just, for Julie was in his arms, spooned against his body, naked, beautiful and sated with loving. It was hard to get his mind past that.

Past her.

But the world was edging in. The wind had risen. He could hear the sound of the gums outside creaking under the weight of it.

Wind. Smoke. Morning.

'Jules?'

'Mmm.' She stirred, stretched like a kitten and the sensation of her naked skin against his had him wanting her all over again. He could…

He couldn't. Wind. Smoke. Morning.

Somehow he hauled his watch from under his woman.

Eight-thirty.

Eight-thirty!

Get out by nine at the latest, the authorities had warned. Keep listening to emergency radio in case of updates.

*Eight-thirty.*

Somehow he managed to roll away and flick on the

bedside radio. But even now, even realising what was at stake, he didn't want to leave her.

The radio sounded into life. Nothing had changed in this house. He'd paid to have a housekeeper come in weekly. The clock was still set to the right time.

There was a book beside the radio. He'd been halfway through it when…when…

Maybe this house should burn, he thought, memories surging back. Maybe he wanted it to.

'We should sell this house.' She still sounded sleepy. The implication of sleeping in hadn't sunk in yet, he thought, flicking through the channels to find the one devoted to emergency transmissions.

'So why did you come back?' he asked, abandoning the radio and turning back to her. The fire was important, but somehow…somehow he knew that words might be said now that could be said at no other time. Certainly not four years ago. Maybe not in the future either, when this house was sold or burned.

Maybe now…

'The teddies,' she told him, still sleepy. 'The wall-hanging my mum made. I…wanted them.'

'I was thinking of the fire engines.'

'That's appropriate.' Amazingly, she was smiling.

He'd never thought he'd see this woman smile again.

And then he thought of those last words. The words that had hung between them for years.

'Julie, it wasn't our fault,' he said and he watched her smile die.

'I…'

'I know. You said *you* killed them, but I believed it was me. That day I brought you home from hospital. You stood here and you said it was because you were sleeping and I said no, it wasn't anyone's fault, but there was such a big part of me that was blaming myself that I couldn't go any further. It was like…I was dead. I couldn't even speak. I've thought about it for four years. I've tried to write it down.'

'I got your letters.'

'You didn't reply.'

'I thought…the sooner you stopped writing the sooner you'd forget me. Get on with your life.'

'You know the road collapsed,' he said. 'You know the lawyers told us we could sue. You know it was the storm the week before that eroded the bitumen.'

'But that I was asleep…'

'We should have stayed in the city that night. We shouldn't have tried to bring the boys home. That's the source of our greatest regret, but it shouldn't be guilt. It put us in the wrong place at the wrong time. I've been back to the site. It was a blind curve. I rounded it and the road just wasn't there.'

'If we'd come up in broad daylight, when we were both alert…'

How often had he thought about this? How often had he screamed it to himself in the middle of troubled sleep?

He had to say it. He had to believe it.

'Jules, I manoeuvred a blind bend first. A tight curve. I wasn't speeding. I hit the brakes the moment I rounded the bend but the road was gone. If you'd been awake it wouldn't have made one whit of difference. Julie, it's not only me who's saying this. It was the police, the paramedics, the guys from the accident assessment scene.'

'But I can't remember.' It was a wail, and he tugged her back into his arms and thought it nearly killed him.

He was reassuring her but regardless of reason, the guilt was still there. *What if…? What if, what if, what if?*

Guilt had killed them both. Was killing them still.

He held her but her body had stiffened. The events of four years ago were right there. One night of passion couldn't wash them away.

He couldn't fix it. How could it be fixed, when two small beds lay empty in the room next door?

He kissed her on the lips, searching for an echo of the night before. She kissed him back but he could feel that she'd withdrawn.

Same dead Julie…

He turned again and went back to searching the radio channels. Finally he found the station he was looking for—the emergency channel.

'…*evacuation orders are in place now for Rowbethon, Carnarvon, Dewey's Creek… Leave now. Forecast is for forty-six degrees, with winds up to seventy kilometres an hour, gusting to over a hundred. The fire fronts are merging…*'

And all his attention was suddenly on the fire. It had to be. Rowbethon, Carnarvon, Dewey's Creek… They were all south of Mount Bundoon.

The wind was coming from the north.

'*Fire is expected to impact on the Mount Bundoon area within the hour,*' the voice went on. '*Bundoon Creek Bridge is closed. Anyone not evacuated, do not attempt it now. Repeat, do not attempt to evacuate. Roads are cut to the south. Fire is already impacting to the east. Implement your fire plans but, repeat, evacuation is no longer an option.*'

'We need to get to a refuge centre.' Julie was sitting bolt upright, wide-eyed with horror.

'There isn't one this side of the creek.' He glanced out of the window. 'We're not driving in this smoke. Besides, we have the bunker.' Thank God, they had the bunker.

'But…'

'We can do this, Jules.'

And she settled, just like that. Same old Jules. In a crisis, there was no one he'd rather have by his side.

'The fire plan,' she said. 'I have it.'

Of course she did. Julie was one of the most controlled people he knew. Efficient. Organised. A list-maker extraordinaire.

The moment they'd moved into this place she'd downloaded a Fire Authority Emergency Plan and made him go through it, step by step, making dot-points for every eventuality.

They were better off than most. Bush fire was always a risk in Australian summers and he'd thought about it carefully when he'd designed this place. The house had been built to withstand a furnace—though not an inferno. There'd been fires in Australia where even the most fireproof buildings had burned. But he'd designed the house with every precaution. The house was made of stone, with no garden close to the house. They had solar power, backup generators, underground water tanks, pumps and sprinkler systems. The tool shed doubled as a bunker and could be cleared in minutes, double-doored and built into earth. But still there was risk. He imagined everyone else in the gully would be well away by now and for good reason. Safe house or not, they were crazy to still be here.

But Julie wasn't remonstrating. She was simply moving on.

'I'll close the shutters and tape the windows while you clear the yard,' she said. Taping the windows was important. Heat could blast them inwards. Tape gave them an extra degree of strength and they wouldn't shatter if they broke.

'Wool clothes first, though,' she said, hauling a pile out of her bottom bedroom drawer, along with torches, wool caps and water bottles. Also a small fire extinguisher. The drawer had been set up years ago for the contingency of waking to fire. Efficiency plus.

Was it possible to still love a woman for her plan-making?

'I hope these extinguishers haven't perished,' she said, pulling a wool cap on her head and shoving her hair up into it. It was made of thick wool, way too big. 'Ugh. What do you think?'

'Cute.'

'Oi, we're not thinking cute.' But her eyes smiled at him.

'Hard not to. Woolly caps have always been a turn-on.'

'And I love a man in flannels.' She tossed him a shirt. 'You've been working out.'

'You noticed?'

'I noticed all night.' She even managed a grin. 'But it's time to stop noticing. Cover that six-pack, boy.'

'Yes, ma'am.' But he'd fielded the shirt while he was checking the fire map app on his phone, and what he saw made any thought of smiling back impossible.

She saw his face, grabbed the phone and her eyes widened. 'Rob…' And, for the first time, he saw fear. 'Oh, my…Rob, it's all around us. With this wind…'

'We can do this,' he said. 'We have the bunker.' His hands gripped her shoulders. Steadied her. 'Julie, you came up here for the teddies and the wall-hanging. Anything else?'

'Their…clothes. At least…at least some. And…'

She faltered, but he knew what she wanted to say. Their smell. Their presence. The last place they'd been.

He might not be able to save that for her, but he'd sure as hell try.

'And their fire engines,' he added, reverting, with difficulty, to the practical. 'Let's make that priority one. Hopefully, the pits are still clear.'

The pits were a fallback position, as well as the bunker. They'd built this house with love, but with clear acceptance that the Australian bush was designed to burn. Many native trees didn't regenerate without fire to crack their seeds. Fire was natural, and over generations even inevitable, so if you lived in the bush you hoped for the best and prepared for the worst. Accordingly, they'd built with care, insured the house to the hilt and didn't keep precious things here.

Except the memories of their boys. How did you keep something like that safe? How did you keep memories in fire pits?

They'd do their best. The pits were a series of holes behind the house, fenced off but easily accessed. Dirt dug from them was still heaped beside them, a method used by those who'd lived in the bush for generations. If you wanted to keep something safe, you buried it: put belongings inside watertight cases; put the cases in the pit; piled the dirt on top.

'Get that shirt on,' Julie growled, moving on with the efficiency she'd been born with. She cast a long regretful look at Rob's six-pack and then sighed and hauled on her sensible pants. 'Moving on… We knew we'd have to, Rob, and now's the time. Clearing the yard's the biggie. Let's go.'

The moment they walked out of the house they knew they were in desperate trouble. The heat took their breath away. It hurt to breathe.

The wind was frightening. It was full of dry leaf litter, blasting against their faces—a portent of things to come. If these leaves were filled with fire… She felt fear deep in her gut. The maps she'd just seen were explicit. This place was going to burn.

She wanted to bury her face in Rob's shoulder and block this out. She wanted to forget, like last night, amazingly, had let her forget.

But last night was last night. Over.

Concentrate on the list. On her dot-points.

'Windows, pits, shovel, go,' Rob said and seized her firmly by the shoulders and kissed her, hard and fast. Making a mockery of her determination that last night was over. 'We can do this, Jules. You've put a lot of work into that fire plan. It'd be a shame if we didn't make it work.'

They could, she thought as she headed for the shutters. They could make the fire plan work.

And maybe, after last night… Maybe…

Too soon. Think of it later. Fire first.

She fixed the windows—fast—then checked the pits. They were overgrown but the mounds of dirt were still loose enough for her to shovel. She could bury things with ease.

She headed inside, grabbed a couple of cases and headed into the boys' room.

And she lost her breath all over again.

She'd figured yesterday that Rob must have hired someone to clean this place on a regular basis. If it had been left solely to her, this house would be a dusty mess. She'd walked away and actively tried to forget.

But now, standing at their bedroom door, it was as if she'd just walked in for the first time. Rob would be carrying the boys behind her. Jiggling them, making them laugh.

Two and a half years old. Blond and blue-eyed scamps. Miniature versions of Rob himself.

They'd been sound asleep when the road gave way, then

killed in an instant, the back of the car crushed as it rolled
to the bottom of a gully. The doctors had told her death
would have been instant.

But they were right here. She could just tug back the
bedding and Rob would carry them in.

Or not.

'Aiden,' she murmured. 'Christopher.'

Grief was all around her, an aching, searing loss. She
hadn't let herself feel this for years. She hadn't dared to.
It was hidden so far inside her she thought she'd grown
armour that could surely protect her.

But the armour was nothing. It was dust, blown away
at the sight of one neat bedroom.

It shouldn't be neat. It nearly killed her that it was neat.
She wanted those beds to be rumpled. She wanted...

She couldn't want.

She should be thinking about fire, she thought desperately. The warnings were that it'd be on them in less than
an hour. She had to move.

She couldn't.

The wind blasted on the windowpanes. She needed to
tape them. She needed to bury memories.

Aiden. Christopher.

What had she been thinking, wondering if she could
move on? What had she been doing, exposing herself to
Rob again? Imagining she could still love.

She couldn't. Peeling back the armour, even a tiny part,
allowed in a hurt so great she couldn't bear it.

'Julie?' It was a yell from just outside the window.

She couldn't answer.

'Julie!' Rob's second yell pierced her grief, loud and
demanding her attention. 'Jules! If you're standing in that
bedroom thinking of black you might want to look outside instead.'

How had he known what she was doing? Because he felt the same?

Still she didn't move.

'Look!' he yelled, even more insistent, and she had to look. She had to move across to the window and pull back the curtains.

She could just see Rob through the smoke haze. He was standing under a ladder, not ten feet from her. He had the ladder propped against the house.

He was carrying a chainsaw.

As she watched in horror he pulled the cord and it roared into life.

'What's an overhanging branch between friends?' he yelled across the roar and she thought: *He'll be killed. He'll be...*

'Mine's the easier job,' he yelled as he took his first step up the ladder. 'But if I can do this, you can shove a teddy into a suitcase. Put the past behind you, Julie. Fire. Now. Go.'

He was climbing a ladder with a chainsaw. Rob and power tools...

He was an architect, not a builder.

She thought suddenly of Rob, just after she'd agreed to marry him. He'd brought her to the mountains and shown her this block, for sale at a price they could afford.

'This can be our retreat,' he'd told her. 'Commute when we can, have an apartment in the city for when we can't.' And then he'd produced his trump card. A tool belt. Gleaming leather, full of bright shiny tools, it was a he-man's tool belt waiting for a he-man. He'd strapped it on and flexed his muscles. 'What do you think?'

'You're never thinking of building yourself?' she'd gasped and he'd grinned and held up a vicious-looking... she didn't have a clue what.

'I might need help,' he admitted. 'These things look scary. I was sort of thinking of a registered builder, with maybe a team of registered builder's assistants on the side. But I could help.'

And he'd grinned at her and she'd known there was nothing she could refuse this man.

Man with tool belt.

Man with ladder and chainsaw.

And it hit her then, with a clarity that was almost frightening. Yesterday when she'd woken up it had been just like the day before and the day before that. She'd got up, she'd functioned for the day, she'd gone to bed. She'd survived.

Life went on around her, but she didn't care.

Yesterday, when she'd told her secretary she was heading up to the Blue Mountains, Maddie had been appalled. 'It's dangerous. They're saying evacuate. Don't go there.'

The thing was, though, for Julie danger no longer existed. The worst thing possible had already happened. There was nothing else to fear.

But now, standing at the window, staring at Rob and his chainsaw, she realised that, like it or not, she still cared. She could still be frightened for someone. For Rob.

But fear hurt. Caring hurt. She didn't want to care. She couldn't. Somehow she had to rebuild the armour. But meanwhile...

Meanwhile Rob was right. She had to move. She had to bury teddies.


He managed to get the branches clear and drag them into the gully, well away from the house.

He raked the loose leaves away from the house, too, easier said than done when the wind was blasting them back. He blocked the gutters and set up the generator so they could use the pump and access the water in the tanks even if they lost the solar power.

He worked his way round the house, checking, rechecking and he almost ran into Julie round the other side.

The smoke was building. It was harder and harder to see. Even with a mask it hurt to breathe.

The heat was intense and the wind was frightening.

How far away was the fire? There was no way to tell. The fire map on his phone was of little use. It showed broad districts. What he wanted was a map of what was happening down the road. He couldn't see by looking. It was starting to be hard to see as far as the end of his arm.

'We've done enough.' Julie's voice was hoarse from the smoke. 'I've done inside and cleared the back porch. I've filled the pits and cleared the bunker. All the dot-points on the plan are complete.'

'Really?' It was weird to feel inordinately pleased that she'd remembered dot-points. Julie and her dot-points... weird that they turned him on.

'So what now?' she asked. 'Oh, Rob, I can't bear it in these clothes. All I want is to take them off and lie under the hose.'

It gave him pause for thought. *Jules, naked under water...* 'Is that included on our dots?' Impossible not to sound hopeful.

'Um...no,' she said, and he heard rather than saw her smile.

'Pity.'

'We could go inside and sit under the air-conditioning while it's still safe to have the air vents open.'

'You go in.' He wouldn't. How to tell what was happening outside if he was inside? 'But, Jules, the vents stay closed. We don't know where the fire is.'

'How can we tell where it is? How close…?' The smile had gone from her voice.

'It's not threatening. Not yet. We have thick smoke and wind and leaf litter but I can reach out my hand and still—sort of—see my fingers. The fire maps tell us the fire's cut the access road, but how long it takes to reach this gully is anyone's guess. It might fly over the top of us. It might miss us completely.' There was a hope.

'So…why not air-conditioning?'

'There's still fire. You can taste it and you can smell it. Even if the house isn't in the firing line, there'll be burning leaf litter swirling in the updraught. On Black Saturday they reckoned there were ember attacks five miles from the fire front. We'd look stupid if embers were sucked in through the vents. But you go in. I'll keep checking.'

'For…how long?' she faltered. 'I mean…'

'For as long as it takes.' He glanced upward, hearing the wind blasting the treetops, but there was no way he could see that far. The smoke was making his throat hurt, but still he felt the need to try and make her smile. 'It looks like we're stuck here for Christmas,' he managed. 'But I'm sure Santa will find a way through. What's his motto? *Neither snow nor rain nor heat nor gloom of night shall stay St Nicholas from the swift completion of his appointed rounds.*'

'Isn't that postmen?' And amazingly he heard the smile again and was inordinately pleased.

'Maybe it is,' he said, picking up his hose and checking pressure. They still had the solar power but he'd already swapped to the generators. There wouldn't be time to do it when…if…the fire hit. 'But I reckon we're all in the same union. Postmen, Santa and us. We'll work through whatever's thrown at us.' And then he set down his hose.

'It's okay, Jules,' he said, taking her shoulders. 'We've

been through worse than this. We both know…that things aren't worth crying over. But our lives are worth something and maybe this house is worth something as well. It used to be a home. I know the teddies and fire engines and wall-hanging are safe but let's see this as a challenge. Let's see if we can save…what's left of the rest of us.'

They sat on the veranda and faced the wind. It was the dumbest place to sit, Julie thought, but it was also sensible. The wind seared their faces, the heat parched their throats but ember attacks would come from the north.

Their phones had stopped working. 'That'll be the transmission tower on Mount Woorndoo,' Rob said matter-of-factly, like it didn't matter that a tower not ten miles away had been put out of action.

He brought the battery radio outside and they listened. All they could figure was that the valley was cut off. All they could work out was that the authorities were no longer in control. There were so many fronts to this fire that no one could keep track.

Most bush fires could be fought. Choppers dropped vast loads of water, fire trucks came in behind the swathes the choppers cleared; communities could be saved.

Here, though, there were so many communities…

'It's like we're the last people in the world,' Julie whispered.

'Yeah. Pretty silly to be here.'

'I wanted to be here.'

'Me, too,' he said and he took her hand and held.

And somehow it felt okay. Scary but right.

They sat on. Surely the fire must arrive soon. The waiting was almost killing her, and yet, in a strange way, she felt almost calm. Maybe she even would have stayed if Rob hadn't come, she thought. Maybe this was…

'We're going to get through this,' Rob said grimly and she hauled her thoughts back from where they'd been taking her.

'You know, those weeks after the boys were killed, they were the worst weeks of my life.' He said it almost conversationally, and she thought: *don't. Don't go there.* They hadn't talked about it. They couldn't.

But he wasn't stopping. She should get up, go inside, move away, but he was waiting for ember attacks, determined to fight this fire, and she couldn't walk away.

Even if he was intent on talking about what she didn't want to hear.

'You were so close to death yourself,' he said, almost as if this had been chatted about before. 'You had smashed ribs, a punctured lung, a shattered pelvis. But that bang on the head... For the first few days they couldn't tell me how you'd wake up. For the first twenty-four hours they didn't even know whether you'd wake up at all. And there I was, almost scot-free. I had a laceration on my arm and nothing more. There were people everywhere—my parents, your parents, our friends. I was surrounded yet I'd never felt so alone. And at the funeral...'

'Don't.' She put a hand on his arm to stop him but he didn't stop. But maybe she had to hear this, she thought numbly. Maybe he had to say it.

'I had to bury them alone,' he said. 'Okay, not alone in the physical sense. The church was packed. My parents were holding me up but you weren't there... It nearly killed me. And then, when you got out of hospital and I asked if you'd go to the cemetery...'

'I couldn't.' She remembered how she'd felt. Where were her boys? To go to the cemetery...to see two tiny graves...

She'd blocked it out. It wasn't real. If she didn't see the

graves, then maybe the nightmare would be just that. An endless dream.

'It was like our family ended right there,' Rob said, staring sightlessly out into the smoke. 'It didn't end when our boys died. It ended...when we couldn't face their death together.'

'Rob...'

'I don't know why I'm saying this now,' he said, almost savagely. 'But hell, Julie, I'm fighting this. Our family doesn't exist any more. I can't get back...any of it. But once upon a time we loved each other and that still means something. So if you're sitting here thinking it doesn't matter much if you go up in flames, then think again. Because, even though I'm not part of your life any more, if I lose you completely, then what's left of my sanity goes, too. So prepare to be protected, Jules. No fire is going to get what's left of what I once loved. Of what I still love. So I'm heading off to do a fast survey of the boundary, looking for embers. It'd be good if you checked closer to the house but you don't need to. I'll do it for both of us. This fire...I'll fight it with everything I have. Enough of our past has been destroyed. This is my line in the sand.'

# CHAPTER FOUR

THE SOUND CAME before the fire. Before the embers. Before hell.

It was a thousand freight trains roaring across the mountains, and it was so sudden that they were working separately when it hit. It was a sweeping updraught which felt as if it was sucking all the air from her lungs. It was a mass of burning embers, not small spot fires they could cope with but a mass of burning rain.

Stand and fight… They knew as the rumble built to a roar that no man alive could stay and fight this onslaught.

Julie was fighting to get a last gush of water onto the veranda. A branch had blasted in against the wall and Rob had been dragging it away from the building. She couldn't see him.

He was somewhere out in the smoke, heading back to her. Please, she pleaded. Please let him be heading back to her.

She had the drill in her head. *When the fire hits, take cover in your designated refuge and wait for the front to pass. As soon as the worst has passed, you can emerge to fight for your home, but don't try and fight as the front hits. Take cover.*

Now.

'Rob…' Where was he? She was screaming for him but she couldn't even hear herself above the roar. The heat was blasting in front of the fire, taking the temperature to unbearable levels. She'd have to head for the shelter without him...

Unthinkable!

But suddenly he was with her. Grabbing her, hauling her off the veranda. But, instead of heading towards the bunker, he was hauling her forward, into the heat. 'Jules, help me.'

'Help?' They had to get to the bunker. What else could they do?

'Jules, there are people next door.' He was yelling into her ear. 'There's a woman—pregnant, a mum. She was trying to back her car out of the driveway and she's hit a post. Jules, she won't come with me. We need to make her see sense. Forcibly if need be, and I can't do it by myself.'

And, like it or not, sensible or not, he had her arm. He was hauling her with him, stumbling across their yard, a yard which seemed so unfamiliar now that it was terrifying.

There were burning embers, burning leaves hitting her face. They shouldn't be here. They had to seek refuge. But...

'She's lost...a kid...' Rob was struggling to get enough breath to yell over the roar of impending fire. 'When the car hit, the dog got out. The kid's four years old, chasing his dog and she can't find him. I have to...' But then a blast of heat hit them, so intense he couldn't keep yelling. He just held onto her and ran.

But she wanted to be safe. She wanted this to be over. Why was Rob dragging her away from the bunker?

A child... Four years old? She tried to take it in but her mind wouldn't go there.

And then they were past the boundary post, not even visible now, only recognised because she brushed it as they passed. Then onto the gravel of the next-door neighbour's house. There was a car in the driveway, visible only as they almost ran into it.

She didn't know the neighbours. This house had been owned by an elderly couple when they'd built theirs. The woman had since died, her husband had left to live with his daughter and the house had stood empty and neglected for almost the entire time they'd lived here.

Last night she'd been surprised to see the lights. She and Rob had both registered that there'd been someone there, but then they'd both been so caught up...

And then her thoughts stopped. Through the wall of smoke, there was a woman. Slight. Shorter than she was.

Very, very pregnant.

Rob reached to grab her and held.

'I can't find him.' The woman was screaming. 'Help me! Help me!' The scream pierced even the roar of the fire and it held all the agony in the world. It was a wail of loss and desperation and horror.

'We will.' Rob grabbed Julie's arm, thrust the woman's hand into hers and clamped his own hand on top. 'Julie, don't let go and that's an order. Consider it a dot-point, the biggest one there is. Julie, Amina; Amina, Julie. Amina, Julie's taking you to safety. You need to go with her now. Julie, go.'

'But Danny...' The woman was still screaming.

'I'll find him. Julie, the bunker...'

'But you have to come, too.' Julie was screaming as well. Already they were cutting things so close they mightn't make it. The blackness was now tinged with burning orange, flashes looming out of the blasting heat. Dear God, they had to go—but they had to go together.

But Rob was backing away, yelling back at her over the roar of the fire. 'Jules, there's a little boy.' His voice held a desperation that matched hers. 'He ran to find his dog. I won't let this one die. I won't. Go!'

And his words stopped her screaming. They stopped her even wanting to scream.

She checked for a moment, fought for air, fought for sanity. A wave of wind and heat smashed into her, almost knocking her from her feet. Burning embers were smashing against their clothes.

The woman was wearing a bulky black dress but it didn't hide her late pregnancy. Another child. Dear God…

And they didn't have to wait until the fire front hit them; the fire was here now.

'Jules, go!' Rob was yelling, pushing.

But still… 'I can't…leave you.'

'Danny…' The woman's scream was beyond terror, beyond reason, almost drowning Julie's, but Rob had heard her.

'Jules.' He touched her once, briefly, a hand on her cheek. A touch of reassurance where there was no reassurance to be had. A touch for courage. Then he pushed her again.

'Keep her and her little one safe. You can do this,' he said fiercely. 'But stay safe. I won't lose…more. I'll find him,' he said fiercely. 'Go!'

The woman had to be almost dragged to the bunker. Somewhere out there was her son, and Julie could feel her terror, could almost taste it, and it was nearly enough to drown her own fear.

Left on her own she'd be with Rob, no question. Did it matter if she died? Not much. But she was gripping her neighbour's hand and the woman looked almost to term. Two lives depended on her and Rob had told her what he expected.

And she expected it of herself. That one touch and she knew what she was doing couldn't be questioned.

But by now it was almost impossible to move. She hardly knew where the bunker was. The world was a swirling blast of madness. Trees loomed from nowhere. She could see nothing. How could she be lost in her own front yard?

She couldn't. She wouldn't. She had the woman's hand in a grip of iron and she kept on going, tugging the woman behind her.

Finally she reached the side of the house. There was no vision left at all now. The last of the light had gone. The world was all heat and smoke and fear.

She touched the house and kept touching as she hauled the woman along behind her. The woman had ceased fighting, but she could feel her heaving sobs. There was nothing she could do about that, though. Her only thought was to get to the rear yard, then keep going without deviation and the bunker would be right there.

But Rob…

*Don't think of Rob.*

There was so much smoke. How could they breathe?

And then the bunker was right in front of her groping arm. She'd been here earlier, checked it was clear. She should have left the door open. Now it was all she could do to haul it wide. She had to let Amina go and she was fearful she'd run.

If it was her little boy out there she'd run.

*Christopher. Aiden…*

Don't think it. That was the way of madness.

But Amina had obviously made a choice. She was no longer pulling back. Her maternal instincts must be tearing her apart. Her son was in the fire but she had to keep her baby safe. She was trusting in Rob.

*Do not think of Rob.*

Somehow she managed to haul open the great iron door Rob had built as the entrance to the bunker. The bunker itself was dug into the side of the hill, with reinforced earth on the sides and floor and roof, with one thick door facing the elements and a thinner one inside.

She got the outer door open, shoving the woman inside, fighting to keep out embers.

She slammed it shut behind her and it felt as if she was condemning Rob to death.

Inside the inner door was designed to keep out heat. She couldn't shut that. No way. The outer door would have to buckle before she'd consider it. One sheet of iron between Rob and safety was more than she could bear; two was unthinkable.

The woman was sobbing, crumpling downward. There were lamps by the door. She flicked one on, took a deep, clean breath of air that hardly had any smoke in it and took stock.

She was safe here. They were safe.

She wasn't sure what was driving her, what was stopping her crumbling as well, but she knew what she had to do. The drill. Her dot-points. Rob would laugh at her, say she'd be efficient to the point where she organised her own funeral.

He loved her dot-points.

She allowed herself one tiny sob of fear, then swallowed it and knelt beside the woman, putting her arm around the woman's shoulders.

'We're safe,' she told her, fighting to keep her voice steady. 'You and your baby are safe. This place is fireproof. Rob's designed it so we have ventilation. We have air, water, even food if we need. We can stay here until it's all over.'

'D…Danny.'

'Rob is with Danny,' she said with a certainty she had to assume. But suddenly it wasn't assumed. Rob had to be with Danny and Rob had to be safe. Anything else was unthinkable.

'Rob will have him,' she whispered. 'My...my husband will keep him safe.'

'Danny! Luka!' Why was he yelling? Nothing could be heard above the roar of the fire. He could see nothing. To stay out here and search for a child in these conditions was like searching in hot, blasting sludge. A child would be swallowed, as he was being swallowed.

He'd asked for the dog's name. 'Luka,' Amina had told him through sobs. 'A great big golden retriever my husband bought to keep us safe. Danny loves him.'

So now he added Luka to his yelling. But where in this inferno...?

He stopped and made himself think. The boy had followed the dog. Where would the dog go?

Back to the house, surely. He'd escaped from the car. He'd be terrified. If Danny had managed to follow him...

The heat was burning. He'd shoved a wool cap over his head. Now he pulled it right down over his eyes. He couldn't see anyway and it stopped the pain as embers hit. He had his hands out, blundering his way to the front door.

At least Julie was safe. It was the one thing that kept him sane, but if there was another tragedy out of this day...

He knew, none better, how close to the edge of sanity Julie had been. He knew how tightly she held herself together. How controlled...

He hadn't been able to get past that control and in the end he'd had to respect it. He'd had to walk away, to preserve them both.

If he died now maybe Julie's control would grow even

deeper. The barriers could become impenetrable—or maybe the barriers would crumble completely.

Either option was unthinkable.

Last night he'd seen a glimmer of what they'd once had. Only a glimmer; the barriers had been up again this morning. But he'd seen underneath. How vulnerable…

He could go to her now. Save himself.

And sit in the bunker while another child died?

He had his own armour, his own barriers, and they were vulnerable, too. Another child's death…

'Danny! Luka!' He was screaming, and his screams were mixing with the fire.

'Please…'

*Please.*

She said it over and over again. She'd found water bottles. She'd given one to Amina, and watched her slump against the back wall, her face expressionless.

Her face looked dead.

Her face would look like that too, Julie thought. Maybe it had looked like that for four years?

She slumped down on the floor beside her. Fought to make her mind work.

What was safety when others weren't safe? When Rob was out there?

'Do you think…?' Amina whispered.

'I can't think,' Julie told her. She took a long gulp of water and realised just how parched she'd been. How much worse for Rob…

'So…so what do we do?' Amina whispered.

'Wait for Rob.'

'Your husband.'

'Yes.' He still was, after all. It was a dead marriage but the legalities still held.

'My…my husband will be trying to reach us,' Amina whispered. 'He's a fly in, fly out miner. He was flying back in last night. He rang from the airport and told us not to move until he got here. I'm not very good in the car but in the end I couldn't wait. But then I crashed.'

'What's his name?' She was trying so hard to focus on anything but Rob.

'Henry,' Amina said. 'He'll come. I know he will. I…I need him.'

*You need Rob,* Julie thought, but she didn't say it.

And she didn't say how much her life depended on Rob pushing through that door.

Amina's house had caught fire. Dear God, he could see flames through the blackness. The heat was almost unbearable. No, make that past unbearable.

He had to go. He was doing nothing staying here. He was killing himself in a useless hunt.

But still… His hand had caught the veranda rail. He steadied. One last try…

He hauled himself onto the veranda and gave one last yell.

'Danny! Luka!'

And a great heavy body shoved itself at his legs, almost pushing him over.

Dog. He couldn't see him. He could only crouch and hold.

He searched for his collar and found…a hand. A kid, holding the dog.

'Danny!' There was nothing of him, a sliver of gasping fear. He couldn't see. He hauled him into his arms and hugged, steadying for a moment, taking as well as giving comfort. Taking strength.

*God, the heat…*

'Mama…' the little boy whimpered, burying his face in Rob's chest, not because he trusted him, but to stop the heat.

Rob was holding him with one arm, unbuttoning his wool flannel shirt with the other. Thank God the shirt was oversized. The kid was in shorts and sandals!

He buttoned up again, kid inside, and the kid didn't move. He was past moving, Rob thought. He could feel his chest heaving as he fought for breath. His own breathing hurt.

He had him. Them. The dog was hard at his side, not going anywhere.

He had to get to the bunker. It was way past a safe time for them to get there but there was nowhere else.

Julie would be at the bunker. If she'd made it.

And he had something to fight for. For Rob, the last four years had passed in a mist of grey. He'd tried to get on with his life, he'd built his career, he'd tried to enjoy life again but, in truth, every sense had seemed dulled. Yet now, when the world around him truly was grey and thick with smoke, every one of his senses was alert, intent, focused.

He would make it to the bunker. He would save this kid.

He would make it back to Julie.

*Please…*

'Hold on,' he managed to yell to the kid, though whether the little boy could hear him over the roar of the flames was impossible to tell. 'Hold your breath, Danny. We're going to run.'

Amina was crying, not sobbing, not hysterical, but tears were running unchecked down her face.

Julie was past crying. She was past feeling. If Rob was safe he'd be here by now. The creek at the bottom of the gully was dry. Even if it had been running it was overhung with dense bush. There was no safe place except here.

She was the last, she thought numbly. Her boys had gone. Now Rob, too?

Last night had been amazing. Last night it had felt as if she was waking up from a nightmare, as if slivers of light were finally breaking through the fog.

She hadn't deserved the light. She might have known…

'Your husband…' Amina managed, and she knew the woman was making a Herculean effort to talk. 'He's… great.'

'I…yeah.' What to say? There was nothing to say.

'How long have you been married?'

She had to think. Was she still married? Sort of. Sort of not.

'Seven years,' she managed.

'No kids?'

'I…no.'

'I'm sorry,' Amina whispered, and the dead feeling inside Julie turned into the hard, tight knot she knew so well. The knot that threatened to choke her. The knot that had ended her life.

'It's too late, isn't it?' Amina whispered. 'They would have been here by now. It's too…'

'I don't know…'

And then she stopped.

A bang. She was sure…

It was embers crashing against the door. Surely.

She should have closed the inner door. It was the last of her dot-points.

Another bang.

She was up, scrambling to reach the door. But then she paused, forcing herself to be logical. She was trying desperately to think and somehow she managed to make her mind see sense. To open the outer door mid-fire would suck every trace of oxygen from the bunker, even if the fire didn't blast right in. She couldn't do that to Amina.

Follow the dot-points. Follow the rules.

The banging must have been flying embers. It must. But if not…

She was already in the outer chamber, hauling the inner door closed behind her, closing herself off from the inner sanctuary. 'Stay!' she yelled at Amina and Amina had the sense to obey.

With the inner door closed it was pitch-dark, but she didn't need to see. She was at the outer door. She could feel the heat.

She hauled up the latch and tugged, then hauled.

The door swung wide with a vicious blast of heat and smoke.

And a body. A great solid body, holding something. Almost falling in.

A huge, furry creature lunging against her legs.

'Get it…get it sh—'

Rob. He was beyond speech. He was beyond anything. He crumpled to his knees, gasping for air.

She knew what he'd been trying to say. She had to get the door shut. She did it but afterwards she never knew how. It felt as if she herself was being sucked out. She fought with the door, fought with everything she had, and finally the great latch Rob had designed with such foresight fell into place.

But still…the smoke… There was no air. She couldn't breathe.

It took effort, will, concentration to find the latch on the inner door but somehow she did. She tugged and Amina was on the other side. As soon as the latch lifted she had it open.

'Danny…' It was a quavering sob.

'He's here,' Rob managed and then slumped sideways into the inner chamber, giving way to the all-consuming black.

Rob surfaced to water. Cool, wondrous water, washing his face. Someone was letting water run over him. There was water on his head. The wool cap was nowhere. There was just water.

He shifted a little and tasted it, and heard a sob of relief.

'Rob…'

'Julie.' The word didn't quite come out, though. His mouth felt thick and swollen. He heard a grunt that must have been him but he couldn't do better.

'Let me hold you while you drink.' And she had him. Her arm was supporting his shoulders, and magically there was a bottle of water at his lips. He drank, gloriously grateful for the water, even more grateful that it was Julie who had him. He could see her by the dim light of the torch lamp. Julie…

'The…the boy…' Maybe it came out, maybe it didn't, but she seemed to understand what he said.

'Danny's safe; not even burned. His mother has him. They're pouring water over Luka's pads. His pads look like your face. You both look scorched, but okay. It's okay, Rob.' Her voice broke. 'You'll live. We'll all live, thanks to you.'

# CHAPTER FIVE

How LONG DID they stay in the shelter? Afterwards they tried to figure it out, but at the time they had no clue. Time simply stopped.

The roar from outside built to a crescendo, a sound where nothing could be said, nothing heard. Maybe they should have been terrified, but for Julie and for Amina too, they'd gone past terror. Terror was when the people they loved were outside, missing. Now they were all present and accounted for, and if hell itself broke loose, if their shelter disintegrated, somehow it didn't matter because they were there.

Rob was there.

He roused himself after a while and pushed himself back against the wall. Julie wasn't sure where the black soot ended and burns began. None of his clothes were burned. His eyes seemed swollen and bloodshot, but maybe hers did too. There were no mirrors here.

Amina was cuddling Danny, but she was also cuddling the dog.

The dog had almost cost her son his life, Julie thought wonderingly, but as Amina poured water over Luca's paws and his tail gave a feeble wag of thanks, she thought: *this dog is part of their family.*

No wonder Danny ran after him. He was loved.

*Love...*

It was a weird concept. Four years ago, love had died. It had shrivelled inside her, leaving her a dried out husk. She'd thought she could never feel pain again.

But when she'd thought she'd lost Rob... The pain was still with her. It was like she'd been under anaesthetic for years, and now the drug had worn off. Leaving her exposed...

*The noise...*

She was sitting beside the dirt wall, next to Rob.

His hand came out and took hers, and held. Taking comfort?

Her heart twisted, and the remembered pain came flooding back. Family...

She didn't have family. Her family was dead.

But Rob was holding her hand and she couldn't pull away.

She stirred at some stage, found cartons of juice, packets of crackers and tinned tuna. The others didn't speak while she prepared a sort of lunch.

Danny was the first to eat, accepting her offering with pleasure.

'We didn't have breakfast,' he told her. 'Mama was too scared. She was trying to pack the car; trying to ring Papa. I wanted toast but Mama said when we got away from the fire.'

'We're away from the fire now,' she told him, glancing sideways at Rob. She wasn't sure if his throat was burned. She wasn't sure...of anything. But he cautiously sipped the juice and then tucked into the crackers like there was no tomorrow.

The food did them all good. It settled them. *Nothing like a good cup of tea*—Julie's Gran used to say that, and she grinned. There was no way she could attempt to boil water. Juice would have to do as a substitute, but it seemed to be working just as well.

The roaring had muted. She was scarcely daring to hope, but maybe the front had passed.

'It's still too loud and too hot,' Rob croaked. 'We can't open the door yet.'

'My Henry will be looking for us,' Amina said. 'He'll be frantic.'

'He won't have been allowed through,' Rob told her. 'I came up last night and they were closing the road blocks then.'

'You were an idiot for coming,' Julie said.

'Yep.' But he didn't sound like he thought he was an idiot. 'How long have you lived here?' he asked Amina, and Julie thought he was trying hard to sound like things were normal. Like this was just a brief couple of hours of enforced stay and then they'd get on with their lives.

Maybe she would, she thought. After all, what had changed for her? Maybe their house had burned, but she didn't live here anyway.

Maybe more traces of their past were gone, but they'd been doomed to vanish one day. Things were just…things.

'Nearly four years,' Amina said. 'We came just after Danny was born. But this place…it's always been empty. The guy who mows the lawns said there was a tragedy. Kids…' And then her hand flew to her mouth. 'Your kids,' she whispered in horror. 'You're the parents of the twins who died.'

'It was a long time ago,' Rob said quietly. 'It's been a very long time since we were parents.'

'But you're together?' She seemed almost frantic, over-whelmed by past tragedy when recent tragedy had just been avoided.

'For now we are,' Rob told her.

'But you don't live here.'

'Too many ghosts,' Julie said.

'Why don't you sell?' She seemed dazed beyond belief. Horror piled upon horror...

'Because of the ghosts,' Julie whispered.

Amina glanced from Julie to Rob and back again, her expression showing her sheer incomprehension of what they must have gone through. Or maybe it wasn't incomprehension. She'd been so close herself...

'If you hadn't saved Danny...' she whispered.

'We did,' Rob told her.

'But it can't bring your boys back.'

'No.' Rob's voice was harsh.

'There's nothing...' Amina was crying now, hugging Danny to her, looking from Julie to Rob and back again. 'You've saved us and there's nothing I can do to thank you. No way... I wish...'

'We all wish,' Rob said grimly, glancing at Julie. 'But at least today we have less to wish for. A bit of ointment and the odd bandage for Luka's sore paws and we'll be ready to carry on where we left off.'

*Where we left off yesterday, though,* Julie thought bleakly. *Not where we left off four years ago.*

What had she been about, clinging to this man last night? The ghosts were still all around them.

The ghosts would never let them go.

'We're okay,' Rob said and suddenly he'd tugged her to him and he was holding. Just holding. Taking comfort or giving it, it didn't matter. His body was black and filthy and big and hard and infinitely comforting and she had a huge urge to turn and kiss him, smoke and all. She didn't. She couldn't and it wasn't just that they were with Amina and Danny.

The ghosts still held the power to hold them apart.

\* \* \*

An hour later, Rob finally decreed they might open the bunker doors. The sounds had died to little more than high wind, with the occasional crack of falling timber. The battery-operated radio Rob had dug up from beneath a pile of blankets told them the front had moved south. Messages were confused. There was chaos and destruction throughout the mountains. All roads were closed. The advice was not to move from where they were.

They had no intention of moving from where they were, but they might look outside.

The normal advice during a bush fire was to take shelter while the front passed, and then emerge as soon as possible and fight to keep the house from burning. That'd be okay in a fast-moving grass fire but down in the valley the bush had caught and burned with an intensity that was never going to blow through. There'd been an hour of heat so intense they could feel it through the double doors. Now…she thought they'd emerge to nothing.

'What about staying here while we do a reconnaissance?' Rob asked Amina and the woman gave a grim nod.

'Our house'll be gone anyway; I know that. What's there to see? Danny, can you pass me another drink? We'll stay here until Rob and Julie tell us it's safe.'

'I want to see the burned,' Danny said, and Julie thought this was becoming an adventure to the little boy. He had no idea how close he'd come.

'You'll see it soon enough.' Rob managed to keep the grimness from his voice. 'But, for now, Julie and I are the fearless forward scouts. You're the captain minding the fort. Take care of everyone here, Danny. You're in charge.'

And he held out his hand to Julie. 'Come on, love,' he said. 'Let's go face the music.'

She hesitated. There was so much behind those words.

Sadness, tenderness, and…caring? How many years had they been apart and yet he could still call her *love*.

It twisted her heart. It made her feel vulnerable in a way she couldn't define.

'I'm coming,' she said, but she didn't take his hand. 'Let's go.'

First impression was black and smoke and heat. The wash of heat was so intense it took her breath away.

Second impression was desolation. The once glorious bushland that had surrounded their home was now a black-ened, ash-filled landscape, still smouldering, flickers of flame still orange through the haze of smoke.

Third impression was that their house was still standing.

'My God,' Rob breathed. 'It's withstood… Julie, Plan D now.'

And she got it. Their fire plan had been formed years before but it was typed up and laminated, pasted to their bathroom door so they couldn't help but learn it.

Plan A: leave the area before the house was threat-ened. When they'd had the boys, this was the most sensible course of action. Maybe it was the most sensible course of action anyway. Their independent decision to come into a fire zone had been dumb. But okay, moving on.

Plan B: stay in the house and defend. They'd abandon that plan if the threat was dire, the fire intense.

Plan C: head to the bunker and stay there until the front passed. And then implement Plan D.

Plan D: get out of the bunker as soon as possible and try to stop remnants of fire destroying the house.

The fire had been so intense that Julie had never dreamed she'd be faced with Plan D but now it had hap-pened, and the list with its dot-points was so ingrained in her head that she moved into automatic action.

The generator was under the house. The pump was under there too. If they were safe they could pump water from the underground tanks.

'You do the water, spray the roof,' Rob snapped. 'I'll check inside, then head round the foundations and put out spot fires.' It was still impossibly hard to speak. Even breathing hurt, but somehow Rob managed it. 'We can do this, Julie. With this level of fire, we might be stuck here for hours, if not days. We need to keep the house safe.'

*Why?* There was a tiny part of her that demanded it. *Why bother?*

For the same reason she'd come back, she thought. This house had been home. It no longer was, or she'd thought it no longer was. But Rob was already heading for the bricked-in cavity under the house where they'd find tools to defend.

Rob thought this place was worth fighting for—the remnants of her home?

Who knew the truth of it? Who knew the logic? All she knew was that Rob thought this house was worth defending and, for now, all she could do was follow.

They worked solidly for two hours. After the initial checks they worked together, side by side. Rob's design genius had paid off. The house was intact but the smouldering fires after the front were insidious. A tiny spark in leaf litter hard by the house could be enough to turn the house into flames hours after the main fire. So Julie sprayed while Rob ran along the base of the house with a mop and bucket.

The underground water tank was a lifesaver. The water flowing out seemed unbelievably precious. Heaven knew how people managed without such tanks.

They didn't, she thought grimly as finally Rob left her

to sentry duty and determinedly made his way through the ash and smoke to check Amina's house.

He came back looking even grimmer than he had when he'd left.

'Gone,' he said. 'And their car... God help them if they'd stayed in that car, or even if they'd made it out onto the road. Our cars are still safe in the garage, but a tree's fallen over the track leading into the house. It's big and it's burning. We're going nowhere.'

There was no more to be said. They worked on. Maybe someone should go back to Amina to tell her about her house, but the highest priority had to be making sure this house was safe. Not because of emotional ties, though. This was all about current need.

Mount Bundoon was a tiny hamlet and this house and Amina's were two miles out of town. Thick bush lay between them and the township. There'd be more fallen logs—who knew what else—between them and civilisation.

'We'll be stuck here till Christmas,' Julie said as they worked, and her voice came out strained. Her throat was so sore from the smoke.

'Seeing as Christmas is tomorrow, yes, we will,' Rob told her. 'Did you have any plans?'

'I...no.'

'Do we have a turkey in the freezer?'

'I should have left it out,' she said unsteadily. 'It would have been roasted by now. Oh, Rob...' She heard her voice shake and Rob's arms came round her shoulders.

'No matter. We've done it. We're almost on the other side, Jules, love.'

But they weren't, she thought, and suddenly bleakness was all around her. What had changed? She could cling to Rob now but she knew that, long-term, they'd destroy each other. How could you help ease someone else's pain when you were withered inside by your own?

'Another half hour and we might be able to liberate Amina,' Rob said and something about the way he spoke told her he was feeling pretty much the same sensations she was feeling. 'The embers are getting less and Luka must be just about busting to find a tree by now.'

'Well, good luck to him finding one,' she said, pausing with her wet mop to stare bleakly round at the moonscape destruction.

'We can help them,' Rob said gently. 'They've lost their house. We can help them get through it. I don't know about you, Jules, but putting my head down and working's been the only thing between me and madness for the last four years. So keeping Amina's little family secure—that's something we can focus on. And we can focus on it together.'

'Just for the next twenty-four hours.'

'That's all I ever think about,' Rob told her, and the bleakness was back in his voice full force. 'One day at a time. One hour at a time. That's survival, Jules. We both know all about it so let's put it into action now.'

*One day at a time?* Rob worked on, the hard physical work almost a welcome relief from the emotions of the last twenty-four hours but, strangely, he'd stopped thinking of now. He was putting out embers on autopilot but the rest of his brain was moving forward.

Where did he go from here?

Before the fire, he'd thought he had almost reached the other side of a chasm of depression and self-blame. There'd been glimmers of light when he'd thought he could enjoy life again. 'You need to move on,' his shrink had advised him. 'You can't help Julie and together your grief will make you self-destruct.' Or maybe that wasn't what the shrink had advised him—maybe it was what the counselling sessions had made him accept for himself.

But now, working side by side, with Julie a constant presence as they beat out the spot fires still flaring up against the house, it was as if that thinking was revealed for what it was—a travesty. A lie. How could he move on? He still felt married. He still *was* married.

He'd fallen in love with his dot-point-maker, his Julie, eight years ago and that love was still there.

Maybe that was why he'd come back—drawn here because his heart had never left the place. And it wasn't just the kids.

It was his wife.

So… Twenty-four hours on and the mists were starting to clear.

*Together your grief will make you self-destruct.* It might be true, he conceded, but Julie chose that moment to thump a spark with a wet mop. 'Take that, you—' she grunted and swiped it again for good measure and he found himself smiling.

She was still under there—his Julie.

*Together they'd self-destruct?* Maybe they would, he conceded as he worked, but was it possible—was there even a chance?—that together they could find a way to heal?

It was time to get Amina and Danny and Luka out of the bunker.

It was dark, not because it was night—it was still midafternoon—but because the smoke was still all-enveloping. They'd need to keep watch, take it in turns to check for spot fires, but, for now, they entered the house together.

Rob was holding Amina's hand. He'd been worried

she'd trip over the mass of litter blasted across the yard. Danny was clinging to his mother's other side. Luka was pressing hard against his small master. The dog was limping a little but he wasn't about to leave the little boy.

Which left Julie bringing up the rear. She stood aside as Rob led them indoors and for some crazy reason she thought of the day Rob had brought her here to show her his plans. He'd laid out a tentative floor plan with string and markers on the soil. He'd shown her where the front door would be and then he'd swung her into his arms and lifted her across.

'Welcome to your home, my bride,' he'd told her and he'd set her down into the future hall and he'd kissed her with a passion that had left her breathless. 'Welcome to your Happy Ever After.'

*Past history. Moving on.* She followed them in and felt bleakness envelop her. The house was grey, dingy, appalling. There were no lights. She flicked the switch without hope and, of course, there was none.

'The cabling from the solar system must have melted,' Rob said, and then he gave a little-boy grin that was, in the circumstances, totally unexpected and totally endearing. 'But I have that covered. I knew the conduit was a weak spot when we built so the electrician's left me backup. I just need to unplug one lot and plug in another. The spare's in the garage, right next to my tool belt.'

And in the face of that grin it was impossible not to smile back. The grey lifted, just a little. Man with tool belt, practically chest-thumping...

He'd designed this house to withstand fire. Skilled with a tool belt or not, he had saved them.

'It might take a bit of fiddling,' Rob conceded, trying —unsuccessfully—to sound modest. 'And the smoke will be messing with it now. But even if it fails completely we have the generator for important things, like pumping water. We have the barbecue. We can manage.'

'If you're thinking of getting up on the roof, Superman...'

'When it cools a little. And I'll let you hold the ladder.' He offered it like he was offering diamonds and, weirdly, she wanted to laugh. Her world was somehow righting.

'Do you mind...if we stay?' Amina faltered and Julie hauled herself together even more. Amina had lost her home. She didn't know where her husband was and Julie knew she was fearful that he'd have been on the road trying to reach her. What was Julie fearful about? Nothing. Rob was safe, and even that shouldn't matter.

But it did. She looked at his smoke-stained face, his bloodshot eyes, his grin that she knew was assumed— she knew this man and she knew he was feeling as bleak as she was, but he was trying his best to cheer them up— and she thought: *no matter what we've been through, we have been through it.*

*I know this man.* The feeling was solid, a rock in a shifting world. Even if being together hurt so much she couldn't bear it, he still felt part of her.

'Of course you can stay.' She struggled to sound normal, struggled to sound like a friendly neighbour welcoming a friend. 'For as long as you like.'

'For as long as we must,' Rob amended. 'Amina, the roads will be blocked. There's no phone reception. I checked and the transmission towers are down.' He hesitated and looked suddenly nervous. 'When...when's your baby due?'

'Not for another four weeks. Henry works in the mines, two weeks on, two weeks off, but he's done six weeks in a row so he can get a long leave for the baby. He was flying in last night. He'll be frantic. I have to get a message to him.'

'I don't think we can do that,' Rob told her. 'The phones are out and the road is cut by fallen timber. It's over an hour's walk at the best of times down to the highway and frankly it's not safe to try. Burned trees will still be falling. I don't think I can walk in this heat and smoke.'

'I wouldn't want you to, but Henry…'

'He'll have stopped at the road blocks. He'll be forced to wait until the roads are cleared, but the worst of the fire's over. You'll see him soon.'

'But if the fire comes back…'

'It won't,' Rob told her. 'Even if there's a wind change, there's nothing left to burn.'

'But this house…'

'Is a fortress,' Julie told her. 'It's the house that Rob built. No fire dare challenge it.'

'He's amazing,' Amina managed as Rob headed out to do another mop and bucket round—they'd need to keep checking for hours, if not days. 'He's just…a hero.'

'He is.'

'You're so lucky…' And then Amina faltered, remembering. 'I mean… I can't…'

'I am lucky,' Julie told her. 'And yes, Rob's a hero.' And he was. Not her hero but a hero. 'But for now…for now, let's investigate the basics. We need to make this house liveable. It's Christmas tomorrow. Surely we can do something to celebrate.'

'But my Henry…'

'He'll come,' Julie said stoutly. 'And when he does, we need to have Christmas waiting for him.'


Rob made his way slowly round the house, inspecting everything. Every spark, every smouldering leaf or twig copped a mopful of water, but the threat was easing.

The smoke was easing a little. He could almost breathe.

He could almost think.

He'd saved Danny.

It should feel good and it did. He should feel lucky and he did. Strangely, though, he felt more than that. It was like a huge grey weight had been lifted from his shoulders.

Somehow he'd saved Danny. Danny would grow into a man because of what he'd achieved.

It didn't make the twins' death any easier to comprehend but somehow the knot of rage and desolation inside him had loosened a little.

Was it also because he'd held Julie last night? Lost himself in her body?

*Julie.*

'I wish she'd been able to save him, too,' he said out loud. Nothing and no one answered. It was like he was on Mars.

But Julie was here, right inside the door. And Amina and the kid he'd saved.

If he hadn't come, Julie might not have even made it to the bunker. Her eyes said maybe that wouldn't matter. Sometimes her eyes looked dead already.

How to fix that? How to break through?

He hadn't been able to four years ago. What was different now?

For the last four years he'd missed her with an ache in his gut that had never subsided. He'd learned to live with it. He'd even learned to have fun despite it, dating a couple of women this year, putting out tentative feelers, seeing if he could get back to some semblance of life. For his overtures to Julie had been met with blank rebuttal and there'd been nothing he could do to break through.

Had he tried hard enough? He hadn't, he conceded, because he'd known it was hopeless. He was part of her tragedy and she had to move on.

He'd accepted his marriage was over in everything but name.

So why had he come back here now? Was it really to save two fire engines? Or was it because he'd guessed Julie would be here?

One last hope…

If so, it had been subconscious, acting against the advice of his logic, his shrink, his new-found determination to look forward, to try and live.

But the thing was…Julie was here. She was here now, and it wasn't just the bleak, dead Julie. He could make this Julie smile again. He could reach her.

But every time he did, she closed off again.

No matter. She was still in there, in that house, and he wielded his mop with extra vigour because of it. His Julie was still Julie. She was behind layers of protection so deep he'd need a battering ram to knock them down, but hey, he'd saved a kid and his house had withstood a firestorm.

All he needed now was a battering ram and hope.

And a miracle?

Miracles were possible. They'd had two today. Why not hope for another?


The house was hot, stuffy and filled with smoke but compared to outside it seemed almost normal. It even felt normal until she hauled back the thick shutters and saw outside.

The once glorious view of the bushland was now devastation.

'I don't know what to do,' Amina whimpered and Julie thought: *neither do I*. But at least they were safe; Rob was outside in the heat making sure of it. The option of whimpering, too, was out of the question.

She looked at Amina and remembered how she'd felt

at the same stage in pregnancy. Amina wasn't carrying twins—at least she didn't think so—but this heat would be driving her to the edge, even without the added terrors of the fire.

'We have plenty of water in the underground tank,' she told her. 'And we have a generator running the pumps. If you like, you could have a bath.'

'A bath...' Amina looked at Julie like she'd offered gold. 'Really?'

'Really.'

'I'm not sure I could get in and out.' She gazed down at her bulk and even managed a smile. 'I used to describe it as a basketball. Now I think it's a small hippopotamus.'

'There are safety rails to help you in and out.'

'You put them in when you were pregnant?' It was a shy request, not one that could be snapped at.

'Yes.'

'You and Rob didn't come back here because this is where your boys lived?' Amina ventured, but it wasn't really a question. It was a statement; a discovery.

'Yes.' There was no other answer.

'Maybe I'd have felt the same if I'd lost Danny.' Danny was clinging to her side but he was looking round, interested, oblivious to the danger he'd been in mere hours before. 'Danny, will you come into the bathroom with me?'

But Danny was looking longingly out of the window. He was obviously aching for his adventure to continue, and the last thing Amina needed, Julie thought, was her four-year-old in the bathroom with her.

Luka had flopped on the floor. The big dog gave a gentle whine.

'I'll see to his pads,' Amina said but she couldn't disguise her exhaustion, or her desolation at postponing the promised bath.

'Tell you what,' Julie said. 'You go take a bath and Danny and I will take Luka into the laundry. There's a big shallow shower/bath in there. If he's like any golden retriever I know he'll like water, right?'

'He loves it.'

'Then he can stand under the shower for as long as he wants until we know his pads are completely clean. Then I'll find some burn salve for them. Danny, will you help me?'

'Give Luka a shower?' Danny ventured.

'That's the idea. You can get undressed and have a shower with him if you want.' And Julie's mind, unbidden, was taking her back, knowing what her boys loved best in the world. 'We could have fun.'

*Fun...* Where had that word come from? Julie McDowell didn't do fun.

'Will Rob help, too?' Danny asked shyly and she nodded.

'When he's stopped firefighting, maybe he will.'

'Rob's big.' There was already a touch of hero worship in the little boy's voice.

'Yes.'

'He made me safe. I was frightened and he made me safe.'

'He's good at that,' Julie managed, but she didn't know where to take it from there.

Once upon a time Rob had made her feel safe. Once upon a time she'd believed safe was possible.

Right now, that was what he was doing. Keeping them safe.

*One day at a time,* she thought. She'd been doing this for years, taking one day at a time. But now Rob was outside, keeping them safe, and the thought left her exposed.

*One day at a time?* Right now she was having trouble focusing on one *moment* at a time.

* * *

Rob did one final round of the house and decided that was it; he didn't have the strength to stay in the heat any longer. But the wind had died, there was no fire within two hundred yards of the house and even that was piles of ash, simmering to nothing. He could take a break. He headed up the veranda steps and was met by the sound of a child's laughter.

It stopped him dead in his tracks.

He was filthy. He was exhausted. All he wanted was to stand under a cold shower and then collapse, but the shower was in the laundry.

And someone was already splashing and shouting inside.

He could hear Julie laughing and, for some weird reason, the sound made him want to back away.

*Coward*, he told himself. He'd faced a bush fire and survived. How could laughter hurt so much? But it took a real effort to open the laundry door.

What met him was mess. Huge mess. The huge laundry shower-cum-bath had a base about a foot deep. It had been built to dump the twins in when they'd come in filthy from outside. The twins had filled it with their chaos and laughter and it was filled now.

More than filled.

Luka was sitting serenely in the middle of the base. The water was streaming over the big dog, and he had his head blissfully raised so the water could pour right over his eyes. Doggy heaven.

Danny had removed his clothes. He was using…one of the twins' boats?…to pour water over Luka's back. Every time he dumped a load, Luka turned and licked him, chin to forehead. Danny shrieked with laughter and scooped another load.

Julie was still fully dressed. She'd hauled off her boots and flannel overshirt but the rest was intact. Dressed or not, though, she was sitting on the edge of the tub, her feet were in the water and she was soaking. Water was streaming over her hair. She was still black but the black was now running in streaks. She looked like she didn't care.

She was helping Danny scoop water. She was laughing with Danny, hugging Luka.

*Silly as a tin of worms...*

Once upon a time Rob's dad had said that to him. Angus McDowell, Rob's father, was a Very Serious Man, a minister of religion, harsh and unyielding. He'd disapproved of Julie at first, though when Julie's business prowess had been proven he'd unbent towards her. But he'd visited once and listened to Julie playing with the twins at bathtime.

*'She's spoiling those two lads. Listen to them. Silly as a tin of worms.'*

Right now her hair was wet, the waves curling, twisting and spiralling. He'd loved her hair.

He loved her hair.

How had he managed without this woman for so long?

The same way he'd managed without his boys, he told himself harshly. One moment at a time. One step after another. Getting through each day, one by one.

Julie must feel the same. He'd seen the death of the light behind her eyes. Being together, their one-step-at-a-time rule had faltered. They could only go on if they didn't think, didn't let themselves remember.

But Julie wasn't dead now. She was very much alive. Her eyes were dancing with pleasure and her laughter was almost that of the Julie of years ago. Young. Free.

She turned and saw him and the laughter faded, just like that.

'Rob!' Danny said with satisfaction. 'You're all black. Julie says she doesn't have enough soap to get all the black off.'

'There's enough left.' Julie rose quickly—a little too quickly. Before he could stop himself he'd reached out and caught her. He held her arms as she stepped over the edge of the bath. She was soaking. She'd been using some sort of lemon soap, the one she'd always used, and suddenly he realised where that citrus scent came from. She smelled... She felt...

'You're not clean yet,' he managed and she smiled. She was only six inches away from him. He was holding her. He could just tug...

He didn't tug. This was Julie. She'd been laughing and the sight of him had stopped that laughter.

They'd destroy each other. They'd pretty much decided that, without ever speaking it out loud. Four years ago they'd walked away from each other for good reason.

How could you live with your own hurt when you saw it reflected in another's eyes, day after day? Moment after moment.

A miracle. He needed a miracle.

*It's Christmas,* he thought inconsequentially. *That's what I want for Christmas, Santa. I've saved Danny. We're safe and our house is safe, but I'm greedy. A third miracle. Please...*

'I'm clean apart from my clothes,' Julie managed, shaking her hair like a dog so that water sprayed over him. It hit his face, cool and delicious. Some hit his lips and he tasted it. Tasted Julie?

'I'll go change if you can take over here,' Julie said. 'Danny, is it okay if Rob comes under the water, too?'

'Yes,' Danny said. 'He's my friend. But you can both fit.'

'I need to find some clean clothes and something your

mum can wear,' Julie told him. 'And some dog food. And some food for us.'

'The freezer...'

'I've hooked it to the generator so I can save the solar power for important stuff,' she said and deliberately she tugged away from him. It hurt that she pulled back. He wanted to hold her. 'Like the lights on the Christmas tree.'

'So we have Christmas lights and there's enough to eat?' he asked, trying hard to concentrate on practicalities.

'If need be, we have enough to live on for weeks.'

'Will we stay here for weeks?' Danny asked and Rob saw a shadow cross Julie's face. It was an act then, he thought, laughing and playing with the child. The pain was still there. She'd managed to push it away while she'd helped Danny have fun but it was with her still. Every time she saw a child...

And every time she saw him. She glanced up at him and he saw the hurt, the bleakness and the same certainty that this was a transient, enforced connection. If they were to survive they had to move on.

He knew it for the truth. It was time it lost the power to hurt.

Miracles were thin on the ground. They'd already had two today. Was it too much to ask for just one more?

How long was frozen food safe? Where was the Internet when she needed it? Finally she decided to play safe. Using the outside barbecue—well, it had been outside but Rob had hauled it under the house during the fire so now it could be wheeled outside again—she boiled dried spaghetti and tipped over a can of spaghetti sauce. The use-by dates on both were well past, but she couldn't figure how they could go off.

'I reckon, come Armageddon, these suckers will survive,' she told Rob, tipping in the sauce.

'We might have to do something a bit more imaginative tomorrow,' Rob told her. Washed and dressed in clean jeans and T-shirt, he'd found her in the kitchen. He was now examining the contents of the freezer. 'Shall I take the turkey out?'

'Surely the roads will be open by tomorrow.'

'Don't count on it,' he said grimly. 'Jules, I've been listening to the radio and the news is horrendous. We're surrounded by miles of burned ground and the fire's ongoing. The authorities won't have the resources to get us out while they're still trying to protect communities facing the fire front.'

'Turkey it is, then,' she said, trying to make it sound light. As if being trapped here was no big deal.

As if the presence of this man she'd once known so well wasn't doing things to her head. And to her body.

She'd known him so well. She *knew* him so well.

One part of her wanted to turn away from the barbecue right now and tug him into her arms. To hold and be held. To feel what she used to take for granted.

Another part of her wanted to leave right now, hike the miles down the road away from the mountains. Sure, it would entail risks but staying close to this man held risks as well. Like remembering how much she wanted him. Like remembering how much giving your heart cost.

It had cost her everything. There was simply…nothing left.

'Can…can I help?' Amina stood at the doorway, Danny clinging by her side. She was dressed in a borrowed house robe of Julie's. She looked lost, bereft, and very, very pregnant.

'Put your feet up inside,' Rob said roughly and Julie

knew by his tone that he was as worried as she was about the girl. 'It's too hot out here already and Julie's cooking. Hot food!'

'You tell me where we can get sandwiches or salad and I'll open my purse,' Julie retorted. 'Sorry, Amina, it's spaghetti or nothing.'

'I'd like to see my house,' she said shyly and Julie winced.

'It's gone, Amina.'

'Burned,' Danny said. The adventure had gone out of the child. He looked scared.

'Yes, but we have this house,' Julie said. 'That's something. You can stay here for as long as you want.'

'My husband will be looking for us,' Amina whispered.

'If he comes next door the first place he'll look will be here.'

'Will Santa know to come here?' Danny asked. His dog was pressed by his side. He looked very small and very frightened. It was his mother's fear, Julie thought. He'd be able to feel it.

'Santa always knows where everyone is,' Rob said, squatting before Danny and scratching Luka's ears. It was intuitive, Julie thought. Danny might well recoil from a hug, but a hug to his dog was pretty much the same thing. 'I promise.'

'He's found us before,' Amina managed, but this time she couldn't stop a sob. 'I can't…we were just…'

'Where are you from?' Rob asked gently, still patting Luka.

'Sri Lanka. We left because of the fighting. My husband… He's a construction engineer. He had a good job; we had a nice house but we…things happened. We had to come here, but here he can't be an engineer. He has to retrain but it's so expensive to get his Australian accreditation. We're working so hard, trying to get the money so he can do the transition course. Meanwhile, I've been working as a cleaner.' She tilted her chin. 'I work for the firm that cleans this house. My job's good. We couldn't believe it when we were able to rent our house. We thought...this is heaven. But Henry has to work as a fly in, fly out miner. He'll be so worried right now and I'm scared he might have tried to get here. If he's been caught in the fire...'

Rob rose and took her hands. She was close to collapse, weak with terror.

'It won't have happened,' he said firmly, strongly, in a voice that Julie hadn't heard before. It was a tone that said: *don't mess with me; this is the truth and you'd better believe me.* 'They put road blocks in place last night. No one was allowed in. I was the last, and I had to talk hard to be let through. If your husband had come in before the blocks were in place, then he'd be here now. He can't have. He'll be stuck at the block or even further down the mountain. He'll be trying to get to you but he won't be permitted. He'll be safe.'

Danny was looking up at Rob as if he were the oracle on high. 'Papa's stuck down the mountain?'

'I imagine he's eating his dinner right now.'

'Where will he eat dinner?'

'The radio says a school has been opened at the foot of the mountains. Anyone who can't get home will be staying at the school.'

'Papa's at school?'

'Yes,' Rob said in that same voice that brooked no argument. 'Yes, he is. Eating dinner. Speaking of dinner... how's it coming along?'

'It's brilliant,' Julie said. 'Michelin three star, no less.'

'I don't doubt it,' Rob said, and grinned at her with the same Rob-grin that twisted her heart with pain and with pleasure. 'Do we have enough to give some to Luka?'

'If Luka eats spaghetti he'll get a very red moustache,' Julie said and Danny giggled.

And Julie smiled back at Rob—and saw the same pain and pleasure reflected in his eyes.

# CHAPTER SIX

DANNY AND ROB chatted. It was their saving grace; otherwise their odd little dinner would have been eaten in miserable silence. Too much had happened for Julie to attempt to be social.

Amina was caught up in a pool of misery. Julie's heart went out to her but there was little she could do to help.

She pressed her into eating, with limited success, and worried more.

'When's your baby due?' she asked.

'The twentieth of January.' Amina motioned to Danny. 'We were still in the refugee camp when we had Danny. This was supposed to be so different.'

'It is different.'

'Refugees again,' Amina whispered. 'But not even together.'

'You will be soon,' Julie said stoutly, sending a fervent prayer upward. 'Meanwhile we have ice cream.'

'Ice cream!'

'It's an unopened container, not a hint of ice on it,' she said proudly. 'How's that for forethought? I must have pre-prepared, four years ago.'

There was an offer too good to refuse. They all ate ice cream and Julie was relieved to see Amina reach for seconds.

There was another carton at the base of the freezer. Maybe they could even eat ice cream for breakfast.

Breakfast… How long would they be trapped here?

'Now can I go next door?' Amina asked as the last of the ice cream disappeared.

Rob grimaced. 'You're sure you don't want me to check and report back?'

'I need to see.'

'Me too,' Danny said and his mother looked at him and nodded.

'Danny's seen a lot the world has thrown at us. And his father would expect him to be a man.'

Danny's chest visibly swelled.

Kids. They were all the same. Wanting to be grown-up. Wanting to protect their mum?

It should be the other way round. She should have been able to protect…

'Stop it, Jules,' Rob said in his boss-of-the-world voice, and she flinched. Stop it? How could she stop? It was as if the voices in her head were on permanent replay.

'We need to focus on Santa,' he told her, and his eyes sent her a message that belied his smile. 'Moving on.'

*Move on.* How could she ever? But here there was no choice. Amina was looking at her and so was Danny. Even Luka… No, actually, Luka was looking at the almost empty ice cream container in her hand.

Move on.

'Right,' she said and lowered the ice cream to possibly its most appreciative consumer. 'Danny, you're going to have to wash your dog's face. Spaghetti followed by chocolate ice cream is not a good look. Meanwhile, I'll see if I can find you some sturdy shoes, Amina, and I have a jogging suit that might fit over your bump. It's not the most gorgeous outfit you might like but it's sensible, and Sensible R Us. Let's get the end of this meal cleared up and then go see if the fire's left anything of your house.'

It hadn't left a thing.

A twisted, gnarled washing line. The skeleton of a washing machine. A mass of smouldering timbers and smashed tiles.

Amina stood weeping. Julie held her and Danny's hands as Rob, in his big boots, stomped over the ruins searching for... Anything.

Nothing.

He came back to them at last, his face bleak. 'Amina, I'm sorry.'

'We didn't have much,' Amina said, faltering. 'My sister...she was killed in the bombing. I had her photographs. That was what I most...' She swallowed. 'But we've lost so much before. I know we can face this too. As long as my Henry is safe.'

'That's a hell of a name for a Sri Lankan engineer,' Rob said and Amina managed a smile.

'My mother-in-law dreamed of her son being an Englishman.'

'Will Australian do instead?'

'It doesn't matter where we are—what we have. It's a long time since we dreamed of anything but our family being safe.'

And then she paused.

The silence after the roar of the fire had been almost eerie. The wind had dropped after the front had passed. There was still the crackle of fire, and occasionally there'd be a crash as fire-weakened timber fell, but there'd been little sound for hours.

Now they heard an engine, faint at first but growing closer.

Rob ushered his little group around Amina's burned car, around the still burning log that lay over their joint driveways and out onto the road. Rob was carrying Danny— much to Danny's disgust, but he had no sensible shoes. And if anyone was to carry him, it seemed okay that his hero should. Thus they stood, waiting, seeing what would emerge out of the smoky haze.

And when it came, inevitably, magically but far too late, it was a fire engine. Big, red, gorgeous.

Julie hadn't realised how tense she'd been until she saw the red of the engine, until she saw the smoke-blackened firefighters in their stained yellow suits. Here was contact with the outside world.

She had a sudden mad urge to climb on the back and hitch a ride, all the way back to Sydney, all the way back to the safety of her office, her ordered financial world.

*Ha.* As if this apparition was offering any such transport.

'Are you guys okay?' It was the driver, a grim-faced woman in her fifties, swinging out of the cab and facing them with apprehension.

'No casualties,' Rob told her. 'Apart from minor burns on our dog's feet. But we have burn cream. And ice cream. And one intact house.'

'Good for you.' The guys with her were surveying Amina's house and then looking towards their intact house with surprise. 'You managed to save it?'

'It saved itself. We hid in a bunker.'

'Bloody lucky. Can you stay here?'

'Amina's pregnant,' Rob said. 'And her husband will be going out of his mind not knowing if she's safe.'

The woman looked at Amina, noting Danny, noting everything, Julie thought. She had the feeling that this woman was used to making hard decisions.

'We'll put her on the list for evacuation,' she said. 'How pregnant are you?'

'Thirty-six weeks,' Amina whispered.

'No sign of labour?'

'N…no.'

'Then sorry, love, but that puts you down the list. We're radioing in casualties and using the chopper for evacuation, but the chopper has a list a mile long of people with burns, accidents from trying to outrun the fire or breathing problems. And it's a huge risk trying to take anyone out via the road. There's so much falling timber I'm risking my own team being here. Do you have water? Food?'

'We're okay,' Rob told her. 'We have solar power, generators, water tanks, freezers and a stocked pantry. We have plenty of uncontaminated water and more canned food than we know what to do with.'

'Amazing,' the woman told him. 'It sounds like you're luckier than some of the towns that have been in the fire line. We managed to save houses but they're left with no services. Meanwhile, there are houses further up the mountain that haven't been checked. Our job's to get through to them, give emergency assistance and detail evacuation needs for the choppers, but by emergency we're talking life-threatening. That's all we can do— we're stretched past our limits. But we will take your name and get it put up on the lists at the refuge centres to say you're safe,' she told Amina. 'That should reassure your husband. Meanwhile, stay as cool as you can and keep that baby on board.'

'But we have no way of contacting you if anything… happens,' Rob said urgently and the woman grimaced.

'I know and I'm sorry, but I'm making a call here. We'll get the road clear as soon as we can but that'll be late tomorrow at the earliest, and possibly longer. There's timber still actively burning on the roadside. It's no use driving anyone out if a tree's to fall on them, and that's a real risk. You have a house. Your job is to protect it a while longer and thank your lucky stars you're safe. Have as good a Christmas as you can under the circumstances—and make sure that baby stays where it is.'

They watched the fire truck make its cautious way to the next bend and disappear. All of them knew what they were likely to find. It was a subdued little party that picked its way through the rubble and back to the house.

Luka greeted them with dulled pleasure. His paws obviously hurt. Rob had put on burn cream and dressings. They were superficial burns, he reported, but they were obviously painful enough for the big dog to not want to bother his bandages.

Danny lay down on the floor with him, wrapped his arms around his pet's neck and burst into tears.

'My husband wanted a dog to protect us when he was away,' Amina volunteered, and she sounded close to tears herself. 'But Luka's turned into Danny's best friend. Today Luka almost killed him—and yet here I am, thanking everything that Danny still has him. I hope...I hope...'

And Julie knew what she was hoping. This woman had gone through war and refugee camps. She'd be thinking she was homeless once again. With a dog.

Once upon a time as a baby lawyer, Julie had visited a refugee camp. She couldn't remember seeing a single dog.

'It's okay, Amina,' she told her. 'If you've been renting next door, then you can just rent here instead. This place is empty.'

'But...' Rob said.

'We never use it.' Julie cast him an uncertain glance. 'We live...in other places. I know you have a lot to think about and this will be something you and your husband need to discuss together, but, right now, don't worry about accommodation. You can stay here for as long as you want.'

'But don't...don't *you* need to discuss it with your husband?' Amina asked, casting an uncertain glance at Rob.

Her husband. Rob. She glanced down at the wedding ring, still bright on her left hand. She still had a husband—and yet she hadn't made one decision with him for four years.

'Rob and I don't live together,' she said, and she couldn't stop the note of bleakness she could hear in her own words. 'We have separate lives, separate...homes. So I'm sure you agree, don't you, Rob. This place may as well be used.'

There was a moment's pause. Silence hung, and for a moment she didn't know how it could end. But then... 'It should be a home again,' Rob said. 'Julie and I can't make it one. It'd be great if you and Henry and your children could make it happy again.'

'No decisions yet,' Amina urged. 'Don't promise anything. But if we could... If Henry's safe—' She broke off again and choked on tears. 'But it's too soon for anything.'

Rob went off to check the perimeter with his mop and bucket again. They had a wide area of burned grass between them and any smouldering timber. The risk was pretty much over but still he checked.

Amina and Danny went to bed. There was a made-up guest room with a lovely big bed, but Danny had spotted the racing-car beds. That was where he wanted to sleep—so Amina tugged one racing car closer to the other and announced that she was sleeping there, with her son.

She was asleep almost as her head hit the pillow. Had she slept at all last night? Julie wondered. She thought again of past fighting and refugee camps and all this woman had gone through.

Danny was fast asleep too. He was sharing his car-bed with Luka. Julie stood in the doorway and looked at them, this little family who'd been so close to disaster.

Disaster was always so close...

*Get over it,* she told herself harshly. *Move on.* She needed work to distract herself. She needed legal problems to solve, paperwork to do—stuff that had to be done yesterday.

Rob was out playing fireman but there was no need for the two of them to be there. So what was she supposed to do? Go to bed? She wasn't tired or if she was her body wasn't admitting it. She felt weird, exposed, trapped. Standing in her children's bedroom watching others sleep in their beds... Knowing a man who was no longer her husband was out protecting the property...

What to do? What to do?

Christmas.

The answer came as she headed back down the hall. There in the sitting room was her Christmas tree. Was it only last night that she'd decorated it? Why?

And the answer came clear, obvious now as it hadn't been last night. Because Danny needed it. Because they all needed it?

'Will Santa know to come here?' Danny had asked and Rob had reassured him.

'Santa knows where everyone is.'

That had been a promise and it had to be kept. She wouldn't mind betting Danny would be the first awake in the morning. Right now there was a Christmas tree and nothing else.

Santa had no doubt kept a stash of gifts over at Amina's house, but there was nothing left there now except cinders. Amina had been too exhausted to think past tonight.

'So I'm Santa.' She said it out loud.

'Can I share?'

And Rob was in the doorway, looking at the tree. 'I thought of it while I mopped,' he told her. 'We need to play Father Christmas.'

They could. There was a stash from long ago…

If she could bear it.

Of course she could bear it. Did she make her decision based on emotional back story or the real, tomorrow needs of one small boy? What was the choice? There wasn't one. She glanced at Rob and saw he'd come to the same conclusion she had.

Without a word she headed into their bedroom. Rob followed.

She tugged the bottom drawer out from under the wardrobe, ready to climb—even as toddlers the twins had been expert in finding stuff they didn't want them to find. She put a foot on the first drawer and Rob took her by the waist, lifted her and set her aside.

'Climbing's men's work,' he said.

'Yeah?' Unbidden, came another memory. Their town house in the city. Their elderly neighbour knocking on the door one night.

'Please, my kitten's climbed up the elm outside. He can't get down. Will you help?'

The elm was vast, reaching out over the pavement to the street beyond. The kitten was maybe halfway up, mewing pitifully.

'Right,' Rob had said manfully, though Julie had known him well and heard the qualms behind the bravado.

'Let me call the fire brigade,' she'd said and he'd cast her a look of manly scorn.

'Stand aside, woman.'

Which meant twenty minutes later the kitten was safely back in her owner's arms—having decided she didn't like Rob reaching for her, so she'd headed down under her own steam. And Julie had finally called the fire department to help her husband down.

So now she choked, and Rob glowered, but he was laughing under his glower. 'You're supposed to have forgotten that,' he told her. 'Stupid cat.'

'It's worth remembering.'

'Isn't everything?' he asked obliquely and headed up his drawer-cum-staircase.

And then they really had to remember.

The Christmas-that-never-was was up there. Silently, Rob handed it down. There were glove puppets, a wooden railway set, Batman pyjamas. Colouring books and a blow-up paddling pool. A pile of Christmas wrapping and ties they'd been too busy to use until the last moment. The detritus of a family Christmas that had never made it.

Rob put one of the puppets on his too-big hand. It was a wombat. Its two front paws were his thumb and little finger. Its head had the other fingers stuffed into its insides.

The little head wobbled. 'What do you say, Mrs McDowell?' the little wombat demanded in a voice that sounded like a strangled Rob. 'You reckon we can give me to a little guy who needs me?'

'Yes.' But her voice was strained.

'I'm not real,' the little wombat said—via Rob. 'I'm just a bit of fake fur and some neat stitchery.'

'Of course.'

'But I represent the past.'

'Don't push it, Rob.' Why was the past threatening to rise up and choke her?

'I'm not pushing. I'm facing stuff myself. I've been facing stuff alone for so long…' Rob put down his wombat and picked up the Batman pyjamas. 'It hurts. Would it hurt more together than it does separately? That's a decision we need to make. Meanwhile, we bought these too big for the twins and Danny's tiny. These'll make him happy.'

She could hardly breathe. What was he suggesting? That he wanted to try again? 'I…I know that,' she managed but she was suddenly feeling as if she was in the bunker again, cowering, the outside threats closing in.

Dumb. Rob wasn't threatening. He was holding Batman pyjamas—and smiling at her as if he understood exactly how she felt.

*I've been facing stuff alone for so long…* She hadn't allowed herself to think about that. She hadn't been able to face his hurt as well as hers.

Guilty…and did she need to add *coward* to her list of failings as well?

'Would it have been easier if it all burned?' Rob asked gently and she flinched.

'Maybe. Maybe it would.'

'So why did you come?'

'You know why.'

'Because it's not over? Because they're still with us?' His voice was kind. 'Because we can't escape it; we're still a family?'

'We're not.'

'They're still with me,' he said, just as gently. 'Every waking moment, and often in my sleep as well, they're with me.'

'Yeah.'

'They're not in this stuff. They're in our hearts.'

'Rob, no.' The pain… She hadn't let herself think it. She hadn't let herself feel it. She'd worked and she'd worked and she'd pushed emotion away because it did her head in.

'Jules, it's been four years. The way I feel…'

'Don't!'

He looked at her for a long, steady moment and then he looked down at the wombat. And nodded. Moving on? 'But we can pack stuff up for Danny?'

'I…yes.'

'We need things for Amina as well.'

'I have…too many things.' She thought of her dressing table, stuffed with girly things collected through a lifetime. She thought of the house next door, a heap of smouldering ash. Sharing was a no-brainer; in fact Amina could have it all.

'Wrapping paper?' Rob demanded. The emotion was dissipating. Maybe he'd realised he'd taken her to an edge that terrified her.

'I have a desk full of it,' she told him, grateful to be back on firm ground.

'Always the organised one.' He hesitated. 'Stockings?'

She took a deep breath at that and the edge was suddenly close again. Yes, they had stockings. Four. Julie, Rob, Aiden, Christopher. Her mother had embroidered names on each.

But she could be practical. She could do this. 'I'll unpick the names,' she said.

'We can use pillowcases instead.'

'N…no. I'll unpick them.'

'I can help.' He hesitated. 'I need to head out and put a few pans of water around for the wildlife, and then I'm all yours. But, Jules…'

'Mmm?'

'When we're done playing Santa Claus…will you come to bed with me tonight?'

This was tearing her in two. If she could walk away now she would, she thought. She'd walk straight out of the door, onto the road down to the highway and out of here. But that wasn't possible and this man, the man with the eyes that saw everything there was to know, was looking at her. And he was smiling, but his smile had all her pain behind it, and all his too. They had shared ghosts. Somehow, Rob was moving past them. But for her... The ghosts held her in thrall and she was trapped.

But for this night, within the trap there was wriggle room. She'd remove names from Christmas stockings. She'd wrap her children's toys and address them to Danny. She'd even find the snorkel and flippers she had hidden up on the top of her wardrobe. She'd bought them for Rob because she loved the beach, she'd loved taking the boys there and she was...she had been...slowly persuading Rob of its delights.

Did he go to the beach now? What was he doing with his life?

Who knew, and after this night she'd stop wondering again. But on Christmas morning the ghosts would see her stuffing the snorkel and flippers in his stocking. He'd head out into the burned bush with his pails of water so animals wouldn't die and, while he did, she'd prepare him a Christmas.

And the ghosts would see her lie in his arms this night.

'Yes,' she whispered because the word seemed all she could manage. And then, because it was important, she tried for more. 'Yes, please, Rob. Tonight...tonight I'd like to sleep with you once more.'

Christmas morning. The first slivers of light were making their way through the shutters Rob had left closed because there was still fire danger. The air was thick with the smell of a charred landscape.

She was lying cocooned in Rob's arms and for this moment she wanted nothing else. The world could disappear. For this moment the pain had gone, she'd found her island and she was clinging for all she was worth.

He was some island. She stirred just a little, savouring the exquisite sensation of skin against skin—her skin against Rob's—and she felt him tense a little in response.

'Good, huh?'

He sounded smug. She'd forgotten that smugness.

She loved that smugness.

'Bit rusty,' she managed and he choked on laughter

'Rusty? I'll show you rusty.' He swung up over the top of her, his dark eyes gleaming with delicious laughter. 'I've been saving myself for you for all this time...'

'There's been no one else?'

She shouldn't have asked. She saw the laughter fade, but the tenderness was there still.

'I did try,' he said. 'I thought I should move on. It was a disaster. You?'

'I didn't even try,' she whispered. 'I knew it wouldn't work.'

'So you were saving yourself for me too.'

'I was saving myself for nobody.'

'Well, that sounds a bit bleak. You know, Jules, maybe we should cut ourselves a little slack. Put bleakness behind us for a bit.'

'For today at least,' she conceded, and tried to smile back. 'Merry Christmas.'

'Merry Christmas to you, too,' he said, and the wickedness was back. 'You want me to give you your first present?'

'I...'

'Because I'm about to,' he said and his gorgeous muscular body, the body she'd loved with all her heart, lowered to hers.

She rose to meet him. Skin against skin. She took his

MARION LENNOX 109

body into her arms and tugged him to her, around her, merging into the warmth and depth of him.

Merry Christmas.

The ghosts had backed off. For now there was only Rob, there was only this moment, there was only now.

They surfaced—who could say how much later? They were entwined in each other's bodies, sleepily content, loosely covered by a light cotton sheet. Which was just as well as they emerged to the sound of quiet but desperate sniffs.

Danny.

They rolled as one to look at the door, as they'd done so many times with the twins.

Danny was in the doorway, clutching Luka's collar. He was wearing a singlet and knickers. His hair was tousled, his eyes were still dazed with sleep but he was sniffing desperately, trying not to cry.

'Hey,' Rob said, hauling the sheet a little higher. 'Danny! What's up, mate?'

'Mama's crying,' Danny said. 'She's crying and crying and she won't stop.'

'That'll be because your house is burned and your dad's stuck down the mountain,' Rob said prosaically, as if this was the sort of thing that happened every day. 'I guess your dad won't be able to make it here for a while yet, so maybe it's up to us to cheer her up. What do you think might help?'

'I don't know,' Danny whispered. 'Me and Luka tried to hug her.'

'Hugs are good.' Rob sat up and Julie lay still and watched, trying not to be too conscious of Rob's naked chest, plus the fact that he was still naked under the sheet, and his body was still touching hers and every sense…

No. That was hardly fair because she was tuned to Danny.

She'd been able to juggle…everything when they were a family. She glanced at her watch. Eight o'clock. Four years ago she'd have been up by six, trying to fit in an hour of work before the twins woke. Even at weekends, the times they'd lain here together, they'd always been conscious of pressure.

Yeah, well, both of them had busy professional lives. Both of them thought…had thought…getting on was important.

'You know, hugs are great,' Rob was saying and he lay down again and hugged Julie, just to demonstrate. 'But there might be something better today. Did you remember today is Christmas?'

'Yes, but Mama said Santa won't be able to get through the burn,' Danny quavered. 'She says…Santa will have to wait.'

'I don't think Santa ever waits,' Rob said gravely. 'Why don't you go look under the Christmas tree while Julie and I get dressed? Then we'll go hug your mama and bring her to the tree too.'

'There might be presents?' Danny breathed.

'Santa's a clever old feller,' Rob told him. 'I don't think he'd let a little thing like a bush fire stop him, do you?'

'But Mama said…'

'Your mama was acting on incorrect information,' Rob told him. 'She doesn't know Australia like Julie and I do. Bush fires happen over Australian Christmases all the time. Santa's used to it. So go check, but no opening anything until we're all dressed and out there with you. Promise?'

'I promise.'

'Does Luka promise, too?'

And Danny giggled and Julie thought she did have senses for something—for someone—other than Rob.

To make a child smile at Christmas… It wasn't a bad feeling.

Actually, it was a great feeling. It drove the pain away as nothing else could.

And then she thought…it was like coming out of bleak fog into sunlight.

It was a sliver, the faintest streak of brilliance, but it was something that hadn't touched her for so long. She'd been grey for years, or sepia-toned, everything made two-dimensional, flat and dull.

Right now she was lying in Rob's arms and she was hearing Danny giggle. And it wasn't an echo of the twins. She wasn't thinking of the twins.

She was thinking this little boy had been born in a refugee camp. His mother had coped with coming from a war-torn country.

She'd wrapped the most beautiful alpaca shawl for Amina, in the softest rose and cream. She knew Amina would love it; she just knew.

And there was a wombat glove puppet just waiting to be opened.

'Go,' she ordered Danny, sitting up too, but hastily remembering to keep her sheet tucked around her. 'Check out the Christmas tree and see if Rob's right and Santa's been. I hope he's been for all of us. We'll be there in five minutes, and then we need to get your mama up and tell her things will be okay. And they will be okay, Danny. It's Christmas and Rob and I are here to make sure that you and your mama and Luka have a very good time.'

They did have a good time. Amina was teary but, washed and dressed in a frivolous bath robe Rob had once given Julie, ensconced in the most comfortable armchair in the living room, tears gave way to bemusement.

Julie had wrapped the sensible gifts, two or three each, nice things carefully chosen. Rob, however, had taken wrapping to extremes, deciding there was too much wrapping paper and it couldn't be wasted. So he'd hunted the house and wrapped silly things. As well as the scarf and a bracelet from Africa, Amina's stocking also contained a gift-wrapped hammer, nails, a grease gun—'*because you never know what'll need greasing*', Rob told her—and a bottle of cleaning bleach. They made Amina gasp and then giggle.

'Santa thinks I might be a handyman?'

'Every house needs one,' Rob said gravely. 'In our house I wear the tool belt but Santa's not sexist.'

'My Henry's an engineer.'

'Then you get to share. Sharing a grease gun—that's real domestic harmony.'

Amina chuckled and held her grease gun like it was gold and they moved on.

Julie's stocking contained the nightdress she'd lusted after four years before and a voucher for a day spa, now long expired. *Whoops*.

'The girls at the spa gift-wrapped it for me four years ago,' Rob explained. 'How was I to know it had expired?' Then, 'No matter,' he said expansively. 'Santa will buy you another.'

He was like a bountiful genie, Julie thought, determined to make each of them happy.

He'd made her happy last night. Was it possible…? Did she have the courage…?

'You have another gift,' Rob reminded her and she hauled her thoughts back to now.

Her final gift was a wad of paper, fresh from their printer. Bemused, she flicked through it.

It was *Freezing—the Modern Woman's Survival Guide*,

plus a how-to manual extolling the virtues of ash in compost. He'd clearly got their printer to work while she'd gift-wrapped. He'd practically printed out a book.

She showed Amina and both women dissolved into laughter while Rob beamed benevolently.

'Never say I don't put thought into my gifts,' he told them and Julie held up the spa voucher.

'An out-of-date day spa?'

'They cancel each other out. I still rock.'

They chuckled again and then turned their attention to Danny.

Danny was simply entranced. He loved the pyjamas and his fire engine but most of all he loved the wombat puppet. Rob demonstrated. Danny watched and was smitten.

And so was Julie. She watched the two of them together and she thought: *I know why I fell in love with this man.*

*I know why I love this man?*

Was she brave enough to go there?

As well as snorkel and flippers—which Rob had received with open enjoyment before promising Danny that they could try them out in the bath later—Julie had given Rob a coat—a cord jacket. She remembered buying it for him all those years ago. She'd tried it on herself, rushing in her lunch hour, last-minute shopping. It had cost far more than she'd budgeted for but she'd imagined it on Rob, imagined holding him when he was wearing it, imagined how it'd look, faded and worn, years hence.

She should have given it to him four years ago. Now he shrugged himself into it and smiled across the room at her and she realised why she hadn't given it to him. Why she'd refused to have contact with him.

She was afraid of that smile.

Was she still? Tomorrow, would she...?

No. Tomorrow was for tomorrow. For now she needed

to watch Danny help Luka open a multi-wrapped gift that finally revealed a packet of biscuits scarily past their use-by date. Oatmeal gingernuts. 'They'll be the closest thing Santa could find to dog biscuits,' Rob told Danny.

'Doesn't Santa have dog biscuits at the North Pole?'

'I reckon he does,' Rob said gravely. 'But I think he'll have also seen all this burned bush and thought of all the animals out here who don't have much to eat. So he might have dropped his supply of dog biscuits out of his sleigh to help.'

'He's clever,' Danny said and Rob nodded.

'And kind.'

*He's not the only one,* Julie thought, and her heart twisted. Once upon a time this man had been her husband. If she could go back…

Turn back time? As if that was going to happen.

'Is it time to put the turkey on?' Rob asked and Julie glanced at him and thought *he's as tense as I am*. Making love didn't count, she thought, or it did, but all it showed was the same attraction was there that had always been there. And with it came the same propensity for heartbreak.

He was still wearing his jacket. He liked it. You could always tell with Rob. If he loved something, he loved it for ever. And she realised that might just count for her too.

Whether she wanted that love or not.

Switch to practical. 'We still need to use the barbecue,' she said. 'We don't have enough electricity to use the oven.'

'That's us then,' Rob said, puffing his chest. 'Me and Danny. Barbecuing's men's work, hey, Dan?'

'Can my wombat help?'

'Sure he can.'

'I'm not sure what we can have with it,' Julie said. 'There doesn't seem to be a lot of salad in the fridge.'

'Let me look at what you have,' Amina said. 'I can cook.'

'Don't you need to rest?'

'I've had enough rest,' Amina declared. 'And I can't sleep. I need to know my husband's safe. I can't rest until we're all together.'

*That's us shot then,* Julie thought bleakly. For her family, together was never going to happen.

They ate a surprisingly delicious dinner—turkey with the burned-from-the-freezer bits chopped off, gravy made from a packet mix and couscous with nuts and dried fruit and dried herbs.

They had pudding, slices fried in the butter she'd bought with the bread, served with custard made from evaporated milk.

They pulled bon-bons. They wore silly hats. They told jokes.

But even Danny kept glancing out of the window. He was waiting for his father to appear.

So much could have happened. If he'd tried to reach them last night... All sorts of scenarios were flitting through Julie's mind and she didn't like any of them.

Once catastrophe struck, did you spend the rest of your life expecting it to happen again? Of course you did.

'He'll be fine.' Astonishingly, the reassurance came from Amina. Had she sensed how tense Julie was? 'What you said made sense. He'll be at the road block. And, as for the house... We've seen worse than this before. We'll survive.'

'Of course you will.'

'No, you have to believe it,' Amina said. 'Don't just say it. Believe it or you go mad.'

What had this woman gone through? She had no idea. She didn't want to even imagine.

'I'd like to do something for you,' Amina said shyly. 'If

you permit... In the bathroom I noticed a hair colour kit. Crimson. Is it yours?'

'Julie doesn't colour her hair,' Rob said, but Julie was remembering a day long ago, a momentary impulse.

She'd be a redhead for Christmas, she'd thought. Her boys would love it, or she thought they might. But of course she hadn't had time to go to a salon. On impulse she'd bought a do-it-yourself kit, then chickened out at the last minute—of course—and the kit had sat in the second bathroom since.

'I'm a hairdresser,' Amina said, even more shyly. 'In my country, that's what I do. Or did. My husband has to retrain here for engineering but there are no such requirements for hairdressing, and I know this product.' She gazed at Julie's hair with professional interest. 'Colour would look good, but I don't think all over. If you permit, I could give you highlights.'

'I don't think...'

'Jules,' Rob said, and she heard an undercurrent of steel, 'you'd look great with red highlights.'

She'd hardly touched her ash-blonde curls for four years. She tugged them into a knot for work; when they became too unruly to control she'd gone to the cheap walk-in hairdresser near work and she'd thought no more about it.

Even before the boys died... When had she last had time to think about what her hair looked like?

When she'd met Rob she'd had auburn highlights. He'd loved them. He'd played with her curls, running his long, strong fingers through them, massaging her scalp, kissing her as the touch of his fingers through her hair sent her wild...

Even then she hadn't arranged it herself. Her mother had organised it as a gift.

*'I bought this voucher for you, pet. I know you don't*

*have time for the salon but you need to make a little time
for yourself.'*

Her parents were overseas now, having the holiday of a
lifetime. They wouldn't be worried about her. They knew
she'd be buried in her work.

They'd never imagine she'd be here. With time…

'I don't think…'

'Do it, Jules,' Rob said and she caught a note of steel
in his voice. She looked at him uncertainly, and then at
Amina, and she understood.

This wasn't about her. Rob wasn't pushing her because
he wanted a wife…an ex-wife…with crimson highlights.
He was pushing her because Amina needed to do something to keep her mind off her burned house and her missing husband. And she also needed to give something back.

She thought suddenly of the sympathy and kindness
she'd received during the months after the boys' deaths
and she remembered thinking, more than once: *I want to
be the one giving sympathy. I want to give rather than take.*

Amina was a refugee. She would have been needing
help for years. Now, this one thing…

'I'd love highlights,' she confessed and Amina smiled,
really smiled, for the first time since she'd met her. It was
a lovely smile, and it made Danny smile too.

She glanced at Rob and his stern face had relaxed.

Better to give than receive? Sometimes not. Her eyes
caught Rob's and she knew he was thinking exactly the
same thing.

He'd have been on the receiving end of sympathy too.
And then she thought of all the things he'd tried to make
her feel better—every way he could during those awful
weeks in hospital, trying and trying, but every time she'd
pushed him away.

'Don't get soppy on us,' Rob said, and she blinked and

he chuckled and put his arm around her and gave her a fast, hard hug. 'Right, Amina, we need a hair salon. Danny, I need your help. A chair in the bathroom, right? One that doesn't matter if it gets the odd red splash on it.'

He set them up, and then he disappeared. She caught a glimpse of him through the window, heading down to the creek, shovel over his shoulder.

She guessed what he'd be doing. He'd left water for wildlife, but there'd be animals too badly burned…

'He's a good man,' Amina said and she turned and Amina was watching her. 'You have a good husband.'

'We're not…together.'

'Because of your babies?'

'I…yes.'

'It happens,' Amina said softly. 'Dreadful things…they tear you apart or they pull you together. The choice is yours.'

'There's no choice,' she said, more harshly than she intended, but Danny was waiting in the bathroom eyeing the colouring kit with anticipation, and she could turn away and bite her lip and hope Amina didn't sense the surge of anger and resentment that her words engendered.

*Get over it…* It was never said, not in so many words, but, four years on, she knew she was pretty much regarded as cool and aloof. The adjectives were no longer seen as a symptom of loss—they simply described who she was.

And who she intended to be for the rest of her life?

Thinking ahead was too hard. But Rob was gone, off to do what he could for injured wildlife, and Danny was waiting in the bathroom and Amina was watching her with a gaze that said she saw almost too much.

*Do something.*

Back in the office, she'd be neck-deep in contracts.

It was Christmas Day.

Okay, back home, she'd have left her brother's place

after managing to stay polite all through Christmas dinner and now she'd be back in her apartment. Neck-deep in contracts.

But now...neck-deep in hair dye?

'Let's get this over with,' she muttered and Amina took a step back.

'You don't have to. If you don't want...'

She caught herself. If Rob came back and found her wallowing in self-pity, with her hair the same colour and Amina left alone...

See, there was the problem. With Rob around she couldn't wallow.

Maybe that was why she'd left him.

Maybe that was selfish. Maybe *grief* was selfish.

It was all too hard. She caught herself and forced a smile and then tried even harder. This time the smile was almost natural.

'Rob is a good man,' she conceded. 'But he needs a nicer woman than me. A happier one.'

'You can be happier if you try,' Amina told her.

'You can be happy if you have red hair,' Danny volunteered and she grinned at his little-boy answer to the problems of the world.

'Then give me red hair,' she said. 'Red hair is your mum's gift to me for Christmas, and if there's one thing Christmas needs it's gifts. Are you and Luka going to watch or are you going to play with your Christmas presents?'

'Me and Luka are going to watch,' Danny said, and he wiggled his glove puppet. 'And Wombat. Me and Luka and Wombat are going to watch you get happy.'

Almost as soon as they started, Julie realised that agreeing to this had been a mistake.

Putting a colour through her hair would have been a relatively easy task—simply applying the colour, leaving it to take and then washing it out again.

Amina, though, had different ideas. 'Not flat colour,' she said, just as flatly. 'You want highlights, gold and crimson. You'll look beautiful.'

Yeah, well, she might, but each highlight meant the application of colour to just a few strands of hair, then those strands wrapped in foil before Amina moved to the next strands.

It wasn't a job Amina could do sitting down. She also didn't intend to do a half-hearted job.

'If I put too much hair in each foil, then you'll have flat clumps of colour,' she told Julie as she protested. 'It won't look half as good. And I want some of them strong and some diluted.'

'But you shouldn't be on your feet.' She hadn't thought this through. Amina was eight months pregnant, she'd had one hell of a time and now she was struggling.

She looked exhausted. But…

'I need to do this,' Amina told her. 'Please…I want to. I need to do something.'

She did. Julie knew the worry about her husband was still hanging over her, plus the overwhelming grief of the devastation next door. But still…

'I don't want you to risk this baby,' she told her. 'Amina, this is madness.'

'It's not madness,' Amina said stubbornly. 'It's what I want to do. Sit still.'

So she sat, but she worried, and when Rob appeared as the last foil was done she felt a huge wash of relief. Not that there was anything Rob could do to help the situation but at least…at least he was here.

She'd missed him…

'Wow,' Rob said, stopping at the entrance to the bath-room and raising his brows in his grimy face. 'You look like a sputnik.'

'What's a sputnik?' Danny demanded.

'A spiky thing that floats round in space,' Rob told him. 'You think we should put Julie in a rocket launcher and send her to the moon?'

Danny giggled and Amina smiled and once again there was that lovely release of tension that only Rob seemed capable of producing. He was the best man to have in a crisis.

'Amina's exhausted, though,' Julie told him. 'She needs to sleep.'

'You need to keep those foils in for forty minutes,' Amina retorted. 'Then you need a full scalp massage to get the colour even and then a wash and condition. Then I'll rest.'

'Ah, but I'm back now,' Rob said, and Julie knew he could see the exhaustion on Amina's face. He'd have taken in her worry at a glance. 'And if anyone's going to massage my wife it's me. Forty minutes?' He glanced at his watch. 'Amina, I came to ask if there was anything precious, any jewellery, anything that might have survived the fire that you'd like us to search for. The radio's saying it may rain tonight, in which case the ash will turn to concrete. Sputnik and I could have a look now.'

Julie choked. *Sputnik?* She glanced in the mirror. She was wearing one of Rob's shirts, faded jeans, and her head was covered in silver spikes. Okay, yep. Sputnik.

'I could be a Christmas decoration instead,' she volunteered. 'One of those shiny spiky balls you put on top of the tree.'

'You'll be more help sifting through ash. I assume you can put a towel around the spikes—the wildlife has had enough scares for the time being without adding aliens to the mix. Amina, is that okay with you?'

'I will look,' Amina said but Rob caught her hands. He had great hands, Julie thought inconsequentially. He was holding Amina and Julie knew he was imparting strength, reassurance, determination. All those things…

He was a good man. Her husband?

'The ground's treacherous,' he told her. 'Your house is a pile of ash and rubble and parts of it are still very hot. Julie and I have the heavy boots we used to garden in, we have strong protective clothing and we're not carrying a baby. You need to take care of your little one, and of Danny. We won't stay over there for long—it's too hot—but we can do a superficial search. If you tell us where to look…'

'Our bedroom,' Amina told him, meeting his stern gaze, giving in to sense. 'The front bay window…you should see the outline. Our bed started two feet back from the window and was centred on it. The bed was six foot long. On either side of the bed was a bedside table. We each had a box…'

'Wood?' Rob asked without much hope.

'Tin.'

'Well, that's possible. Though don't get your hopes up too much; that fire was searing and tin melts. We'll have a look—but only if you try and get some rest. Danny, will you stand guard while your mum sleeps?'

'I want to help with the burn.'

'There'll be lots of time to help with the burn,' Rob said grimly. 'But, for now, you need to be in charge of your mother. Go lie down beside her, play with your toys while she sleeps, but if she tries to get up, then growl at her. Can you do that?'

Danny considered. 'Because of the baby?'

'Yes.'

'Papa says I have to look after her because of the baby.'

'Then you'll do what your papa asked?'

'Yes,' Danny said and then his voice faltered. 'I wish he'd come.'

'He will come,' Rob said in a voice that brooked no argument. 'He will come. I promise.'

# CHAPTER SEVEN

'IT SHOULD HAVE been ours.' Julie stood in the midst of the devastation that was all that was left of Amina's house, she glanced across at their intact home and she felt ill.

'Fire doesn't make sense,' Rob told her, staring grimly round the ruin.

'No. And I understand that it was your design that saved it. But Amina's house was…a home.'

'Our place will be a home again. If we rent it out to them, Amina will make it one. I suspect she's been making homes in all sorts of places for a long time.'

'I know. Home's where the heart is,' Julie said bleakly. 'They all say it. If you only knew how much I hate that saying.'

'We're not here for self-pity, Jules,' Rob said, hauling her up with a start. He sounded angry, and maybe justifiably. This was no time to wallow. 'If it rains, then there'll be little chance of finding anything. Let's get to it.' He handed her a pair of leather gloves and a shovel. 'Watch your feet for anything hot. Sift in front of you before you put your feet down. Don't go near anywhere that looks unstable.'

There wasn't much that looked unstable. The house had collapsed in on itself. The roof was corrugated iron, but Rob must have been here before, because it had been hauled off site.

The bedroom. They could see the outline of the bay window.

'You focus on either side of where the bed would have been,' Rob told her. 'I'm doing a general search.'

What a way to spend Christmas afternoon. Overdressed, hot, struggling to breathe with the wafts of smoke still in the air, her hair in spikes, covered by a towel, squatting, sifting through layer upon layer of warm ash...

She found the first tin almost immediately. It had melted—of course it had—but it had held enough of its shape to recognise it for what it was.

Who knew what was inside? There was no time now to try and open it. She set it aside and moved to the other side of where the bed would have been and kept on searching.

And was stopped in her tracks by a whoop.

She looked up and Rob was standing at the rear of the house, where the laundry would have been. He'd been shovelling.

'Jules, come and see.'

She rose stiffly and made her way gingerly across the ruin.

It was a safe. Unmistakably it was a safe and it must be fireproof, judging by the fact that it looked intact, even its paintwork almost unscathed.

'It must have been set in the floor,' Rob said. 'Look, it's still in some sort of frame. But I can get it out.'

'Do you think Amina knew it was there?'

'Who knows? But we'll take it next door. How goes the tin hunt?'

'One down.'

'Then let's find the other.' He grabbed her and gave her a hard unexpected hug. 'See, good things can happen. I just hope there's something inside that safe other than in-surance papers.'

'Insurance papers would be good.'

'You and I both know that's not important. And we have five minutes to go before sputnik takes off. Tin, Jules, fetch.'

And, amazingly, they did fetch—two minutes later their search produced a tin box even more melted than the first. Three prizes. Rob brought the barrow from their yard, then they heaved the safe into it and carted it back. 'I feel like a pup with two tails,' Rob said.

Julie grinned and thought: *fun*.

That had been fun. She'd just had fun with Rob. How long since…?

She caught herself, a shaft of guilt hitting her blindside as it always did when she started forgetting. She had no right…

They parked their barrow on the veranda and went to check on Amina. She was fast asleep, as was Danny, curled up beside her. Luka was by their bedside, calmly watchful. The big dog looked up at them as if to say: *What's important enough to wake them up?*

Nothing was. But the foils had to come off.

'I can take them off myself,' Julie said, but dubiously, because in truth they were now overdue to come off and, by the time she took off every last one, the fine foils would be well overdone. What happened if you cooked your hair for too long? Did it fall out? She had no idea, and she had no intention of finding out.

'I'll take them out,' Rob said and looked ruefully down at himself. 'Your beautician, though, ma'am, is filthy.'

'In case you hadn't noticed, your client is filthy too. Can you imagine me popping into a high-class Sydney salon like this?'

'You'd set a new trend,' Rob told her, touching her foils with a grin. 'Smoked Sputnik. It'd take off like a bush fire.'

'Of course it would,' she lied. She'd reached the bathroom now and looked at the mirror. 'Ugh.'

'Let's get these things off then,' he said. 'Sit.'

So she sat on the little white bathroom stool, which promptly turned grey with soot. Rob stood behind her and she watched in the mirror as he slid each foil from her hair.

He worked swiftly, dextrously, intently. He was always like this on a job, she remembered. When he was focused on something he blocked out the world.

When he made love to her, the world might well not exist.

He was standing so close. He smelled of fire, of smoke, of burned eucalyptus. His fingers were in her hair, doing mundane things, removing foils, but it didn't feel mundane. It felt…it felt…

Too soon, the last of the foils was gone, heaped into the trash. Her hair was still spiky, looking very red. Actually, she wouldn't mind if it was green, she thought, as long as she could find an excuse to keep Rob here with her. To stretch out this moment.

'I can…' Her voice wobbled and she fought to steady it. 'I can go from here. I'll shower it off.'

'You need a full scalp massage to even the colour,' Rob told her, but his voice wasn't steady either. It was, however, stern. 'I'm Amina's underling. She's given us orders. The least we can do is obey.'

'I can do it by myself.'

'But you don't have to,' he said, and he bent and touched her forehead with his mouth. It was a feather touch, hardly a kiss, just a fleeting sensation, but it sent shivers through her whole body. 'For now, just give in and forget about facing things alone.'

So she gave in. Of course she did. She sat perfectly still while Rob massaged her scalp with his gorgeous, sensuous fingers and her every nerve ending reacted to him.

He was filthy, covered with smoke and ash. If you met this man on a dark night you'd scream and run, she thought, catching his reflection in the mirror in the split second she allowed herself to glance at him. For she couldn't watch. Feeling him was bad enough...or good enough...

*Good* was maybe too small a word. Her entire body was reacting to his touch. Any more and she'd turn and take him. She wanted...

'Conditioner,' Rob said, only the faintest tremor cutting through the prosaic word. 'Amina said conditioner.'

'It's in the shower.'

'Then I suggest,' he said, bending down so his lips were right against her ear, 'that we adjourn to the shower.'

'Rob...'

'Mmm?'

'N...nothing.'

'No objections?'

'We...we might lock the door first.'

'What an excellent idea,' he said approvingly. 'I have a practical wife. I always knew I had a practical wife. I'd just forgotten...'

And seemingly in one swift movement the door was locked and she was swept into his arms. He pushed the shower screen back with his elbow and deposited her inside.

It was a large shower. A gorgeous shower. They'd built it...well, they'd built it when they were in love.

It was wide enough for Rob to step inside with her and tug the glass screen closed after them.

'Clothes,' he said. 'Stat?'

'Stat?'

'That's what they say in hospitals in emergencies. Oxygen here, nurse, stat.'

'So we need clothes?'

'We don't need clothes. If this was a hospital and I was a doctor, that's what I'd be saying. Nurse, my wife needs her clothes removed. Stat.'

'Rob...'

'Yes?'

She looked at him and she thought she needed to say she wasn't his wife. She should say she didn't have the courage to take this further. She was too selfish, too armoured, too closed.

But he was inches away from her. He smelled of bush fire. His face was grimy and blackened. As was she.

The only part of her that wasn't grimy or blackened was her hair. Crimson droplets were dripping onto the white shower base, mixing with the ash.

How much colour had Amina put in? How had she trusted a woman she didn't know to colour her hair?

Rob was standing before her, holding her.

She trusted this man with all her heart, and that was the problem. She felt herself falling...

Where was her armour?

She'd find it tomorrow, she told herself. This was an extraordinary situation. This was a time out, pretend, a disaster-induced remarriage that would dissolve as soon as the rest of the world peered in. But for this moment she was stranded in this time, in this place...

In this shower.

And Rob was tugging her shirt up over her head and she was lifting her arms to help him. And then, as the shirt was tossed over the screen, as he turned his attention to her bra, she started to undo the buttons of his shirt.

Her hands were shaking.

He took her hands in his and held. Tight. Hard. Cupping her hands, completely enfolding them.

'There's no need for shaking, Jules. I'd never hurt you.'

'I might…hurt you.'

'I'm a big boy now,' he told her. 'I can take it.'

'Rob, I need to say…this is for now. I don't think…I still can't think…'

'Of course you can't.' He held her still. 'But for now, for this moment, let's take things as they come. Let our bodies remember why we fell in love. Let's start at the beginning and let things happen.'

And then he kissed her, and that kiss made her forget every other thing. Everything but Rob.

Water was streaming over them. Somehow they managed to stop, pull back, give themselves time to haul their clothes off and toss them out, a sodden, stained puddle to be dealt with later.

Everything could be dealt with later, Julie thought hazily as she turned back to her beautiful naked Rob. For now there was only Rob. There was only this moment.

Water was running in rivulets down his beautiful face, onto his chest, lower. He was wet and glistening and wonderful. His hands were on the small of her back, drawing her into him, and the feel of wet hands on wet skin was indescribably erotic.

For now there was no pain. There was no yesterday. There was only this man, this body. There was only this desire and the only moment that mattered was now.

'You think we should have a nap now, too?' Rob asked.

Somehow they were out of the shower, sated, satisfied, dazed.

Maybe she should make that almost satisfied, Julie thought. Rob was drying her. She was facing the mirror, watching him behind her. The feel of the towel was indescribably delicious.

He pressed her down onto the bathroom stool and started drying her hair. Gently. Wonderfully.

If she could die now, she'd float to heaven. She was floating already.

'If we go anywhere near the bed I can't be held responsible for what happens,' she managed and Rob chuckled. Oh, she remembered that chuckle. She'd forgotten how much she'd missed it.

How much else had she forgotten?

Had she wanted to forget...all of it?

'Maybe you're right. But maybe it's worth not being responsible,' Rob growled. 'But I want to see your hair dry first.'

Her hair. She'd had colour foils put in. Every woman in her right senses regarded the removing of colour foils with trepidation, hoping the colour would work. For some reason Julie had forgotten all about it.

'It looks good wet,' Rob said, stooping and kissing her behind her ear. 'Let's see it dry.'

She tried to look at it in the mirror. Yeah, well, that was a mistake. Rob was right behind her and he was naked. How was a woman to look at her hair when her hairdresser was...Rob?

'I...I can do it,' she tried but he was already hauling the hairdryer from the cabinet. This place was a time warp. Everything had simply been left. It had been stupid, but coming back here four years ago had been impossible. She'd simply abandoned everything...which meant she had a hairdryer.

And, stupid or not, that had its advantages, she decided, as Rob switched on the dryer and directed warm air at her hair. As did the solar panels he'd installed on the roof and the massive bank of power batteries under the house.

They had electricity, and every cent they'd paid for such a massive backup was worth it just for this moment. For the power of one hairdryer.

She couldn't move. Her body seemed more alive than she could remember. Every nerve was tingling, every sense was on fire but she couldn't move. She was paralysed by the touch of his hands, by the warmth of the dryer, by the way he lifted each curl and twisted and played with it as he dried it.

By the way he watched her in the mirror as he dried.

By the way he just…was.

He was lighting her body.

He was also lighting her hair. Good grief, her hair…

It was almost dry now, and the colours were impossible to ignore. They were part of the same magical fantasy that was this moment, but these colours weren't going to go away with the opening of the bathroom door.

What had happened?

She'd bought auburn highlights, but what Amina had done… She must have mixed them in uneven strengths, done something, woven magic…because what had happened *was* magic.

Her mousey-blonde hair was no longer remotely mouse. It was a shiny mass of gold and chestnut and auburn. It was like the glowing embers of a fire, flickering flames on a muted background.

Rob was lifting her curls, watching the light play on them as he made sure every strand was dry. Her hair felt as if it was their centre. Nothing else mattered.

If only nothing else mattered. If only they could move on from this moment, forgetting everything.

But she didn't want to forget. The thought slammed home and she saw Rob's eyes in the mirror and knew the thought had slammed into him almost simultaneously. They always had known what each other was thinking.

One mind. One body.

'Jules, we could try again,' he said softly, almost as if

talking to himself. 'We've done four years of hell. Does it have to continue?'

'I don't see how it can't.'

'We don't have to forget. Going forward together isn't a betrayal. Does it hurt, every time you look at me, because of what we had?'

'No. Yes!'

'I've seen a shrink. There I was, lying on a couch, telling all.' He smiled down at her and lifted a curl, then letting it drop. 'Actually, it was a chair. But the idea's the same. I'm shrunk.'

'And what did he...she...tell you?'

'She didn't tell me anything. She led me round and round in circles until I figured it out. But finally I did. Four people weren't killed that day, though they can be if we let them.'

'You can live...without them?'

'There's no choice, Jules,' he said, his voice suddenly rough. 'Look at us. It's Christmas, our fourth Christmas without them, yet it's all about two little boys who are no longer here. Out there is a little boy who's alive and who needs us to make him happy. We can help Amina be happy, at least for the day. We can do all sorts of things, make all sorts of people happy if we forget we're the walking dead.'

'I'm not...'

'No. You're not the walking dead. Look at your hair. This is fun hair, fantastic hair, the hair of a woman who wants to move forward. And look at your body. It's a woman's body, Jules, your body, and it gives you pleasure. It still can give you pleasure. Maybe it could even give you another child.'

'No!'

'Are you so closed?'

'Are you? You said you've been seeing other women?'

'I said I've been trying,' he said, and once again his fingers started drifting in her curls. 'The problem is they're not you.'

'You can't still love me.'

'I've never stopped.'

'But there's nothing left to love.' She was sounding desperate, negative, harsh. She'd built up so much armour and he'd penetrated it. It was cracking and she was fighting desperately to retain it. If it shattered…how could she risk such hurt again? She felt as if she was on the edge of an abyss, about to fall.

'Jump,' Rob said softly. 'I'll catch you.'

But she had to keep trying. She had to make him see. 'Rob, there are so many women out there. Undamaged. Women who could give you a family again.'

'Are you offering me up for public auction? I'm not available,' he said, more harshly still. 'Julie, remember the first time we came here? Deciding to camp? Me nobly giving you our only single air bed, then the rain at two in the morning and you refusing to move because you were warm and dry and floating?'

'I did move in the end.'

'Only because I tipped you off into six inches of water.'

'That wasn't exactly chivalrous.'

'Exactly. The thing is, Jules, that with you I've never felt the need to be chivalrous. What happens between us just…happens.'

'You did rescue the kitten…sort of.'

'That's what comes of playing the hero. You end up laughing.'

'I didn't laugh at you.'

'No,' he said and he stooped and took her hands in his. 'You laugh with me. Every time I laugh, I know you're laughing too. And every time I'm gutted it's the same.

That's what's tearing me apart the most. I've known, these last four years, that you haven't been laughing. Nor have you been gutted because I would have felt it. You've just been frozen. But I want you, Jules. I want my lovely, laughing Julie back again. We've lost so much. Do we have to lose everything?'

He was so close. His hands enfolded hers. It would be so easy to fall…

But it was easier to make love to him than what he was asking her now. She remembered that closeness. That feeling that she was part of him. That even when he drove her crazy she understood why, and she sort of got that she might be driving him crazy too.

They'd fought. Of course they'd fought. Understanding someone didn't mean you had to share a point of view and often they hadn't.

She'd loved fighting with him and often she hadn't actually minded losing. A triumphant Rob made her laugh.

But to start again…

Could she?

She so wanted to, but…but…

She was like the meat she had taken out from the freezer, she thought tangentially. On the surface she was defrosting but at her core there was still a deep knot of frozen.

If she could get out of here, get away from Rob, then that core would stay protected. Her outer layers could freeze again as well.

Was that what she wanted?

'Jules, try,' Rob said, drawing her into his arms and holding her. 'You can't waste all that hair on legal contracts. Waste it on me.'

'What do you think I'm doing now?'

'But long-term? After the fire.'

'I don't know.' The panic was suddenly back, all around

her—the panic that had overwhelmed her the first time she'd walked into the twins' empty bedroom, the panic that threatened to bring her down if she got close to anyone. The abyss was so close…

'I won't push you,' Rob said.

'So making love isn't pushing?'

'That wasn't me,' he said, almost sternly. 'It was both of us. You know you want me as much as I want you.'

'I want your body.'

'You want all of me. You want the part that wants to be part of you again. The part that wants to love you and demands you love me back.'

'Rob…I can't!' How could she stop this overwhelming feeling of terror? She wanted this man so much, but…but…

She had to make one last Herculean effort. One last try to stay…frozen.

'It's…time to get dressed,' she managed, and he nodded and lifted his fingers through her curls one last time.

'I guess,' he said ruefully, achingly reluctant. 'But let's try. Let the world in, my Julie. Let Amina see what her magic produced.'

'Only it's not magic,' she whispered. 'We can't cast a happy-ever-after spell.'

'We could try.'

'We could destroy each other.'

'More than we already have?' He sighed. 'But it's okay. Whatever you decide has to be okay. I *will not* push.' He kissed her once again, on the nape of her neck, and it was all she could do not to turn and take him into her arms and hold him and hold him and hold him. She didn't. The panic was too raw. The abyss too close.

But he was twisting a towel around his hips. It nearly killed her to see his nakedness disappear. If the world wasn't waiting…

Someone was banging on the front door. Luka started barking.

The world was indeed waiting. It was time to dress. It was time to move on.

Rob reached the front door first. He'd hauled jeans on and left it at that. Amina and Danny must be still asleep, or waking slowly, because only Luka was there, barking hysterically.

The knocking started again as he reached the hall, but for some reason his steps slowed.

He didn't want the world to enter?

Maybe there was a truck outside, emergency personnel offering to take them down the mountain, evacuate them to safety. The authorities would want everyone off the mountain. This place was self-sufficient but most homes were dependent on essential services. That first truck had been the precursor to many. The army could even have been called in, with instructions to enforce evacuation.

He didn't want to go.

Well, that was dumb. For a start, Amina desperately needed evacuation. It wasn't safe for an eight months pregnant woman to be here, with no guaranteed way out if she went into labour. With the ferocity of the burn and the amount of bushland right up to the edges of the roads, normal traffic would be impossible for weeks. So many burned trees, all threatening to fall... They needed to get out as soon as it was safe to go.

And yet...and yet...

And yet he didn't want to leave.

Maybe he could send Amina and Danny away and keep Julie here.

As his prisoner? That was another dumb thought. He couldn't keep her against her will, nor would he want to, but, even so, the thought was there. The last twenty-four hours had revealed his wife again. He knew she was still hurting. He knew that breaking down her armour required a miracle, and he also knew that once they were off the mountain, then that miracle couldn't happen. She'd retreat again into her world of finance and pain.

'She has to deal with it in her own time.' The words of his shrink had been firm. 'Rob, you've been wounded just as much as she has, but you're working through it. For now it's as much as you can do to heal yourself. You need to let Julie go.'

But what if they could heal together? These last hours had shown him Julie was still there—the Julie he'd loved, the Julie he'd married.

But he couldn't lock her up. That wasn't the way of healing and he knew it.

What was? Holding her close? She'd let him do that. They'd made love, they'd remembered how their bodies had reacted to each other, yet it had achieved…nothing.

Could he keep trying? Dare he? These last years he'd achieved a measure of peace and acceptance. Would taking Julie to him open the floodgates again? Would watching her pain drive him back to the abyss? Only he knew how hard it had been to pull himself back to a point where he felt more or less at peace.

He knew what his shrink would say. *Move away and stay away. Leave the past in the past.*

Only the past was in their shared bedroom, with hair that glistened under his hands, with eyes that smiled at him with…hope? If he could find the strength… If, somehow, he could drag her to the other side of the nightmare…

Enough of the introspection. The knocking continued and he'd reached the door. He tugged it open, Luka launched himself straight out—and into the arms of a guy standing on the doorstep.

The man was shorter than Rob, and leaner. He looked in his forties, dark-skinned and filthy. He looked…haggard. His eyes were bloodshot and he hadn't shaved for a couple of days. He was leaning against the door jamb, breathing heavily, but as Luka launched himself forward he grabbed him and held him as if he was drowning.

He met Rob's eyes over Luka's great head, and his look was anguished.

'Amina?' It was scarcely a croak.

'Safe,' Rob said quickly. 'And Danny. They're both here. They're safe. You're Henry?' He had to be. No one but Amina's husband could say her name with the same mix of love and terror.

'Yes. I am. I went…next door. Oh, God, it's…'

'We got them here before the house went up,' Rob said, speaking quickly, cutting through Henry's obvious terror. 'They're tired but well. They're asleep now but they've been as worried about you as you seem to be about them. They're safe.'

The man's knees sagged. Rob grabbed the dog and hauled him back, then took Henry's elbows under his hands, holding him up. He looked beyond exhaustion.

'They're safe,' he said again. 'I promise. Happy Christmas, Henry. I know your house is burned and I'm sorry, but things can be replaced. People can't. Everything else can wait. For now, come in and see your wife.'

And Henry burst into tears.

After that things seemed to happen in a blur.

There was a whimper behind him. Rob turned and Amina was there, staring in incredulity. And then somehow she was in Rob's place, holding her husband, holding and holding. Weeping.

And then Danny, flying down the hall. 'Papa...' He was between them, a wriggling, excited bundle of joy. 'My Papa's come,' he yelled to anyone who'd listen and then he was between them, sandwiched, muffled but still yelling. 'Papa, our house burned and burned and Luka was lost and I was scared but Rob found me and then we hid in a little cave and we've been here for lots and lots and Santa came and we had turkey but we didn't have chocolates. Mama had them for us but they've been burned as well, but Mama says we can get some more. Papa, come and see my presents.'

Rob backed away and then Julie was beside him, in her gorgeous crimson robe with her gorgeous crimson hair, and she was sniffing. He took her hand and held and it felt...right.

They finally found themselves in the kitchen, watching Henry eat leftover Christmas lunch like he hadn't eaten for a week—but he still wasn't concentrating on the food. He kept looking from Amina to Danny and back again, like he couldn't get enough of them. Like he was seeing ghosts...

His plane last night, a later one than Rob's, had been diverted—landing in Melbourne instead of Sydney because of the smoke. He'd spent the night trying to get any information he could, going crazy because he couldn't contact anyone.

This morning he'd flown into Sydney at dawn, hired a car, hit the road blocks, left the car, dodged the road blocks and walked.

It didn't take any more than seeing his smoke-stained face and his bloodshot eyes to tell them how fraught that walk had been. And how terror had stayed with him every inch of the way.

But he was home. He had his family back again. Julie watched them with hungry eyes, and Rob watched Julie and thought that going back was a dream. A fantasy. He couldn't live with that empty hunger for ever.

'We've plenty of water. Go and take a bath,' he told Henry, and Danny brightened.

'Luka and I will help,' he announced and they disappeared towards the bathroom, with the sounds of splashing and laughter ensuing. Happy ever after...

'I'll go get dressed,' Julie said, sounding subdued, and Amina touched her hair.

'Beautiful.'

'Yes. Thank you.'

'Don't waste it,' Amina said sternly with a meaningful glance at Rob, and Julie flinched a little but managed a smile.

'I promise I won't wear a hat for months.'

Which wasn't what Amina had meant and they all knew it but it was enough for Julie to escape.

Which left Amina with Rob.

'You love her still,' she said, almost as if she was talking of something mundane, chatting about the weather, and Rob had to rerun the words in his mind for a bit before he could find an answer.

'Yes,' he said at last. 'But our grief threatened to destroy us. It's still destroying us.'

'You want...to try again?'

'I don't think we can.'

'It takes courage,' she whispered. 'So much courage. But you...you have courage to spare. You saved my son.'

'It takes more than courage to wake up to grief every morning of your life.'

'It's better than walking away,' she said softly. 'Walking away is the thing you do when all else fails. Walking away is the end.'

'Amina…'

'I shall cook dinner,' she announced, moving on. 'Food is good. Food is excellent. When all else fails, eat. I need to inspect this frozen-in-time kitchen of yours.'

'You need to rest.'

'I have rested,' she said. 'I have my husband back. My family is together and that's all that matters. We need to move on.'

Christmas dinner was a sort of Middle Eastern goulash made with leftover turkey, couscous, dried herbs, packet stock and raisins. It should have tasted weird—half the ingredients were well over their use-by dates—but it tasted delicious. The house had a formal dining room but no one was interested in using it. They squashed round the kitchen table meant for four, with Luka taking up most of the room underneath, and it felt right.

*Home*, Rob thought as he glanced at his dinner companions. That was what this felt like. Outside, the world was a bleak mess but here was food, security, togetherness.

Henry couldn't stop looking at Amina and Danny. From one to the other. It was like he was seeing a dream.

That was what looking at Julie felt like too, Rob thought. A dream. Something that could never be.

But still… Henry had made a quick, bleak foray across to the ruins of his house and came back grimly determined.

'We can build again,' he'd said. 'We've coped with worse than this.'

Building again… Could he and Julie? A building needed foundations, though, Rob thought, and their foundations hardly existed any more. At least, that was what Julie thought. She thought their foundations were a bed of pain,

of nightmares. Could he ever break through to foundations that had been laid long before the twins were born?

   Did he have the strength to try?

'You have our safe,' Henry said as the meal came to
an end and anxiety was in his voice again. 'You said you
managed to haul it out.'

'I did,' Rob told him. 'I'm not sure whether the contents
have withstood the fire.'

'It's built to withstand an inferno. And the contents…
it's not chocolate.'

'I'd like some chocolate,' Danny said wistfully, but there
was ice cream. Honestly, wrapped containers might cope
with a nuclear blast, Rob thought as they sliced through the
layers of plastic to ice cream that looked almost perfect.

But Amina didn't want any. She was looking exhausted
again. Julie was watching her with concern, and Rob
picked up on it.

'You want to go back to bed?' he asked her. 'All of you.
Henry's had a nightmare twenty-four hours and you've
made us a feast of a Christmas dinner. You've earned some
sleep.'

'I'm fine,' Amina said, wincing a little. 'I just have a
backache. I need a cushion, that's all.'

In moments she had about four and they moved into
the living room, settled in the comfortable lounge suite…
wondering where to go from here.

He'd quite like to carry Julie back to the bedroom, Rob
thought. It was Christmas night. He could think of gifts
he'd like to give and receive…

But Danny had slept this afternoon, and he was wide
awake now. He was zooming back and forth across the
floor with his new fire truck. In Danny's eyes, Christmas was still happening. There was no way he was going
calmly to bed, and that meant the adults had to stay up.

Henry was exhausted. He'd slumped into his chair, his face still grey with exhaustion and stress.

Amina also looked stressed. The effort of making dinner had been too much for her. She had no energy left.

Rob sank to the floor and started playing with Danny, forming a makeshift road for his fire engine, pretending the TV remote was a police car, conducting races, making the little boy laugh. Doing what he'd done before…

It nearly killed her. He was doing what she'd seen him do so many times, what she'd loved seeing him do.

Now he was playing with a child who wasn't his.

He was *getting over it*?

*Get over it.* How many times had those words been said to her? 'It'll take time but you will get over it. You will be able to start again.'

She knew she never would, but Rob just might. It had been a mistake, coming back here, she thought. Connecting with Rob again. Reminding themselves of what they'd once had.

It had hurt him, she thought. It had made him hope…

She should cut that hope off right now. There was no chance she could move on. The thought of having another child, of watching Rob romp with another baby… It hurt.

*Happy Christmas,* she thought bitterly. This was worse than the nothing Christmases she'd had for the last few years. Watching Rob play with a child who wasn't his.

She glanced up and saw Amina was watching her and, to her surprise, she saw her pain reflected in the other woman's eyes.

'Are you okay?' she asked. 'Amina…?'

'It's only the backache,' she said, but somehow Julie knew it wasn't. 'Henry, the safe… Could you check? I need to know.'

'I'll do it in the morning,' Henry said uneasily but Amina shook her head.

'I need to see now. The television…does it work?'

'We have enough power,' Rob told her. 'But there won't be reception.'

'We don't need reception. I just need to see…'

'Amina, it'll hurt,' Henry said.

'Yes, but I still need to see,' she said stubbornly. 'Henry, do this for me, please. I need to see that they're still there.'

Which explained why, ten minutes later, Rob and Henry were out on the veranda, staring at a fire-stained safe. The paint had peeled and charred, but essentially it looked okay.

'Do you want to open it in privacy?' Rob asked, but Henry shook his head.

'We have nothing of value. This holds our passports, our insurance—our house contents are insured, how fortunate is that?'

'Wise.'

'The last house we lost was insured too,' Henry said. 'But not for acts of war.'

'Henry…'

'No matter. This is better. But Amina wants her memories. Do you permit?'

He wasn't sure what was going on but, two minutes later, Henry had worked the still operational combination lock and was hauling out the contents.

Papers, documents…and a couple of USB sticks.

'I worried,' Henry said. 'They're plastic but they seem okay. It would break Amina's heart to lose these. Can we check them on your television?'

'Of course. Julie and I can go to bed if you want privacy.'

'If it's okay with you,' Henry said diffidently, 'it's better to share. I mean…Amina needs to…well, her history seems more real to her if she can share. Right now she's hurting. It would help…if you could watch. I know it'll be dull for you, other people's memories, but it might help. The way Amina's looking… Losing our house. Worrying about me. The baby… It's taken its toll.'

'Of course we can watch.' It was Julie in the doorway behind them. 'Anything that can help has to be okay by us.'

The television worked. The USB worked. Ten minutes later they were in Sri Lanka.

In Amina and Henry's past lives.

The files contained photographs—many, many photographs. Most were amateur snaps, taken at family celebrations, taken at home, a big, assorted group of people whose smiles and laughter reached out across distance and time.

And, as Julie watched her, the stress around Amina's eyes faded. She was introducing people as if they were here.

'This is my mother, Aisha, and my older sister Hannah. These two are my brothers. Haija is an architect like you, Rob. He designs offices, wonderful buildings. The last office he designed had a waterfall, three storeys high. It wasn't built, but, oh, if it had been… And here are my nieces and nephews. And Olivia…' She was weeping a little but smiling through tears as the photograph of a teenage girl appeared on the screen, laughing, mocking the camera, mischief apparent even from such a time and distance. 'My little sister Olivia. Oh, she is trouble. She'll be trouble still. Danny, you remember how I told you Olivia loves trains?' she demanded of her son. 'Olivia had a train set, a whole city. She started when she was a tiny child, wanting and wanting trains. "What are you interested in those for?" my father asked. "Trains are for boys." But Olivia wanted and wanted and finally he bought her a tiny train and a track, and then another. And then our father helped her build such a city. He built a platform she could raise to the roof on chains whenever my mother wanted the space for visitors. Look, here's a picture.'

And there they were—trains, recorded on video, tiny locomotives chugging through an Alpine village, with snow-covered trees and tiny figures, railway stations, tunnels, mountains, little plastic figures, a businessman in a bowler hat endlessly missing his train...

Danny was entranced but he'd obviously seen it before. 'Olivia's trains,' he said in satisfaction and he was right by the television, pointing to each train. 'This green one is her favourite. Mama's Papa gave it to her for her eighth birthday. Mama says when I am eight she'll try and find a train just like that for me. Isn't it lucky I'm not eight yet? If Mama had already found my train, it would have been burned.'

'Do you...still see them?' Rob asked cautiously.

Amina smiled sadly and shook her head. 'Our house was bombed. Accidentally, they said, but that's when Henry and I decided to come here. It's better here. No bombs.'

'Bush fires, though,' Rob said, trying for a smile and, amazingly, Amina smiled back at him, even as she put her hand to her obviously aching back.

'We can cope with what we have to cope with,' she said simply. She looked back at the television to where her sister was laughing at her father. Two little steam engines lay crashed on their side on the model track, obviously victims of a fake disaster. 'You get up and keep going,' she said simply. 'What choice is there?'

*You can close down,* Julie thought. *You can roll into a tight ball of controlled pain, unbending only to work.* That was what she'd done for four long years.

'Would you like to see our boys?' Rob asked and her eyes flew wide. What was he saying? Shock held her immobile and it was as if his voice was coming from the television, not from him. But, 'I'd like to show you our sons,' he was saying. 'They're not here either, but they're still in our hearts. It'd be great to share.'

*No. No!* She wanted to scream it but she couldn't.

'Would you like us to see them, Julie?' Amina asked shyly, tentatively, as if she guessed Julie's pain. As she must. She'd lost so much herself.

'We lost our boys in a car accident four years ago,' Rob told Henry. 'But it still feels like they're here.'

'But it hurts Julie?' Amina said. 'To talk about them? To see them? Is it better not?'

*Yes,* Julie thought. *Much better.* But then she looked at Rob, and with a shock she realised that his face said it wasn't better at all.

His expression told her that he longed to talk about them. He longed to show these strangers pictures of his sons, as they'd shown him pictures of their family.

'It's up to Jules, though,' Rob said. 'Julie, do you know where the disc is of their birthday?'

She did, but she didn't want to say. She never spoke of the boys. She never looked at their photographs. They were locked inside her, kept, hers. They were dead.

'Maybe not,' Amina said, still gently. 'If Julie doesn't want to share, that's her right.'

Share…share her boys… She wanted to say no. She wanted to scream it because the thought almost blindsided her. To talk about them…to say their names out loud…to act as if they still had a place in her life…

To see her boys on the screen...

'Jules?' Rob said gently and he crossed the room and stooped and touched her chin with his finger. 'Up to you, love. Share or not? No pressure.'

But it was pressure, she thought desperately, and it was as if the pressure had been building for years. The containment she'd held herself in was no longer holding.

To share her boys... To share her pain...

Rob's gaze was on her, calmly watchful. Waiting for the yay or nay.

No pressure.

Share... Share with this man.

A photo session, she thought. That was all he was asking. To see his kids as they'd been when they'd turned two. How hard was that?

'Don't do it if it hurts,' Amina whispered and Julie knew that it would hurt. But suddenly she knew that it'd hurt much more not to.

They were her boys. Hers and Rob's. And Rob was asking her to share memories, to sit in this room and look at photographs of their kids and let them come to life again, if only on the screen. To introduce them, to talk of them as Amina had talked of her family.

'I...I'll get it,' she said and Rob ran a finger the length of her cheek. His eyes said he did understand what he was asking, and yet he was still asking.

His gaze said he knew her hurt; he shared it. He shared...

She rose and she staggered a little, but Rob was beside her, giving her a swift, hard hug. 'I love that video,' he said but she knew he hadn't seen it for four years. It had been hidden, held here in limbo. Maybe it was time...

She couldn't think past that. She gave Rob a tight hug in return and went to fetch the disc.

\* \* \*

And there they were. Her boys. It had been the most glorious birthday party, held here on the back lawn. All the family had been here—her parents, Rob's parents, their siblings, Rob's brother's kids, Rob's parents' dog, a muddle of family and chaos on the back lawn.

A brand-new paddling pool. Two little boys, gloriously happy, covered in the remains of birthday cake and ice cream, squealing with delight. Rob swinging them in circles, a twin under each arm.

Julie trying to reach Aiden across the pool, slipping and sprawling in the water. Julie lying in the pool in her jeans and T-shirt, the twins jumping on her, thinking she'd meant it, squealing with joy. Rob's laughter in the background. Julie laughing up at the camera, hugging her boys, then yelling at Rob's dad because the dog was using the distraction to investigate the picnic table.

The camera swivelled to the dog and the remains of the cake—and laughter and a dog zooming off into the bushes with half a cake in his mouth.

Family…

She'd thought she couldn't bear it. She'd thought she could never look at photographs again, but, instead of crying, instead of withering in pain, she found she was smiling. Laughing, even. When the dog took off with the cake they were all laughing.

'Luka wouldn't do that,' Danny decreed. 'Bad dog.'

'They look…like a wonderful family,' Amina said and Rob nodded.

'They are.'

They were. She'd never let them close. She'd seen her remaining family perfunctorily for the last four years, when she had to, and she'd never let anyone talk of the boys.

'Aiden and Christopher were…great.'

She said their names now out loud and it was like turning a key in a rusty lock. She hadn't said their names to anyone else since…

'They're the best kids,' Rob said, smiling. He was gripping her hand, she realised, and she hadn't even noticed when he'd taken it. 'They were here for such a short time, but the way they changed our lives… You know, in the far reaches of my head, they're still with me. When I get together with my parents and we talk about them, they're real. They're alive. I understand why you need your family tonight, Amina. For the same reason I need mine.'

Julie listened, and Rob's words left her stunned. His words left her in a limbo she didn't understand. Like an invitation to jump a crevice…but how could she?

The recording had come to an end. The last frame was of the twins sitting in their pool, beaming out at all of them. She wanted to reach out and touch them. She felt as if her skin was bursting. That she could look at her boys and laugh… That she could hold Rob's hand and remember how it had felt to be a family…

'Thank you for showing us,' Henry said, gravely now, and Julie thought that he knew. This man knew how much it hurt. He'd lost too, him and Amina, but now he was tugging his wife to her feet, holding her…moving on.

'We need to sleep,' he said. 'All of us. But thank you for giving us such a wonderful, magical Christmas. Thank you for saving my family, and thank you for sharing yours.'

They left.

Rob flicked the television off and the picture of their boys faded to nothing.

Without a word, Rob went out to the veranda. He stood at the rail and stared into the night and, after a moment's hesitation, Julie followed. The smouldering bushland gave no chance of starlight but, astonishingly, a few of the solar lights they'd installed along the garden paths still glowed. The light was faint but it was enough to show a couple of wallabies drinking deeply from the water basins Rob had left.

'How many did you put out?' Julie said inconsequentially. There were so many emotions coursing through her she had no hope of processing them.

'As many containers as I could find. I suspect our veranda was a refuge. There are droppings all over the south side. All sorts of droppings.'

'So we saved more than Amina and Danny and Luka.'

'I think we did. It's been one hell of a Christmas.' He hesitated. 'So…past Christmases…Julie, each Christmas, each birthday and so many times in between, I've tried to ring. You know how often, but I've always been sent straight through to voicemail. I finally accepted that you wanted no contact, but it hasn't stopped me thinking of you. I've thought of you and the boys every day. But at Christmas…for me it's been a day to get through the best way I can. But, Julie, how has it been for you? I rang your parents. The year after…they said you were with them but you didn't want to talk to me. The year after that they were away and I couldn't contact you.'

How to tell him what she'd been doing? The first year she'd been in hospital and Christmas had been a blur of pain and disbelief. The next her parents had persuaded her to spend with them.

Doug and Isabelle were lovely ex-hippy types, loving their garden, their books, their lives. They'd always been astonished by their only daughter's decision to go into law and finance, but they'd decreed anything she did was okay by them. Doug was a builder, Isabelle taught disadvantaged kids and they accepted everyone. They'd loved Rob and their grandsons but, after the car crash, they'd accepted Julie's decision that she didn't want to talk of them, ever.

But it had left a great hole. They were so careful to avoid it, and she was so conscious of their avoidance. That first Christmas with them had been appalling.

The next year she'd given them an Arctic cruise as a Christmas gift. They'd looked at her with sadness but with understanding and ever since then they'd travelled at Christmas.

And what had Julie been doing?

'I work at Christmas,' she said. 'I'm international. The finance sector hardly closes down.'

'You go into work?'

'I'm not that sad,' she snapped, though she remembered thinking if the entire building hadn't been closed and shut down over Christmas Day she might have. 'I have Christmas dinner with my brother. But I do take contracts home. It takes the pressure off the rest of the staff, knowing someone's willing to take responsibility for the urgent stuff. How about you?'

'That's terrible.'

'How about you?' she repeated and she made no attempt to block her anger. Yeah, Christmas was a nightmare. But he had no right to make her remember how much of a nightmare it normally was, so she wasn't about to let him off the hook. 'While I've been neck-deep in legal negotiations, what have you been doing?'

'To keep Santa at bay?'

'That's one way of looking at it.'

'I've skied.'

It was so out of left field that she blinked. 'What?'

'Skied,' he repeated.

'Where?'

'Aspen.'

She couldn't have been more astounded if he'd said he'd been to Mars. 'You hate the cold.'

'I hated the cold. I'm not that Rob any more.'

She thought about that for a moment while the stillness of the night intensified. The smell of the smoke was all-consuming but…it was okay. It was a mist around them, enveloping them in a weird kind of intimacy.

Rob in the snow at Christmas.

Without her.

Rob in a life without her.

It was odd, she thought numbly. She'd been in a sort of limbo since the accident, a weird, desolate space where time seemed to stand still. There was no future and no past, simply the piles of legal contracts she had in front of her. When she'd had her family, her work had been important. When she hadn't, her work was everything.

But, meanwhile, Rob had been doing…other stuff. Skiing in Aspen.

'Are you any good?' she asked inconsequentially and she heard him smile.

'At first, ludicrous. A couple of guys from work asked me to go with them. I spent my first time on the nursery slopes, watching three-year-olds zoom around me. But I've improved. I pretty much threw my heart and soul into it.'

'Even on Christmas Day?'

'On Christmas Day I pretty much have the slopes to myself. I ski my butt off, to the point where I sleep.'

'Without nightmares?'

'There are always nightmares, Jules,' he said gently. 'Always. But you learn to live around them.'

'But this Christmas—you didn't go to Aspen?'

'My clients finished the house to die for in the Adelaide Hills. They were having a Christmas Eve party. My sister asked me to join her tribe for Christmas today.

I'd decided…well, I'd decided it was time to stay home. Time to move on.'

*Without me?* She didn't say it. It was mean and unfair. She'd decided on this desolate existence. Rob was free to move on as best he could.

But…but…

He was right here, in front of her. Rob. Her beloved Rob, who she'd turned away from. She could have helped…

Or she could have destroyed him.

He reached out and touched her cheek, a feather touch, and the sensation sent shivers through her body. *Her Rob.*

'Hell, Julie, how do we move on from this?' His voice was grave. Compassionate. Loving?

'I don't know,' she whispered. 'I can't think how to escape this fog.'

There was a moment's hesitation and then his voice changed. 'Escape,' he said bitterly. 'Is that what you want? Do you think Amina was escaping by coming here?'

'I don't know.'

'Well, I do,' he said roughly, almost angrily. 'She wasn't escaping. She was regrouping. Figuring out how badly she and her family had been wounded, and how to survive. And look at her. After all she's been through, back she goes, to her memories, to talking about the ones she loves. You know why I wasn't going to Aspen this Christmas? Because I've finally figured it out. I've finally figured that's what I want, Jules. I want to be able to talk about Aiden and Christopher without hurting. Call it a Christmas list if you want, my Santa wish, but that wish has been with me for four years. Every day I wake up and I want the same thing. I want people to talk of Christopher and Aiden like Amina does of her family. I want to admit that Christopher bugged me when he whined for sweets. I want to remember that Aiden never wanted me to go the bathroom by myself. I want to be able to say that you sometimes took all the bedcovers…'

'I did not!'

'And the one time I got really pissed off and pinned them to my side of the bed you ripped them. You did, too.'

'Rob!'

'Don't sound so outraged.' But then he gave a rueful smile and shrugged. 'Actually, that's okay. Outrage is good. Anything's good apart from silence. Or fog. We've been living with silence for years. Does it have to go on for ever?'

'I'm…safe where I am.'

'Because no one talks about Aiden or Christopher? Or me. Do they talk about me, Julie, or am I as dead to you as the boys are?'

'If they did talk…it hurts.'

But he was still angry. Relentless. The gentle, compassionate Rob was gone. 'Do you remember the first time we climbed this mountain?' he demanded, and he grabbed her hand and hauled her round so she was facing out to where the smoke-shrouded mountain lay beyond the darkened bush. 'Mount Bundoon. You were so unfit. It was mean of me to make you walk, but you wanted to come.'

'I only did it because I was besotted with you.'

'And I only made you come because I wanted you to see. Because I knew it was worth it. Because I knew you'd think it was worth it.' His hand was still holding hers, firm and strong. 'So you struggled up the track and I helped you…'

'You pushed. You bullied!'

'So I did and you got blisters on blisters and we hadn't taken enough water and we were idiots.'

'And then we reached the top,' she said, remembering.

'Yeah,' he said in satisfaction and hauled her against

him. 'We reached the top and we looked out over the gorge and it's the most beautiful place in the whole world. Only gained through blisters.'

'Rob...'

'And what do you remember now?' he demanded, rough again. 'Blisters?'

'No.'

'So? Does my saying Aiden's name, Christopher's name, my name—does it hurt so much you can't reach the top? Because you know what I reckon, Jules? I reckon that saying Aiden's name and Christopher's, and talking of them to each other, that's the top. That's what we ought to aim for. If we could start loving the boys again...together...could we do that, Jules? Not just now? Not just for Christmas? For ever?'

And she wanted to. With every nerve in her body she wanted to.

'Do you know what I've done every Christmas?' he asked, gently now, holding her, but there was something implacable about his voice, something that said he was about to say something that would hurt. 'And every birthday. And so many times in between...I've taken that damned recording out and watched it. And you know what? I love it. I love that I have it. I love that my kids—and my Julie—can still make me smile.'

'You...you have it?' She was stammering. 'But tonight...I had to find the disc.'

'That's because tonight had to be your choice. I have a copy. Jules, I've made my choice. I'm living on, with my kids, with my memories and I've figured that's the way to survive. But you have to do your own figuring. Whether you want to continue blocking the past out for ever. Whether you want to let the memories back in. Or maybe...maybe whether you dare to move forward. With me or without. Julie, I still want you. You're still my wife. I still love you, but the rest…it's up to you.'

The night grew even more still. It was as if the world was holding its breath.

He was so close and he was holding her and he wanted her. All she had to do was sink into him and let him love her.

All she had to do was love in return.

But what did she have to give? It'd be all one way, she thought, her head spinning. Rob could say he loved her, he could say he still wanted her but it wasn't the Julie of now that he wanted. It was the Julie of years ago. The Julie she'd seen on replay. Today's Julie was like a husk, the shed skin of someone she had once been.

Rob deserved better.

She loved this man; she knew she did. But he deserved the old Julie and, confused or not, dizzy or not, she knew at some deep, basic level that she didn't have the energy to be that woman.

'Jules, you can,' he said urgently, as if he knew what she was thinking—how did he do that? How did he still have the skill?

How could she still know him when so much of her had died?

She wanted him, she ached for him, but it terrified her. Could she pretend to be the old Julie? she wondered. Could she fake being someone she used to be?

'Try for us,' Rob demanded, and his hands held her. He tugged her to him, and she felt…like someone was hauling the floor from under her feet.

Rob would catch her. Rob would always catch her.

She had to learn to catch herself.

'Maybe I should see the same shrink,' she managed. 'The one who's made you brave enough to start again.'

'The shrink didn't make me brave. That's all me.'

'I don't want…'

'That's just it. You have to want. You have to want more than to hide.'

'You can't make me,' she said, almost resentfully, and he nodded.

'I know I can't. But the alternative? Do you want to walk away? Once the road is reopened, once Christmas is over, do you want to go back to the life you've been existing in? Not living, existing. Is that what you want?'

'It's what I have to want.'

'It's not,' he said, really angry now. 'You can change. Ask Danny. His Christmas list was written months ago. Amina said he wanted a bike but he got a wombat instead and you know what? Now he thinks that's what he wanted all along.'

'You think I can be happy with second best? Life without our boys?'

'I think you can be happy. I think dying with them is a bloody waste.'

'There's no need…'

'To swear? No, I suppose not. There's no need to do anything. There's no need to even try. Okay, Jules, I'll back off.'

'Rob, I'm…'

'Don't you dare say you're sorry. I couldn't bear it.'

But there was nothing to say but sorry so she said nothing at all. She stood and looked down at her feet. She listened to the soft scuffles of the wallabies out in the garden. She thought…she thought…

'Please?'

And the outside world broke in. The one word was a harsh plea, reverberating through the stillness and it came from neither of them. She turned and so did Rob.

Henry was in the open doorway, his hands held out in entreaty.

'Please,' he said again. 'Can either of you...do either of you know...?'

'What?' Rob said. 'Henry, what's wrong?'

'It's Amina,' Henry stammered. 'She says the baby's coming.'

# CHAPTER EIGHT

ALL THE WAY to the bedroom Julie hoped Henry might be mistaken. They reached the guest room, however, and one look told her that there could be no mistake about this. Amina was crouched by the bed, holding onto the bed post, clinging as if drowning. She swung round as Julie entered and her eyes were filled with panic.

'It can't come. It's too early. I can't…last time it was so… I can't do this.'

*Right. Okay.*

'And it's breech,' Amina moaned. 'It was supposed to turn; otherwise the doctor said I might need a Caesarean…'

Breech! A baby coming and breech! Things that might best have been known when the fire crew was here, Julie thought wildly. They'd had that one chance to get away from here. If they'd known they could have insisted on help, on helicopter evacuation. Amina would surely have been a priority. But now…it was nine o'clock on Christmas night and they'd already knocked back help. What was the chance of a passing ambulance? Or a passing anything?

They were trapped. Their cars were stuck in the garage. The tree that had fallen over the driveway was still there, huge and smouldering. It had taken Henry almost twelve hours to walk up from the road blocks and he'd risked his life doing so.

'The phone…' she said without much hope, and Rob shook his head.

'I checked half an hour ago.' He rechecked then, flipping it from his pocket. 'No reception. Zip. Jules, I'll start down the mountain by foot. I might find someone with a car.'

'I didn't see an occupied house all the way up the mountain.' Henry shook his head. 'The homes that aren't burned are all evacuated. Amina, can't you stop?'

Amina said something that made them all blink. Apparently stopping was not on the agenda.

'What's wrong with Mama?' It was Danny, standing in the hall in his new Batman pyjamas. The pyjamas Julie had bought for her sons. The pyjamas that she'd thought would make her feel…make her feel…

But there wasn't time for her to feel anything. Danny's voice echoed his father's fear. Amina looked close to hysterics. Someone had to do something—now.

She was a lawyer, Julie thought wildly. She didn't do babies.

But it seemed she had no choice. By the look of Amina, this baby was coming, ready or not.

*Breech.*

'You'll be fine,' she said with a whole lot more assurance than she was feeling. 'Rob, take Danny into the living room and turn on a good loud movie. He had a nap this afternoon; he won't be sleepy. Isn't that right, Danny?'

'But what's wrong with Mama?'

She took a deep breath and squatted beside the little boy. Behind her, Henry was kneeling by his wife—remonstrating? For heaven's sake—as if Amina could switch anything off. And Danny looked terrified.

And suddenly Julie was done with terror. *Enough.*

'Danny, your mama is having a baby,' she told him.

'There's nothing to worry about. There's nothing wrong, but I suspect this is a big baby and your mama will hurt a bit as she pushes it out.'

'How will she push it out?'

'Rob will tell you,' she said grandly, 'while he finds a movie for you to watch. Won't you, Rob?'

'Um…yeah?' He looked wild-eyed and suddenly Julie was fighting an insane desire to grin. A woman in labour or teaching a kid the facts of life—what a choice.

'And your papa and I will help your mama,' she added. But…

'No.' It was Amina, staring up at them, practically yelling. 'No,' she managed again, and this time it was milder. 'It's okay, Danny,' she managed, making a supreme effort to sound normal in the face of her son's fear. 'This is what happened when I had you. It's normal. Having babies hurts, but only like pulling a big splinter out.' *As if*, Julie thought. *Right*.

'But Papa's not going to stay here.' Amina's voice firmed, becoming almost threatening, and she looked up at Julie and her eyes pleaded. 'Last time…Henry fainted. I was having Danny and suddenly the midwives were fussing over Henry because he cut his head on the floor when he fell. Henry, I love you but I don't want you here. I want you to go away.'

Which left…Julie and Rob. They met each other's gaze and Julie's chaotic thoughts were exactly mirrored in Rob's eyes.

Big breath. No, make that deep breathing. A bit of Zen calm. Where was a nice safe monastery when she needed one?

'Give us a moment,' she said to Amina. 'Henry, no fainting yet. Help Amina into bed, then you and Danny can leave the baby delivering to us. We can do this, can't we, Rob?'

'I…'

'*You* won't faint on me,' she said in a voice of steel.

'I guess I won't,' Rob managed. 'If you say so—I guess I wouldn't dare.'

She propelled him out into the passage and closed the door. They stared at each other in a moment of mutual panic, while each of them fought for composure.

'We can't do this,' Rob said.

'We don't have a choice.'

'I don't have the first clue…'

'I've read a bit.' And she had. When she was having the twins, the dot-point part of her—she was a lawyer and an accountant after all, and research was her thing— had read everything she could get her hands on about childbirth. The fact that she'd forgotten every word the moment she went into labour was immaterial. She knew it all. In theory.

'You're a lawyer, Jules,' Rob managed. 'Not an obstetrician. All you know is law.'

And she thought suddenly, fleetingly: *that's not all I have to be.*

Why was it a revelation?

Weirdly, she was remembering the day she'd got the marks to get into law school. Her hippy parents had been baffled, but Julie had been elated. From that moment she'd been a lawyer.

Even when the twins were born…she'd loved Rob to bits and she'd adored her boys but she was always a lawyer. She'd had Rob bring files into hospital after she'd delivered, so she wouldn't fall behind.

*All you know is law…*

For the last four years law had been her cave, her hiding place. Her all. The night the boys were killed they'd been running late because of her work and Rob's work.

Rob had started skiing, she thought inconsequentially and then she thought that maybe it was time she did something different too. Like delivering babies?

The whole concept took a nanosecond to wash through her mind but, strangely, it settled her.

'We don't even have the Internet,' Rob groaned.

'I have books.'

'Books?'

'You know: things with pages. I bought every birth book I could get my hands on when the twins were due. They'll still be in the bookcase.'

'You intend to deliver a breech baby with one hand while you hold the book in the other?'

'That's where you come in, Rob McDowell,' she snapped. 'From this moment we're a united team. I want hot water, warm towels and a professional attitude.'

'I'm an architect!'

'Not tonight you're not,' she told him. 'It's still Christmas. You played Santa this morning. Now you need to put your midwife hat on and deliver again.'

She'd sounded calm enough when she'd talked to Rob but, as she stood in front of her small library of childbirth books, she felt the calm slip away.

*What...? How...?*

*Steady*, she told herself. *Think.* She stared at the myriad titles and tried to decide.

Not for the first time in her life, she blessed her memory. Read it once, forget it never. Obviously she couldn't remember every detail in these books—some parts she'd skimmed over fast. But the thing with childbirth, she'd figured, was that almost anyone could do it. Women had been doing it since time immemorial and they'd done it without the help of books. Ninety-nine times out of a hundred there were no problems; all the midwife had to do was encourage, support, catch and clean up.

But the one per cent…

Julie had become just a trifle obsessive in the last weeks of her pregnancy. She therefore had books with pictures of unthinkable outcomes. She remembered Rob had found her staring in horror at a picture of conjoined twins, and a mother who'd laboured for days before dying. *Extreme Complications of Pregnancy*. He'd taken that book straight to the shredder, but she had others.

Breech, she thought frantically, fingering one title after another. There were all sorts of complications with breech deliveries and she'd read them all.

But…but…

*Ninety-nine per cent of babies are born normally,* she told herself and she kept on thinking of past reading. *Breech is more likely to be a problem in first time mothers because the perineum is unproven.* Or words to that effect? She'd read that somewhere and she remembered thinking if her firstborn twin was breech it might be a problem, but if the book was right the second twin would be a piece of cake regardless.

'You're smiling!'

Rob had come into the living room and was staring at her in astonishment.

'No problem. We can do this.' And she hauled out one of the slimmest tomes on the shelf, almost a booklet, written by a midwife and not a doctor. It was well thumbed. She'd read it over and over because in the end it had been the most comforting.

She flicked until she found what she was looking for, and there were the words again. *If the breech is a second baby it's much less likely to require intervention*. But it did sound a warning. *Avoid home birth unless you're near good medical backup.*

There wasn't a lot of backup here. One architect, one lawyer, one fainting engineer and a four-year-old. Plus a first aid box containing sticking plasters, tweezers and antiseptic.

*Breech...* She flipped to the page she was looking for and her eyes widened. Rob looked over her shoulder and she felt him stiffen. 'My God...'

'We can do this.' *Steady*, she told herself. *If I don't stay calm, who will?* 'Look,' she said. 'We have step by step instructions with pictures. It's just like buying a desk and assembling it at home, following instructions. Besides, if we need to intervene, we can, but it says we probably won't need to. It's big on hands off.'

'But if we do? You know me and kit furniture—it always ends up with screws left over and one side wonkier than the other. And look what it says! If it's facing upward, head for hospital because...'

'There's no need to think like that,' she snapped. 'We need to stay positive. That means calm, Rob.' And she thought back, remembering. 'Forget the kit furniture analogy. Yes, you're a terrible carpenter but as a first time dad you were great. You are great. You need to be like you were with me, every step of the way. No matter how terrified I was, you were there saying how brave I was, how well I was doing, and you sounded so calm, so sure...'

'I wasn't in the least sure. I was a mess.'

'So you're a good actor. Put the act on again.'

'This isn't you we're talking about. Jules, I could do it when I had to.'

'Then you have to now.' She took a long, hard look at the diagrams, committing them to memory. Hoping to heaven she wouldn't need them. 'Amina has us. Rob, together we can do this.'

'Okay.' He took a deep breath while he literally squared his shoulders. 'If you say so, maybe we can.' Then suddenly he tugged her to him and hugged her, hard, and gave her a swift firm kiss. 'Maybe that's what I've been saying all along. Apart we're floundering. Together we might...'

'Be able to have a baby? Do you have those towels warming?' The kiss had left her flustered, but she regrouped fast.

'Yes, ma'am.'

'I'll need sterilised scissors.'

'I already thought of that. They're in a pot on the barbecue. So all we need is one baby.' He cupped her chin and smiled down at her. 'Okay, Dr McDowell, do you have your dot-point plan ready? I hope you do because we're in your hands.'

Breech births were supposed to be long. Weren't they? Surely they were supposed to take longer than normal labours, but no one seemed to have told Amina's baby that. When Rob and Julie returned to her room she was mid-contraction and one look at her told them both that this was some contraction. Surely a contraction shouldn't be as all-consuming if it was early labour.

Henry and Danny were looking appalled but Henry was looking even more appalled than his son. He'd fainted at Danny's birth, but then refugees did it tough, Rob thought, and who knew what the circumstances had been? Today he'd literally walked through fire to reach his family. He must be past exhaustion. He'd cut him some slack—and, besides, if Henry left with Danny, it would be Henry who'd have to explain childbirth to his son.

He put his hand on Henry's shoulder and gripped, hard.

'We can do this, mate,' he said. 'At least, Julie can and I'm here to assist. Julie suggested I take Danny into the living room and turn on a movie. If it's okay with Amina, how about you take my place? We have a pile of kids' movies. Pick a loud, exciting one and watch it until you both go to sleep. Hug Luka and know everything's okay. Danny, your mama's about to have a baby and she needs to be able to yell a bit while she does. It's okay, honest, most mamas yell when they have babies. So if you hear yelling, don't you worry. Snuggle up with your papa and Luka, and when you wake up in the morning I reckon your mama will have a baby to show you. Is that okay, Henry?'

'I'll stay,' Henry quavered. 'If you want me to, Amina...'

'Leave,' Amina ordered, easing back from the contraction enough to manage a weak smile at her husband and then her son. 'It's okay, sweetheart,' she told Danny. 'This baby has to push its way out and I have to squeeze and squeeze and it's easier for me if I can yell when I squeeze. Papa's going to show you a movie and Julie and Rob are going to stay with me to take care of the baby when it's born.'

'Can I come back and see it—when it's born?'

'Yes.'

'And will it be a boy?'

'I don't know,' Amina told him. 'But, Danny, take your papa away because I have to squeeze again and Papa doesn't like yelling. You look after Papa, okay?'

'And watch a movie?'

'Yes,' Amina managed through gritted teeth. Julie got behind Henry and practically propelled him and his son through the door and closed it behind them, and it was just as well because Amina was true to her word.

She yelled.

* * *

*Hands off. Do not interfere unless you have to.* That was the mantra the little book extolled and that was fine by Julie because there didn't seem to be an alternative.

She and Rob both washed, scrupulously on Julie's part, the way she'd seen it done on television. Rob looked at her with her arms held out, dripping, and gave a rueful chuckle. 'Waiting for a nurse to apply latex gloves?'

'The only gloves I have are the ones I use for the washing-up. I'm dripping dry,' she retorted and then another contraction hit and any thought of chuckling went out of the window.

'Hey,' Rob said, hauling a chair up by Amina's bedside. 'It's okay. Yell as much as you want. We're used to it. You should have heard Julie when she had the twins. I'd imagine you could have heard her in Sri Lanka.'

'But…but she knows…what to do? Your Julie?'

'My Julie knows what to do,' Rob told her, taking her hand. 'My Julie's awesome.'

And how was a woman to react to that? Julie felt her eyes well, but then Rob went on.

'My Julie's also efficient. She'll help you get through this faster than anyone I know. And if there's any mucking around she'll know who to sue. She's a fearsome woman, my Julie, so let's just put ourselves in her hands, Amina, love, and get this baby born.'

Which meant there was no time for welling eyes, no time for emotion. There was a baby to deliver.

By unspoken agreement, Rob stayed by Amina's side and did what a more together Henry should have done, while Julie stayed at the business end of the bed.

The instructions in her little booklet played over and over in her head, giving her a clear plan of action. How close? Julie had no clue. She couldn't see the baby yet but, with the power of these contractions, it surely wouldn't be long before she did.

She felt useless, but at the other end of the bed Rob was a lot more help.

'Come on, Amina, you can do this. Every contraction brings your baby closer. You're being terrific. Did anyone ever teach you how to breathe? You do it like this between contractions...' And he proceeded to demonstrate puffing as he'd learned years before in Julie's antenatal classes. 'It really works. Julie said so.'

Julie had said no such thing, she thought. She'd said a whole lot of things during her long labour but she couldn't remember saying anything complimentary about anything.

And Amina was in a similar mood. When Rob waited until the next contraction passed and then encouraged Amina to puff again, he got told where he could put his puffing.

'And it's breech,' she gasped. 'Julie doesn't know about breech.'

'Julie knows everything,' Rob declared. 'Memory like a bull elephant, my Julie. Tell us the King of Spain in 1703, Jules.'

'Philip Five,' Julie said absently.

'Name a deadly mushroom?'

'Conocybe? Death caps? How many do you want?'

'And tell me what's different about breech?'

'I might have to do a little rotating as the baby comes out,' Julie said, trying to sound as if it was no big deal.

'There you go, then,' Rob approved as Amina disappeared into another contraction. 'She knows it all. This'll be a piece of cake for our Julie.'

Only it wasn't. Rob had managed to calm Amina; there no longer seemed to be terror behind the pain, but there was certainly a fair bit of terror behind Julie's façade of competence.

One line in the little book stood out. *If the baby's presenting face up then there's no choice; it must be a Caesarean.*

Any minute now she'd know. *Dear God...*

Her mind was flying off at tangents as she waited. Was there any other option? They couldn't go for help. They couldn't ring anyone. For heaven's sake, they couldn't even light a fire and send out smoke signals. If it was face up...

'And my Julie always stays calm,' Rob said, and his voice was suddenly stern, cutting across the series of yelps Amina was making. 'That's what I love about her. That's why you're in such good hands, Amina. Are you sure you don't want to puff?'

Amina swore and slapped at his hand and a memory came back to Julie—she'd done exactly the same thing. She'd even bruised him. The day after the twins were born she'd looked at a blackening bruise on her husband's arm, and she'd also seen marks on his palm where her nails had dug in.

Her eyes met his and he smiled, a faint gentle smile that had her thinking...*memories can be good.* The remembrance of Rob's comfort. Her first sight of her babies.

The love...

Surely that love still deserved to live. Surely it shouldn't be put away for ever in the dusty recesses of her mind, locked away because letting it out hurt?

Surely Rob was right to relive those memories. To let them make him smile...

But then Amina gasped and struggled and Rob supported her as she tried to rise. She grasped her knees and she pushed.

Stage two. Stage two, stage two, stage two.

Face up, face down. *Please, please, please...*

There was a long, loaded pause and Amina actually puffed. But still she held her knees while the whole world seemed to hold its breath.

Another contraction. Another push.

Julie could see it. She could see...what? *What?*

A backside. A tiny bottom.

Face down. *Oh, God, face down. Thank you, thank you, thank you.* She glanced up at Rob and her relief must have shown in her face. He gave her a fast thumbs-up and then went back to holding, encouraging, being...Rob.

She loved him. She loved him with all her heart but now wasn't the time to get corny. Now was the time to try and deliver this baby.

*Hands off.* That was what the book said. *Breech babies will often deliver totally on their own.*

*Please...*

But they'd been lucky once. They couldn't ask for twice. Amina pushed, the baby's bottom slid out so far but as the contraction receded, so did the baby.

Over and over.

Exhaustion was starting to set in. Time for Dr Julie to take a hand? Did she dare?

Another glance at Rob, and his face was stern. He'd read the book over her shoulder, seen the pictures, figured what was expected now. His face said: *do it.*

*So do it.*

She'd set out what she'd need. Actually, she'd set out what she had. The book said if the head didn't come, then forceps might be required. She didn't actually have forceps or anything that could be usefully used instead.

*Please don't let them be needed.* It was a silent prayer said over and over.

*Don't think forward.* One step at a time. First she had to deliver the legs.

Dot-point number one. Carefully, she lubricated her fingers. One leg at a time. One leg…

*Remember the pictures.*

'Jules is about to help your baby out,' Rob said, his voice steady, calm, settling. 'Next push, Amina, go as far as you can and then hold. Puff, just like I said. Keep the pressure on.'

Next contraction… The baby's back slid out again. Deep breath and Julie felt along the tiny leg. What did the book say? *Manoeuvre your finger behind the knee and gently push upward. This causes the knee to flex. Hold the femur, splint it gently with your finger to prevent it breaking. This should allow the leg to…*

It did! It flopped out. *Oh, my…*

Calm. Next. Dot-point number two.

The other leg was easier. Now the baby could no longer recede. *Manoeuvre to the right position. Flex.*

Two legs delivered. She was almost delirious with hope. *Please…*

Dot-point number three. *Gently rotate the baby into the side position to allow delivery of the right arm.* Easier said than done but the illustrations had been clear. If only her hands weren't so slippery, but they had to be slippery.

'Fantastic, Jules,' Rob said. 'Fantastic, Amina. You're both doing great.'

She had the tiny body slightly rotated. Enough? It had to be. Her finger found the elbow, put her finger over the top, pressured gently, inexorably.

An arm. She'd delivered an arm. The dot-points were blurring, but she still had work to do. She was acting mostly on instinct, but thank God for the book. She'd write to the author. No, she'd send the author half her kingdom. All her kingdom.

She suddenly thought of the almost obscene amount of money she'd been earning these past years and thought...

And thought there was another arm to go and then the head, and the head was...

'Jules. We're doing great,' Rob growled and she glanced up at him and thought he'd seen the shiver of panic and he was grounding her again.

He'd always grounded her. She needed him.

Her hands held the tiny body, took a grip, lifted as the book said, thirty degrees so the left arm was in position for delivery. She twisted as the next contraction eased. The baby rotated like magic.

She found the elbow and pushed gently down. The left arm slithered out.

Now the head. *Please, God, the head.* She didn't have forceps. She wouldn't have the first clue what to do with forceps if she had them.

'Lift,' Rob snapped and he was echoing the book too. 'Come on, Jules, you know what the book says. Come on, Amina. Our baby's so close. We can do this.'

*Our baby...*

It sounded good. It sounded right.

'Next contraction, puff afterwards, ease off until Jules has the baby in position,' Rob urged Amina, and magically she did.

Amina was working so hard. Surely she could do the same.

She steadied. Waited. The next contraction passed. Amina puffed, Rob held her hand and murmured gentle words. 'Hold, Amina, hold, we're so close...'

*Do it.*

She held the baby, resting it on her right hand. She manoeuvred her hand so two fingers were on the side of the tiny jaw. With her other hand she put her middle finger on the back of the baby's head.

It sounded easy. It wasn't. She lifted the baby as high as she could, remembering the pictures, remembering…

So much sweat. She needed…she needed…

'You're doing great, Jules,' Rob said. 'Amina, your baby's so close. Maybe one more push. This is fantastic. Let's do this, people. Okay, Jules?'

'O…Okay.' She nodded. She'd forgotten how to breathe. *Please…*

'Okay, Amina, push,' Rob ordered and Amina pushed—and the next second Julie had a healthy, lusty, slippery bundle of baby girl in her arms.

She gasped and staggered but she had her. She had Amina's baby.

Safe. Delivered.

And seconds later a tiny girl was lying on her mother's tummy. Amina was sobbing with joy, and a new little life had begun.

After that things happened in a blur. Waiting for the afterbirth and checking it as the book had shown. Clearing up. Watching one tiny girl find her mother's breast. Ushering an awed and abashed Henry into the room, with Danny by his side.

Watching the happiness. Watching the little family cling. Watching the love and the pride, and then backing out into the night, their job done.

Julie reached the passage, leaned against the wall and sagged.

But she wasn't allowed to sag for long. Her husband had her in his arms. He held her and held her and held her, and she felt his heart beat against hers and she thought: *here is my home.*

*Here is my family.*

*Here is my heart.*

'Love, I need to check the boundaries again,' he said at last, ruefully, and she thought with a jolt: *fire.* She hadn't thought of the fire for hours. But of course he was right. There'd still be embers falling around them. They should have kept checking.

'We should have told Henry to check,' she managed.

'Do you think he would have even seen an ember? You take a shower. I'll be with you soon.'

'Rob...' she managed.

'Mmm?'

'I love you,' she whispered.

'I love you too, Dr McDowell.' He kissed her on the tip of the nose and then put her away. 'But then, I always have. All we need to do now is to figure some way forward. Think of it in the shower, my Jules. Think of me. Now, go get yourself clean again while I rid myself of my obstetric suit and put on my fireman's clothes. Figuring roles for ourselves... This day's thrown plenty at us. Think about it, Jules, love. What role do you want for the rest of your life?'

And he was gone, off to play fireman.

While Julie was left to think about it.

There was little to think about—and yet there was lots. She thought really fast while she let the water stream over her. Then she towelled dry, donned her robe and headed back out onto the veranda.

Rob was just finishing, heading up the steps with his bucket and mop.

'Not a single ember,' he announced triumphantly. 'Not

a spark. After today I doubt an ember would dare come close. Have I told you recently that we rock? If I didn't think Amina might be asleep already I'd puff out my chest and do a yodel worthy of Tarzan.'

'Riiiight…'

'It's true. In fact I feel a yodel coming on right this minute. But not here. Do you fancy wandering up the hill a little and yodelling with me?'

And it was such a crazy idea that she thought: *why not?* But then, she was in a robe and slippers and she should…

*No.* She shouldn't think of reasons not to. *Move forward.*

'That's something I need to hear,' she said and grinned. 'A Tarzan yodel… Wow.' She grabbed his mop, tossed it aside, took his hand and hauled him out into the night.

'Jules! I didn't mean…'

'To yodel? Rob McDowell, if you think I'm going through what we've gone through without listening to you yodel, you're very much mistaken.'

'What have I done?' But Rob was helpless in her hands as she hauled him round the back of the bunker, up through the rocks that formed the back of their property, along a burned out trail that led almost straight up—it was so rocky here that no trees grew, which made it safe from the remnants of fire—and out onto a rock platform where usually she could see almost all over the Blue Mountains.

She couldn't see the Blue Mountains tonight. The pall of smoke was still so thick she could hardly see the path, but the smoke was lifting a little. They could sometimes see a faint moon, with smoke drifting over, sending them from deep dark to a little sight and back again. It didn't matter, though. They weren't here to see the moon or the Blue Mountains. They were here…to yodel.

'Right,' Julie said as they reached the platform. 'Go ahead.'

'Really?'

'Was it all hot air? You never meant it?'

He chuckled. 'It won't be pretty.'

'I'm not interested in pretty!'

'Well, you asked for it.' And he breathed in, swelled, pummelled his chest—and yodelled.

It was a truly heroic yodel. It made Julie double with laughter. It made her feel…feel…as if she was thirteen years old again, in love for the first time and life was just beginning.

It was a true Tarzan yodel.

'You've practised,' she said accusingly. 'No one could make a yodel sound that good first try.'

'My therapist said I should let go my anger,' he told her. 'It started with standing in the shower and yelling at the soap. After a while I started experimenting elsewhere.'

'Moving on?'

'It's what you have to do.'

'Rob…'

'I know,' he said. 'You haven't. But you will. Try it yourself. Open your mouth and yell.' And he stood back and dared her with his eyes. He was laughing, with her, though, not at her. Daring her to laugh with him. Daring her to yodel?

And finally, amazingly, it felt as if she could. How long had it been since she'd felt this free? This alive? Maybe never. Even when they were courting, even when the twins were born, she'd always felt the constraints of work. The constraints of life. But now…

Rob's hands were exerting a gentle pressure but that pressure was no constraint. She was facing outward into the rest of the world.

She was facing outward into the rest of her life.

'Can you do it?' Rob asked, and he kissed the nape of her neck. 'Not that I doubt you. My wife can do anything.'

And she could. Or at least maybe she could.

Deep breath. Pummel a little.

Yodel.

And she was doing it, yodelling like a mad woman, and she took another breath and tried again and this time Rob joined her.

It was crazy. It was ridiculous.

It was fun.

'We've delivered a Christmas baby,' Rob managed as finally they ran out of puff, as finally they ran out of yodel. 'A new life. And we're learning Christmas yodelling duets! Is there nothing we're not capable of? Happy Christmas, Mrs McDowell, and, by the way, will you marry me? Again? Make our vows again? I know we're not divorced but it surely feels like we have been. Can we be a family? Can we take our past and live with it? Can we love what we've had, and love each other again for the rest of our lives?'

And the smoke suddenly cleared. Everything cleared. Rob was standing in front of her, he was holding her and the future was hers to grasp and to hold.

And in the end there was nothing to say except the most obvious response in the whole world.

'Why, yes, Mr McDowell,' she whispered. 'Happy Christmas, my love, and yes, I believe I will marry you again. I believe I will marry you—for ever.'

# CHAPTER NINE

A RETAKING OF weddings vows shouldn't be as romantic as the first time around. That was what Julie's mother had read somewhere, but she watched her daughter marry for the second time and she thought: *what do 'they' know?*

People go into a second marriage with their eyes wide open, with all the knowledge of the trials and pitfalls of marriage behind them, and yet they choose to step forward again, and step forward with joy. Because they know what love is. Because they know that, despite the hassles and the day-to-day trivia, and sometimes despite the tragedy and the heartache, they know that love is worth it.

So Julie's mother held her husband's hand and watched her daughter retake her vows, and felt her heart swell with pride. They'd ached every step of the way with their daughter. They'd ached for their grandsons and for the hurt they'd known their son-in-law must be feeling. But in the end they'd stopped watching. Julie had driven them away, as she'd driven away most people in her life. But somehow one magical Christmas had brought healing.

It was almost Easter now. Julie had wanted to get on with their lives with no fuss, but Rob wasn't having any part of such a lame new beginning. 'I watch people have parties for their new homes,' he'd said. 'How much more important is this? We're having a party for our new lives.'

And they would be new lives. So much had changed.

They'd moved—Julie from her sterile apartment in Sydney, Rob from his bachelor pad in Adelaide—but they'd decided not to move back to the Blue Mountains. Amina and Henry were in desperate need of a house—'and we need to move on,' they'd told them.

Together they'd found a ramshackle weatherboard cottage on the beach just south of Sydney. They'd both abandoned their jobs for the duration and were tackling the house with energy and passion—if not skill. It might end up a bit wonky round the edges, but already it felt like home.

But... *Home. Home is where the heart is,* so somehow, some way, it felt right that their vows were being made back here. On the newly sprouting gardens around Amina and Henry's home in the Blue Mountains, where there was love in spades. Amina and Henry had been overjoyed when Rob and Julie had asked to have the ceremony here.

'Because your love brought us together again,' Julie had told Amina. 'You and Henry, with your courage and your love for each other.'

'You were together all the time,' Amina had whispered, holding her baby daughter close. 'You just didn't know it.'

Rob and Julie were now godparents. More. They were landlords and they were also sponsoring Henry through retraining. There'd be no more working in the mines. No more long absences. This family deserved to stay together.

As did Julie and Rob.

'I asked you this seven years ago,' the celebrant said, smiling mistily at them. She must have seen hundreds of weddings, but did she mist up for all of them? Surely not. 'But I can't tell you the joy it gives me to ask you again. Rob, do you take Julie—again—to be your lawful wedded wife, to love and to cherish, in sickness and in health, forsaking all others, for as long as you both shall live?'

'I do—and the rest,' Rob said softly, speaking to Julie and to Julie alone. 'Beyond the grave I'll love you. Love doesn't end with death. We both know that. Love keeps going and going and going, if only we let it. Will we let it? Will we let it, my love?'

'Yes, please,' Julie whispered, and then she, too, made her vows.

And Mr McDowell married Mrs McDowell—again—and the thing was done.

Christmas morning.

Julie woke early and listened to the sounds of the surf just below the house. She loved this time of day. Once upon a time she'd listened to galahs and cockatoos in the bush around their house. Now she listened to the sounds of the waves and the sandpipers and oystercatchers calling to each other as they hunted on the shore of a receding tide.

Only that wasn't right, she told herself. She'd never lain in bed and listened to the sounds of birds in the bush. She'd been too busy working. Too busy with her dot-points.

But now… They'd slowed, almost to a crawl. Her dot-points had grown fewer and fewer. Rob worked from home, his gorgeous house plans sprawled over his massive study at the rear of the house. Julie commuted to Sydney twice a week, and she, too, worked the rest of the time at home.

But they didn't work so much that they couldn't lie in bed and listen to the surf. And love each other. And start again.

She'd stop commuting soon, she thought in satisfaction. She could maybe still accept a little contract work, as long as it didn't mess with her life. With her love.

With her loves?

And, unbidden, her hand crept to her tummy, where her secret lay.

She couldn't wait a moment longer. She rolled over and kissed her husband, tenderly but firmly.

'Wake up,' she told him. 'It's Christmas.'

'So it is.' He woke with laughter, reaching for her, holding her, kissing her. 'Happy Christmas, wife.'

'Happy Christmas, husband.'

'I have the best Christmas gift for you,' he said, pushing himself up so he was smiling down at her with all the tenderness in the world. 'I bet you can't guess what it is.'

She choked on laughter. Last night he'd driven home late and on the roof rack of his car was a luridly wrapped Christmas present, complete with a huge Christmas bow. It was magnificently wrapped but all the wrapping in the world couldn't disguise the fact that it was a surfboard.

'I have no idea,' she lied. 'I can't wait.'

They'd come so far, she thought, as Rob gathered her into his arms. This year would be so different from the past. All their assorted family was coming for lunch, as were Amina and Henry and their children. For family came in all sorts of assorted sizes and shapes. It changed. Tragedies happened but so did joys. Christmas was full of memories, and each memory was to be treasured, used to shape the future with love and with hope and memories to come.

And dot-points, she thought suddenly. There were—what?—twenty people due for lunch. Loving aside, smugness aside, she had to get organised. Dot-point number one. Stuff the turkey.

But Rob was holding her—and she had her gift for him.

So: *soon*, she told her dot-point, and proceeded to indulge her husband. And herself.

'Do you want your present now?' she asked as they finally resurfaced, though she couldn't get her mind to be practical quite yet.

'I have everything I need right here.'

'Are you sure?'

'What more could a man want?'

She smiled. She smiled and she smiled. She'd been holding this secret for almost two weeks and it had almost killed her not to tell him, but now… She tugged away from his arms, then kissed him on the nose and settled on her back. And tugged his hand to her naked tummy.

She could scarcely feel it herself. Could he…? Would he…?

But he got it in one. She saw his eyes widen in shock. He was clever, her husband. He was loving and tender and wise. He was a terrible handyman—her kitchen shelves were a disaster and she was hoping her dad might stay on long enough to fix them—but a woman couldn't have everything.

Actually, she did. She did have everything. Her husband was looking down at her with awe and tenderness and love.

'Really?' he whispered.

'Really.'

And she saw him melt, just like that. A blaze of joy that took her breath away.

Joy… They had so much, and this baby was more. For it was true what they said: *love doesn't die*. The memories of Christopher and Aiden would stay with them for ever—tender, joyous, always mourned but an intrinsic part of her family. Their family. Hers and Rob's.

'Happy Christmas, Daddy,' she murmured and she kissed him long and hard. 'Happy Christmas, my love.'

'Do you suppose it might be twins again?' he breathed, awed beyond belief, and she smiled and smiled.

'Who knows? Whoever it is, we'll love them for ever.

Like I love you. Now, are you going to make love to me again or are you going to let me go? I hate to mention it but I have all these dot-points to attend to.'

'But here is your number one dot-point,' he said smugly, and gathered her into his arms yet again. 'The turkey can wait. Christmas can wait. Number one is us.'

\* \* \* \* \*

# REUNITED UNDER THE MISTLETOE

**SUSAN MEIER**

# CHAPTER ONE

"THE QUEEN SENDS her regrets."

*The Queen?*

Autumn Jones stifled a laugh. She knew Ivy Jenkins's society wedding would be packed with a who's who of guests...but the Queen?

She glanced around the office of Ivy's Park Avenue townhouse. Decorated for Christmas, the whole place could have been taken from the pages of a high-end style magazine because Ivy was Manhattan royalty. Autumn, the most average woman on the face of the earth with her mid-length auburn hair and hazel eyes, should have felt out of place, but because of Raise Your Voice, the charity where Ivy volunteered and Autumn worked, she and Ivy had become close. Not just friends. More like sisters.

As Ivy's assistant handed a Tiffany's box to her, a gift in lieu of the Queen's appearance, dark-haired, green-eyed Ivy arched one perfectly shaped eyebrow. "She's seriously not coming? Are you kidding me?"

This time Autumn couldn't hold back the laugh. Sometimes Ivy's life amazed her. "You weren't actually expecting *the* Queen to come to your wedding?"

"No. I just thought she'd RSVP by the November twenty-eighth deadline. Not two days after. For Pete's sake, where is her staff?" She pointed at the seating chart she and Autumn had been reviewing in front of a marble fireplace rimmed with evergreen branches and bright red ornaments. "Look, she has a seat...two. One for her. One for her guest. Because Alexandra, the wedding planner, made this chart based on RSVPs."

Autumn shook her head. It was exactly two weeks until the wedding and though Ivy was as polished as ever, her nerves were beginning to fray. Not a lot. She'd been one of Manhattan's elite her entire life. She knew how to be a lady, and she liked to throw a party— two reasons why Autumn and Ivy had bonded at Raise Your Voice, a charity created to assist underprivileged women who needed help climbing the ranks of corporate America. Ivy had the connections and Autumn had the skills to host events that raised millions.

As Ivy handed the Tiffany's box back to her assistant who walked it to the table with the other wedding gifts, the office door opened again. Sebastian Davis, CEO of one of New York's most exciting tech startups and Ivy's fiancé, entered. Wearing a dark suit and white shirt with a thin gray tie, he looked ready for the board meeting Autumn knew he had that crisp Saturday.

"Good morning, everybody."

Ivy and Autumn said, "Good morning."

He bent down and bussed a quick kiss across Ivy's cheek. "More gifts?"

Ivy rolled her eyes. "And late RSVPs. We're looking at the seating chart before I approve it for Alexandra." She took a quick breath. "Did you know the Queen wasn't coming?"

He winced. "No. But it takes a lot to get her to travel to America these days. Besides, the royals from Adria are coming. That's enough royalty for anybody's wedding." He headed for the door again. "I'll see you at dinner." But he stopped suddenly and pivoted to face them. "By the way, Autumn, your partner for the wedding is having dinner with us tonight and I was hoping you would join us."

Ivy clapped. "Oh, great idea!" She turned to Autumn. "I cannot wait for you to meet Jack."

Autumn happily said, "Okay. I don't think I have plans on my calendar for tonight, but even if I do, I'm sure I can reschedule. Anything you need in the next two weeks, I'm your girl."

"Good," Sebastian said.

Ivy smiled.

She rose from her chair, grabbing her purse and briefcase from the floor beside it. "I should get to work, too."

Sebastian waited for her at the office door. "You're going into your office on a Saturday?"

"Most of our clients have Monday through Friday jobs. Saturdays are when they have time for appointments with our mentors."

Sebastian smiled. "Makes sense. Can I give you a lift?"

"No. I'm fine."

They walked into the main foyer, a space so elegant it could have been in a museum. The sound of their heels clicking on the marble floor echoed around them.

Sebastian opened the black and etched glass front door for her. She stepped out with a murmured, "Thanks," for Sebastian, but when she looked toward the street, she blinked and did a double take.

Leaning against Sebastian's black limo was a big, fat unresolved piece of Autumn's past—

Jack Adams.

Tall and thin and wearing a dark suit and black overcoat in the cold last-day-of-November air, he looked every inch a mogul like Sebastian.

His blue eyes met hers across the sidewalk. He pushed off the fender of the limo.

Sebastian said, "Hey! You're here!"

"I wanted to catch a ride to the board meeting. Thought I could run my new management system by you while we drove."

Sebastian motioned to the car. "Great. Get in." Then he faced Autumn. "Autumn, this is Jack Adams, your partner for the wedding."

Jack held her gaze. He didn't make a move to tell his friend Sebastian they already knew each other. In fact, he extended his hand to shake hers, like they were strangers meeting for the first time.

*Oh, dear God! Maybe he didn't remember her!*

"Jack, this is Autumn Jones."

Their hands met, wrapped around each other and bobbed up and down once. Feeling like a deer in the headlights, Autumn could only stare at him. She'd think she had the wrong guy—Jack Adams was a common name—but she'd remember those blue eyes anywhere. Five years had been very kind to him. Not only did he appear smooth and polished, but also he was just plain gorgeous.

In that second, she could forgive herself for their one-night stand. Because had it been up to her, it would have been more than a one-night stand. But looking at him now, she could see why he hadn't thought of her as anything other than a passing fancy.

He was well dressed, sophisticated, obviously rich.

And she was still Autumn Jones, outreach officer for Raise Your Voice. She had the same car, same apartment, same job… Good God. It was like she was stuck in a time warp.

"It's nice to meet you Mr. Adams…"

He almost smiled. "Jack."

*Or maybe he did remember her?*

Her heart thrummed as she recalled some particularly *interesting* parts of their encounter.

A blush crept up her cheeks. "Sure. Sure. Jack."

Sebastian said, "Sorry, Autumn. Don't mean to rush off but we've got to get going."

"Me too." She pointed to the right. "I'm picking up a birthday cake at the bakery—"

Her voice trailed off and she fought to keep her eyes from squeezing shut in misery. Her biggest claim to fame was that she was the office birthday girl. She remembered the date, bought the cake, got the card signed.

*No fancy job. Not married. Not dating. Still ten pounds overweight.*

Yeah, Fate. She got it. No sense in rubbing salt into the wound.

She pivoted to head to the bakery.

"Nice to meet you, too, Autumn."

Jack's smooth voice stopped her dead in her tracks as it washed over her like good whiskey. Which, if she remembered correctly, had been his drink of choice.

Refusing to think about that night, that wonderful night that could have stayed in her memory like the plot of a favorite movie if he hadn't unceremoniously disappeared from her bed, she faced him again.

She said, "Thanks," then quickly turned to go.

Before she got two steps down the block, Sebastian called, "Don't forget dinner tonight!"

This time she did squeeze her eyes shut. Seriously?

She had to endure dinner with him? She groaned. And the *entire* day of the wedding?

She straightened her shoulders. Damned if she'd let that hurt or upset her. She might be stuck in the past, but she was a mature adult. And no matter how successful he was, he was an oaf. He'd swept her off her feet then sneaked out in the middle of the night. No goodbye. No call the next day. Or the next week. Or the next month.

Yeah. She was over him.

She popped her eyes open then faced Sebastian and Jack again with a smile. "I won't forget!" she said with a wave, hoping to speedily spin around and get out of there—

But her eyes met Jack's and she suddenly felt tall and why-hadn't-she-ever-buckled-down-and-lost-those-ten-pounds? clumsy.

Damn it! What the hell was it about this guy that she couldn't step out of idiot mode?

Waking up in her empty bed the day after the most romantic night of her life had been embarrassing and soul crushing, but she'd moved on.

Really.

Seeing him shouldn't even be a blip on her radar screen!

But if the tightening of her chest was anything to go by, it hadn't quite been the nonevent she'd convinced herself it was.

She said, "Goodbye," pivoted and raced away, her heart heavy.

Yeah. It truly hadn't been the nonevent she'd convinced herself it was.

Jack Adams stared out the darkened window of Sebastian's limo.

Of all the people to be his partner for Sebastian and

Ivy's wedding… Autumn Jones? The woman who reminded him of the worst day of his life?

"You wanted to talk about your new management system?"

"Not really the system itself," he said, glancing at Sebastian. "The provider. I've got it narrowed down to three. I wanted to see if you'd heard of any of them."

Sebastian chuckled. "You mean you wanted to see if I knew any dirt on any of them."

Jack snorted. "Yeah."

"Okay, who are you considering?"

Jack opened his briefcase and handed Sebastian his short list.

Sebastian scanned it. "Two are relatively new. But this one," he said, pointing at a name on the list, "has been around forever. That's always a nudge in their favor…"

"That's the group we were thinking about working with." Jack put the list back in his briefcase.

"So, you're good?"

"Yeah, I'm good."

Sebastian eyeballed him. "You don't look good. You look like you swallowed a live fish."

Jack gaped at him. "A live fish?"

"Yeah. Something that didn't go down well."

This was why Sebastian was rolling in success. A genius with a keen business sense wasn't unheard of. A genius who could read people like short books? Not so easy to find.

"Maybe I'm just making too big of a deal about the management system. After all, there are prepackaged systems for restaurants…especially companies with multiple sites."

"Or maybe you're avoiding the subject."

Jack reached for a bottle of water from the small

fridge beside the limo's minibar. There was no way he'd tell Sebastian about his night with Autumn. Partially because he didn't want to embarrass her. Partially because it had taken him years to erase that night from his brain. He didn't want to bring it up again.

"You know that anybody who runs a company is always thinking. Always preoccupied." He opened the water and took a long drink.

"Yeah, I get it." Sebastian nudged Jack's bicep. "But how about being present tonight. Who knows? You might just hit it off with Autumn."

Jack swallowed so hard and so fast, he almost choked. "She seems like a very nice woman but..."

Sebastian frowned at Jack. "But what? She's not your type?"

"I don't have a type."

"Of course, you do. Cool brunettes who don't ever really get to know you because they're shallow and you pretend to be somebody else. And at least two of them were crazy."

"That's not true."

Sebastian only looked at him. "Not even the one who stole from you? Or the one who burned down your beach house?"

Jack grimaced. He had horrible luck choosing women. Everyone but Autumn because she'd only been a one-night stand. She hadn't had time enough to do something egregious like steal from him, cheat on him or burn down his beach house—

Which was why he now only had one-night stands. He'd gotten engaged three times out of a desperate need to feel connected, to feel normal, to have a normal life. He was over that now. Some people simply were made to stand alone. Be strong. Make their mark as a businessperson, not a family man.

"All right. It's a little true. But I finally figured out it's not a good idea for me to settle down. There are temptations in a billionaire's life." Like things to steal. "And I work hard." Leaving at least one fiancée so lonely, she'd cheated.

Sebastian snorted. "And fiancée number three had a temper."

He held back a groan. She sure had. A person had to be really angry to pour gasoline on someone's sofa, toss a match on it and walk away without a backward glance. "Yeah. She had a temper."

"But I do agree that you work hard. Maybe too hard."

"Probably." But he worked hard for his mom. For her vision. To see that vision realized. She'd come up to him the night of his first and only Raise Your Voice gala and told him she wasn't feeling well and would be taking the limo home. He thought of going with her, but he had already spotted Autumn across the room and felt like lightning had struck him. So, he'd kissed his mom's cheek and let her go.

Then he'd turned off his phone and eased through the groups gathered in the crowded ballroom to introduce himself.

While he and Autumn were laughing, dancing and eventually going back to her apartment, his mom had realized she was having a heart attack, called an ambulance, gotten herself to the hospital and ultimately died.

Seeing Autumn reminded him of his biggest failure, his greatest mistake. If getting engaged to a thief, a cheater and a woman who burned down his beach house had been bad, losing his mom because he's been bedazzled by a woman had been the worst.

He'd be a mature adult and do his part for Sebastian's wedding, but he'd limit the time he spent with Autumn. If only to keep her in the category of one-night stand and not give her the chance to prove yet again that he wasn't a good judge of women and shouldn't have relationships.

He also didn't need to be reminded that Autumn had started his run of bad luck with women.

# CHAPTER TWO

AUTUMN PULLED FOUR DRESSES from her closet, looking for something to wear to dinner. She didn't want to dress up, but she also didn't want to look out of place. Normally with an impromptu invitation she'd go home with Ivy, borrow something to wear and dress at her house. Easy-peasy.

Angry, confused, and even a little confused about why she was so angry, she couldn't risk slipping something to Ivy about Jack—*the guy who'd pretended not to know her*. Her best friend was getting married. She didn't want to spoil anything about the next two weeks for Ivy. So, she couldn't tell her about Jack dumping her. She had to look normal. Happy.

On the other hand, she didn't want Jack Adams to think she'd dressed up for him. The scoundrel. Make love to her as if she was the woman of his dreams then never call? It would be a cold, frosty day in hell before she'd dress up for him. It would be difficult enough to speak civilly to the oaf.

In the end, she chose a simple black dress, high heels and a sparkly clutch bag that she'd gotten at a second-hand store. She left her apartment, raced to the subway, and headed for the Upper East Side and Ivy's town-house again.

\* \* \*

Jack exited his limo and told the driver to return for him in two and a half hours. He was tired after the board meeting that had taken an entire day. But he also knew Sebastian and Ivy would be tired. Not only had Sebastian been with him at his board meeting, but he and Ivy were knee-deep in exhausting wedding preparations. He wouldn't overstay his welcome.

Climbing the steps to the townhouse, he also wouldn't let himself think about Autumn. Though he knew she was probably tired too if she'd spent the day at her office, he couldn't handle the feelings that rumbled through him just recalling her name. Anger with himself and grief had almost paralyzed him that day. He couldn't let seeing her bring all that up again.

He rang the bell and Ivy's longtime butler answered. "Good evening, sir."

"What's on the menu tonight, Frances?" Jack asked as he shrugged out of his overcoat and handed it to butler.

"Seared steak and polenta with *chimichurri*."

His mouth watered. "Ah. Is Chef Randolph tonight's chef?"

"Yes. It's Louis's night off. Randolph asked about you. Maybe you could stop by and say hello after dinner."

"I'll do that."

Frances took the overcoat. "Everyone's in the drawing room."

He smiled at Frances, straightened his jacket and tie and headed into the second room on the right. As soon as he stepped over the threshold, he saw her. Tall and shapely in her black dress with her shoulder-length reddish-brown hair curled in some kind of foo-foo

hairdo, she looked amazing. Feminine, yet sophisticated.

Sebastian rose from the sofa. "There he is."

Jack glanced at his watch. "I'm not late, am I?"

"No. No!" Ivy reassured as she walked over to give
him a hug. "We're just happy to see you."

He shook Sebastian's hand, then—obligated to do
so by social convention—he turned to Autumn. "Good
evening, Autumn."

She politely said, "Good evening," from her Queen
Anne chair across from the sofa. The room had been
decorated for the holiday with red and green ornaments
nestled in evergreen branches. They sat on the mantel,
looped over drapes in the big window and hugged the
bases of lamps.

Sebastian walked to the bar. "What can I get you
to drink?"

"Whiskey."

Autumn shot him a glance. She knew he drank whiskey. They'd had a night together. She *knew* things about
him. Personal, intimate things. Like his ticklish spots.
She'd laughed at them…then ran her tongue along them
to make him crazy.

He took a cleansing breath. That morning, it had
been easy to pretend he didn't know her. Tonight, it
sat like a four-ton elephant in the center of the room.
Something he and Autumn would have to walk around.
Something Sebastian and Ivy would trip over.

Of course, they wouldn't know it. They could say a
million embarrassing things, but as long as he and Autumn ignored them, everything would be fine.

Ivy said, "I heard your board meeting went well
today."

Jack snorted. "Depends on your perspective. I prefer two-hour board meetings to eight-hour board meetings."

Sebastian handed Jack his whiskey. "Then you shouldn't want to expand and need the advice of your board. A board you chose I might add."

Autumn gave him a sideways glance. "The board meeting this morning was for *your* company?"

Pain rippled through him. Any time anyone called Step Inside *his* company, it was like a knife in his chest. Step Inside had been his mother's dream. His mother's baby. Now he was running it, shaping it, enjoying the benefits of its success.

Still, he faced Autumn with a smile, not showing one iota of emotion. "Yes. We were working out details for expanding." Quickly, to prevent Sebastian from telling Autumn things Jack preferred to stay private, he added, "The original five-year plan finishes in six months, and today I was seeking approval and guidance for expansion in the next five years."

"Your plan is ambitious," Sebastian said. "But I've seen you in action. You can do just about anything you put your mind to."

"Interesting," Autumn said. "In other words, if he sets his mind on something, something he really wants…he goes after it?"

"Yes!" Sebastian wholeheartedly agreed.

Jack worked to stay tall in his chair and not slink down in embarrassment. She clearly assumed he hadn't been interested in her after their one-night stand and that was why he hadn't called her. Which was okay. He'd take the hit. From her vantage point, he had treated her terribly. But hearing her say it, backhandedly calling him out, he had to struggle not to wince.

He'd always believed Autumn had been the first in

his string of bad choices about women…so why did he suddenly feel like the villain?

Autumn said, "That's wonderful."

Before she could ask him another question or toss a barb, he smiled and said, "What about you, Autumn? You work at Raise Your Voice, right?"

She cleared her throat. "Yes."

"That's an interesting charity."

She pulled in a long breath. Her expression became like a thundercloud, as if he'd somehow insulted her.

Ivy said, "She's the go-to girl for everything. She manages their PR and is the public face of the company. She organizes most events. She supervises staff *and* the mentors who have 'office' hours on Saturdays."

A bit surprised, he peeked over at Autumn. They'd spent most of their night together dancing and making love, but he did remember she had organized the gala where they'd met.

A blush crept up her cheeks. Was she embarrassed?

In the five years since they'd seen each other, he'd taken over a company and she was still in the job she'd said was a steppingstone to—

He'd forgotten what it was a steppingstone to, but as he looked into her pretty hazel eyes, more memories formed. He remembered her in bed, naked with a tousled mess of sheets covering bits and pieces of her legs and torso, her eyes shining as she talked about things she wanted out of life. Happiness first and foremost, but also the kind of position that would come with respect.

Since she was still in the same job, he supposed the *respect* aspect of her future might not have materialized.

But all those mundane recollections were edged out by the memory of how soft she was. How touching her had felt like coming home. How she kissed in a way that made him feel he was sinking into something important.

He shook his head to dislodge the images. Those were the things that he couldn't let himself think about. Not merely to prevent the next thoughts—the phone call that woke him, racing to the hospital and being told his mother had died—but also so he wouldn't wonder what might have been.

Like the Prince in *Cinderella*, he'd felt he'd found something special, maybe even the woman of his dreams, but he'd been the one to race away and go back to his real life. Not that it was drudgery—

Frances stepped into the wide doorway. "Dinner is served, ma'am."

Sebastian rose and took Ivy's hand to help her stand. "Thank you, Frances."

With a quick nod of acknowledgment, the butler left.

Sebastian motioned Autumn and Jack to the door. As the foursome walked down the hall to the elaborate dining room that had been decorated with tinsel, and shiny red ornaments, Jack wasn't sure what to do with his hands. Should he guide Autumn to the dining room with a hand on the small of her back? Should he keep his distance?

In the sitting room, actually talking to Autumn, too many memories had assaulted him. Good and bad. Happy and devastating. It was no wonder he'd forgotten common courtesy.

Sebastian seated Ivy. Jack followed suit and seated Autumn, who cast him a confused look. He wanted to tell her he was simply following Sebastian's lead not getting familiar, but that would break their cover.

He took the chair beside Autumn, across from Ivy and Sebastian who had chosen the more intimate seating arrangement rather than sitting at the head and foot of the long table.

Ivy smiled. Looking elegant and sophisticated in her slim red dress and pixie-haircut, she lit the room. "No more talk of business. No more talk of companies. We want you and Autumn to get to know each other."

He glanced at Autumn, who smiled at Ivy. "Oh, I think we know each other well enough to be partners in a wedding."

Jack fought back a wince.

"Let's talk about something more interesting than me and Mr. Adams."

The insult of her use of his formal name rumbled through him and he quietly said, "Jack. My name is Jack. Remember?"

She turned and smiled, but if the woman wanted to be on Broadway, she'd never make it. Her smile was so fake it was a wonder her face didn't crack.

"Of course, *Jack*."

Until that moment, he'd never looked at their one-night stand from her perspective. First, he'd been grieving his mom. Then he'd been busy. Then he'd had a string of terrible engagements that had rendered him totally incapable of having a relationship. But tonight, he suddenly realized he'd hurt her.

And why not? They had been like soul mates who'd found each other after a long separation. They'd instinctively known each other's whims and wishes—

Then he'd never called.

A thought hit him like a boulder falling on a road in the Rocky Mountains.

What if that night hadn't just been the worst night of his life?

What if his not calling had made it the worst night of hers?

What if she wasn't the first in his string of bad encounters with women but the last in his string of good encounters?

And if any of that was true, what was he going to do about it?

# CHAPTER THREE

AUTUMN WASN'T ENTIRELY sure how it happened. But after dinner and a glass of Cognac, somehow she and Jack announced they were leaving at the same time.

Ivy grinned. "That's great! This way Jack can give you a lift home."

"I'm in Queens," Autumn quickly reminded her. "That's too far. I can take the subway."

"Nonsense," Sebastian said, handing Autumn her black wool coat. "It's not like Jack has anywhere else to go."

Jack smiled stiffly.

And how could Autumn blame him? She hadn't exactly taken *every* jab at him she could, but she'd used more than one of the opportunities presented to remind him he was pond scum.

Watching him try to get them out of this one would be her last mean thing. She swore. On the day of the wedding, she would be nothing but sweet to him. Or at least sort of friendly.

He caught her gaze, and she lifted her chin in challenge. *Go ahead, rich kid. Get us out of this.*

His blue eyes flickered with something that looked like humor and her resolve shook. *Had he gone from squirming to enjoying this? How could he possibly enjoy this?*

"You know what? I'm happy to give Autumn a ride home."

Her eyes bugged. He wasn't enjoying this! He was turning everything back on her!

"That's not necessary."

He smiled at her. "Of course, it is. I'm not totally familiar with the route, but don't you have to take a bus to get to a subway stop?"

"I can get a ride share."

"Don't be ridiculous. What kind of a gentleman would I be to let a lady go through all that this late at night?"

"One who knows that the lady is perfectly capable of getting herself home."

"Of course, she is," Jack said, motioning for her to walk to the door. "But a gentleman still enjoys doing a kindness."

Ivy laughed as he kissed her cheek when he said goodbye. "Such a smooth talker."

Sebastian slapped his back, then hugged Autumn before she stepped out of the townhouse.

"I'll see you on Monday," Ivy called, waving goodbye.

Then the townhouse door closed.

Autumn turned on Jack. "I am not letting you drive me home!"

Jack talked through a big smile he had pasted on his face. "You better. Sebastian and Ivy are at the window, watching us."

"Damn it!"

He waved off his driver before he could open the limo door and handled it himself, directing Autumn to get inside. "Is that any way for a lady to talk?"

"What do you care if I'm a lady or not?" She turned

back to look at the window. The drapes had closed. She was free. She sidestepped Jack. "They're gone. I'll see myself home."

"Wait!"

She ignored Jack's call and headed up the street, pulling her phone from her pocket so she could call a ride share.

The sound of tires crunched beside her. Through her peripheral vision she saw the limo inching along the curb next to her.

The back window lowered. Jack said, "Come on. Get in. Let us take you home."

"I already ordered a ride share."

"Seriously," Jack said as the limo crawled along. "It is no problem for me to give you a ride."

"Maybe it's a problem for me?"

"Really?"

"Maybe I don't want to spend thirty minutes in a car with you trying to figure out what to say. I don't like you. You dumped me. Our spending time together is the definition of awkward."

He said nothing.

*Ah. He agreed.*

"At least let me wait for your ride share."

"It's a free country, but you look like you're stalking me driving up beside me like that."

"Okay, here's the thing. I know you're mad that I left after our night together and didn't call. But there were extenuating circumstances."

The limo continued to inch along beside her and she sighed. "Don't be so smug, thinking I'm still mad after five years. I'm a mature adult. Sometimes things just aren't what they seem. I have moved on."

"You'd never prove it by me."

"Hey, just because I got past what happened doesn't mean I want to be friends with you."

He winced.

"I'm serious. You played me for a fool."

"What if I told you that had it not been for the extenuating circumstances, I would not have played you for a fool."

Something hopeful rippled through her and she cursed it. Seriously? She could not give him a pass, have fun with him at the wedding then have him drop out of her life again. "What might have happened doesn't matter. What does matter is that you're a scoundrel. An oaf."

"An *oaf*? No one says *oaf* anymore."

She glanced at her phone. "Hey, my ride's around the corner. He must have just dropped someone off."

She stepped back so she could peer down the street to see when the car turned. Within seconds the blue sedan was driving toward her.

She waved her arm and the car eased to the curb. She fake-smiled at Jack. "See you at the wedding."

She got into the car and they sped off, leaving Jack's limo in the dust. Grateful she didn't have to see him until the rehearsal dinner, she leaned back on the seat, and relaxed for the first two minutes. But then her phone buzzed with a message. She glanced down. It was from Ivy.

Hey everyone!
I was thinking about our introduction dances for the reception, and I decided we needed something more special than a plain announcement of your names as you enter the dance floor. So, I've decided that each couple will have a "piece" of a bigger dance routine

to be performed by the entire bridal party. I've hired a dance instructor to do the choreography and he'll also teach each couple the routine. Because everyone's part is different, there's no need to practice together. Each couple only need to learn their segment of the routine! We think it will only take three sessions.

Isn't this fun? Greg will text your practice times. I've given him all of your numbers.

Autumn groaned. She didn't want to be with Jack at all. But three "sessions" learning a dance routine? Being in his arms? Swaying up against each other?

That was one step too far!

If she didn't know better, she'd think Ivy either knew about their one-night stand or suspected something.

But how could she? No one knew. At least Autumn didn't think so.

She swung around in the back of the sedan, spotting Jack's limo behind them before it turned right and disappeared.

Could *he* have told Sebastian?

She groaned. After the way he pretended they didn't know each other when they saw one another that morning, forcing her to follow his lead, she would clobber him if he had!

Jack showed up at the dance studio Monday evening at six. Sunday morning, he'd called Sebastian and as smoothly as possible tried to get himself and Autumn out of this. But happy Sebastian seemed oblivious to Jack's maneuvering.

Sunday afternoon, he'd received a text from the dance instructor with the times of his practices with Autumn. So here he was. He removed his suit jacket and tie, hanging them on a hook near the door and rolled the sleeves of his white shirt to the elbows. He still wore his loafers from work that day, but he decided that was fine. At the wedding, he'd be dancing in a tux and good shoes. His current clothes were close to that. It would be good practice.

Autumn, however, would be dancing in a gown.

He sniffed a laugh. Wonder how she planned to accommodate that?

Not that he'd been thinking about her. At least not too much. And he wasn't thinking about her as much as working to figure out a way that being with her for the entire day of the wedding wouldn't be too awkward.

He'd apologized. He'd told her as much of his story as he was comfortable sharing. He wasn't sure what else to do.

After introducing himself to the dance instructor, Greg, an average-sized, average-looking guy in jeans and a T-shirt, who beamed with happiness, Jack edged over to the balance barre and glanced at his phone. Autumn was two minutes late.

Hope built that she'd talked Ivy out of this idea, but then the glass door of the studio opened, and Autumn blew in with a gust of wind. Snowflakes frosted her hair. Laughing, she brushed them off. Then she saw him and deflated.

His chest tightened. All these years, if he ever thought of Autumn at all it was to consider her the first in his string of bad luck with women. Now that he'd begun seeing things from her perspective, he felt like a crumb, a snake, someone who owed *her*.

"I couldn't talk Sebastian out of this," he said as she approached him.

"I couldn't talk Ivy out of it either."

The normal tone of her voice encouraged him. "At least we agree about something."

She sniffed and removed her wool coat, revealing black yoga pants and a pink T-shirt that outlined her curves. He remembered those curves warm and silky beneath his palms and took a quick breath to dispel the memory.

"Sorry about the yoga pants. I keep them in my office for when I work late." She glanced down at them, then up at Jack. "I should have practiced in my dress. At least that's somewhat like a gown."

"You look…" *Really hot.* Hot enough that his chest tightened and spectacular memories of their night together cascaded through his brain again. "Fine."

She tossed her coat on an available hook and sat on the bench against the wall to remove her clunky boots. Then she rummaged through her huge purse and pulled out…

"Are those ballet slippers?" He caught her gaze. "You took ballet?"

"A very acceptable thing for girls to do when I was growing up."

He frowned.

"What? You think because I'm clumsy I couldn't possibly dance?"

She was not clumsy. Especially not in bed. She was smooth and graceful.

"No. I was wondering what purpose it serves to learn our part in ballet slippers when you'll be wearing wedding shoes when we actually dance."

She rose. "Not if I slip into these under the table before we're introduced."

He laughed, remembering why he'd liked her so much the night he'd met her. Her blissful pragmatism.

Greg ambled over. Glancing at Jack, he said, "This is your partner for the wedding?"

He and Autumn simultaneously said, "Yes."

Autumn added, "I'm Autumn."

Happy Greg grinned. "Then let's get started." He walked to the opposite side of the room and motioned for Autumn and Jack to stay where they were. "Your dance begins with a series of twirls that gets you to the center of the floor."

Jack balked. "I'm twirling?"

"No. You twirl your partner."

He relaxed. "Thank God."

Autumn giggled. "What? Twirling is a threat to your masculinity?"

"No. I don't want to look like a fool. There'll be lots of important people at that wedding. Most of them eat at my restaurants. I don't want to look like the guy who can't twirl."

"*You're* the one worried about being clumsy?"

"Hey, I didn't laugh at you when you insinuated you were clumsy." He hadn't laughed because he'd remembered her in bed. Definitely not clumsy.

"Oh, poor baby."

Another memory shot through him. The night they'd stayed together, he'd complained about a meeting the following afternoon and she'd walked her fingers up his chest and said, "Oh, poor baby," before she'd completely annihilated him with a kiss.

He sucked in a breath. He had to stop thinking about that night.

"Take your partner's hand and raise her arm enough that you can twirl her out to the floor. I'm guessing it will be three or four twirls before you get to the center of the dance area."

Jack did as he was told. He wasn't completely clue-less. He'd actually learned the basics of dancing in lessons his mom had insisted on when he was fourteen because she believed a polished gentleman should be able to dance. He'd groaned and argued, but once he'd begun going to charity events, he'd realized how smart of a decision that had been.

He raised Autumn's arm and twirled her three times, mesmerized by the way she sprang to her toes and made the simple movement of twirling look majestic and elegant.

Her ability gave him confidence and they did two more twirls to get to the center.

"Lovely." Greg smiled at Autumn. "You've taken lessons."

"Only every Saturday morning for what seemed like an eternity."

He laughed.

Jealousy crept up on Jack, but he stopped it because it was wrong. There'd never be anything between him and Autumn. She disliked him and three failed engagements was enough to make any man take a step back and evaluate. He clearly wasn't relationship material.

Greg walked over and positioned them. "When you come out of the twirl, I want you to stand like this." He motioned for Jack to stay where he was and turned Autumn to face Jack.

"Now," Greg continued. "I want you both to shift right, then left, as if you're trying to see over each other's shoulder—"

Jack grimaced. "What kind of dance is this?"

"It's free style. Ivy wants us to tell the story of her relationship with Sebastian. Apparently, she and Sebastian were at odds when they first met and had to grow to love each other. Because you two are the first couple, you'll be demonstrating that discord."

Autumn said, "Should be a piece of cake for us to demonstrate discord."

Jack sniffed a laugh.

Greg smiled. "Well, those movements are only about two seconds of your dance. Lean left, lean right, get into the waltz position. Then it's a waltz around the floor until you are beside Ivy and Sebastian where you will stop, and the next couple will be introduced."

"Okay." Waltz? He loved to waltz. "Sounds easy."

Greg faced Autumn. "Agree?"

"Absolutcly."

Greg clapped. "Then let's start at the beginning. Twirl, twirl, twirl. Lean left. Lean right. Waltz hold. Then a waltz around the dance floor."

# CHAPTER FOUR

AUTUMN AND JACK returned to the side of the room. He took her hand and twirled her to the center of the dance floor, where they stopped and faced each other before they leaned left and right. Then he stepped toward her to get into the waltz hold.

His hand sliding across her back almost made her stumble, but her trusty ballet shoes saved her. Still, that didn't stop the warmth that spread up her spine causing tingles of awareness that spawned a million memories. Mostly of how they'd laughed at the gala where they'd met. He'd snagged champagne for her from passing waiters and bribed one of them to always have a glass of whiskey on his tray. By the end of the night, they were both tipsy. And happy. They'd seemed like two peas in a pod. Especially when they'd danced.

She put her hand on his shoulder and the memories multiplied. She could almost feel them gliding along the floor, gazing into each other's eyes as if they couldn't believe their luck in finding each other. But more than that, she knew what he felt like beneath that shirt. She could picture his muscled shoulders, back and chest.

She swallowed.

"You okay?"

She raised her eyes to meet his gaze. Those stunning blue eyes almost did her in. She glanced away, saying, "Yes. Fine."

Jack took the first step to lead her in the waltz. His feet were sure. His movements balanced.

Greg clapped. "Stop! Stop! Stop!" He ambled over. "Seriously? You had hundreds of dance lessons, but you don't know you're to look your partner in the eye?"

Autumn stepped out of the hold. "Yes. I'm sorry. I'm just a little scattered today."

Jack's head tilted as he studied her.

"Long day at work," she qualified.

Greg sighed. "It doesn't take a lot of energy to look in your partner's eyes."

She took a breath. "I know."

"Good. Then let's start from the top."

She and Jack walked back to the side of the room. Greg said, "Go."

Jack took her hand and twirled her four times to get her to the center of the dance floor. They leaned left, then right. He stepped toward her and joined their hands as he slid his other arm around her waist.

Her palm tingling, she placed her fingers on his shoulder, then raised her eyes to meet his gaze.

The world upended. Memories of dancing together at the gala whispered through her, then making love. They'd been as close as two people could be and now they were pretending not to know each other.

He effortlessly waltzed them in a circle around the dance floor. But with her gaze connected to his, everything inside her shivered. Not merely with remembered sensations. But with the feeling of rejection. With the sense that she wasn't good enough. The sense that— just as her dad always said—she was average, made to be a worker bee. That she should keep her head down and do her job and hopefully find a man who could take care of her.

The thoughts penetrated so deep, she faltered, tripping as she was gazing into the eyes of the man she'd thought she could fall in love with.

Jack covered her misstep and effortlessly got them to their stopping place. Yanking her gaze from his, she jerked out of his arms.

Greg said, "That was lovely. Jack, you waltz like a dream. You have nothing to be afraid of." He turned to Autumn. "Since you'll be wearing a gown. No one will even notice if you bobble a step."

*I will.*

*Jack will.*

*And he already thinks there's something wrong with me. A reason not to ever call again. A reason to never see me again.*

She did not want to be unbalanced or foolish in his arms.

Damn it. She was not what her father thought. She did not want Jack to think she was. She would not trip in his arms again.

She took a cleansing breath and pasted on a smile for Greg. "Thank you. That was fun and honestly I think we have the hang of it."

Jack continued to study her.

Greg glanced at his phone. "Second couple will be here in five minutes. Do you want to go over it one more time or do you think you have it?"

"We're fine," Autumn quickly said, then smiled to take the sting out of it. "I'm tired. I had that bad day, remember?" She smiled again.

"Honestly, you two have the easiest of the dances,"

Greg said. "One more run through on Wednesday and you should be solid."

"Sounds great," Autumn agreed as she headed for her coat and clunky boots. She slid them on and walked to the door. "I'll see you on Wednesday night."

"See you then," Greg replied, but Jack said nothing.

Which was fine. They had one more dance lesson, the rehearsal dinner and one wedding to get through, then they'd never see each other again. She might be in the same job she'd been in five years ago, but she was extremely good at it. The current CEO was getting up in years and would eventually retire and she would step into his shoes.

That was her plan.

She was not less than. She was a smart woman, gifted in fundraising. With a plan. A good, solid plan to move into the job she was born to do.

One guy who dumped her and one misstep on the dance floor changed nothing.

Tuesday morning, Autumn got a call from Ivy, who bubbled over with excited questions. Making a cup of coffee, Autumn told the bride-to-be that the dance lesson had been fine.

"That's all? Just fine?"

"It's a very simple dance," Autumn said, smiling in the hope the positivity of it would translate to her voice.

"Maybe too simple?"

"No. It's lovely. I love to waltz and Jack's a great dancer. In fact, we did so well last night Greg thinks we only need one more lesson."

After a few seconds of silence, Ivy said, "Jack didn't say anything offensive, did he?"

Autumn laughed. "As we were both focused on learning a dance?"

"Jack can be chatty."

"Does he typically say offensive things when he's chatty?"

"No." Ivy's voice turned petulant. "It's just that I thought you'd enjoy the lessons."

"Dancing was fun," Autumn said, scrambling for something positive to say. Everything about the wedding was important to Ivy. She wanted everyone to love every step of the process as much as she did. And Autumn loved how happy Ivy was and wanted to keep her that way. "The dance is going to be really cool. I think it will be entertaining for the guests."

"Good. Great. You'll all have fun and it will be brilliant. I am glad I thought of it and I'm glad you like it."

Autumn frowned. Ivy was babbling and she never babbled. "Is everything okay with the wedding?"

"Yes! Wonderful. Meeting with the florist again today."

"Oh, that's fun."

"Yes. It really is."

But Ivy had that strange tone in her voice again. Still, she didn't probe any deeper about the dance lesson with Jack, so when she said goodbye Autumn went back to dressing for work.

As she walked out the door, a weird sensation spiraled through her and she stopped on the little porch of her second-floor apartment. She'd told Ivy she didn't think she and Jack needed the final two lessons—

Then Ivy had changed the subject even though she'd been asking questions—

Was Autumn crazy to notice that or did that mean something?

She shook her head with a laugh. She was monitoring the bride for signs of nerves, but that subject change had been meaningless.

She hoped.

Because when Ivy had a bee in her bonnet about something she wouldn't rest until she resolved it.

Jack stepped out of the elevator into the reception area for the corporate offices of Step Inside when his phone rang. Seeing the caller was Sebastian, he said, "What's up?"

"I have a favor to ask."

"Anything for the groom to be."

"We're cake tasting this afternoon."

Jack grimaced at his friend's plight. "I thought you'd chosen a cake."

"We thought we had too. Thing is… Ivy's decided everyone should get their own tiny wedding cake to take home and she wants everybody to have a choice of flavor. She's going for goofy things. New flavors designed by the baker. I'm sort of campaigning for just plain chocolate cake."

"Your favorite."

"Is that so wrong?"

Jack laughed.

"We've already chosen four, but up to this point, chocolate never made the grade. This afternoon at the bakery, I want you to help me get chocolate into the rotation."

Jack laughed at the way he said rotation as if the cake was vying to be a starting pitcher for the Yankees, then he realized what Sebastian had said. "You want me to taste cakes?"

"Yes. As a former chef, your opinion holds weight.

If you come prepared to taste the chocolate and say it's the best thing ever created, Ivy will listen."

It was a bit odd. But he'd seen how stressful the wedding plans had become, so Jack could be a good sport and help out his friend. "Okay. I'll be there." He stepped into his office. Furnished in an ultra-modern minimalist style, with a pale wood desk and a buttery brown leather for the chair, the clean lines of both the room and the furnishings forced him to keep his big, shiny desk empty. He walked over to the hidden closet where he stored his coat. "Text me the address."

"Okay. Three o'clock. I'll see you then."

"Right. See you at three."

Turning away from the closet, he stopped as a weird sensation washed through him. He hadn't thought about being a chef in years. When his mom ran Step Inside, he'd been the head chef of their flagship restaurant. That was where he'd created the menu that had made them so successful that they could put restaurants in the five boroughs and expand into New Jersey. Before she'd died, they'd been discussing creating a research and development kitchen where he could create and test recipes to come up with dishes that would rotate, keeping their menu original and innovative.

He shook his head to clear it. That had been the culmination of their dream. His mom running the business end and him creating. But when she died, he'd taken over the business and found a way to update the menu by subcontracting chefs like Randolph to create new meals. It was that decision that solidified his ability to take over the business with the board his mother had chosen.

*It was that decision that had made him who he was today. One hell of a businessman.*

So why did it feel so odd suddenly? Like Sebastian mentioning he'd been a chef had dragged him further back in time than seeing Autumn had—

Actually, he could probably blame these new feelings on seeing Autumn, too.

That night had changed so much about his life. He stopped being a son, stopped being a chef, literally lost his entire family and had to pick up the ball and finish the game for his mother.

But it had worked and worked well. He wouldn't question it or analyze choices that had succeeded.

With a ton of emails in his inbox, he dismissed his thoughts and spent an hour reading before he met with the company's chief financial officer and his team who would handle crafting the financials for the new five-year plan.

At one o'clock, he had lunch at one of his own restaurants. He'd changed from his suit into jeans and a sweater with a black leather jacket. No one recognized him, so it gave him the perfect opportunity to observe.

And maybe to be a little bit proud that he'd brought his mother's vision to glorious life.

But on the heels of that pride came the sorrow and the longing to have watched *her* live her dream. He recognized that Sebastian's throwaway comment had spawned memories of the years of dedication it had taken to turn Step Inside into something remarkable. But it felt wrong to be proud of himself. Wrong to enjoy the success.

So, he'd forget all that, forget Autumn, forget Sebastian's throwaway comment and focus on the wedding. When his driver arrived with his limo, he texted the address Sebastian had given him to his driver and settled into the backseat, reading emails on his phone during the ride to the cake tasting. Twenty minutes later, the limo pulled up at a townhouse.

"This is it?"

Arnie, his driver, turned around on his seat. "This is the address."

"Stay close a minute while I make sure Sebastian didn't transpose a number or something."

He got out of the limo, walked up to the townhouse door and rang the bell. Sebastian answered. "Come in. We're all in the kitchen."

He waved to Arnie and headed inside. "This is a house."

"The home of the baker Ivy chose to make our cakes."

Sebastian led him down a hall replete with antiques and Oriental rugs. They walked into an open kitchen with stunning white cabinets, quartz counter tops and tall-backed stools around the biggest island Jack had ever seen.

It was also very similar to what he and his mom had planned for his test kitchen. The memory of meeting with the architect and even approving plans rippled through him.

"Here he is now," Ivy said, racing over to kiss Jack's cheek. "I can't wait for you to test the strawberry cream filled."

He shoved the unwanted memories to the back of his mind and returned Ivy's cheek kiss. "Meaning, you're on team strawberry?"

"Yes. We have one slot to fill. I adore the strawberry. Sebastian likes the chocolate. And Autumn is team lemon."

He saw her then. Sitting on one of the tall-backed stools at the island, she had five or six pieces of cake in front of her. But her hair hung straight, almost to her shoulders and she wore a slim red dress that came to her knees and high-high heels that he was positive would make her look tall and sexy.

"Autumn."

She glanced at him. "Jack."

Even after three times seeing each other there was still something off in the way they treated each other. He'd thought dancing together had melted some of the ice between them, but she'd gotten odd at the end of the session and raced away so quickly he hadn't even heard her say goodbye.

Anybody who wasn't wrapped up in wedding preparations would realize they barely tolerated each other—

Or maybe somebody who *was* wrapped up in wedding preparations had noticed. And maybe that's why Ivy kept throwing them together.

Ivy slid her hand beneath his arm and led him to the spot right beside Autumn.

*Yeah. She'd noticed.*

"Here's your cake set up." The happy bride pointed at the plate holding the yellow slice and said, "That's the lemon."

She then pointed at the pink "strawberry cream," then at two nondescript versions with names like "tangerine torte" and "special birthday," and finally she pointed at the chocolate. "And that, of course, is Sebastian's pick."

Jack said, "Yum. I'm a big fan of chocolate."

Ivy snorted. "You're a friend of the guy who likes chocolate. You don't get to make your choice until you've tasted all of them."

He winced. "Even that special birthday thing that looks like the color of a zombie?"

Autumn laughed unexpectedly and his gaze jumped to her.

"I knew it reminded me of something. I just couldn't figure out what it was."

Jack's lips lifted into a hopeful smile. Maybe some of the ice had melted after all?

The baker sighed. "It's a theme color." Older, stout and dressed in a traditional chef's uniform of white coat and toque blanche, he gave Jack a you-should-know-that look as he ambled over to the island. "It was created for the birthday party of Angelina Montgomery last year. Guests couldn't get enough of it."

"Oh, yes, Mark! I remember!" Ivy said. "Guests gushed about that cake for months."

Mark took a breath, lifting his nose in the air as if he were looking down on them. "They're still gushing."

Autumn pressed her lips together to keep from laughing and caught Jack's gaze again. He was totally with her. He understood the pride of the great chefs and bakers. He'd been proud of every damned thing he'd created. But sometimes the pretense was just a little bit funny.

He rolled his eyes and Autumn nodded. They were absolutely on the same page.

Memories of the click he'd felt with her five years ago poured through him. He hadn't been born into this life the way Ivy had. Neither had Autumn. Both had worked to get here and worked even harder to belong here. But they'd both also hung on to their normal lives, their normal values.

Ivy turned to Jack. "Jack, this is Mark Patel. His cakes are divine."

Jack offered his hand across the big island. "It's a pleasure to meet you."

Stretching forward, the baker took Jack's hand to shake. "A pleasure to meet you too."

Autumn slid one of Jack's slices closer to him. "Try the zombie one. It's actually pretty good."

Mark nodded approvingly. "I accomplish that gray color with blueberry juice which also gives the cake just a bit of a tangy flavor."

"That had been what I thought," Jack said as he took the seat beside Autumn and picked up the fork. He cut a bite of the cake and ate it. Flavor burst on his tongue.

"Oh, that *is* good."

The baker stuck his nose in the air again. "Of course, it is."

"But, Jack," Sebastian reminded him. "You like chocolate."

"I do," Jack agreed, sliding the zombie cake away and reaching for the chocolate. He took a bite. "Oh, my God." He jerked his gaze to the baker. "Are you kidding me? This is the best cake I've ever eaten."

Sebastian leaned in and whispered, "Don't over sell it."

"I'm not overselling." He caught Mark's gaze again. "This is amazing."

"And Jack knows amazing," Sebastian said, glancing over at Mark. "He owns Step Inside."

Mark's expression said he was impressed. "I've eaten there. And also heard good things from your chefs."

Autumn said, "You *own* Step Inside?"

He winced, expecting some sort of wise crack. The ice might be thawing but it hadn't melted completely. "Yes."

"I love those restaurants."

Pride rolled through him. He tried to stop it. After all, he was only following his mother's plans. But it bubbled up. He swore he could feel his chest swelling.

"And I like the chocolate too."

Autumn's voice filled the sudden void in the kitchen.

Surprised that Autumn had sided with him on the chocolate cake, Jack peeked over at her. The click of rightness they'd shared the night they'd spent together tiptoed back. Too busy having fun, they hadn't shared facts of their lives until she'd told him a bit about her job when they were lying in bed together.

But that night, the past hadn't mattered. Only the present had. The connection they'd felt. The fun they'd had being themselves.

Jack was glad when Ivy broke the spell by groaning and Sebastian laughed. "It looks like I get chocolate after all."

Ivy sighed dramatically. "All right. You win. Chocolate it is."

With the decision made, Mark nudged the plates closer to his guests. "Eat! These cakes are too good to throw away."

Steeped in conflicting emotions, Jack quietly said, "You could donate them to homeless shelters."

Mark batted a hand. "Everything but the pieces on the plates can definitely go to the shelters. Pieces on the plates must be eaten." He grinned. "Can I get anyone a glass of wine?"

Sebastian said, "I'd love one."

Ivy agreed. "Me too. Though I'm only eating one piece of cake because I have a wedding gown to fit into."

Autumn seconded that. "I have a dress to fit into, too. I also have a long trip home." She rose from her stool. "So, if you don't mind, I'll be leaving."

Mark jumped into action, scooping up the plate with her slice of lemon cake that had only one bite taken out. "Let me box this up for you." He grinned. "For breakfast tomorrow."

Autumn glanced at the cake with longing in her eyes. "It would make a great breakfast."

Jack almost told her she was perfect just the way she was. She didn't need to diet. She had curves in all the right places. But not only was this the wrong place and time, the urge itself confused him. She didn't like him. He didn't do relationships. There was no reason for them to get personal. All he needed was for the ice to thaw a little more. He didn't even want to be her friend. After this wedding they'd go their separate ways.

"It will make a fabulous breakfast!" Mark slid the cake into a handy takeout container. Obviously, this wasn't the first cake tasting in his house.

Autumn happily took it. "Thank you."

Mark said, "You're welcome."

She turned to Ivy. "If you need me, call."

"Okay."

Then she waved to Sebastian before she left the kitchen, cake in hand, and slipped out the front door.

Jack blinked, surprised at how quickly she was gone and even more surprised no one had asked him to give Autumn a ride home. Then he remembered the cold war feeling he'd sensed he and Autumn were throwing off when he first arrived.

They might have warmed up over her love of his restaurants, the proud baker and the chocolate cake, but she'd barely acknowledged him when she left.

No. She hadn't acknowledged him at all.

She'd thanked Mark, told Ivy to call if she needed anything and waved to Sebastian.

And nothing to him.

He waited for Ivy to say something about Autumn. Maybe to call him out over the way they barely spoke to each other. She didn't. He expected Sebastian to say something twenty minutes later when he walked Jack to the door. He didn't. He simply said a happy goodbye.

Jack walked down the sidewalk to his limo with the godawful feeling that it wasn't other people who didn't like the cold war between him and Autumn. It was *him*.

He'd hurt her. Good excuse or not, he'd hurt her.

And if he wanted the two of them to get along for this wedding, he was going to have to tell her why.

# CHAPTER FIVE

AUTUMN STOPPED AT the door of the dance studio and took a long breath. Fat white snowflakes fell to the sidewalk, making the city a winter wonderland and covering the hood of her down jacket. But she needed a minute to remind herself she was a strong woman who refused to be attracted to a man who was probably a player, someone who had lots of one-night stands and countless pretty girls willing to go anywhere he wanted any time he wanted. The man *owned* Step Inside. One of the best restaurants she'd ever eaten at.

He was way out of her league.

Unfortunately, he hadn't behaved like a rich guy at the cake testing. In fact, he'd been the Jack she'd met at the summer gala five years before. He'd made her laugh at least twice. And, God help her, now that she knew he owned Step Inside, she *did* understand how busy and demanding his life had probably been for the past few years.

She couldn't remember him mentioning what he did for a living the night they'd met at the gala. They'd been preoccupied gazing into each other's eyes and having fun. But now that he'd told her he managed a string of highly successful restaurants, the problem was clear.

Of course, she liked him. He was gorgeous, funny, rich.

But she was Autumn Jones. Average at best. Not the girl Prince Charming would choose to dance with at the ball—unless there was no one else around. Historically, young singles were at a premium at a gala planned to entice wealthy people to donate money.

She hadn't been a choice that night. She'd been the only option.

Which was why she needed the minute to regroup. If she continued to think back to the gala and remember how attuned they seemed to be, she could forget that they weren't two peas in a pod. Plus, she wasn't the same woman she was when she had met him. She might have always wanted to be CEO of Raise Your Voice, but now that goal was in reach. Gerry was old enough that he would soon be retiring.

She couldn't afford a misstep. She couldn't afford to become so involved with a man that she'd end up part of his life rather than having her own life. She'd seen enough of that with her parents. Her mom waited on her dad hand and foot and threw herself into making sure her kids had good lives, but she didn't seem to have a life of her own. Autumn wanted a career. She wanted to help hundreds of people achieve their goals. She didn't have time for a man or a family.

Her resolve to keep her distance restored, she entered the dance studio.

Unlike their first lesson, Jack wasn't yet there.

She couldn't breathe a sigh of relief that she wouldn't see him that night. Even if he wasn't available for a lesson, they'd have to make it up. She wanted to get this final session over with. She didn't want any more confusing encounters. Didn't want to understand him anymore. Didn't want to see peeks of the guy she'd met at the Raise Your Voice gala. She just wanted them to do their part for the wedding and never see each other again.

She took off her coat and sat on the bench to put on her ballet slippers. The door opened and Jack walked in. "Cold out there."

"And lots of snow," Greg agreed, ambling into the studio from a door in the back. "I hope you have a dependable way home."

Before Jack could say anything, Autumn said, "I usually stay with Ivy and Sebastian when it snows this much."

Jack said, "There's no need. I can take you."

Now that she had a solid understanding of what had happened between them, she ventured a smile. "Ivy wants to go over some things about the wedding." Thank God. She and Jack might be getting along but that didn't mean she wanted to spend almost an hour in a car with him, trying to think of things to talk about without getting too chummy, causing her to remember how very much she'd liked him that night.

"And speaking of Ivy," Greg said. "She's changed your dance a bit."

Jack groaned. He removed his overcoat and walked it to the row of hooks on the wall by the big window, revealing a dark suit. After he took off his jacket, he turned to face Greg and Autumn's heart fluttered. He looked amazing in the dark trousers and white shirt. He rolled the sleeves to his elbows then took off his tie and he looked even better. Professional sexy.

Walking to Greg, he said, "I liked what we had."

"You pulled off the waltz like a pro—"

"Because I had about six lessons as a kid and learning to waltz took up most of them."

Greg batted a hand. "You'll get this too. Especially

since the new version isn't much more difficult. We're going to add the basic Charleston step right after the look left, look right move."

Her shoes on, Autumn rose from the bench. Greg reached for her hand and guided her onto the dance floor. "So, you're going to look left, then look right," he said as he reminded her of the move that she and Jack already knew. "Then you do a twirling pivot that puts you beside Jack."

He demonstrated the step so that he stood beside Autumn. "Then you do the basic Charleston step. Take a step back with the right foot. Then swing the left leg back in a kicking motion. Bring the left foot forward again and return to the starting position. Then, with the right foot loose, kick it forward. Bring it back. Blah. Blah. Blah. We're going to repeat that step five times. Meaning the left foot gets five kicks and so does the right."

Jack stared at him.

Autumn pressed her lips together to keep from laughing. It was fun to find something he wasn't good at. Though with the way he waltzed, he'd probably get this easily.

Greg smiled encouragingly. "It's really a very simple dance once you master the primary step."

Looking like a deer in the headlights, Jack said, "But I'll be in front of people. Every additional step adds to the potential embarrassment."

"Why don't we try learning the move, before we ease it into the routine?" Autumn asked, taking pity on him. "Plus, I know the Charleston. Just follow my lead."

Greg glanced at Jack. Autumn smiled hopefully. Jack took a breath.

"Okay. Yeah. Sure. But Ivy does realize this could

backfire, right? Any one of us could go on that dance floor and make a fool of ourselves."

"And you know what?" Greg said supportively. "The guests will love it. They will love that you tried. Everyone roots for an underdog."

Autumn motioned for Jack to stand beside her on the dance floor.

He approached, mumbling, "I do not want to be the underdog."

She held back a snort as he lined up beside her. Now that she knew who he was it was easy to see his objections as funny. He could end up on the wrong side of a society page critic's article.

Greg said, "All right. Let's have a go at this. Take a step back on the right leg. Swing the left leg back in a kicking motion. Bring the left foot forward again and return to the starting position. Then with the right foot loose, kick it forward. Bring it back."

Autumn put her hand on Jack's forearm to stop him. "Forget the words. Watch my feet."

He frowned. She motioned for him to look at her feet before she brought her right leg back, then her left, then kicked it forward.

He brought his right leg back, then his left, then kicked it forward.

"I feel stupid kicking."

"Pretend you're playing for the Giants. You've got the center holding the football up for you and you're going to kick it through the uprights."

One of his eyebrows rose.

"I'm serious. You might not want to kick your leg as high as the kicker on a football team does. But it's the same basic concept. It's also a little more manly that way. Something you can sink your teeth into."

She repeated the step and he followed until they were able to string five of them together.

When they were done, Greg clapped. "Very nice. Now, let's try the thing from the top. Go back to the side. Twirl onto the dance floor. Look left, look right. Charleston step five times. Waltz hold. Waltz."

They walked to the side of the dance floor but before he gave them the signal to start, Greg added music. The song began with a gentle gathering of notes that made it easy for Jack to twirl her to the dance floor, then the music changed subtly for the look left, look right, then it shifted again for the Charleston steps, which Jack bungled.

He sighed. She smiled at him and said, "Let's just go over it one more time."

"Yeah. And are we going to go over it at the wedding before we do the dance?"

She shrugged. "If it will help, we can find a private room and go over the whole routine after dinner, before the dance, so it's fresh in your mind."

He ran his hand along the back of his neck. "Actually, that probably would help."

"Then that's what we'll do."

They walked back to the side of the dance floor and Greg restarted the music, but he stopped it again. "What do you say we run through the entire dance. No matter how poorly you think you've done, Jack, I want you to push through it."

Jack took a breath. "You know why he said that, don't you?"

Autumn peered up at him. "To show us that the dance works?"

"No, he wants me to get practice screwing up and

soldiering on. So, when I screw up at the wedding, I'll just keep going."

She laughed.

Greg hit the music and Jack twirled Autumn onto the dance floor. They looked left then right, then she did the Charleston step and he followed as best he could. Then they got into the waltz hold and began to dance.

He relaxed completely. This was the part he knew.

"Look how well you're doing."

"This is the dance I took lessons for, remember?"

She held back a wince. "You did okay on the Charleston steps."

"Not really. But thanks."

The waltz ended and they headed back to the edge of the dance floor. Greg turned on the music and they started the routine from the top.

This time, maybe because the Charleston steps went a little smoother, when Jack took Autumn into his arms for the waltz and looked into her eyes, he felt like he had gone back in time to their night at the gala. His comfort with the waltz meshed with how comfortable he'd been with her five years ago and emotions tumbled around him. He remembered thinking how logical it was for them to go back to her apartment and make love because everything between them was so effortless—

He wasn't the only one who had felt it. She had too. Which was why he owed her an explanation for why he hadn't called.

What they'd had that night was once-in-a-lifetime perfect. Something he hadn't felt before or since and probably wouldn't ever feel again. Technically, he'd ruined what might have been their chance at permanent happiness.

Or maybe better said, Fate had stolen it and she deserved to know that.

Suddenly the sound of Greg applauding filled the dance studio. "That was beautiful, Jack. You certainly have command of the waltz."

He stepped away from Autumn, but their gazes held. Feelings from the night they met swamped him. The sense of finding something that would change his life.

"You can let go of my hand now."

The spell broken, he released her hand. He might be having feelings from all those years ago, but she wasn't. Not only did he have to remember that, and explain what had happened, but also those resurrected emotions weren't valid anymore. They weren't the same people they had been five years ago. They weren't going to pick up where they left off. Especially since neither of them wanted to.

"One more time, then we're done for the night."

They walked back to the edge of the dance floor. Jack twirled her to the center. They looked left and right, did a clumsy version of the Charleston step and began the waltz. Their gazes connected as he whirled them around the floor, and he felt like he could see the whole way into her soul. She didn't have secrets like he did. She didn't tell lies. She'd had a simple upbringing like his and didn't try to pretend she hadn't. She liked who she was. At least, she had liked who she was the night of the highly successful gala for Raise Your Voice that she'd planned and executed to perfection.

Was it any wonder he'd been so drawn to her?

Once again, it was Greg clapping that brought Jack back to the present. He stepped out of the waltz hold, but let go of her hand slowly. As if bewitched, he couldn't stop staring at her, wondering what would have happened between them if that night had ended differently.

"Jack? Are you with us?"

He shook his head and faced Greg. "I'm sorry. I missed what you said."

"I said you're doing very well."

That would have made him laugh if it wasn't so sad that a couple of steps had him tied up in knots. "We both know I'm not."

Autumn said, "Look at it this way. You ace the twirl. Any fool can look left then right. And you are a master at the waltz. You own this dance—"

"Except for the Charleston steps."

"Which you will get. This is only our first day with those steps."

"Yes. But this is our second session. And it's supposed to be our last."

She frowned. "That's right."

Greg said, "Ivy has paid me to provide as many lessons as you want. Technically, Monday was the last lesson Ivy had scheduled for you, the one we thought you wouldn't need. But that's still five days away from the wedding. That gives you a little too much time to forget everything you learned here…or time enough to have another lesson or two."

He glanced at Autumn. "Do you think we can handle one more lesson?"

"Of course we can."

Her easy acceptance relaxed him, reminding him of what a sweet woman she was, and doubled down on his need to tell her what had happened after their one-night stand.

Greg said, "Okay. Monday it is. Now scoot. I have another couple coming in ten minutes."

She changed into her boots then walked to the hooks on the wall and slipped into her coat and gloves. When he saw Autumn wore mittens he smiled.

His resolve to tell her had never been stronger. She also seemed very receptive.

This was his shot.

They stepped out into the falling snow and she laughed. "You know, come February we're going to be really sick of snow, but the first couple of snowfalls are like magic."

He glanced around. "I remember how I used to wait for snow to go sledding."

"My brothers and I did too."

He hit the button on his key fob to unlock his Mercedes. "You have brothers?"

"Two. Both accountants. Both work on Wall Street."

"Yet you chose a charity?"

"For a couple of really good reasons. First and foremost, I couldn't see myself sitting in an office all day talking numbers."

He laughed. "That does get old quickly."

"Second, I like the idea of using my time to help people." Under the light of a streetlamp, she looked up at him. "What about you?"

"Me?"

"How many brothers and sisters do you have?"

He faltered but realized this was actually a perfect introduction to the conversation they needed to have, though chatting on the street wasn't exactly ideal. "No brothers. No sisters. Only child."

"Oh, that must be fun!"

"Yes and no. Look, let me drive you to Ivy and Sebastian's."

She turned her face up into the snow. "Are you kidding? Miss a chance to walk in the snow?"

He couldn't fault her for that. The wet snow indicated that the temps were around freezing. Warmish for a winter night. And the snow was beautiful.

"Can I walk with you?"

"This is a low crime neighborhood. I'll be fine."

"I know you will. There's just a couple of things we need to talk about."

She headed down the street, starting the four-block walk that would get them to Ivy's townhouse. "You mean like how Ivy and Sebastian keep setting us up for things?"

It wasn't what he wanted to discuss, but now that she mentioned it, they probably should talk about that too.

He hit the button on his key fob to relock his Mercedes and fell in step with her. "I think they noticed we were a little icy to each other."

She laughed. "You think?"

He winced. "All right. I *know.*"

She laughed again. The sound echoed around them on the almost empty street. "Maybe we should tell them we met before."

"Maybe." Slowing his steps, he faced her. "Not total disclosure though."

"Oh, God no. If we told Ivy we went home together that night, she'd want every detail."

"Could get embarrassing."

She nudged his shoulder with hers. "Or we could twist it into an opportunity to brag."

Her comment was so unexpected, he burst out laughing. "We were pretty good together."

"Pretty good?" she asked, her pace increasing and

her steps getting longer. "We could have done a demo video for YouTube."

He laughed again, his own voice sounding warmer and happier than he could ever remember hearing it. They'd been bold that night. Brazen, really. And so damn happy.

They walked a block in silence. Then she mentioned Christmas shopping she had to do, and he didn't stop her. Didn't try to change the subject. He loved the sound of her voice. He loved the conversation about something so simple, yet so important to someone who had a family.

"My dad is definitely a Christmas sweater guy. I think the new sweater I get him every year is the only update to his winter wardrobe."

"I understand that. I actually have a shopper who keeps my closet full of updated clothes."

She stopped. Looked at him. "Really? You have someone who makes sure you have clothes?"

"Underwear and socks too."

She shook her head and started walking again. "Are you going to come in with me so we can tell Ivy and Sebastian they should cool it?"

"Are we going to tell them we know each other?"

"If you think about it, it's part of the explanation."

"True. So, we say we'd met before at the gala but leave everything else out."

She peeked at him. "The good parts."

"Yeah, no sense making them more focused on us than they already are."

"Or steal the thunder from the wedding."

"I think we'd only steal their thunder if we do the YouTube video."

She chortled and his heart swelled. This was how

they were the night of the gala. Easy with each other. Happy.

"You're so fixated on the video that I have to wonder if you aren't looking for a little validation."

"No. I don't need validation. I just think…" He glanced over at her. "Making the video recreating that night might be fun."

Time stopped. Even the snowflakes seemed to hang in midair. He remembered peeling off her pretty gown the night they met. Remembered kisses so hot and deep his blood had crackled. Remembered tucking her beside him when she began to fall asleep.

Finally, he said, "I thought that would make you laugh."

She combed her fingers through her hair. "I should have laughed."

But she hadn't. For the same reason his heart was thrumming now. That night had not been funny. It had been joyful. If she was remembering any of the things he was remembering, laughter would not be her reaction. Her breath might stall. Her pulse might scramble. A whole bundle of wishes that things had been different also might tiptoe into her mind.

Because right now he wasn't laughing either.

# CHAPTER SIX

At Ivy and Sebastian's townhouse, Autumn took a step away from Jack. His comments had brought back more intimate memories of that night and her body tingled with remembered passion even as her heart swelled with the disappointment of the weeks that followed.

Shaking off the feeling, she headed to the steps of the front door. "Are you coming in with me?"

He took a step back. "This might not be the right time to tell them about the night we met."

She stopped.

*Yeah. He might be right.* How could either one of them talk about meeting at a gala and spending the night together without thinking about all the things his video comment brought back? She'd stumble over her words. She might even flush.

She walked back to him. "Maybe I'll have a private talk with Ivy."

He caught her gaze. Snowflakes fell around him. The night was so silent she could hear her own breathing. "You're sure?"

"Yes. And maybe you could mention it to Sebastian."

"Maybe." He looked away then met her gaze again. "For what it's worth. That was probably the best night of my entire life."

She almost said, *I doubt that*, then noticed how serious he was. The light of a streetlight softened his features. His eyes searched hers.

She couldn't lie to a man whose eyes were so sincere or avoid the question that hung in the air. "Yeah. It ranked pretty high on my best night scale too."

The cold space between them suddenly warmed. They really were coming to terms with this. Making peace with it. Maybe even getting to know each other in a way they hadn't had time to do the night they'd met

Time stood still again. Neither of them made a move to leave.

And then the oddest thing struck her. It felt like a moment for a first kiss. Romantic snow. Just enough nervousness to amplify the attraction that wouldn't let them alone. And curiosity. Sweet, sweet curiosity if everything she remembered was true. Seconds spun into a minute with them gazing into each other's eyes. Feeling the connection they had the night of the gala. Remembering things probably best left forgotten.

Slowly, regretfully, he took a step back. "I've got a four-block trek to my Mercedes. So, I'll see you."

"I'll see you." She was *not* disappointed that he hadn't kissed her. That would have only confused things. Made her blood race. Filled her heart with that indescribable something only he seemed to inspire. Caused her to yearn for things that couldn't be.

She knew he was out of her league. And his not wanting a relationship with her had made sense. Still, the best-night-of-his-life comment fluttered through her brain again. The expression in his eyes. The warmth in his voice.

Her resolve weakened. Before he could turn to head to his car, she said, "Monday, right?"

Walking backward up the street, he said, "That's our third lesson."

"We can talk about whether or not we need a fourth."

A solid five feet away from her now, he smiled. "Okay."

"Okay." Before she could do something foolish or say something worse, she raced up the steps to Ivy's townhouse, slipped through the door and walked into the foyer.

Her wishful-thinking soul imagined that Jack stood where he had been, staring at the door.

Her heart warmed again, but she forced herself to remember how excited she'd been the first few days after their night together. Every ring of the phone had her heart racing. But he hadn't called. He hadn't texted. He hadn't emailed. Nothing.

The first week she'd been excited. The second week she'd been nervous, the realization that he probably wasn't going to call following her like a zombie. The third week, she knew he hadn't meant a damned word he'd said.

So, no. She wouldn't let that best-night-of-his-life comment change anything.

Thursday whipped by like a normal day. With Raise Your Voice's Valentine's Day Ball a mere two months away, work had begun to multiply enough that Autumn didn't have time to think about Jack Adams.

And if a wayward thought did slide into her brain, she booted it out, reminding herself that no matter how wistful he sounded, they were wrong for each other.

Friday morning, Raise Your Voice CEO Gerry Harding walked to her desk, tapped his fingers on the rim and said, "How about dinner tonight? I like Becco. It's a casual Italian place. I'll meet you there around…" He pondered that. "Let's say seven."

She blinked. The unexpected invitation threw her. The only thing she and Gerry ever spoke about was work. What could he possibly want to discuss with her for an entire dinner—?

*Oh, Lord! Maybe he was retiring?*

Her heart sped up. If he was, all those dreams she'd created as a little girl were about to come true. She'd be the boss. And not just of any old company, but a charity that helped people. She'd finally be the person she'd known was inside her all along.

Still, she couldn't panic or look overeager. "Sure. Seven is great and I love Italian food."

He knocked on her desk again. "I'll meet you there. Don't bring your bank card. This is Raise Your Voice business."

"Okay."

He walked away and she took a long, life-sustaining breath. Holy cats. Raise Your Voice business? Could that be anything other than Gerry's retirement?

Oh, dear God, it was happening—

Or at least she thought it was happening. She would not jump the gun. That was another thing Jack ghosting her had taught her. Never, ever, ever make assumptions.

A great debate raged in her head the rest of the day as she worked to figure out anything else Gerry might want to discuss with her other than to tell her he was retiring.

Nothing came.

She stayed at the office until six forty-five and took a ride share to West Forty-Sixth Street. Gerry was waiting for her inside the door of the restaurant. She hung her black wool coat, and a hostess began leading them through the tables. Halfway there she swore she saw the back of Jack's head.

Which was stupid. Ridiculous. *How could she recognize the back of his head?* Still, curiosity had her gaze swinging around after they'd passed his table and sure enough. It was him.

"'Of all the gin joints...'" Autumn mumbled as she seated herself across from her boss and—damn it!—across from Jack.

Gerry said, "I'm sorry. I missed what you said."

"Old movie quote. From *Casablanca*."

"Great movie," Gerry said, opening his menu. "Are you an old movie buff or a romantic?"

"Old movie buff," she said, refusing to let anyone think she might be romantic. That was another notion Jack ghosting her had squashed.

Her phone pinged with a text. Out of habit, she glanced at it.

Dating grandpas now?

Her head jerked up and her eyes homed in on Jack, who sat smirking at her. She didn't know what he was smirking about. He was single, sitting with two couples.

Gerry peeked over the top of his menu. "Everything okay?"

"Yes. Fine." She smiled again, though her nerve endings jangled.

"Is the text something you need to answer?"

"Actually, it is. It's the kind of text you can't ignore."

He chuckled. "Must be your mom."

Not wanting to lie, she only smiled.

"My wife goes nuts if the kids don't answer a text."
He motioned to her phone. "Go ahead."

"Thanks."

The waiter walked up to the table with water and
Gerry told him they needed a few minutes to look at
the menu.

Autumn typed furiously.

Not able to got a date now? You're the only single in
your group.

Across the room, she saw ridiculous Jack shake his
head, looking like he was chuckling.

Gerry rose from the table. "I'm going to make a quick
trip to wash my hands. You finish your discussion."

Her phone pinged with another text. Gerry left and
she grabbed her phone to see Jack's unwanted reply to
her text.

This is actually a business meeting.

She snorted.

Aren't you the boss? Shouldn't you be saying something profound? Instead of texting me?

Actually, everybody's talking about their kids now.

Oh.

She knew better than to rib him about that. Some
people were sensitive about not having kids. Others
didn't want kids and hated being hassled about that
choice. That was a landmine she didn't want to step on.

Then a snarky comeback came to her and she laughed to herself as she typed.

Sad that you can't keep control of your own meeting.

Just trying to be a generous, understanding employer.

Damn him. She laughed. When her gaze rose and met his across the room, he smiled at her.

Her heart thrummed. Her nerves sparkled like happy glitter.

Gerry returned. "Everything okay with your mom?"

Though it was better that Gerry thought her mom had texted her, it wasn't true. So, she sidestepped, explaining by saying, "It was just a check-in text."

He snorted. "I've sent that text." He glanced across the table at her. "It usually means you haven't visited in a long time." Without giving her a chance to answer, Gerry picked up the menu. "Any of their dishes are wonderful."

"I love Italian." She put down her menu. "And for the record Sunday is our monthly family dinner. They know I'll be there."

"Oh, that's nice! I should tell my wife about that. We're hit or miss with our kids. It would be good to get on everybody's schedule at least once a month."

The waiter returned and they ordered dinner. When he left, Gerry rested his forearms on the table and said, "I asked you to have dinner with me to get an update on the Valentine ball."

She frowned. "You're up to date. We had a meeting yesterday."

"That was our weekly general office meeting." He leaned forward. "You always tell us about your work in broad strokes. I'd like to get some specifics. I'd like to get a feel for how much work planning an event really is. You tell me flowers are ordered. But I want to know how much work actually goes into ordering flowers, choosing menus, finding a band, all that stuff."

She sat back on her chair. He did not sound like a man who was retiring. He sounded more like a guy who wanted to replace her.

Uncomfortable, she said, "Everything's sort of intertwined." She paused, trying to think through her answer but her brain was stuck on figuring out why he wanted to replace her.

Unable to come up with a stall, she gave up and decided to tell him what he wanted to know.

"Here's a quick rundown. The staff comes up with a theme for the ball."

"Isn't every Valentine's Day theme love?"

"Yes and no." She fiddled with her napkin. "Remember the one year that everything was silver and white with only red accents?"

He nodded.

"The theme that year was a Winter Wonderland." An idea Ivy had liked so much she decided to use it as the theme of her wedding, except with aqua and blue accents, not red. "The theme determines colors, which determines decorations, which also determines flower choices."

Her phone pinged. She glanced down at it.

Things are getting serious at your table.

He didn't know the half of it.

"After that, the decisions sort of cascade. Once we know the theme, we can determine the menu, choose a band, design decorations and even compile a list of gift bag contents."

He thought for a second. "That makes sense."

Not sure what to say or do, she nodded.

He took a breath. "You came in and took over that position and literally created your own job description."

"You make that sound like a bad thing."

"No. It was a very good thing. But sometimes, like this morning, I realize that most of the time I have no idea what you're doing."

Insulted and confused, she sat up in her chair. "I'm not slacking off if that's what you're insinuating."

He gasped. "Just the opposite. You operate like your own little country." He laughed. "And while that gets great results, if you were hit by a bus or decided to get another job, we'd be lost."

She relaxed, though it did creep her out to think of herself as getting hit by a bus. "I'm not going to leave."

"You say that now, but your events are legendary in the city. I'm surprised someone hasn't approached you with a job offer."

"People have." She shrugged. "I like what I do and want to continue doing it."

Gerry visibly relaxed.

She relaxed.

Her phone pinged.

Everything okay?

The waiter arrived with their food and in the shuffle of plates and bread being set on the table, and water and wine glasses being refilled, she grabbed her phone.

Everything's fine. But this is also a business dinner. I need to focus.

What fun is that?

She looked up from her phone as he glanced over at her, his blue eyes shining. She liked snarky, flirty Jack. But there was no future for them.

I'm not looking for fun.

Even as she typed those words, she realized how pathetic that sounded.

No wonder he was out of her league. Aside from him, the only thing she ever thought about was work.

# CHAPTER SEVEN

SATURDAY NIGHT, JACK unsnapped the cufflinks from his white shirt, then tossed them into the box on the dresser in his massive closet.

Right now, he'd expected to be in Bethany Minor's apartment for after-date drinks that probably would have led to more. But he'd been the worst dinner companion in recorded history. Distracted. Thinking about the texts he'd shared with Autumn at the Italian restaurant. Wondering if she had a date—

It was nuts. And wrong. They'd had their time together. Fate had ruined it…and he'd hurt her. He would not get involved with her again. Period. End of story. Not just because they'd had their one-night stand. But also because he was poison. Not the guy who had long-term relationships. And he refused to hurt her again.

He fell asleep thinking about her and woke Sunday morning restless and bored. After making himself toast and coffee, he pulled out his laptop and started working, but even work couldn't hold his attention.

He thanked God when his phone rang. "Hey, Sebastian! What's up?"

"Ivy's hosting an impromptu brunch. You're invited."

His pulse scrambled. If Ivy was hosting, her best friend would be there.

He told himself not to get excited, then argued that he wasn't going to say or do anything wrong. He simply liked seeing Autumn. He would not make this a big deal.

"Okay. What time?"

"This is impromptu. Put on pants and get here now."

He laughed "Got it."

He dressed quickly but slowed himself down when he got to the sidewalk in front of his building. He didn't want to look overeager... He was *not* overeager. He just liked her. Liked talking to her. Liked teasing her.

He walked the few blocks to Ivy's townhouse, rang the bell, did a little back and forth with Frances and joined everyone in the big dining room where a buffet was set up along the back wall.

He glanced at the table where a lot of people already sat eating the informal, impromptu bunch—

No Autumn.

Ivy walked over and kissed his cheek. "If you want waffles or an omelet, we can call Louis back to the omelet station. But there's scrambled eggs, sausages, cheese blintzes, toast, bagels in the warmers."

"That sounds great," he said, though his heart sank.

He told himself that was wrong, but it wouldn't lift. He ate some eggs, a blintz and a few sausages, talking and laughing with Ivy's guests and leaving as soon as it was decently polite to do so.

He walked out into the falling snow and looked up. He'd said he'd never be able to see a snowfall again without thinking about her. But he was wrong. He didn't need snow. He simply never stopped thinking about her.

* * *

Autumn arrived at her parents' home in time to help her mom put the finishing touches on lunch.

"Where are Aaron and Pete?" she asked as she tied a bib apron over her jeans and white sweater. She didn't care if she got gravy on her jeans—they were washable— but her mother was a stickler about things like aprons, placemats and spoon rests.

"Aaron's mother-in-law is in from Florida and Pete wanted to watch the game in the privacy of his own home."

Autumn held back a laugh. Her dad had a tendency to get vocal and loud when watching the Giants. Pete, a kind, gentle soul, didn't like it.

"So, it's just us?" Autumn picked up the bowl of mashed potatoes and took them to the dining room table, her mom on her heels, carrying the platter of fried chicken.

"Yes. But in a way that's good."

She peered at her mom. "It is?"

"Yes! You rarely talk at our dinners. Your brothers' lives are so interesting that they drown you out." She set down the chicken and looked at her beautifully set table with pride. "It'll be nice to hear about you."

As her mother walked away, Autumn winced. She liked that her brothers monopolized the lunch conversation. That meant she didn't have to lie or embellish what her parents considered her very dull life.

Especially on a day when she was beginning to agree with them.

With everything ready, her mom called her dad and he appeared at the curved archway between the living room and dining room.

"Well, Autumn. Looks like you have us all to yourself today."

"Yes. How's it going, Pop?"

"Same old. Same old. Looking to retire in five years."

"Earlier than most of the guys he works with." Her mom beamed. "He won't be able to get his pension until he's fifty-nine or government money until he's sixty-two, but we've got savings."

"I know," Autumn agreed, taking her seat in the middle of the left side of the table. With her mom on the right and her dad on the left, she felt like she was in an interrogation room.

Telling herself to shift that focus, she faced her dad. "I've always been proud of your ability to save money."

"Thank your brothers," her dad said, lifting the platter of fried chicken. "They found the investments."

"They're so smart," her mom put in, her face glowing with pride.

In that second, she had the odd urge to brag about how she was so independent at her job that her boss worried she would get hit by a bus, and she couldn't squelch it.

"I had an interesting conversation with my boss the other day."

Her mom brightened. "You did?"

"Yes, he took me to dinner…"

Her dad harrumphed. "I'm not sure I like where this is going."

"Lots of bosses and employees go to dinner. In fact, one of my friends was at the restaurant with two of his vice presidents and their spouses. That was also a business dinner. Happens all the time."

Reminding herself of Jack might not have been the right thing to do. Even though she'd had to shut him down, she'd loved that he'd texted with her. Flirted with her, really—

She'd promised herself she wouldn't make too much of that.

But now that she'd reminded herself of it, her brain smiled.

Her mother said, "Tell us about the dinner. Are you getting a raise?"

Glad to be brought back to the present, she said, "No. My boss told me that I do so much that most of the time he doesn't even know what I'm doing."

Her dad waved his fork. "That happens all the time with secretaries."

Her nerves tweaked. The way he thought she was a secretary made her crazy. "I'm not a secretary. I'm in charge of all the event planning. I supervise the mentors."

The table fell silent. Autumn picked up her fork and snared a bite of her chicken, refusing to get angry. Her parents were old school. If a woman worked in an office, she was a secretary or assistant. They couldn't get beyond that and Autumn couldn't change fifty years of conditioning.

"It doesn't matter, dear," her mom said. "One of these days you'll find a nice young man and settle down."

She took a breath. They'd been over this a thousand times. "Mom, it isn't that I don't want to get married." It simply wasn't in her life plan. "Right now, I'm focused on my career. I know you guys don't understand my job but it's pretty important and what I do makes a difference."

"You know who makes a difference?" her dad asked, stabbing his fork at her. "Your brothers. That's how I got savings enough to retire. That's why Aaron has that big house in Connecticut. That's making a difference."

"And making money," her mom agreed.

Autumn nodded. They might not understand her job, but she did and that was what mattered.

"So, any nice young men in your life?"

She said, "No." But Jack was. Sort of. They had a dance lesson tomorrow and maybe another one before they'd spend Friday night at the rehearsal dinner and Saturday at the wedding.

She didn't want to be excited over that. But, surely, she could admit to herself that she liked him as a friend.

That didn't sound too bad.

And thinking about him, about spending time with him, about how silly he'd been with the texting, was more fun than having her parents diss her job and ask about boyfriends she didn't have.

For goodness sake, she wasn't even looking for a boyfriend. Which might be why Jack was so appealing. He wasn't looking at her as a girlfriend. They'd had their shot and he'd ended it.

There'd never be anything serious between them.

But did that mean they couldn't have some fun?

Her dad went on chattering about her successful brothers as her mom chimed in with other wonderful accomplishments of her two male siblings and she thought about Jack.

And everybody at the table was happy.

When Jack arrived at the dance studio on Monday night, Autumn was seated on the bench changing into her ballet slippers. The door closed behind him and she glanced over. Their gazes caught and held. A million feelings rippled through him, mostly happiness at seeing her. But that was wrong.

He broke their connection and slipped out of his overcoat, then his jacket and tie. As he rolled his shirt sleeves to his elbows, Greg came out of the back room.

"Okay, favorite couple. Are we ready to tackle that Charleston step?"

Jack winced. "Actually, I looked it up on YouTube. I should ace it now."

Greg laughed. "Better to look it up than to worry about being embarrassed."

"Exactly."

"All right then. Let's take it from the top."

Without a word, Autumn lined up at the edge of the dance floor and Jack joined her. Greg started the music.

Jack took Autumn's hand and twirled her out to the center. They looked left then right, did five perfect Charleston steps, then he pulled her into his arms for the waltz.

As Greg had instructed them, they looked into each other's eyes. He told himself they had only done it because Greg had told them they had to, but there was something more in Autumn's eyes tonight. Something curious and inviting.

He waltzed her around the circle of the dance floor, flowing with her as if they were floating, as if they were made to be dance partners. Something deep and profound seemed to connect them. For twenty seconds, there was no one else in the room.

They stopped, but she didn't try to slide out of his arms, and he didn't try to pull away. They simply stared at each other.

Greg clapped. "That was magnificent! My God,

Jack, you were born to waltz and Autumn you were born to twirl."

She pulled away, laughing at Greg. "Born to twirl? Really? You sound like my mom and dad."

"In the world of dance being born to twirl is not an insult. It's me telling you that you probably don't need another lesson."

She walked over and hugged him. "I know. I'm sorry. I had lunch with my parents yesterday and they always make me overthink everything anyone says."

He batted a hand. "I have parents too. I know the drill."

She laughed again as Jack sauntered over to them. "So, should we take it from the top?"

"Only if you want to," Greg said happily. "You two are gorgeous together."

Autumn's face reddened. "I wouldn't go that far."

"I would. But if you want to continue practicing, the floor is yours for fifteen more minutes. If not, I will be rooting for you at the wedding."

"You're going to the wedding?"

"Ivy's a family friend. She and my wife are on some board together."

Autumn glanced at Jack and she smiled an I-told-you-so smile. They'd discussed the possibility that Ivy had looked for ways to force them together. Her connection to Greg just about sealed it.

"I don't think we need to run through it again," he said, peeking at Autumn. "Unless you do."

"No. I'm fine."

"Then maybe we could have coffee. There's a little place down the street." When she didn't reply, he added, "There are a few things I need to tell you."

The curiosity returned to her eyes, but this time there

was no invitation. Only caution. Still, she said, "Okay," and walked to the bench to change her shoes while he put on his suit jacket and overcoat.

This time the tension that skimmed his nerve endings wasn't excitement. It was a day-of-reckoning feeling. He'd hurt her. He owed her an explanation, even though he knew full well telling her the truth about their night together would end their attraction.

But that was for the best.

# CHAPTER EIGHT

The coffee shop Jack had mentioned was only two build-ings down from the dance studio. When they reached it, he pushed open the door and let her enter before him.

Not sure what to expect from this conversation, Au-tumn began to slip out of her jacket.

Edging toward the counter of the crowded business, he said, "What can I get you?"

The gesture was simple and maybe even okay given that the place was filled with people on phones and laptops and lines for coffee were long. Still, he'd been weird at the dance studio and she had no idea what he was about to tell her. Best to keep their roles clear.

"I'll get my own."

"No. The place is too full. You get a seat. I'll get the coffee. What do you want?"

She glanced around. Technically, there was only one table with two open seats. She'd let him win this one. "Caramel macchiato."

She wove her way between tables and people to the two high stools at the open table and sat, pulling out her phone as he ordered. No missed calls. No voice mails. Nothing to take her focus away from the fact that he'd said he had a *few things* to tell her.

Of course, she hoped he wanted to explain why he'd

left and never called all those years ago. But that was wishful thinking. Lots of time might have passed, but she wanted to know. At the same time, that lots of time had been *five years*. He could think it irrelevant.

Still, if she eliminated that possibility completely, she had no idea what he wanted to talk about.

She groaned at the way her thoughts had become uncontrollable since he'd reentered her life, before she looked down at her phone and began reading the news.

A few minutes later, he appeared at the table.

He set her drink in front of her. "Caramel macchiato."

"Wow. The big one. Somebody's not sleeping tonight."

He winced. "Sorry."

She waved a hand. "Sleep is overrated." She frowned. "Where's yours?"

"Actually, I sort of just wanted to explain something and then leave."

*Well, that didn't sound good.*

Particularly when his words coupled with the somber expression on his face.

"I wasn't going to explain why I left you that night." He shook his head. "Five years had passed. It seemed... I don't know...irrelevant?"

She'd thought that. But her curiosity spiked, and her nerve endings sat at full attention. "Maybe five years means it won't annoy me as much as it would have if you'd told me right away."

He sniffed a laugh.

Her overly active brain began remembering the conclusions she'd drawn in the weeks after he never called. He'd met someone else. An old love had returned, and he'd realized he still loved her. An old love had returned and told him she was pregnant. An old love had returned holding his baby in her arms—

"I got up in the middle of the night and for whatever reason, I turned on my phone."

So, an old girlfriend had *called* while they'd had their phones off.

"It was the hospital."

That surprised her so much her brain stopped drawing conclusions

"My mom had been admitted and they needed me to come down immediately."

*And, at her apartment, he'd been almost an hour away in Queens.*

"What had happened?"

He took a breath and, seeming exhausted, he slid onto the chair across from her. "She'd had a heart attack. She'd already died by the time I called. I don't know if they weren't allowed to tell me that over the phone, or if something had gotten screwed up. But I raced to the hospital."

She could only stare at him. Remorse filled her. Along with nearly overwhelming compassion for him. "Oh, my God, I'm so sorry."

"I was stunned. She was in her fifties. Healthy. No. She was robust. She was one of those people who had tons of energy. She'd started Step Inside. It was her baby. Her vision. I was the chef for the original restaurant, then I eased into research and development, but the day after her funeral, I had ten restaurants to run."

She leaned back on her chair. "That's a lot."

"It was. She had a good assistant and a knowledgeable vice president who operated as chief financial officer. They literally taught me the ropes of the business."

She remembered him saying something about a five-

year plan at Ivy and Sebastian's house, and realized that
for the past five years he'd been building his mother's
dream.

"You sort of dropped off my radar."

She had no idea what to say. He'd been a chef forced
to become a businessman and he'd done a great job if
the little she knew about Step Inside was anything to
go by. But he'd also lost his mom—

And he had no brothers and sisters. He'd told her he
was an only child.

"I'm so sorry."

He slid off the stool. "That's it. That's what I wanted
to tell you. It's clear that we like each other but I knew
we'd never really ever be able to even be friends if I
didn't tell you."

Not knowing what to say, she took a breath before
she settled on, "I'm glad you did."

He sort of smiled, nodded and headed for the door.

She watched him walk out into the few flurries of
snow that swirled in a light breeze. He flipped up his
collar and headed down the street to his car.

She stared straight ahead, her caramel macchiato
forgotten.

Technically, he was all alone in the world.

Autumn was so gobsmacked by Jack's revelation that
she wondered about him all week. Even standing outside
the restaurant for the rehearsal dinner, she thought about
him while waiting for her parents. It was a tradition in
Ivy's family that the parents of the entire bridal party
also be invited to the wedding and rehearsal dinner. Her
dad had driven into the city and her latest text from her
mom said they were walking up the street.

She glanced left and right, then winced. She didn't

want to run into Jack out on the street, where they'd be alone, and conversation would be awkward. She wanted the protection of other wedding participants, so they didn't have that awkward moment where he realized she knew his secrets. She knew his past. She knew his pain.

She wasn't uncomfortable with it. But from the way he'd left the coffee shop, she knew he was.

Her parents came bounding up the street. Her mom's cheeks were red from the cold. Dressed in his best overcoat and only suit, her dad looked like he'd rather be shot than enter the restaurant.

She straightened the collar of his overcoat. "Ivy's parents might be wealthy, but they are very nice."

Her dad rolled his eyes.

"Sebastian grew up middle class."

"Thought his dad was a lawyer."

"He is, but not all lawyers are wealthy." Though Sebastian's company had taken his dad's mediocre law firm and made it great when it became the firm's biggest client.

She decided to change tactics. "This is a totally mixed crowd of people. You're going to love them."

Her mom nodded happily. Her dad sighed.

They walked into the restaurant where the maître d' motioned for someone to get their coats, then led them to the private room for the rehearsal dinner.

Ivy's and Sebastian's parents stood at the door greeting guests. Ivy's mom, Lydia, with the same short black hair and green eyes as Ivy, immediately reached out and took Autumn's hands before kissing both of her cheeks. "It's so lovely to see you again, darling."

"Thanks, Lydia."

Ivy's dad stepped forward, hugging Autumn. "And

who are these two?" he asked referring to Autumn's parents.

"Lydia, Robert, these are my parents. Mary and Jim."

Robert immediately shook Autumn's dad's hand. He motioned to Sebastian's parents, who were chatting with another couple, but turned around when they realized more people had come to the door. "These are Sebastian's parents. Mike and Emily."

Mike and Emily shook everyone's hand. "Such a pleasure to meet you. We've heard a great deal about your daughter from Sebastian."

Another couple entered behind them and Autumn said, "I'm sure we'll have a minute to chat later." Then she led her parents away from the door and into the small group of round tables with elegant white linen tablecloths and centerpieces made with bright red Christmas ornaments arranged in bouquets of white flowers. Some couples had already seated themselves. Others stood between the tables talking.

She immediately homed in on her parents' place cards. "It looks like you're sitting here."

Her mother frowned. "Where are you sitting?"

"I'm in the bridal party. I'll probably be at the main table," she said, pointing to a table at the head of the room.

"We'll be alone?"

"You're sitting with six other people."

"Jim?"

A tall, barrel-chested man approached her dad. He extended his hand to shake Jim's. "What the heck are you doing here?"

To Autumn's surprise, her dad laughed. "My daughter's in the wedding." Jim turned and introduced Autumn and her mom to Paul Fabian. "We used to work together."

Mary said, "Really?"

Jim snorted. "Yeah, then he got the bright idea to buy a business."

"Sebastian's dad handled the deal and we've been friends ever since. My daughter's a flower girl." He glanced around. "Where are you sitting?"

Her dad pointed. "Here."

"So are we. I'll go get my wife."

He was back in the blink of an eye, but Autumn barely noticed. Jack entered, kissed Ivy's mom's cheek, shook hands with her dad and moved on to Sebastian's parents.

He looked amazing in a dark suit with a white shirt and a blue tie. The night she'd met him, she'd felt like she'd been struck by lightning. Tonight, a lot of those same feelings came tumbling back, but so did respect and an odd kind of empathy. She knew what it was like to fight her way through life. Now, she knew he did too.

The small room filled quickly, and Sebastian's dad announced that everyone should find their seats. She eased to the bridal table and wasn't surprised that she and Jack were seated next to each other.

"Hey."

He pulled his seat closer to the table. "Hey."

He seemed uncomfortable so she said the first thing that popped into her head. "How was your week?"

He glanced at her as if to remind her they'd spent bits and pieces of that week together, including the hour-long rehearsal only a few minutes before, where they'd learned their part for the wedding ceremony.

Eventually he said, "Exhausting."

She ignored the one-word answer that might have been a sign that he didn't want to talk. Their entire relationship had been built on drama. First, the lightning strike when they met. Going home together. Him getting a call that his mom was in the hospital, only to discover she was already gone. Her waking up alone. Then not seeing each other again for five years.

Maybe it was time to drop the drama and behave like normal people. "Mine was exhausting too." She faced him fully. "I spent most of it wondering about that dinner I had with my boss."

Obviously glad she wasn't going to talk about what he'd told her at the coffee shop, he perked up. "Oh, yeah. Why?"

"He told me he didn't exactly know my job." She paused, took a breath. "I should probably start at the beginning. Gerry is retirement age. When he told me we needed a private conversation, I thought he was going to tell me he was retiring and I was in line for his position."

Jack's brain clicked with a new memory. He'd remembered she'd talked about her job but couldn't remember everything she'd said. Now, he recalled her mentioning to him that someday she wanted to run the charity where she worked. She wanted to be CEO. She wanted to prove herself.

He waited for the recollection from that night to sour his stomach or make him feel guilty. Instead, it felt like a breath of fresh air—or like a clearing of the uncomfortable air that always hung between them. Maybe what they needed was a little more normal conversation about inconsequential things to whisk away the power that night seemed to hold over them.

He shifted on his chair to face her. "I sort of remember that. But I take it that wasn't why he'd wanted an out of the office meeting."

"No. I got the impression he felt odd about not knowing exactly what I do."

"What do you do?"

"Lots. My job overlaps. I plan and execute all events, but I also monitor the mentors and the cases they handle. That way, I know exactly what we're doing and can also be the PR person."

"Wow. You raise the money, talk to the press and handle clients?"

She inclined her head. "Yes."

"Do you have any accounting experience?"

A white-coated waiter stopped to fill his glass with champagne before he filled Autumn's. As if wanting privacy, she waited until he had moved on to the next couple in the bridal party before she said, "I took classes at university but never did the job."

He considered that. "Your boss might have been feeling you out to see if you are a candidate to replace him. You know the business. You have a basic understanding of the accounting." He shrugged. "I wouldn't worry too much about the meeting."

"Thanks."

He barely had time to say, "You're welcome," before the toasts began.

Ivy's toast to her future husband was funny. Sebastian's toast to Ivy was sentimental and romantic.

After the meal, the rehearsal dinner went on in an almost ordinary fashion, with people leaving their tables and mingling. He talked with Sebastian's best man Gio then Sebastian's dad. Then found himself in a group of laughing people. Autumn stood in the circle, enjoying the crowd, and the mixed feelings he had about her when they first sat down together dissolved even more. She loved to laugh, and he loved hearing her laugh.

She didn't seem crushed or embarrassed or even guilty at having heard the story of his mom. But he supposed she shouldn't. They hadn't really known each other that night. And though she'd been sad about his mom's passing and truly had seemed concerned about him, the way she'd spoken so normally to him had soothed wounds he didn't even remember he had.

Suddenly he could put a name to the feeling he had around her.

Normalcy.

*She made him feel normal.*

He'd spent his entire life being slightly off center. After his dad had abandoned him and his mom, there were only the two of them and they'd formed a team. At little league and soccer, he hadn't been an outcast. There were lots of single parent kids. But he'd always been *that* kid whose father had left and started another family, as if Jack and his mom were somehow substandard. Then he'd become a chef and quickly rose to be everybody's boss at the business his mom owned. Then she'd died and *he'd* owned the business. Hundreds of people depended on him for a living. Plus, he'd had a dream to fulfill. His mom's.

He'd never had a minute to breathe and just be himself.

She let him be himself.

People began to leave. Sebastian and Ivy stood at the door, excited for the big day and telling everyone they would see them at the wedding.

As the crowd thinned, Jack also walked to the door, telling Ivy and Sebastian he would be at the townhouse first thing in the morning, and ambling over to the coatroom.

An older man and woman were sliding into jackets beside Autumn who already wore her black wool coat.

As he stepped inside, Autumn said, "Mom, Dad, this is Jack. He's my partner in the wedding."

He shook Autumn's dad's hand and said, "It's nice to meet you."

Her mom said, "So you're Autumn's partner?"

"Yes. For the wedding. She knows Ivy. I know Sebastian."

Her mom beamed. "It's going to be so beautiful."

"Ivy has impeccable taste," he agreed.

Autumn gathered her parents and headed for the door. "Time to go. You still have a long drive ahead of you."

Jack said, "You drove?"

Autumn's dad puffed out his chest. "I've been driving into this city for forty years. No reason not to."

Impressed, Jack nodded. Autumn said, "We'll see you, Jack." Then got her parents out the door.

He grabbed his overcoat, slid into it and walked out of the restaurant to the sidewalk, where Autumn stood alone.

He frowned. "Where are your parents?"

"Walking to their car."

He peered down the street. "Where'd they park?"

She laughed. "I don't know."

"Are they coming back to pick you up?"

"No. They live in Hunter. I live in Queens."

He glanced down the street again. "Oh."

"Don't ask me if I need a ride. I have a car coming."

He almost chuckled. She was so predictable in her need to be her own person. But he supposed he understood that now that she'd reminded him about her desire to rise to the top of her organization. She was capable and didn't want anyone to minimize that. "Okay."

"And you can go. I don't need a babysitter."

His lips lifted. She was so adamant in her independence, it never occurred to her that he wanted to stay to get some time with her. "What about someone to keep you company?"

She frowned as if that confused her.

"Come on. It could be fifteen or twenty minutes before your ride gets here. It's better to have company. I can give you my opinion on what your boss was thinking at dinner the other night."

"You already did."

"Okay. We can talk about the wedding."

"You want to talk about flower girl dresses and silver decorations that sparkle?"

He grimaced. "Probably not."

"How about the decision that the bridesmaids should wear champagne-colored dresses?"

He laughed. "Lord, no."

"I didn't think so."

"I am curious about what you've been doing the past five years."

She stiffened defensively. "Why? Because I'm still in the same job?"

"No. Because five years is a long time, and you aren't the same, but you aren't really different either."

She shrugged. "It would be odd if I hadn't changed at least a bit in five years."

"Yeah. I guess."

He looked up the street and down again, trying to think of something to say. What came to him surprised him, but he knew he had to say it. "When we're together like this, you know, kind of by ourselves, I realize that I missed you over the past five years. Just never really knew it."

"You couldn't miss me. You didn't know me. And

you were mourning your mom as you worked your butt off. There was no room for me."

"That's just it. I always had this little tweak way deep down inside. I think that was the memory of you trying to surface but not being able to because of all the other things bogging me down."

She laughed but her heart almost exploded from the romance of it. The night they'd met he'd swept her off her feet with simple sincerity. He had a way of looking at things, phrasing things, that was so honest she knew he truly believed what he said.

Not accustomed to anyone having that kind of feelings for her, she brushed it off. "That's silly."

He took a step closer. "Really?"

Her breath stuttered. Memories of their first kiss tumbled into her brain. How much she'd liked him. How eager she'd been for him to kiss her. The same feelings coursed through her now. Stealing her breath. Prickling along her nerve endings.

"I'd never met anybody like you before. Never experienced the love-at-first-sight feeling." He edged closer. "I was so smitten, and you were so perfect." He slid his hands to her shoulders. "How could you not have known only a real disaster would have blotted you out of my mind?"

He bent his head and brushed his lips across hers. Just like the first time he'd kissed her, she totally melted. He eased his mouth along hers a few times, raising goose bumps and igniting something hot and sweet deep inside her. Memories of their past drifted into nothing, as the present drove away everything but the feeling of him against her and the way their mouths fit so perfectly.

Dangerous longing woke in her soul. She'd felt this before and he'd left her. But right now, he was very solid under the hands she had gripping his biceps, as his tempting mouth teased her into believing every wonderful word he said.

The honk of a horn broke them apart. She glanced up to see the light blue sedan from her ride share request.

She pulled away but had to swallow before she could say, "That's my ride."

"You sure you don't want me to take you home?"

And have another goodnight kiss? One that might lead her to invite him inside? For a night of wonderful sex, deep, personal conversations and a dollop of silliness?

Her heart stumbled. Fear of rejection battled with yearning.

The car honked again.

She'd made this decision lightly once. She would not make it lightly again.

"I want to be rested for the wedding."

He laughed, then ran his hand along her hair. "If past experience is anything to go by we'd be walking zombies tomorrow if we went home together."

She held his gaze almost wishing they could have another night. That she could be strong enough to face the inevitable rejection.

But she knew she couldn't.

She headed to the ride share. "See you tomorrow."

His smiled, but his eyes filled with regret. "See you tomorrow."

# CHAPTER NINE

SEBASTIAN AND IVY'S wedding was the most beautiful Autumn had ever seen. Men always looked resplendent in tuxes. But with four gentlemen as handsome as Sebastian, his brother-in-law, the best man Gio and, of course, Jack, she would bet the pulse of every woman in the room had scrambled.

Ivy's mom had forgone the typical pink for the bride's mother and had chosen a rich burgundy dress in a simple A-line style that cruised her tall, slim figure. Sebastian's mom wore an icy sapphire dress that suited her skin tone and white hair to perfection.

Add all those black tuxes and the champagne-colored dresses of the bridesmaids to the Winter Wonderland theme of the reception venue and Autumn truly felt she was in an enchanted forest. Well placed lights dramatized the small evergreens that had been sprinkled with silver glitter and scattered throughout the room. Round tables covered in linen cloths as white as snow held centerpieces of frosted evergreen adorned with blue and aqua Christmas ornaments. A huge white wedding cake sparkled in the center of the room. Accent lights of blue and aqua took turns illuminating the glittering confection, making it look like magic.

But the real beauty was Ivy. Wearing a simple white

velvet gown and white floral fascinator with netting that angled down one side of her forehead, she looked like a princess or the heroine from a fairytale. Slim, tall, regal. Her face glowed when she looked at Sebastian.

Jack slid his hand along the small of Autumn's back. "How long *is* this reception line?"

Though the feeling of his palm on her bare back sent shivers through her, she casually replied. "I don't know. Every time I turned around the guest list changed. I have no idea how many people are here."

He chuckled and temptation to look at him over-whelmed her. She glanced at him and let her breath stall at how sexy he looked in a tux. But just like the night of the gala—when he had been the most gorgeous man in attendance—she didn't feel less than. That night she'd worn one of Ivy's gowns and knew she looked as good as she felt. Tonight, she wore a backless dress. The high collar in the front was slenderizing. The dip of the back that slid the whole way down, stopping only three or four inches above her bottom, was sophisticatedly sexy.

If there was ever a night she truly felt his equal it was tonight.

For a few minutes there was chaos as the reception line continued and guests found their seats. Autumn shifted the beautiful bouquet the florist, Hailey, had made from her right hand to her left and back again, accepting hugs and greeting guests as they walked from the bride and groom to the bridal party.

When the line slimmed to thirty or so people, she and Jack skirted the edge of the room to go to the bridal table on a platform on the far end. Working to keep the confusion to a minimum, they sat as soon as they reached their chairs. Sebastian's sister and brother-in-law did too. And soon Gio and the maid of honor followed.

Ivy and Sebastian walked into the noisy room, a spotlight finding them for guests and following them. The room fell silent. They walked up an aisle created in the center of the round tables that led to the bridal table, while a version of "Silvery Moon" played. It was both a nod to Ivy's dad who loved old music and the theme of the room. Autumn marveled at the beautiful job done by wedding planner Alexandra.

The bride and groom seated themselves at the bridal table, laughing, holding hands. Gio immediately took his glass of champagne and delivered his toast.

But Autumn's gaze kept sliding to Jack, and his arm kept sliding to the back of her chair. They were like a magnet and metal. If they were close, they wanted to touch. She'd fought it the night before, through the ceremony and the wedding photos. She could be strong now too.

Gio finished his toast and to everyone's surprise Sebastian's sister rose to give a toast to her brother. Her comments were light and silly, making Sebastian laugh and his parents sit like two proud peacocks.

Champagne flowed like water. The whole room shimmered as if it had been touched by an angel.

Dinner was served, then Ivy and Sebastian cut the big white cake in the center of the room and it was distributed to the guests along with a small box containing the cakes made as a favor for each guest.

The room buzzed with appreciation and happiness. Ivy and Sebastian left the bridal table and mingled for a minute as the band returned. Then the MC announced their first dance and Ivy and Sebastian glided onto the floor.

Autumn sighed. "They look made for each other."

Jack said, "They are."

"When her dad retires, her life's not going to be easy."

"Sure, it will," he said, refilling her champagne glass from a magnum left by one of the waiters at Jack's request. "Sebastian's already working on software that will do most of her work."

She laughed and drank a little more of the delicious champagne before she turned to him. "We can't drink too much of this. We have a dance to do. In fact, I promised we'd practice before our performance."

"No need. Thanks to YouTube. Plus, there's no time for practice."

"True. We should probably head to the dance floor now to be ready once Ivy and Sebastian's dance is over."

Jack rose and pulled out her chair. "Let's go."

They eased off the raised platform of the bridal table and walked along the edge of the room until they were parallel with the dance floor.

The song shifted to the bridal party dance and Jack and Autumn hurried to get to the rim of the dance floor.

"And now here's the bridal party." The MC motioned for them to come forward. "First, bridesmaid Autumn Jones and groomsman Jack Adams."

Jack expertly twirled her out onto the floor. Then they faced each other, looked left and looked right. She twirled to stand beside him. They did five perfect Charleston steps and then he slid his hand across her bare back again, putting them in the waltz position to dance them over to Ivy and Sebastian.

Remembering Greg's training, she linked her gaze to Jack's and everything inside her stilled. Every time she touched him, every time she looked into his eyes, she felt a connection so strong she wondered if they hadn't been lovers in another life.

The music flowed and Jack smoothly led them around

the floor, his hand resting on the bare flesh of her back. She tried to focus her attention away from the way her nerve endings sparked, sending desire through her. But it was no use. Their chemistry was off the charts.

And maybe it was foolish to ignore that?

With their gazes locked, and whirling around the large dance floor as if they were made to be partners, it definitely seemed foolish to ignore it. What would it be like to roll the dice and see where this would go?

They finally reached Ivy and Sebastian. Their steps slowed, then stopped as they settled in beside the happy bride and groom, and Sebastian's sister and brother-in-law took the floor. After their few fun dance steps, they waltzed over to Jack and Autumn, stopping so close, they nudged Autumn up against Jack's side.

As if it were the most natural thing in the world, he slid his arm across her shoulders, making room for Sebastian's sister and brother-in-law.

Gio and his partner took the floor, did their steps and waltzed over. The dance ended. The MC introduced them again and they took a bow, before the band began playing a song designed to get people out of their seats and onto the dance floor.

It filled in seconds. Ivy and Sebastian headed into the crowd to mingle. Sebastian's sister and brother-in-law danced their way back to the floor. Gio disappeared.

Jack slid his arm from around her shoulders, as someone walked up to him. Clearly a business acquaintance, he motioned for Jack to move to a quieter area and then he was gone.

It seemed odd at first that he'd left her side. Being partners meant they'd been together all day. But this was the party portion of the program. They were no longer obligated to be together.

Her heart tweaked with disappointment, but she took a breath and found her parents who were still seated at their table. She asked her dad if he wanted a drink and plucked two glasses of champagne off the tray of a passing waiter.

"So fancy," her mom said reverently.

Her dad mumbled, "I'd rather have a beer."

"Let me take you over to the bar. I'm guessing Ivy has everything any guest could want."

He rose from the table.

"Wanna come, Ma?"

"No. I think I'll just sit here, sip my champagne and enjoy how beautiful everything is."

Temptation rippled through her. She nearly told her mom that Ivy's wedding might be top of the line, but she planned galas every bit as elegant for Raise Your Voice.

Still, she knew her mom didn't want to hear that. She walked her dad to the bar and after he got his favorite beer, they turned to go back to his seat. But Ivy stopped her.

She caught her hand and pulled her toward the dance floor. "I love this song. Come on. Dance with me."

Her dad motioned for her to go. "If I can find my way in this enormous city, I can find my way back to the table."

"You're sure?"

"Your mom and I aren't dorks."

Ivy laughed. "Your dad has a point."

"Okay. I'll be back after this song, Dad."

"No. You go have fun."

For once his words didn't sound condescending. Though she watched him as he returned to his table, he easily found his way.

She threw herself into the dance with Ivy and one

dance turned into three before Sebastian joined them. Feeling like a third wheel, she eased away and bumped into Gerry and his wife.

"Such a beautiful wedding!" Gerry's wife gushed. "And you look perfect! Wonderful!"

She blushed. "Thanks. Ivy has good taste."

"And you have good bones," Gerry's wife said. "I always knew that outside of that office you went from a duckling into a swan."

"Matilda!"

"What? Lots of women dress down for their job. It's a matter of being respected for the work they do. Not how they look." She reached out and pinched Autumn's cheek. "But outside the office? She's a glamour girl."

Autumn snorted. "Not a glamour girl."

"Ha!" Matilda said. "You cannot say that with a straight face tonight. I'm doing the same thing when Gerry and I move to Florida. I might have been dowdy here, but once we get our condo I'm going to dress up. We'll be the youngest of the old people down there and I will be fabulous."

Gerry groaned and shook his head.

Matilda frowned. "What? I'm talking about when you retire."

Though she laughed at Matilda's enthusiasm, the mention of Gerry's retirement caused Autumn's eyebrows to rise.

Gerry groaned again. "This is neither the time nor the place."

Matilda shrugged. "Whatever."

Gerry leaned into Autumn and said, "She's had a little champagne."

"It *is* good champagne."

"Marvelous champagne," Matilda said.

Gerry motioned to the door. "I think we might be leaving early."

Autumn said, "Have a safe trip home," watching them as they made their way through the crowd out of the ballroom to the coatroom. When she added Gerry's surprise dinner at the Italian restaurant to Matilda's happy thoughts about retiring in Florida, her breath stuttered with hope. What if he was in the planning stages for retirement? What if all of her career goals were about to materialize?

She told herself not to get ahead of things.

Still, she could almost see her name on the door to the CEO's office. This time next year, she could be running the charity that meant so much to her.

Her shoulders shifted back. Her chest filled with excitement.

*She was doing it.* She was accomplishing what she'd set out to do. She was the woman she'd always wanted to be.

She spent more time with her parents, even persuading her mom to dance. Then, drifting through the room, she chatted with other members of the Raise Your Voice staff who had been invited to the wedding, a new confidence rippling through her.

Her gaze found Jack in the crowd a few times. Once or twice their eyes had met. And he'd smiled at her as if they had a secret—

Well, technically they did. She hadn't gotten around to telling Ivy they already knew each other. And from the lack of comment from Sebastian or Ivy she suspected Jack hadn't either.

She returned his smile before she was pulled away by some employees of Raise Your Voice to dance. Far too soon, Ivy and Sebastian did their final dance, then took the microphone to thank everyone for coming and he carried her out of the venue and to a waiting limo. Everyone applauded and the band continued playing, but the night was drawing to a close.

She helped her parents get their coats and waved goodbye to them from the entryway as they waited for the valet to get their car.

She raced back to the big ballroom, hoping to dance the last few songs, and almost ran into Jack. "Hey."

"I thought you might be leaving."

"Nope, just sending the parents off."

"They're nice people."

"They told me you found them and had a chat."

He winced. "Nothing serious."

The band announced the last song of the evening and her heart sunk but Jack said, "Wanna dance?"

New, confident Autumn who'd been lurking under the surface all along said, "Sure. I'd love to."

He pulled her into his arms for the slow song and she melted into him. The connection was stunning. They didn't merely have chemistry. They truly liked each other…and she was a little tired of fighting something she wanted.

"I stayed away from you through the night to give you a chance to mingle."

She leaned back to look at him. "Really?"

"Sure. People from your office were here. So was your board of directors."

She wrinkled her nose. "I steered clear of them."

He chuckled. "I thought you'd take the opportunity to suck up to them."

She laughed joyously. It felt ridiculously wonderful that the universe seemed to be lining up for her. Career plans materializing. The man she wanted gazing at her adoringly.

If there was ever a time to be herself, to take instead of wait, this was it.

To hell with worry that she couldn't handle another rejection. If she looked at this as a one-night stand, a chance to be with a wonderful man again, she wouldn't get hurt.

She wasn't that naive anymore.

She sucked in a breath, marshalled her courage and said, "Want to come back to my apartment?"

He smiled hopefully. "Mine's closer."

Anticipation built then exploded. Her life had never been so perfect. No man had ever been so perfect.

"Sounds good to me."

# CHAPTER TEN

JACK SHOT A quick text to Arnie and his limo was outside the wedding venue in a few minutes. He and Autumn slid into the back. He raised the partition between the driver and the passengers, then pulled her to him for a long, lush kiss.

Everything inside him told him this was right. He'd considered making the suggestion himself, but he needed to be sure this was what she wanted. Having her ask—without even a dropped hint from him—proved they were on the same page.

When they arrived at his building, he ushered her through the ornate lobby and into the elevator, where he kissed her again. The doors opened on his penthouse and they kissed their way through the living room and down the hall to the bedroom where they tumbled onto his California king bed.

It amazed him that a dress that essentially had no back, also gave no clue as to how he was supposed to get it off.

She broke their kiss, reached up and undid three almost invisible buttons that fastened in the back of the high band around her neck. Then she let them go and the front of the dress billowed down, exposing her creamy skin.

His breath caught. Reverence for the moment wrestled with need.

She didn't give him time to think. She slid her hands under his jacket, over his shoulders and slipped it down his arms. He shucked it off, then undid his tie and began to unbutton his shirt.

She slapped his hands away. "That's my fun."

"I let you unbutton your dress…"

"Yeah, because you couldn't find the buttons!"

"They were craftily hidden." He laughed, then kissed her as she worked her way down the buttons of his shirt. When she reached the last one, she yanked the shirt out of his trousers and he rose, reaching for his belt.

"If you want to get fancy, we can do it another time. I've waited too long. Remembered too many wonderful things." He slid out of his pants and sat beside her on the bed. "I want you now."

Longing shuddered through Autumn. She wanted him too. But it was more the things he said that filled her with need. How could she not be comfortable with a man who called their last night together wonderful?

*The best of his life.*

He pushed her back on the bed, then gave one quick yank that slid her dress off. His lips met the sensitive skin of her neck as his hand fell to her breast and she groaned with pleasure, smoothing her hands down his back, enjoying the solidness of the muscle and flesh.

But everything seemed off somehow and she realized they were too sedate. They'd played like two warring tiger cubs their last night together. And that's what she wanted. She wanted them desperate and assertive. So eager to have fun that politeness was not invited into their game.

With a quick jab against his shoulder, she shifted him enough that he rolled to his back and she straddled him. Before he could react, she brought her mouth to his neck. He groaned, but she bit and teased until a quick move from him reversed their positions again.

She laughed. This was what she wanted. The raw honesty.

He ran his hands over her quickly, hungrily, as he suckled her breast. The crazy need that had cruised her nerve endings burst into fire. Putting her hands on his cheeks, she lifted his face for a kiss that went from hot to scorching so fast she didn't even realize he'd positioned himself to take her.

The unexpectedness of it sent lightning through her. Their scorching kiss ramped up another notch. His pace became frantic. Need swelled to a pleasure pain that exploded into almost unbearable joy. She felt his release immediately after, as ripple after ripple of aftershock stole her breath.

He rolled away and she closed her eyes savoring the sweet feeling of complete satisfaction and the happiness at realizing she had not imagined the intensity and fun of their first night all those years ago.

As if to reinforce that, he angled her to him and kissed her deeply.

"That was nice."

She disagreed. "That was explosive."

Their legs tangled. She smiled. He smiled, then kissed her again. He broke the kiss and nestled her against him. The simplicity of it warmed her, as they all but purred with satisfaction. Her ridiculously high comfort level with him relaxed her to the point that she could have fallen asleep. After the long day that they'd had, sleep seemed like a good idea. Cuddled next to him, with his arm around her protectively and his whole body brushing hers, she felt like she was in heaven.

His hand skimmed her spine. Her hands trickled up his chest. Desire began to hum and build until the next thing she knew they were making love again. Kissing deeply, their bodies gliding against each other sensually. The slower movements suited them as well as the frenetic lovemaking had. But as the need grew, light touches became caresses. Inquisitive hands became bold. They only needed to roll together to connect again. The arousal so deep and profound it rose to a pitch that couldn't be sustained. It burst like a hot bubble that rained pleasure through her. She gasped for breath and let it take her.

This time when they cuddled, she swore she could feel his happiness. Everything about their first night together came into focus again. Why she'd been so sure they were about to become an item. Why it had been so devastating when he hadn't called.

Her eyes closed. She told herself none of that mattered. She did not want to fall into that pit again where her expectations didn't match what actually happened. Especially since her own life was up in the air right now.

He ran his lips from her neck to her belly button. "We are ridiculously hot together. And fast. That could be construed as a bad thing, but I've never felt anything so intense that I couldn't control it. And I liked letting go."

"Me too."

His lips grazed the sides of her belly. "You know how I mentioned the other night at the coffee shop that there were *things* I wanted to tell you?"

His question was so unexpected, she opened her eyes. *Talk about expectations being off-kilter.* The last thing she'd envisioned right now was conversation.

She opened her eyes to find him staring at her. "I remember."

He lifted himself away from her and lay down on his pillow again. "Essentially I told you only one of them."

"You sort of intimated a couple of other things in that one admission, like how you had to take over your mom's business...which made you very busy."

"Yeah." He hesitated. "But there were other...things."

With her life up in the air right now and too many complications from that warring for her head space, she wished they'd go back to pillow talk. "Did you rob a bank?"

He laughed. "No."

"Then why are you so glum? We're dynamite, heaven and fun all rolled into one. You should be savoring that."

"I like to be honest."

She liked that he was honest too. It was one of his best traits. As much as poetry and kisses, silliness and fun would have made things easier for her, she couldn't discourage that. "Okay."

"The other things aren't pretty."

She sat up and peered down at him. "I'm getting the feeling your last five years were very different from mine."

"I guess it all depends on your dating history."

She didn't think he'd been celibate for the past five years, but she had to admit she was curious enough to give him a few details of her own life, so he'd be comfortable giving her his.

"My dating history wasn't extensive. Three short relationships. A few dates scattered in between them."

"I had three longish relationships."

"Five whole years did pass."

"The first woman stole things from my house and sold them."

Once again, his comment was so far from what she expected that she couldn't control her reaction and she gasped. "What?"

"We had a miscommunication about her place in my life. In her mind, the things she took and sold were her attempt at balancing the power."

"She told you that?"

"I recognized it as her way of saying she got angry with me and sold things to buy herself something to make up for what she considered to be neglect."

Definitely someone who couldn't possibly be right for a serious guy like Jack. "That's…interesting."

"Honestly, that was easier to deal with than girlfriend number two who cheated on me and girlfriend number three who burned down my beach house."

Her eyebrows rose so high she swore she lost them in her hairline. "Is this your way of telling me that you don't have good luck with women?"

"No. This is my way of telling you that I'm so busy I often forget things like dinner plans."

"I get that."

"Because you also work?"

"The other loves of your life didn't?"

He snorted at her reference to his girlfriends as loves of his life. "No."

"Well, no wonder number one stole from you. Unless she was an heiress, she probably needed money."

"She was a trust fund baby. She didn't need money. She needed attention. I never saw it." He reached up and stroked Autumn's face. "I don't want to hurt you again."

Ah. Now she understood. He wasn't exactly fishing

to get her take on things. But he was trying to make sure they were on the same page with where they were going.

He held her gaze. "I'm committed to my company. Technically the first five years was the testing ground for the idea. The next five years will tell the tale of if the idea is strong enough that it can be replicated on a large scale in different markets and maintain a high level of success."

"I know you're busy. So am I. Raise Your Voice had only been in existence two years before I came on board. It's why I could wear so many hats and almost pick and choose my jobs. But in our infancy, I had to be a jack of all trades. Everybody did. We were always all-hands-on-deck. But as the charity got older and established itself, things settled down, our mission found its focus and we hired more people. Still, in those first few years I wouldn't have had time for a boyfriend."

"True."

"It also means, if I take over Gerry's job, I may want to look at reorganizing some things. I may want to find ways to improve services. Add services." She took a breath. "If Gerry really does retire—and his somewhat tipsy wife more or less confirmed he was considering it earlier tonight—I'll be as busy as you are. And I don't want to blow this chance. My mom could have never had a job outside the home. She threw herself into her family. She has the happiest husband and children on the face of the earth. So, I'm grateful. But it's not what I want. In my heart and soul, I am a businesswoman."

He rolled her to her back again. "So, we'll be like this wonderfully busy power couple who understand each other."

Relief poured through her. "Yes."

"We'll rule Manhattan."

She laughed. "I wouldn't go that far, but I will tell you that we'll understand each other. We won't push for things that can't be. And maybe we'll both simply be happy for what we have."

He smiled. "I like that." He kissed her. "And I like this. And I like you."

"I like you too." The power of honesty surged through her again. But so did the power of being his equal. She wasn't her mom, the little woman who ran the household. Though she knew it took more skill and strength to be a stay-at-home mom than most people realized, she wasn't made to stay home. She was made to be in the workforce, negotiating, building, mentoring. He understood that.

She ran her toe down the back of his leg. "Remember that thing we did as soon as we got to my apartment five years ago?"

He chuckled. "How could I forget?"

"Let's do that."

# CHAPTER ELEVEN

THEY WOKE THE next morning to the sound of his phone chirping. He groaned, rolled away from Autumn and answered with a groggy, "Hello?"

"Hey, Jack!"

"Sebastian, why aren't you on a honeymoon?"

"We leave Wednesday, remember?"

He ran his hand down his face. He'd had about thirty seconds of sleep. He was lucky he could remember his last name. "Sure."

"We're sitting here wondering where you are. You're supposed to come to the townhouse for the after-wedding brunch."

He sat up. Another brunch. At the townhouse. It had all been in Ivy's last memo to the bridal party. "I forgot."

"Don't worry. Looks like Autumn forgot too."

He nudged her with his foot, his eyes widening as he pointed at his phone to let her know they were in trouble or at the very least about to get caught spending the night together.

"Anyway, Ivy's going to call her now. We'll keep the blintzes warm for you."

With that he disconnected the call.

Jack had only time enough to say, "Ivy's about to call you," before her cell phone rang.

She sat up, her pale skin glowing in the morning sun that poured in through the wall of window facing east. "Hey, Ivy," she said, catching Jack's gaze. "Oh, darn. I slept in." She bit her lower lip and shook her head, as if embarrassed by the lie. But she had a look of devilment in her eyes.

"I'll get there as soon as I can."

She hung up the phone and looked at Jack. "How the heck am I going to get to a brunch when the only clothes I have are a bridesmaid's dress and heels that are way too high."

He leaned in and kissed her. A discussion about dresses and shoes was not the appropriate way to greet the woman who had rendered him speechless the night before. Holding her gaze, he pulled away and said, "Good morning."

She smiled. "Good morning. I don't suppose you have a size eight dress and seven and a half shoes in your closet?"

"No. But I have a neighbor about your size who might be willing to lend you a something."

"I'll take it."

He hit a speed dial number on his phone to ask Regina if she had anything Autumn could borrow. Then he called Arnie and asked to have the limo outside in fifteen minutes.

When he was done with his calls, she bounced out of bed and they headed for the shower. Luckily, they knew Arnie was on his way with the limo and Regina would soon drop by with a dress and shoes or the sight of her all soapy would have delayed their trip to Ivy and Sebastian's even more.

She got out first, towel dried and slipped into one of his robes as the elevator bell rang.

He leaned out of the all-glass shower. "That's probably Regina. I gave her today's code. She'll be standing in the entry when you get out there."

She saluted and ran off. He finished his shower and when he walked into the bedroom, she stood by the bed, wearing an ivory sweater dress and black high heels.

"Luckily, I had emergency lipstick and mascara in my purse."

He slid his hands around her from behind and kissed her hair. "Yes. Luckily."

She laughed and pushed him away. "If we want our arrival to be realistic, we need to arrive separately."

He took a regretful breath. "Okay. Fine."

She opened the little black evening bag she'd taken to the wedding to get a credit card and book a ride share on her phone.

He dressed in casual chinos and a sweater, topped with a black leather jacket. They walked outside together, and her car awaited her. She got into the black SUV. He got into his limo.

Despite their efforts at concealment, they arrived at Ivy's simultaneously and walked up to the door together. When Sebastian opened it, he frowned.

"Her ride share pulled up the same time that Arnie and I did."

Sebastian said, "Convenient."

Jack smiled at Autumn. "Yeah. It was."

They ambled into the dining room behind Sebastian. Food warmed on the buffet on the back wall. Ivy's parents and Sebastian's parents sat at the dining room table talking. Plates pushed away and coffee cups brought forward, they'd obviously finished eating and were chatting.

"Where's everybody?"

"Not everybody showed up and of those who did most zipped off when they were done eating," Ivy said with a wince. "I got the impression lots of people are sick of us."

"Couldn't happen," Jack said, as Autumn said, "You did have a boatload of events."

"It's just so much easier sometimes to have everybody meet here," Ivy said petulantly.

Trying to appease her, Jack said, "The rehearsal dinner was nice."

Sebastian's parents said, "Thanks."

"And the wedding was even prettier," Autumn jumped in, seeing what Jack was trying to do. "Everything about this wedding was elegant and perfect," she said, taking a plate from the buffet and dishing out some eggs and breakfast potatoes.

Ivy laughed. "I loved your dance. You two were amazing."

"Jack had to look up the Charleston step on YouTube."

Everybody laughed.

"Hey. I might have had to do research, but I ended up doing a good job. And, admit it, you liked it."

"I loved it," Sebastian said. "Very manly."

"That's because Autumn told me to pretend that I was the extra-point kicker for the Giants."

The room fell silent as everyone thought that through, then a general rumble of laughter followed.

The tension of the room eased. While Jack and Autumn ate and Ivy and Sebastian's parents drank coffee and chitchatted, Ivy wound down. Sebastian relaxed on the seat at the end of the table.

At noon, Jack and Autumn left, forgetting to assume any kind of pretense that they weren't together. They reached the sidewalk where Arnie awaited, and Jack winced. "We forgot to get you a car." She pulled out her phone, but he stopped her with a hand over hers. "What if you didn't get a ride share?"

"You mean, let your driver take me to Queens?"

"I mean stay another night. It would be much easier to get to work tomorrow from my house than yours."

"Yeah."

She said it wistfully and he laughed. "You know you want to."

"I do. But you do realize that we'd have to run to my apartment now to pick up clothes for work and something that I can hang out in at your house today?"

"We could. Or we could call my personal shopper and ask her to pick up a few things."

She considered that. "Unless *we* did some shopping this afternoon?"

"Shopping?"

"I still have to get that sweater for my dad for Christmas."

He laughed as Arnie opened the limo door for them. "You know… I haven't been Christmas shopping in five years."

"Then it's time."

She climbed in and he slid in beside her. Arnie closed the door. Jack swore he felt the earth shift, as if something significant had happened.

But it hadn't. It couldn't.

He'd learned his lesson about relationships. He was no good at them. Mostly because he had nothing left to offer at the end of the day.

And Autumn didn't want a relationship. If her boss retired and she was promoted, she'd be as busy as he was—

Technically, they were the perfect couple.

He frowned. *Maybe something profound had happened?*

He'd found someone as busy as he was, who wanted what he did.

*Why did that suddenly make him feel uneasy?*

Arnie dropped them off at the entry to Macy's. The place was decorated to the nines with a dramatic Christmas tree on the back wall of the mezzanine above them. Covered in blue lights, it dominated the space. Evergreen branches were everywhere, highlighted with lights, colorful ornaments or pinecones.

He glanced around like an alien on a new planet. He hadn't been shopping in forever and the whole experience of the store amazed him.

Autumn had no such problem. She led him to the women's department, quickly chose a dress for work the next day, yoga pants and a big T-shirt for hanging out and some undergarments. They walked out and Arnie drove them back to the penthouse.

But when they stepped inside the lobby, he noticed the ornate decorations of his admittedly fancy building. Silver tinsel framed the huge windows facing the street. Small red bells looped across the front of the lobby desk. A silver tree decorated with oversize red ornaments sat in the corner. Candles with evergreen branches as bases adorned tables and the credenza leading to the elevators.

He looked at it all, his head turning right and left as he and Autumn made their way to the private elevator that would take them to his penthouse.

"You act like you haven't seen Christmas decorations before."

He didn't want to admit he hadn't paid any attention since his mom died, but her comment hung in the air, leaving him no choice.

"Truth is I hadn't really noticed Christmas decorations the past few years. But the decorations in Macy's were so eye-popping I couldn't help seeing them and they sort of opened my eyes to decorations everywhere."

"You've been hit by the Christmas bug."

He laughed. "There is no such thing as a Christmas bug."

"Sure, there is. It's like the flu except instead of wanting to spend the day in bed until you feel better, you want to spend the day looking at Christmas decorations and be around happy shoppers."

"I have never in my life wanted to be around a happy shopper." He caught her gaze as he carried her packages back to the main bedroom. "I'm not even convinced shoppers are happy. They all looked intense and driven to me."

"That's the look of a person trying to get the right gift."

"Much easier to use a personal shopper."

She shook her head, rummaged through her bags until she found the yoga pants and T-shirt and slipped off Regina's dress. He stared at her, his mouth watering. After all the things they'd done the night before, he shouldn't have the desperate urge that whooshed through him. But he did.

Too soon she slid the T-shirt over her head and jumped into the yoga pants.

"What do you want to do now?"

He wanted to go back to bed. But that sounded a little heavy handed. Besides, after the morning with Ivy and Sebastian and an afternoon of shopping he probably should feed her. "We could order dinner and watch a movie. Or if you're not hungry yet, we could watch a movie and order dinner after."

"How long will it take for dinner to get here?"

"Depends on what we order. Steak from Gallaghers

would probably take an hour because they generally get busy. Pizza could be here in twenty minutes."

"I'm hungry enough to wait for a steak."

He smiled. "Yeah. Me too."

They ordered, watched a movie, eating the steak and French fries when they eventually arrived. He found another movie for them, but she began to yawn.

"Neither one of us had much sleep last night. So rather than tough it out, what do you say we go to bed?"

She yawned again. "Good idea."

Getting ready for bed, exhaustion began to claim him too. Still, once they crawled under the covers, they gravitated like a magnet and steel and fell into bliss.

She drifted off to sleep first and he settled on his pillow. But instead of sleep, an odd feeling of doom filled him. He knew it was because the last time he and Autumn were together terrible things had happened. He told himself to forget their first night, his mom's heart attack and being overwhelmed with work. But even after he drifted off, the sensation invaded his dreams in the form of reminders of the failures and difficulties of the past five years.

He woke almost as tired as when he went to sleep, with the command running through his head that he couldn't get comfortable with this thing he and Autumn were doing. He couldn't get passive. He couldn't let it run them. He had to keep control of this so neither of them got hurt.

Autumn awakened in Jack's bed, though he was nowhere around. She took a second to listen and realized he was in the shower. Naked and happy, she rolled out of bed. After laying out her new work dress, she made her way into the bathroom. Jack was toweling off, but he paused long enough to give her a good morning kiss.

She got into the shower as he left the bathroom to dress.

She should have felt odd. At the very least uncomfortable. They'd known each other a couple of weeks, but they were comfortable naked, comfortable living together.

In fact, her heart slipped a notch when she thought about going home that night. Not because she liked his gorgeous penthouse. Because home was empty. He was here.

If that wasn't a red flag that she was getting in too deep, Autumn didn't know what was. Which meant she was going to have to go home after work that night. She couldn't let things get serious.

She took her time drying her hair and styling it. When she came out of the bathroom, he was nowhere around. But she smelled toast. She slipped into her dress and found him in the kitchen. White cabinets surrounded a huge island with Carrara marble countertops. She pulled out one of the tall stools with black wrought iron backs.

"Toast?"

She sat on the stool. "I'd love some."

"Coffee is there," he said, pointing at a one-cup brewer.

She got off the stool and headed over. "Can I make you a cup?"

He pointed at a half-filled mug by the toaster.

Her fears that they were getting in too deep dissolved into nothing because it appeared things weren't so perfect between them after all. Her heart jerked. Would this have been what it would be like if he'd stayed with her the night of their one-night stand?

Awkward? Silent? That just-get-out-of-here feeling in the air?

He set a small plate containing two pieces of toast in front of her. "Can Arnie and I drop you off at work?"

"I can easily get there from here."

He turned back to the toaster. "Okay."

She ate her toast in silence as he read his phone. Then they went their separate ways.

She tried to be chipper and happy at work, answering everyone's questions and even accepting Gerry's apology when he called her into his office to explain that his wife didn't get out much.

"Well, she certainly intends to fix that when you retire," Autumn replied with a laugh.

He squirmed in his chair. "Yes. About that. I wasn't going to announce until the first of the year but since my wife let the cat out of the bag, I'll be announcing my retirement at tonight's board meeting."

Her heart perked up. "That's…great? I mean, is this what you want?"

"Absolutely. We've been vacationing in Sarasota for years. It's where we want to be."

"Then congratulations!"

"My early announcement means everything will speed up. I'll start interviewing candidates now and probably the board will have someone chosen before the first of the year."

"Oh."

He frowned.

New confident Autumn couldn't stay silent. "I didn't think you'd need to interview." She almost wimped out and stopped with that statement but forced herself to move forward. "I thought I'd replace you."

"You might," he agreed, shifting on his chair again.

"Is there something wrong? Something that makes you think I wouldn't be a good replacement."

He took a breath. "It's not that. Exactly." He winced. "Seriously, you're so tight with Ivy, a board member and major contributor, that nobody's really looked at what you were doing in years."

"I was doing a lot!"

"Of course. And if you apply for the job, you'll have plenty of opportunity to show us all that."

Her heart sunk with disappointment—not that she should have been a shoo-in for the job, and no one noticed, but that no one seemed to have recognized everything she did. Still, she put her shoulders back and decided to take charge of getting the position she wanted.

The only problem was, she wasn't sure how. She'd done mountains of work, solved problems, helped clients…and no one had seen.

Plus, she'd already had one shot at impressing Gerry and, obviously, she'd failed or this conversation would have gone very differently.

She rose. "Thank you for letting me know."

"You're welcome." He smiled at her. "And if you really believe you're a good candidate for the job, I look forward to getting your resume and giving you a chance to interview."

# CHAPTER TWELVE

JACK DIDN'T RETURN from work until after eight that night. That fact alone told him that he was correct in keeping things simple with Autumn. He set his takeout dinner on the big island, grabbed utensils from a drawer and settled in the living room to eat.

He turned on that night's basketball game as he ate his chef's salad, but neither held his attention. The entire penthouse seemed cold and dead. The day had been too long. After weeks of Autumn popping in and out of his life, damn it, he was bored.

He picked up his phone. She answered on the third ring.

"What are you doing?"

"Don't you mean what are you wearing?"

He laughed. "This isn't an obscene phone call." But the exhaustion of the day fell away.

"Too bad. I'm on the subway. I'm bored."

"Still on the subway?"

"Stayed late."

"Lots to catch up on after the wedding?"

There was a pause. A long one. Finally, he said, "Autumn?"

"My boss told me today he's retiring. I must have been under consideration to replace him because he took me to dinner and asked me questions about my job. But I don't think I passed muster."

He settled in on the sofa. "That's ridiculous."

"Not really. He already told me no one knew what I did, but he also mentioned my friendship with Ivy... as if being her friend made me untouchable and they couldn't have that."

"That's a tad insulting to both you and Ivy."

"He told me I could apply for the job. I'd have to interview, etc."

"Which is the perfect opportunity to prove your worth."

She went silent again. Jack waited. Finally, he said, "But you don't want to."

"I wish. The real problem is I don't think I know how. I've worked my ass off for these people for seven long years and no one noticed me?"

"No. No one gave you credit for what you did. Do you have a team that works for you?"

"I have a couple of assistants I delegate to—"

"Do you think one of them might have been taking credit for your work or ideas?"

"I don't know. I can't seem to analyze this situation properly. I never thought I'd have to apply for this job and the comments about my relationship with Ivy just add to the confusion."

"I think the real bottom line is that you didn't make sure your superiors saw what you were doing."

She said nothing.

"Autumn?"

She took a breath then glanced at him. "I don't like to brag."

"There's a difference between bragging and taking credit." And she didn't seem to know that, almost as if there was something holding her back.

"How about this? How about if you bring your resume to the penthouse tomorrow and let me look at it?"

"My resume?"

"We'll tackle this together. Since your resume is the first thing they'll see. That's where we'll start."

"Okay. But the only resume I have is the one I got this job with. I haven't updated it."

"That's okay. Starting from scratch gives us a good opportunity to write something strong. You want your resume to speak for you. You want it to demonstrate your worth. It's your first opportunity to show them your worth."

Her voice brightened. "Right. That's true."

"How does a person who works at an agency that helps women rise through the ranks of corporate America not know this?"

"I planned events, talked to the press, monitored the office, found mentors, assigned clients to them. I never actually *was* a mentor."

"Oh. Okay."

She sighed. "You could have knocked me over with a feather when Gerry told me he didn't know what I did, then criticized my relationship with Ivy. I always believed I knew the system. Now, I'm beginning to see what a lot of our clients go through. It was like a punch in the gut to realize I wasn't a shoo-in for the position. Which is exactly what our clients encounter in their day jobs when they're passed over for promotions. I'm as shellshocked as I'll bet most of them are."

"You do realize that after you go through the process to get that job, you'll be the perfect candidate to run the organization that helps them."

"I guess I could look at this as a good thing."

He smiled. "A learning experience. You will be going through what your clients go through every day…and what better person to guide the organization created to help them than someone who knows their struggle?"

"Yes."

He heard the strength return to her voice and pride expanded his chest. He liked that they were friends and that she didn't hesitate to let him assist her. There wasn't any doubt in his mind that she would get the job. She simply needed to see that for herself and expand the confidence she would get when they ran through mock interviews.

Which meant their spending time together had purpose—

Her coming to his penthouse the following night wouldn't be about them inching toward a relationship that couldn't happen. She needed a boost and an objective opinion, and he could provide it.

So, their getting together wasn't about expanding their relationship.

But that didn't mean they couldn't have some fun.

His voice casual and logical, he said, "Bring clothes and stay over. That way you won't have a subway ride home or to work the next morning."

She laughed. "So, I'm sleeping in the guestroom?"

"Not hardly." Because she couldn't see him, he rolled his eyes at her silliness. "Arnie and I will pick you up about six."

"I might have to stay late—"

"No. Your work now is getting that CEO job. That's where your focus should be."

When she stepped out of the office Tuesday evening at six, the limo awaited her. Jack exited the backseat and held the door for her. She slid inside and he slid in behind her, caught her shoulders, turned her to him and kissed her.

"Hey."

"Hey." Their gazes locked and all the weird feelings she'd had that day disappeared. Not merely the confusing bubble of excitement over seeing him again, but the billion things that popped up all day. Especially wondering how anybody could have missed the level of work she did. She didn't want to be angry...but damn it, how could she not be? The comments about Ivy, as if Ivy had gotten her her job and helped her keep it, were infuriating.

Still, deep down inside she worried that this was her fault. Her parents had always been so focused on her brothers' success, downplaying anything she did, that she'd become accustomed to staying in the background.

Was she actually downplaying her part in the charity's success because she was afraid of success...or afraid she didn't deserve it?

She didn't know, but she did recognize she had to grow beyond any feelings of self-doubt she had because her parents hadn't seen her as a businessperson, the way they had her brothers.

"Thanks for helping me. I'm starting to think I don't know how to take credit for what I've done."

He laughed. "I'm happy to help you see the light."

"I'm serious. This might sound horribly old fashioned, but my parents worked very hard to assure my brothers were educated enough that they could conquer the world if they wanted to. They helped me as much with tuition as they did my brothers, but they motivated my brothers more." She shook her head. "I know it sounds crazy, but I think I might have ended up believing I didn't deserve the career they did."

When she said it out loud, there was no might about it. She'd fought her whole life against becoming a "little woman" the way her mom had been. But she'd never anticipated the subtle damage that had occurred because her parents didn't see her as an equal.

Yet here it was. She'd downplayed her accomplishments. Hadn't sought recognition.

"Those are easy fixes."

Doubt tried to overwhelm her, but she fought it. "I hope so."

They drove to the penthouse and she changed into the sweats and T-shirt she'd brought. When she came out of the bedroom, he was by the stove. Something sizzled in a frying pan.

She sniffed the air. "Oh, man. Whatever that is, it smells great."

"It's the makings of Step Inside's famous fajitas."

"I've had those!"

"Everyone has. This was one of the recipes I created when Mom opened her first restaurant."

Resume in hand, she slid on the stool.

"It's been hacked and put on the internet."

She gasped, but he laughed. "Imitation is the greatest form of flattery."

He motioned to the resume. "Start with your education and move to the job history."

"I don't have much of a job history. I've been at Raise Your Voice since graduating university."

"Then we're going to have to make sure that you highlight everything, and I mean every darned thing you do for the company. Because your accounting experience is limited, we'll have to make sure we set out the classes you had at university and what you learned."

He motioned again for her to read and turned to stir the sizzling fajita makings.

She read her education, which basically said the school she attended and when she graduated. Sliding the fajita makings from pan to platter, he said, "You need to beef that up by listing important classes—especially the accounting courses. When you wrote this, you were applying for an assistant's job. Now you want to run the place. Even if it seems like overkill, you have to list the things that demonstrate that you have the knowledge to do that."

He talked as he warmed the tortillas and filled them with steak, peppers, onion and avocado and she made copious notes. Then he told her to put away the resume and join him in front of the television to eat the fajitas.

He picked up the remote. She picked up her fajita. She expected the TV to spring on. Instead, he stood watching her, waiting for her reaction to her first bite.

She groaned. "Oh, my gosh! That's good."

He grinned. "I know." He sat beside her on the sofa and turned on a basketball game. "Someday, I'm going to make you an omelet."

"Lucky me."

"You are lucky. And so are the Pistons. Have you ever seen them have a year like this?"

"No. But I don't watch basketball as much as I used to before I started working."

He peered over. "Do you like it?"

She shrugged. "I love basketball. I'm on the subway when the games start. I mostly see the second half."

"I have season tickets. Rarely use them."

She gaped at him. "Oh, that ends now."

He laughed. "I usually give the tickets to vendors, employees I want to reward or friends. But if you'd like to be courtside—"

Her eyes widened. "Courtside?"

"Yelling at refs, cheering for the Knicks, I suppose we could arrange it."

She set down her fajita, twisted to face him and

kissed him. Her simple thanks turned into something hot and spicy and they did things on his sofa that made them both breathless.

Their fajitas were cold before they got back to them, but neither cared and the next night they were courtside, watching the Knicks, yelling at refs and cheering on players.

She finished her resume on Thursday and turned it in to Gerry, who smiled and said, "Thanks."

She didn't know how a person could convey coolness in one word, but Gerry pulled it off, zapping her confidence enough that she called Jack.

"He didn't seem thrilled when I gave him my resume."

In his office, looking over yet another draft of the new five-year plan his financial staff had given him, Jack leaned back in his chair. Autumn needing assistance coupled with their mutual love of the Knicks had balanced out their relationship. It wasn't just romance and hearts and flowers and sleeping together. They were becoming friends.

Those were good reasons to continue to be involved. Casual reasons. Nothing serious happening between them.

"I think that means we're going to have to practice your interview skills."

She sighed. "Really?"

"Hey, it's not a big deal. I'll ask you a few questions and then tell you if any red flags pop up in your answers."

"Red flags?"

"Things that make boards of directors cringe. When you become CEO, the Raise Your Voice board becomes your boss. You have to know how to deal with people who will be criticizing your performance and your ideas. If you get huffy or say something that makes you seem difficult, they won't promote you."

"I'm never huffy or arrogant."

"Let me be the judge of that." He waited a second, then said, "You didn't happen to bring extra clothes to work, did you?"

"I have those spare yoga pants I used for our dance lessons."

"Let me call my personal shopper and get you something to wear to work tomorrow. That way we can go over your interview skills tonight."

"Tonight?"

"Yes. This is too important to leave to chance. Plus, because you work in that office, I worry that Gerry will call you in for an impromptu interview and you won't be ready."

"Impromptu interview?"

"Just trying to cover all the bases. He asked you to dinner to question you about your job and never gave you a hint that was coming. It wouldn't surprise me if he didn't just call you into his office someday and start asking interview questions."

"We do tend to lean toward a more casual office."

He relaxed. "Okay. We'll prep you tonight and he can call you into his office tomorrow and you'll be ready."

She laughed. "You bet I will."

"That's the spirit. Size eight on the dress, right?"

"Yes."

"Okay, Arnie and I will pick you up at six."

# CHAPTER THIRTEEN

NOT MORE THAN five seconds after Autumn disconnected the call from Jack, her phone rang with a call from her mother.

"Hey, Ma. What's up?"

"I just wanted to tell you how much we enjoyed the wedding."

She leaned back, relaxing in her chair. "It was beautiful."

"And everyone was so friendly."

"Ivy and Sebastian both have lovely families."

"We spent the longest time talking with your friend Jack."

That made her sit up again. He'd said he'd spoken with her parents, but her mom made it sound like a marathon session. She very carefully said, "He's a nice guy."

"Very nice. Do you know he owns Step Inside?"

"Yes."

"He was a chef."

"I know."

"And now he runs the place. Just like your brother Aaron."

"Aaron's not a chef."

"No. But he started off as an entry-level accountant and now he runs the investment firm."

Excitement over interviewing for the CEO position coupled with hating the way her mom bragged about her brothers and before she knew it, she said, "I might someday run *this* place."

"Raise Your Voice?"

The confusion in her mom's tone boosted the sense that it was time to come clean with her mom and admit she had ambitions. Up until this point it had been easy to pretend she was an average office worker. But with Gerry retiring and a potential new job on the horizon, it seemed right to get this out in the open.

"Yes. My boss made it official that he's retiring. I've been supervising most of the general work of the charity for years. I know more about what goes on here than anyone."

Even as she said the words, she felt her confidence building. To hell with Gerry's skepticism. She could do this, and she would wow that board of directors when it came time to interview with them.

She simply had to wow Gerry first. Jack's coaching would make that possible.

"I'll be interviewing for the job before the end of the year."

"Well, that's lovely," her mom said slowly as if she'd never considered the fact that her daughter might make something of herself. "But don't you want to get married and have kids?"

"You chose to devote your life to your family," Autumn said, not getting upset about the question because she knew her mom's opinions were the result of living a different kind of life, having different goals and purposes. Still, this wasn't the time to have the discussion about *her* choices. That would only lead to an argument or a sermon. She wasn't in the mood for either.

Being deliberately vague, she said, "There are other ways to live."

"Sure. But having kids and running a company would be difficult."

"I'm a strong person," she said, steering clear of a real answer again, though her relationship with Jack popped into her brain. Neither of them was commitment oriented. Both wanted to be the best they could be in their careers. That's why their arrangement would work.

"Yes, you are a strong person, Autumn. You always have been a strong person. And you march to your own drummer."

Autumn cringed, but she recognized her mom meant that as a compliment.

"I also know," her mom continued, "that if you set your mind to do something, you will. And I'm proud of you."

The unexpected praise almost stopped her breathing. "Thanks, Ma."

"You're welcome. Now, the second reason I called was to remind you that I'd love to have you come to the house on Christmas Eve and Christmas Day, but both of your brothers bowed out until Christmas Day. Both said something about visiting in-laws on Christmas Eve." She sighed. "This is what happens when someone gets married. There are two families to accommodate."

"True," she said, biting the inside of her lip, suddenly confused. Maybe it was the talk of her brothers and their in-laws, but she realized she and Jack hadn't talked about the holiday. And she almost didn't think it would be appropriate to bring it up. If he said he had plans, that could get awkward. If he said he didn't but didn't want her around, that could be worse. Both of which meant it was too early to make an issue of it. If he said something, good. If he didn't…she'd be fine.

"Anyway, that means we'll just be doing Christmas Day. Also, you can bring your friend, Jack. Your dad and I like him."

It might be too soon for her to make an issue of it, but it was never too soon for her mother to matchmake.

"He was my partner for the wedding. He wasn't my date."

"Yeah, but he is a nice guy. It would be okay to invite him for dinner."

She squeezed her eyes shut, thinking this through, trying to come up with the response that would stop her mom before she got on a roll.

Her mom sighed. "If there's a reason *you* don't want to invite him, *I* can call him…"

She blanched. Not only would it be weird for her mom to call Jack, but there were eight million ways Jack could misinterpret that kind of call from her mother.

Oh, Lord. Even after all their discussions about not wanting a commitment, her mom could make her look like a bride on the auction block.

There was only one way to handle this. "Okay. If you want me to call him, I will." She'd never talk her mom out of inviting him, so at least if she asked Jack if he wanted to come to dinner, she could control the narrative. "The thing is, just because he and I were partners in a wedding, that doesn't make us friends. If he chooses to come to dinner it will be as *your* friend. Not mine."

"You don't like him?"

She adored him. He was smart, funny and whimsical. But his coming to her parents' home for Christmas dinner wasn't part of their deal. "He's a very nice person. But I can read between the lines. *You* like him and *you* think he'd be a good match for me. If you try to make something happen between us, it will be embarrassing for all of us and ruin Christmas dinner."

Her mom said, "Mmm. Okay. I get it. But he can still come for dinner."

"As *your* friend?"

"Sure. Ask Jack to come to dinner as *my* friend."

After a few more comments about gifts, Autumn disconnected the call shaking her head. If Jack came to Christmas dinner, even if she explained it was because her parents liked him—not an invitation from her—it was going to be awkward. Complicated. Especially if he accepted the invitation and her mom went against her word and tried to matchmake.

She would literally have to warn him that matchmaking was a possibility. Then at dinner, they'd have to pretend they weren't already in a romantic relationship.

And exactly how would that work?

Would they feign a growing interest in each other as dinner went on to keep her mom happy?

Or should they pretend disinterest in each other so her mother would back off?

It seemed…too complicated.

And embarrassing.

And wrong.

Not in their deal.

She lowered her forehead to her computer. Now she remembered why her mom never met any of her boyfriends.

Jack's limo pulled up to the building housing the offices for Raise Your Voice and Autumn came racing out. She slid into the backseat but didn't give him a chance to kiss her hello before she said, "My mom wants you to come to Christmas dinner."

Tired from a long day of work, he wasn't sure he'd heard that right. "What?"

"My mom called me today. She and dad love you. They want you to come to Christmas dinner."

"Because they like me?"

She winced. "Yes and no. They like you but I'm pretty sure my mom is matchmaking. The bottom line is they like you enough to think you're good for me."

He considered that. "That's a compliment, right?"

"Yes. I'm sorry. It *is* a compliment. But it's also confusing. I don't want my parents to get the wrong idea about us. Meaning, the dinner will be complicated."

The stab of disappointment he got when she said she didn't want her parents to get the wrong idea about them surprised him. Still, he saw her point. It would be weird to be at a matchmaking dinner when they already sort of were a match, but not really, and they didn't want anyone to know they were seeing each other.

He couldn't remember when they'd decided that, except they'd pretended they weren't a couple with Ivy and Sebastian the day after their wedding. He supposed they'd set that trend right then and there.

A family dinner with her would also set a precedent.

It almost seemed smarter to come clean and admit things—

Except, they didn't even know what they were doing together. How could they explain it to her family? Her *parents*?

"Give them my regrets and apologies. Say I have a prior commitment."

She met his gaze. "Do you?"

He glanced out the window and saw the happy red and green lights that shimmered in the falling snow. Reminders of Christmases with his mom flitted through his brain. She'd had so many friends that there wasn't a Christmas that wasn't filled with entertaining. He'd cooked. She'd schmoozed. Wine and laughter had flowed like water.

He hadn't missed that until now…because shopping with Autumn had reminded him that he hadn't noticed Christmas for five years. Now he couldn't seem to stop noticing it.

Realizing she was waiting for his answer, he smiled and said, "It's a big city. I always find something to do."

The way her eyes shifted told him she was remembering that his mom had passed, and he was an only child. He hadn't mentioned not having other relatives, but he supposed he didn't have to.

He slid across the seat and put his arm around her, changing the mood by changing the subject. "I've thought of a hundred really good interview questions to ask you tonight when we practice for your big day."

"Really?"

"Yes. And I'm going to cook for you again."

That made her smile. "That sounds promising."

"I thought I'd make something simple tonight. Chicken, sweet potatoes and garlic green beans."

The limo stopped in front of his building as she said, "Yum."

He opened the back door. "I'm using food to make you comfortable as I grill you. It will be like a mental anchor. When you think of interviewing, you'll be reminded of eating my delicious dinner and instantly be in a good mood. Which will make you positive and upbeat with Gerry."

They exited the limo and she cuddled against him as they entered the lobby. "I'll take it."

He kissed her cheek and they walked toward the elevator, Christmas decorations blinking at him, as if they had to work to get his attention. They didn't. Since his mom died, he hadn't felt alone on Christmas. He'd ignored the holiday. Why his subconscious suddenly wanted to be part of it again, he had no idea. But he couldn't it shake it off.

As he prepared the sweet potatoes to go into the oven, she pulled up the notepad app on her phone and sat at the center island. When she was settled, he didn't waste a minute and began asking interview questions.

"You've been working for us for over five years, but no one seems to know what you do... Can you explain that?"

She smiled craftily. "I've actually thought about this question and I realized no one understands what I do because I'm good at my job."

He shook his head. "Be careful. There's a thin line between confidence and arrogance."

She nodded, made a note in her phone, then looked up and tried her answer again. "I've actually thought about this question and I realized no one understands what I do because I work independently. I've been with Raise Your Voice almost from its inception. Back then, everybody pitched in and helped with everything. There were no job descriptions, but we all found our niches. I gravitated toward event planning and public relations, but I also love working with mentors. Those three jobs more or less became mine. Having done them for so long I don't often have questions or need assistance. The broad scope of my duties also gives me a very good feel for the organization. I know the mentors. I can handle the media. I understand our mission."

"I don't see any accounting in your background."

"I took courses at university. I can read and interpret

reports made by the accounting department. In my current position, I also set budgets and meet them."

The questions went on like that as the sweet potatoes baked and the chicken grilled.

They paused long enough to set the island with dishes and utensils and even begin eating. Then the questions started again.

Amazed at her knowledge, Jack couldn't find a way to stump her. She really did know almost everything about Raise Your Voice. She'd lived through most of the history of the charity. She could speak with authority about the Raise Your Voice mission, but also their mistakes. Their learning experiences.

When they were done, he stared at her in awe. "There's a part of me that wonders if you don't know more than your current CEO does, if only because you have this ridiculous ability to remember details."

She laughed. "I think it's all about loving the charity."

With the dishes in the dishwasher, they plopped down on the sofa. "I think you're right. Nothing serves a company better than a leader who loves the company's mission."

"Is that the secret to your success?"

"Yes and no. I know food. I know people. I know how much people like to get together over a good meal. So, I work to assure that our meals are festive and happy."

"From behind a desk?"

"When my mom first started Step Inside, I was the chef. I created our menu. I was supposed to form a whole new division of research and development to ensure our menu was always top of the line." He shrugged. "My being in touch with that end of things is like you understanding how a good event doesn't merely raise money, it raises awareness of your charity's mission."

She nodded, then nestled against his side as they watched a movie. They showered together, laughing and playing, making love under the shower spray before climbing into bed and discovering new and more interesting ways to tease and pleasure each other.

The next morning, he made her an omelet for breakfast and the kiss of thanks she gave him when he dropped her off at the building housing Raise Your Voice almost had him dragging her back to his penthouse to spend the morning in bed.

But he didn't. They both had jobs. They were a power couple. That's what he liked.

Still, he couldn't keep himself from calling her at noon. She no longer seemed surprised by his calls, and he loved hearing the smile in her voice when she said hello.

But when she sighed and told him she'd mentioned to her mom that he was unavailable for Christmas, he got a funny tweak in his heart.

"She's disappointed. She said Daddy will be too. But she certainly understood."

He remembered talking to her parents at the wedding, sitting at their table, feeling at home, drinking a beer with her dad.

They were nice people. Salt of the earth people, his mother would have called them. If he wasn't trying to hide his affair with their daughter, he might have actually taken them up on their invitation.

*Which would only complicate things.*

He had to remember that. What he and Autumn had was perfect. He did not want to ruin it.

# CHAPTER FOURTEEN

Friday night after work, they drove to Queens. He went inside with her while she gathered clothes—including one of the gowns she wore to Raise Your Voice events because he had a Christmas ball to attend and had invited her to join him.

As she packed, he walked around the living space. The kitchen and dining room were combined, but the living room was large enough to accommodate a sectional sofa and oversize chair with an upholstered ottoman. The place was exactly as he remembered. Same furniture. Clean in a way only a single person could accomplish. The faint scent of lavender wafting through the air.

He waited for sadness to settle over him. When it didn't, he decided enough time had passed that he'd disassociated Autumn and his tragedy, but he also realized he'd barely known her the first time he'd been here. Now, they'd spent a couple of weeks together. His only connection to her wasn't a one-night stand. It was more like a friendship that had nothing to do with that one-night stand.

Satisfied with that explanation, he smiled as she walked out of the bedroom and said, "Ready?"

He took the bag from her hand. "Yes." He gave her a quick kiss. "Should be a very fun weekend."

Arnie drove them back to Manhattan. They ate at a cute Italian restaurant near his building, then they walked home through the falling snow.

Saturday afternoon, he asked her a few interview questions, but he was in the mood for lunch out, and they went to the first Step Inside restaurant.

She smiled when they entered. "So pretty. Christmas with a twist. Like Ivy's wedding reception."

"We let every manager decorate their own store." He looked around at the aqua and purple decor and decided he liked it. "We also have a contest. Every employee of the restaurant with the best decorations gets an extra week of vacation."

She turned to him with wide eyes. "Wow. That's incentive!"

"A little something to remember when you're the boss."

Knowing they had an event that evening that included dinner, they ordered only tomato soup and toasted cheese sandwiches. She groaned with pleasure over her sandwich.

"The secret is just a hint of chili powder."

She gaped at him. "Seriously?"

"It goes well with tomato soup."

A weird feeling shuffled through him. The way he kept slipping into chef mode confused him. Of course, Autumn loved his cooking and seemed to love his tidbits of information—

He had to be making too much out of nothing.

They strolled through Central Park in the falling snow, and when they returned to the penthouse it was time to dress for the ball.

A couple hours later, he was in his tux in the living room, watching college football, waiting for her. When she came out of the bedroom, his heart skipped a beat. Wearing a sparkly red gown, with her hair pinned up and dangling earrings that highlighted her long, slender neck, she stole his breath.

He slowly rose from the sofa. "You look amazing."

She walked over and straightened the bow tie, then the lapel of his tux. "You do too." She rose to her tip-toes to kiss him. "Some men were made to wear a tux and you are definitely one of them."

Her praise filled him with pleasure, but as quickly as he realized it, the odd sensation he kept getting all day prickled along his nerve endings. He wasn't the kind of person who needed accolades or compliments. He supposed it was the fact that the praise was from *her* that made it noteworthy.

But it confused him. He didn't behave like this. Usually, he was more disinterested. Almost like more of an observer of life than someone living—

He nearly rolled his eyes at his thoughts. Who cared if he was pleased that she thought he was handsome? It actually worked very well for two people involved romantically. And it was nothing more than that.

They drove to the Waldorf and checked their coats before taking their place in the receiving line.

Autumn had attended her share of charity balls, but there was something about this ball that filled her with awe. The size and scope alone were mindboggling. But the decorations and atmosphere were almost hypnotic.

"I don't know who your friend's party planner is, but…wow…" She glanced around at silver and gold decorations, fine china trimmed in gold on blindingly white linen tablecloths and candy cane lilies in arrangements for centerpieces. All of which were accented by red and silver lights that alternated around the room.

"This is lovely."

"Yeah."

He said it calmly, as if the hundred round tables set up around a turntable bar was something he saw every day, and she suddenly realized he might be accustomed this kind of ball. He might not go to one every week or even every month. But he'd been to his fair share—

Meaning, she'd stepped out of her world and into his. Her breath stuttered at the thought. She might plan high class events, but not this big. Her guests might be the cream of the crop in the city, but this party reached another level. Movie stars casually milled about. Two tech geniuses headquartered on the West Coast chatted by the bar. She swore she saw a prince and two Middle Eastern kings.

They reached the hosts, and Jack introduced her to Paul and Tilly Montgomery. At least eighty, with silver hair set off by a blue gown, Tilly took Autumn's hands in both of hers.

"Oh, my dear, how lovely to see our Jack has finally brought a woman to one of my parties."

Afraid Jack might have been insulted, Autumn hid a wince. "Thank you… I think."

Tilly chortled. "Seriously, Jack. You might have actually found a keeper this time."

Jack leaned in and kissed Tilly's cheek. "I'm still waiting for you."

Her husband, Paul, sighed. "I'm standing right here, Jack. If you're going to flirt with my wife at least have the good graces to do it behind my back."

Jack shook his hand, his face blossoming with fondness for the older couple. "I want you to be aware that your wife has options, so you step up your game."

Chuckling, Paul slapped his back. "It's good to see you happy again, kid."

Jack said, "I'm always happy."

Tilly and Paul exchanged a look that Autumn saw. They truly liked seeing Jack happy. And they didn't for one minute buy his claim that he was always happy.

Jack put his hand on the small of her back and led her into the ballroom, but Tilly's and Paul's comments stayed with her. They liked Jack and loved that he was happy—

*She* made him happy.

Or their arrangement did.

A waiter walked by with champagne and Jack plucked two glasses and handed one to her.

"Thank you."

"We don't have to stay long."

"Are you kidding?" Maybe she was a little high on the power she seemed to have to make Jack happy, but there was no way she wanted to leave. "This room is gorgeous. There's a band. And movie stars!"

"And here I thought you were happy to be with me."

She leaned in and kissed him. "You're the icing on the cake."

He laughed.

"You know I love being with you." Remembering how it felt to realize she made Jack happy, she said, "You make me happy. I always have fun with you."

He smiled as if he didn't have a care in the world, but Tilly's and Paul's comments came back to her. He might be the Jack she remembered from five years ago. Fun, easygoing. But Tilly and Paul had seen another side of him. They'd seen him grieving his mom. They'd seen him alone. They might have also seen him after his fiancées stole his ability to trust.

No wonder Tilly and Paul were pleased to see him happy.

A couple greeted Jack and stopped to wish him a merry Christmas. He turned to Autumn and said, "Tom, Grace, this is Autumn Jones. You might remember her from her work with Raise Your Voice. Autumn, this is Tom and Grace Howell. Tom's on my board of directors."

Autumn shook hands and said, "It's nice to meet you," as the strange feeling rippled through her again. But this time she recognized it. She might have stepped out of her world and into his, but she fit. She didn't feel out of place. She belonged at Jack's side. Not as arm candy, but as herself. She made him happy. She *loved* making him happy.

And he made her happy.

Seated with a group of Jack's friends, they enjoyed lively conversation at dinner. After dessert, Tilly walked up to the microphone and said a few words thanking everyone for coming and encouraging them to celebrate the season with her. Then the band began to play, and she and Jack took to the floor.

Just two short weeks ago, they'd been muddling through dance lessons with Greg, awkward with each other. Now, they fit in each other's arms, laughed when he swung her around, and enjoyed the night.

Then they were taken home in the limo she'd gotten very accustomed to.

When they arrived in his penthouse, he took her into his arms again, this time to kiss her. He looked her in the eye with his beautiful blue orbs and the horrible truth hit her. She didn't merely fit into his world. She loved him.

Again.

This time when he slipped off her gown and she undid the buttons of his shirt there was a familiarity that opened her heart like a blossom in the sun. Touching him took new meaning. Their connection breathed life into her soul. When she kissed him, she wanted him to know that. She wanted him to realize how special he was.

His kisses felt different too. They still played like two happy puppies. But when they were tingling and needy and he rolled her to her back and entered her, their gazes caught and held. Everything she'd been thinking at the ball came into focus. He'd brought her into his world, and she'd belonged there.

Because she belonged with him and he belonged with her.

She made him laugh.

He cooked for her.

She loved touching him.

He stole her breath every time he looked at her—

They were now officially in too deep. Much deeper than they'd intended to go.

And as soon as he saw that, he would be gone.

Sunday, after breakfast and a try at the *Times* crossword puzzle, she walked into the bedroom and came out dressed in jeans and a sweater.

"If you don't mind, I need to finish my shopping."

Tossing the paper to a sofa cushion, he rose. "I don't mind. I'll come with you."

She pulled gloves out of her purse. "That's okay. You don't have to."

He headed for the bedroom to get his coat and shoes. "I want to."

He wanted to see what she looked at in stores. Because he wanted to buy her a Christmas gift. It made him feel equal parts of happy and confused. He'd spent the past five years delegating his Christmas gift buying to his personal shopper, but he suddenly wanted to choose Autumn's present himself, even though he had no idea what she might want or need.

But her search for the perfect sweater for her dad and housecoat for her mom did not help him in the slightest. Neither did the thirty minutes she spent listening to a toy store owner discuss the merits of one train set over another.

"It's for my nephews," she'd told Jack as they walked out of the store with a starter set and onto the busy street again. "I promised my brother I'd get the train that they'll put under their tree. It had to be perfect. Something they can easily add to every year."

He snorted. "I know the importance of the right train. It took me and my mom an entire fall to find the one we eventually bought for under our Christmas tree—"

He stopped himself. The memory didn't hurt, but it did surprise him that he and Autumn had a shared experience. She wanted the right train for her nephews. He understood why.

They'd lived such different lives that it threw him for a second. But he shook his head to bring himself back to the present. Before his mom started Step Inside, he'd been raised in a blue-collar environment. Just as Autumn had been—

Maybe their lives weren't so different after all?

He froze, but quickly started walking again. The

conversation had thrown him back in time for a few seconds, back to roots he'd all but forgotten he had because his life had changed so much, but also because he'd been very busy.

It was not a big deal.

Monday, he didn't even tell Autumn he'd be picking her up at six. Arnie simply pulled the limo in front of her building and she raced out, using her worn briefcase like an umbrella because today's snowflakes were huge and wet.

She jumped into the limo saying, "You were right! Gerry called me in today. We did my interview."

"And?"

She set her briefcase on the floor a few feet away from her boots. "And Friday at two I have a second interview with the board."

"The twenty-seventh?"

"Yeah."

"I thought they said they wanted somebody in place by the first of the year?"

"Looks like they're cutting it close."

"Technically they have until Tuesday."

She laughed. "I guess. But we get out at noon on New Year's Eve—in case anybody has big plans, the charity gives us time to take a nap and get dressed. If they want someone in place when we return to work on January second, that means they have to announce their decision that morning."

He hugged her. "Doesn't matter. You got the second interview! That's great!"

She pondered that a second then said, "It is."

He frowned. "You seem to have lost your enthusiasm."

"There are four people interviewing with the board."

Arnie pulled the limo into traffic, heading for home.

He squeezed her hand. "You'll ace it."

"I think so. But it's difficult for me to get over the fact that I have to jump through hoops for this job."

He shrugged. "That's part of life."

She just looked at him.

"I'm serious. Things happen. And dreams don't fall from the sky. You have to work for them."

"I've been working for this for over five years."

"Look at this as your final push."

"Okay." She grinned at him. "So, what's for dinner?"

"What do you want?"

"First of all, I need to make sure you don't mind cooking."

The fact that she would even ask that shocked him. "I love to cook! I actually miss cooking."

"How good are you with soup?"

"I am *the man* when it comes to soup!"

"Turkey noodle?"

He winced. "Now, see… I have a problem coming up with that on the spur of the moment. I like to start with a carcass. You know, make my own broth."

"Seriously?"

"Think of me like an artist when it comes to food. Just like Picasso didn't do paint-by-number… I'm not a fan of recipes. Unless I create them. I make my own broth. Make my own sauces."

"What can you come up with for a spur of the moment dinner tonight?"

"Steak. Spaghetti—"

Her face brightened. "Oh, let's have spaghetti!"

"Okay. But tomorrow I'm getting a turkey. I'll brine it and stuff it—"

"That could be Christmas dinner!"

"You're having Christmas dinner with your parents."
Her voice turned pouty. "My mom makes ham."

"And you like turkey?"

"I *love* turkey."

The way she said it made him laugh. "Maybe we could eat the turkey on Saturday. By then you'll be sick of ham. I can spoil you."

Autumn liked the sound of that. As long as he was happy, she was happy. And planning dinners was a far cry from the emotionally charged night they'd had after the ball. It almost seemed like a return to normal. The kind of relationship they could handle.

They changed out of work clothes and into casual clothes and she watched him make spaghetti. He pulled out a bag of frozen noodles that he'd prepared from scratch and a bag of frozen sauce.

The whole time he thawed and prepared things, he talked about creating the dishes for Step Inside.

"It was like having a couple thousand anonymous judges. People don't hesitate to criticize you on social media…or compliment. I loved the challenge of it."

She took a sip of wine. "You sound like me when I need to choose the perfect floral arrangements for a summer gala. I never minded the criticism I got on the samples. I use it to make the arrangements better."

He gave her a taste of sauce. "What do you think?"

"I think your abilities are wasted running the company."

He chuckled and turned away, but the truth of that settled into her brain. His food was amazing and he was clearly happy cooking—

"How did you go from being the creative soul of the

company to being the guy who looks at numbers? That couldn't have been easy."

"It was an adjustment."

"I'll bet." But he didn't say anything else. He didn't say, *It was an adjustment but now I love it.* He'd simply acknowledged the adjustment. He also wasn't enthusiastic about his job. Not the way he enjoyed cooking for her.

But he didn't seem to see it.

Just as she'd suspected, the spaghetti was so good, she groaned. "I can't imagine being this talented," she said, pointing at the spaghetti with meat sauce.

He ladled more sauce on her spaghetti as if he thought she hadn't taken enough. "I studied here in New York. After that I was working as a sous chef when Mom decided to open her restaurants. At first, it was just the one, but she had a dream."

"Have you ever considered that you inspired her dream?"

His eyebrows knit together when he frowned. "What?"

"You clearly have talent. She must have seen that and decided to create the vehicle you could use to sky-rocket to stardom."

He laughed. "You have such an interesting way of looking at things."

She studied his face, seeking signs that he saw what was going on in his own life. None came. He was clue-less. "Or maybe I see things that you missed?"

He shook his head and dug into his spaghetti, the conversation dying a natural death as they talked about myriad other things as they ate.

When they were done, he rose to clear their dishes. She motioned him back down. "I'll clean up."

"You're a guest."

After the way they'd made love on Saturday night, that hit her funny and she stopped halfway to picking up his plate. She'd felt the difference in their feelings, the connection, the commitment to each other. Maybe he hadn't. But she had. If she looked at it that way, she knew his calling her a guest was meant to be positive, complimentary.

And, really, she wasn't supposed to be looking at this any other way than casual. That's all he wanted. That's all *she* wanted—

Wasn't it?

She took a breath and reached for his dish again. The short amount of time they'd known each other made his way of categorizing the relationship the smarter one. No matter that their crossover into stronger feelings had happened naturally. It was not in their plan. She had to get herself in line with him or she'd say or do something she'd regret.

She stacked the dishes in the dishwasher and tidied the kitchen while he checked his streaming service for a movie. They stayed up later than usual because neither one of them had work the next day, Christmas Eve. Remembering that, she also realized he didn't have a tree or any sort of Christmas decorations.

It didn't seem right that she'd be waking up Christmas morning in a house that didn't even have a nod to the holiday.

She woke early on Christmas Eve. Leaving him sound asleep in his comfortable bed, she tiptoed into the bathroom. After showering and dressing, she went out into the marshmallow world of accumulating snow. Fat, fluffy flakes tumbled around her as they billowed to the ground, toppling on piles of snow scraped off the sidewalk to the fronts of coffee shops, restaurants and boutiques.

Two hours later, with a small artificial tree and two boxes of ornaments, she had to call a car to take her home. Jack wasn't anywhere around when she stepped off the elevator into the penthouse but that simply made her surprise even better.

Halfway through assembling the tree, her phone rang. She plucked it from the sofa, saw the call was from her mom and answered. "Hey, Ma."

"Hey, yourself."

She'd never heard that discouraged tone from her mom and knew something had happened. "What's up?"

"Oven broke. No one's working on Christmas Eve. I can't get it fixed. And it's too late to go out and buy a new stove. It wouldn't be here by tomorrow. Which by the way is Christmas…so no one is working then, either."

She pressed her lips together to keep from laughing. The problem might be bad, but it wasn't the end of the world. "I'm sorry. I know this ruins your plans for Christmas dinner."

"I wanted a big dinner, but we can make do. I'm thinking tomorrow's lunch could be cold cuts and a cake, if there's a shop that still has a cake this close to Christmas." She sighed. "I should have baked the pies yesterday."

"It's not a big deal, Mom. Cold cuts will be fine."

The elevator door opened, and Jack walked out. He carried two huge bags into the kitchen and put them into the refrigerator before he strolled over to the sofa and bent to kiss her cheek. She smiled up at him.

"The family's accustomed to my brown sugar pineapple ham."

"No one cares about the ham, Ma. Everybody just wants to be together. Besides, without having to spend your morning in the kitchen you'll have more time to play with your grandkids."

"I suppose."

Frowning, Jack sat on the sofa beside her.

"Maybe I could hunt around Manhattan for a cake?"

"Manhattan? Are you at work? It's Christmas Eve! Don't you take a day off?"

She winced, realizing she'd nearly spilled the beans about being at Jack's. "I meant Queens."

"Okay. With all the shopping I have to do to change dinner, I'd appreciate it if you could bring dessert tomorrow."

"Consider it done."

"Thanks. I'll see you tomorrow around noon."

Autumn disconnected the call and Jack pulled her to him for a long, lingering kiss.

"I take it that was your mom."

"Yeah. Poor thing. Her oven broke. She can't bake the family ham and mashed potatoes…or her world-famous pumpkin pies."

"World-famous?"

"Well, maybe not world-famous. But the whole family loves them. They're a tradition. Still, I think she'll be okay with having sandwiches and cake tomorrow." She shrugged. "Not the big dinner she likes to make, but the point is getting the family together. She knows that and she'll be fine."

He nodded, then inclined his head toward the half-assembled Christmas tree. "I was going to ask you where you were when I finally rolled out of bed, but I figured it out. You should have woken me."

She laughed and kissed him again. "I knew you needed the sleep."

He chuckled.

She rose from the sofa and began inserting fake evergreen limbs into the pole that made up the spine of the artificial tree. "I also thought your house could use some holiday spirit."

He picked up one of the branches and examined it. "I haven't had a tree in forever." He caught her gaze. "Not even a fake one."

She'd bet he hadn't had a tree since his mom's passing, but she decided not to mention that. "Where did *you* go?"

"I did some shopping too. Got a turkey."

"Oh, for turkey noodle soup!"

"Yep. Also got a ham. Thought I'd make that for myself tomorrow—"

Jack stopped midsentence. In the butcher shop, choosing a turkey, he'd seen the ham and the Christmas decorations around the display case and suddenly wanted it. But there was a much better purpose for that ham.

"I could make your family's Christmas dinner."

"What?"

"Your family could come here, and I could make Christmas dinner."

Her eyes widened in horror. "Fate stole my mother's chance to make a ham. She's not going to agree to having Christmas anywhere but at her house."

He realized that in his spontaneity he'd forgotten they'd be outing themselves to her parents. She'd be too familiar with his house. He'd be too comfortable having her there. But he wanted to do this—

"Okay. I'll bake the ham here and we'll take it to your parents' house tomorrow."

"That's very nice of you, but—"

"Hey, your mom invited me to dinner. I know I'm welcome."

"Of course, you are! I just don't want you to go out of your way."

"It's not out of my way. We can get up early. I'll bake the ham and make some side dishes." The happy feelings he'd had standing in the butcher shop returned full force. The joy of really celebrating the holiday rushed through him. "It will be fun."

She bit her lower lip. "I should call my mother and tell her you're going to do that."

"You don't want it to be a surprise?"

"I don't want my mom and dad to be eating deli meat from their freezer until August." Happiness suddenly filled her eyes, as if the merit of his idea finally sunk in for her. "Thank you. You're right. This could be fun."

He laughed as she picked up her phone to call her mom, but warmth filled him, as the spirit of Christmas warmed him. He'd liked her parents. It felt good to be able to do something nice for them.

He hadn't felt this way since he was nine, anticipating gifts and a special dinner. Candy in a stocking. Cookies left on the doorstep by neighbors. Carolers going from floor to floor of their apartment building, singing.

Crystal clear memories swept through him. Instead of brushing them away, he smiled and began planning the menu for Christmas dinner.

# CHAPTER FIFTEEN

THEY WOKE EARLY the next morning, as Jack had said they would. He prepared the ham for baking then began making side dishes, sliding each one into storage containers as he completed them, then putting those containers into a thermal carrier.

"You're certainly prepared."

He peeked up at her. "Because I have storage containers?"

"No. The thermal thing. I didn't even know those existed."

He leaned across the center island and kissed her. "Because I'm guessing you don't cook, let alone take things to your mom's."

"Hey, I bought the cake."

"You and I are going to be the hit of the day."

He carted things to his Mercedes in the basement of the building. She scurried after him with the cake box, setting it beside the thermal container in the trunk. He'd baked the ham in an electric roaster not merely for ease of transport but to heat it before lunch. He took that to the car, then returned to the penthouse to help her carry the train for her nephews while she held a shopping bag of presents for her parents.

When they were finally settled on the front seat, she

thought he'd start the car. Instead, he sat there for a few seconds, then reached into the pocket of the leather jacket he wore over a sage green sweater.

He handed her a small gift, obviously a wrapped jeweler's box. "I bought this for you. Merry Christmas."

Her heart stuttered. "Oh, I'm sorry. I didn't think we were doing presents."

He laughed. "If you're saying you didn't get me anything, I'm sort of glad. We've only been in each other's lives a few weeks. Presents might have been premature at this point." He paused to suck in a breath. "But I just wanted to buy you something." He peeked at her. "Myself." He sniffed a laugh. "It sounds weird when I say it out loud."

It sounded wonderful to her. It sounded like a man who was getting real feelings for her. Maybe even a guy who hadn't had real feelings for so long he didn't recognize them.

But she did. As long as she didn't push, he'd eventually come to the right conclusions.

He nudged his chin in the direction of the box. "Open it."

Her fingers shook slightly as she ripped the red foil paper from the box then opened it to reveal a diamond solitaire necklace. She wasn't an expert, but she'd seen one and two-carat solitaires. This one was bigger.

Her gaze jumped to his. "Oh, my God."

"You like it?"

She took it out of the box. When she held it up, the diamond caught even the dim light of the basement garage and sparkled like the sun. "It's beautiful."

"I just kept thinking that you have such a pretty neck, and this would be perfect nestled right there."

He tapped the little dip at the base of her throat before motioning for her to give him the necklace.

She handled it over and pulled her hair off her neck before turning around so he could fasten it at her nape. When he released the chain, the diamond fell exactly where he wanted it.

She faced him again and he smiled approvingly, proudly. "Just as I thought. It's perfect. Merry Christmas."

She'd never seen him so happy. Tears filled her eyes. "Merry Christmas." Such an ordinary thing to say, and an ordinary thing to do on Christmas Day, but the moment softened her bones and found a home in her heart. He might not realize it, but he loved her.

He started the car, but she put her hand on his forearm to stop him from putting it in gear. Then she leaned in and kissed him. "Thank you."

He smiled. "You're welcome."


They arrived at her parents around eleven, an hour before the other guests were to arrive. He pulled the Mercedes into the driveway of a white two-story house with black shutters. Very modest and traditional.

Carrying the roaster first, he followed Autumn to the front door. She entered without knocking. "Ma! Pop! Jack and I are here with lunch."

Her mother scrambled down the stairs as her dad lifted himself out of a recliner in a living room made small by the enormous Christmas tree in the corner.

"I've got the ham," Jack announced trailing Autumn as she led him to the kitchen. "We can plug in the roaster and it will be perfect by the time guests arrive."

Autumn's mom pressed her hands to her face. "This is wonderful!"

Unbuttoning her coat, Autumn leaned in and kissed her mom. "It's fabulous to live with a chef."

Her mom's head tilted in question.

Realizing what she's said, Autumn quickly covered her mistake. "I meant have a chef in your social circle." She shook her head as Jack exited the front door again to get his thermal bag of side dishes.

She quickly faced her mom. If her mom said or did the wrong thing, Jack could react badly. He wasn't skittish. He was careful. And they hadn't known each other long enough for him to endure her mom's well-meaning but pushy comments. This perfect dinner could end their relationship or at least send them back to square one.

"You promised no matchmaking. That also means no making something out of nothing."

Her mom straightened indignantly. "Well, I'm sorry for wanting the best for my daughter."

"And I would like the chance to choose my own partner."

Her mom rolled her eyes. "You've been making up your own mind since you were four. I do not think I'll change you now."

Her mom sauntered away as if she wasn't going to let anything ruin her good mood, and Autumn breathed a sigh of relief. She'd killed two birds with one stone in that short exchange. Her mom had been warned about matchmaking and Jack had been out of earshot.

Things were going well.

As Jack took care of business with lunch, her dad ambled into the kitchen, opened the refrigerator and pulled out two beers. He handed one to Jack, then twisted the cap on the second for himself. Jack reheated side dishes and tended to the ham, and Autumn's dad chitchatted with him about the Knicks.

Aaron soon arrived with his wife Penny and two boys, Mark and Donnie, who bounded over to Autumn, hugging her around the thighs.

She laughed with them, then chased them from the living room, through the dining room, into the kitchen and the foyer and back into the living room again. They shrieked with laughter when she caught them and tickled them, then the whole process started again until Autumn was so tired she had to sit.

Pete and his wife arrived late. But once they were out of their coats and settled in the living room, the opening of gifts began. Autumn sat on the floor beside the recliner, while Mark and Donnie distributed gifts. At six and four, neither could read, so they brought the packages to Autumn who read the tags before the boys took them to the appropriate receiver.

With the gifts opened, they moved to the dining room, where they ate the ham, hot potato salad, peas and pancetta, herb and garlic linguine, and creamed kale and mushrooms.

Her mom said, "This is fantastic."

"I didn't want to overstep by making your pineapple ham and thought this would be a good replacement dinner until next year when your cooking will be the star again. Autumn tells me no one makes a pineapple ham like yours."

Mary blushed. "Well, I don't know about that."

"Your ham is great, Ma," Autumn said.

Aaron said, "Best around," as Pete said, "Absolutely the best."

Autumn smiled across the table at Jack, who winked at her, and she suddenly realized how modest he was. He didn't need to steal the show. He'd helped out— saved Christmas dinner—without making it a big deal.

Four-year-old Donnie strolled over to him with the car he'd gotten as a gift from Pete and Sasha. "It doesn't work."

Jack shifted on his seat and took the car from Donnie. Turning it over, he said, "Ah. You know why? It needs a battery."

Shaggy-haired Donnie blinked up at him.

Jack said, "It's a power source," then realizing who he was talking to he said, "It's what makes the car run."

Autumn bit back a laugh as her heart about exploded in her chest. She adored her nephews and having Jack be so kind to Donnie filled her with pleasure—then something else that made her swallow hard.

*She could see Jack as a daddy.*

No. She could see Jack as the father of *her* children. In this house for holidays. Laughing with her mom, talking about the Knicks with her dad.

She *loved* him. Deeply. Profoundly. So much her heart swelled to its breaking point.

It wasn't what she wanted.

But more than that, he wasn't ready.

Mary scrambled from her seat. "We have some batteries in the junk drawer."

Autumn's dad waved her down. "I'll get them. You eat."

Autumn did a doubletake as her dad rose from his chair and headed for the kitchen. He returned in a minute and handed the batteries to Jack who nimbly installed them and gave the car to Donnie.

"Press that little button there."

Donnie grinned, pressed the button and giggled when the toy car's engine came to life.

"Put it on the floor," Pete encouraged.

Donnie stooped down, placed the car on the floor

and gasped when it raced from the dining room into the kitchen, stopping only when it hit the center island.

Everyone laughed. Donnie ran into the kitchen. Jack set his napkin on his plate and followed the little boy to the car. Mark quickly joined them.

Jack showed the two little boys the clear path for the car to run and they took turns hitting the start button, setting it on the floor, letting it run to the back door, then scooping it up and repeating the process.

Autumn watched them through the twenty minutes they played, wondering if Jack realized how good he was with kids.

And that he wanted a family?

Oh, he'd never say it. And she'd never even hint to him that his longing and joy were evident on his face and he played with her nephews...but it was there. She could see it. He wanted a family and she didn't.

Instead of watching the football game, as Jack assumed they would, the family cleared the table then set it up again for a game of Yahtzee.

At Jack's puzzled expression, Pete caught his elbow and dragged him a few feet back.

"Ma doesn't like football. So we play an hour or two of Yahtzee before we settle in like slugs."

"Okay."

They took seats around the dining table again. This time, instead of being across from Autumn, he found himself seated beside her. He remembered her warning about her mother and matchmaking, but he didn't have the sense that her mom had pushed them together. All he saw was what he believed to be the normal activities of family.

He and his mom had never been alone on Christmas. She had too many friends. But they'd never had the simplicity of connection that he found here with the Jones family.

Kindness and laughter interspersed with teasing that usually led to more laughter.

Not familiar with the game, he'd come in dead last. Autumn's mom won, even letting Donnie roll her dice most of the time. Jim drank more beer, clearly unconcerned with positioning his dice rolls for maximum score. But Pete and Aaron had something of a competition that led to Pete coming in second and Aaron third, but only by three points.

Everybody laughed and joked, but by the time they were in the living room the Yahtzee scores were forgotten.

Around seven that night, it struck him that he hadn't once thought about leaving. He liked it at Autumn's parents' house. It wasn't the Christmas he was accustomed to with his mom. It was Christmas the way he'd imagined it when his friends talked about their holidays. What he believed "real" Christmas should be like.

He knew he was quiet as he drove back to the penthouse and realized neither he nor Autumn questioned where she'd spend the night. He pulled the Mercedes into his parking space. Autumn carried her gifts from her parents, and he carried the roaster which was big enough to hold the empty storage containers and thermal carrier.

They stepped off the elevator into the penthouse, totally silent. He assumed she was exhausted, maybe too tired to talk. It had been a long two days. But he was quiet because it all felt too normal.

Too, too normal.

Technically, he'd known Autumn for five years. But he had really only been in her life a few weeks. He'd met her parents three times. He'd only met her brothers that day.

How could this feel normal?

And why was it he hadn't missed his mom?

Hadn't *thought* of her except in passing all day.

Hadn't even considered going to the mausoleum with flowers as he did some Christmases.

Guilt overwhelmed him. His mother had been the center of his world. She had also provided him with an opportunity to be the creative center of Step Inside. He didn't believe, as Autumn had said, that she'd opened a restaurant to give him a place to showcase his talent. But he did see that those years he'd spent planning menus and creating recipes for her company had been a gift of a sort.

*And he'd forgotten her.*

It rattled through him, made him feel odd, itchy like he couldn't reconcile it in his brain.

"I think I'll shower," he said as they stepped into the bedroom. He walked toward the bathroom, pulling his sweater over his head, not waiting for Autumn's reply.

In the bathroom, he turned on all the jets and grabbed his bodywash. The shower steamed enough that he didn't see Autumn enter until she opened the glass door and walked inside to join him.

Without a word, she slid against his soapy torso, put her arms around his neck and kissed him. He fell into the kiss like a drowning man, which only confused him more. When the diamond solitaire at her throat winked at him, something sensual and possessive raced through him and he kissed her hotly, greedily, as he ran the luffa down her back, then let it fall to the shower floor, replacing it with his hands.

Laughing, she slid away, but he caught her wrist and brought her back, so he could nuzzle the shiny spot at her throat and let his hands touch every inch he couldn't reach with his lips. Sliding both palms up her sides, he let them meet below her breasts, lifting them for his eager mouth. She moaned as he pulled on each one, then she wrapped one leg around his thighs.

Power coursed through him when he realized she'd positioned them perfectly. He angled himself to enter her, then shifted their positions so that he could sit on the shower bench with her straddling him. When they were settled, he let his lips roam from her shoulders to her stomach and back up again. She tensed, trembling and began the rhythm that brought them both to a fever pitch of need.

Her release came first, rippling around him, bringing him to the point of no return.

After that they showered for real, and he'd never felt more energized and yet more exhausted. The crazy push pull between guilt and happiness happening in his brain had been silenced while they were in the shower, but it seemed to be back again. Guilt wanted to drag him down. Even as happiness bubbled through him.

Telling himself to stop thinking, he toweled off Autumn's back and she returned the favor, which led to kissing again.

Wonderful kisses that reached the entire way to his soul and filled up empty places he always knew were there but couldn't reach himself. They kissed their way to the bedroom and fell into bed where they made love again and eventually drifted off into an exhausted sleep.

But in the last seconds of consciousness, it struck

him that even the fleeting thoughts or memories he'd had of his mom had always evaporated into nothing that day.

It was like he couldn't hold on to them.

Like losing her again.

Which made him wonder how in the hell he could allow himself to be happy, when he was forgetting the person who hadn't merely raised him; she'd given him a wonderful life.

# CHAPTER SIXTEEN

HE WOKE THE next morning to find Autumn gone. He rolled out of bed, slid into sweatpants and a sweatshirt and headed for the main area.

When he reached the living room, he saw her in the kitchen, toasting bagels.

She walked over and kissed him. "We had so much rich food to eat yesterday, I thought we should go back to basics...bagels."

Scrubbing his hand across the back of his neck, he laughed. He loved having her with him and wished he could figure out, and to make his peace with, his guilt and sorrow. Especially when Autumn herself was one of the reminders of his remorse. He'd been with her the night his mom had died.

In fact, being with her had taken away his opportunity to change the outcome of that night.

If he hadn't been with Autumn, he might have gotten his mom the medical help she needed—

"I also wanted to thank you for being so good to my parents yesterday. My whole family really."

He fought the guilt, the memories of the night his mom died, and forced himself into the present. "Your family is very easy to get along with."

The toaster popped. She took out two sides of the

first bagel and offered them to him. "You have cream cheese, right?"

"Of course, I have cream cheese."

She laughed, then kissed him again.

The world righted for a few seconds then quickly fell off-kilter again because he could not understand how all this could feel so perfect, so right, when inside he was angry with himself. He stood in the center of his fancy kitchen, holding two halves of a bagel, looking like a tourist in Times Square, not sure which way to turn.

She opened the refrigerator, retrieved the cream cheese and set it on the center island.

He shook his head, hoping to clear these feelings, as he prepared his bagel.

"Of course, we could eat them plain to give our stomachs the chance to balance out."

He said nothing, simply took his bagel to the side of the center island that offered seating, set it on a napkin and then walked to the coffeemaker. Silence hung in the air as she put cream cheese on her bagel and his coffee brewed.

When both were finally seated at the island the silence wasn't merely obvious, it was telling.

He knew he couldn't get himself out of his own head. Couldn't fight the guilt over having had such a good day.

He had no idea why Autumn was quiet.

She took a breath. "Okay, look. I know yesterday had to be hard for you."

"You just said you appreciated how good I was with your family. Now, you're saying you could tell the day was difficult for me?"

"You didn't get quiet until we were in the car. Then you were odd when we got home."

"You didn't seem to think so in the shower."

She laughed and caught his gaze. "You were your normal self then."

He couldn't reply. Not because she was wrong. Because he hated that she wanted to talk about this when he wasn't even sure what to say.

"I think it's perfectly normal for someone to decompress after meeting so many new people, but there's more. You really seemed to enjoy cooking dinner for my parents."

"I did."

"And they loved it and you loved that they loved it."

"What's wrong with that?"

"Nothing. That's my point. You've been cooking and talking about cooking so much that it struck me last night that I think you might be missing how cooking is becoming part of your life again."

That was far, far away from what he'd been thinking last night, but for some reason or another it resonated. Which was stupid considering all the misery and guilt he'd been experiencing. "You think I miss cooking?"

"Yes."

Suddenly, the truth of that rippled through him. Experiencing grief and guilt had tried to drown it out, but she was right. He'd enjoyed making Christmas dinner. He'd enjoyed cooking in a way he hadn't in years—

He blocked the thought, but it wouldn't go away because these feelings weren't new. He'd been having them since he'd begun cooking for Autumn. He'd gotten so good at blocking them he didn't even feel them pop up anymore.

That thought spiraled into more thoughts. He could see himself cooking for her forever. But he could also see that though that might be fulfilling for a while, it was not a permanent solution—

Solution?

To the guilt? That didn't make sense.

"You know, you haven't spoken a lot about your mother, but you've said enough that I've guessed some things."

He glanced over at her.

"You've told me that you're keeping her dream alive. Maybe building her dream."

He cautiously said, "I am."

"And you believe her dream was to have a bunch of really great restaurants."

"A business. Not necessarily restaurants. My mom wanted to run a business. She was incredibly smart. She took night classes at community college, thought things through and ultimately wanted to create a successful business."

Her face softened as she put her hand on his forearm, as if comforting him. "When did the desire to start a chain of restaurants come up for her?"

"After I did some apprenticeships, we both saw that I had some unique abilities and she realized that was her chance."

"What if that wasn't what happened?"

He peered at her.

"What if she saw your potential as a chef and she started her business as a way to give *you* a platform?"

She'd mentioned something like that before, but it didn't fit. "My mom had always wanted to start a business. Because she'd been a waitress and hostess and even a general manager of a diner, restaurants seemed like a good fit."

"Jack, I know I may be overstepping here. But watching you cook for me all week and how you enjoyed it... I felt like I understood what your mom felt watching you. She might have always wanted to start a business, but she didn't even try until you showed promise."

He stared at her.

"I think what she really wanted was for you to continue research and development. To make Step Inside extraordinary because of your talent."

His temper hummed below his skin. "Are you saying Step Inside wasn't her dream?"

"It was very much her dream. Her dream *for you*. I think that when you lost her, you got it backwards. I think she wanted you in R&D. Not taking the place she had."

The hum became red hot anger. "Stop. Just stop. That wasn't how it was."

She held up her hands. "I'm not saying this to make you mad. I'm not saying that you have to change. I'm just giving you something to think about, something to consider."

"Because I've been moody?"

"Sort of. But more because you're wasting your talents."

"Well, thank you very much." He rose from the stool, his anger so hot and so potent he could have easily said something he would regret. Heading for the bedroom, he said, "I'm going in to work today. I'll text Arnie's number to you and you can have him drive you home." He turned and faced her. "Unless you'd rather take the subway. Isn't that what you do? Resist everybody's help or opinion. Even though you don't hesitate to share your own."

"That's not fair! Especially since you all but coached me for the CEO position."

He said, "Hmmm." And headed for the bedroom again. She was right. She had taken his help and now she was offering hers and it infuriated him. Not because he didn't like assistance or opinions but because she was wrong! She thought she had his whole life figured out when he didn't even have his life figured out!

He dressed quickly and was returning to the main area before she'd finished her bagel.

Without a word, he walked past her, shrugging into his leather jacket. Knowing no one else would be in the office, he'd worn jeans and a sweater, so the jacket worked.

And his Mercedes keys were in the pocket.

Autumn watched him go. A million questions swam in her head. She could think their disagreement small, meaningless, a blip, something they would laugh about that evening when he returned.

Except—with his offer of a ride from Arnie—he'd kicked her out.

She bit her lower lip, thinking this through. Technically, they'd been living together. Without getting to know each other they'd fallen into a serious living arrangement and with their first fight hanging in the air, she realized she needed time as much as he needed time.

Whether he saw it or not, he was changing. His life was changing. What he wanted was changing.

And she might be getting her big break. A break that didn't mesh with the new things he wanted.

She didn't call Arnie. Instead, she gathered her things with an eye toward carrying them on the subway. She left behind the dresses and items he'd bought her. Not just because they wouldn't fit into the duffel bag she'd used, but because they weren't hers.

When all the clothes and cosmetics she'd brought were stuffed in the duffel, she touched the solitaire at her throat.

He'd given that to the woman he had fun with. Not the one who'd tried to get him to see that he might have taken his life down the wrong path.

She reached behind her to undo the clasp, slid it off and set it on the table in his walk-in closet. He liked fun Autumn. He didn't seem to like more serious Autumn or maybe he didn't like *anyone* questioning his life choices.

She couldn't say. They hadn't been together long enough for her to know that.

Rolling her duffel behind her, she headed for the main room and the elevator. They definitely needed some time apart. If he called her and they smoothed things over, the solitaire would be on the table in the closet.

If he didn't—

She refused to think about that.

Jack returned home from work, half expecting Autumn to be there. As he rode the private elevator, nerves skittered through him. He didn't want to have a fight, but he didn't want her in the penthouse. No one had the right to question his decisions about Step Inside. Someone who didn't know his mother had even less right to an opinion.

Plus, that morning at work, his world had seemed to right again. All those crazy feelings he'd had at breakfast had disappeared.

So what if his penthouse seemed cold and empty without Autumn? So what if he missed cooking for her, missed the eager expression on her face before she took her first bite of whatever he'd made her? Something about being alone felt right.

* * *

Friday morning his staff returned to work and even more order came to his world. Contracts arrived, resumes for new chefs were stacked on his desk, blueprints for the new restaurants to be built in Pennsylvania were delivered.

He dove in eagerly, but by eleven he'd looked at the details on the drawings so long his eyes crossed. Telling himself that was normal, he called the architects, and they came to his office to meet with him. As they spoke, it struck him that they were competent enough that he shouldn't be making decisions that they were more qualified to make.

Worse, after the architects were gone, he tried to read the five-year plan, but it bored him so much, he stuffed it in his briefcase to read over the weekend while watching a game.

An itchy feeling trembled along his nerve endings. He refused to try to identify it.


Autumn had had her interview with the board of directors for Raise Your Voice Friday afternoon, and as Jack had said, she aced it. She should have been happy. Instead, she kept getting weird thoughts about whether or not a CEO had enough time to raise children.

The very thought shocked her. Never in her life had she thought she'd want to have kids. She loved her nephews, but they hadn't made her long to have her own child until she'd seen Jack with those rambunctious little boys.

Thinking about Jack made her catch her breath. He'd arranged for her to leave Thursday and all of Friday had gone by without a word.

She'd noticed that they were both changing. He

wanted more out of life than to run his mom's company. He wanted a family and suddenly she wanted kids. Not to accommodate him but because it seemed right.

But he wouldn't talk about it. He hated when she mentioned his returning to research and development. What would he think if she brought up kids?

He'd probably explode as he had the morning after Christmas.

*Had she pushed him? Had she believed she'd seen something that wasn't there?*

She knew she hadn't. She knew what she'd seen. She'd been trying to help, but he didn't want help. So now she knew his boundaries. She wouldn't breach them again. She'd forget about having kids. Forget about Step Inside. Not second guess anything about his life.

Because he would call. He was a smart guy. They had a casual relationship. Eventually, his anger would cool, and he'd remember how much fun they'd had.

But when he didn't call Friday night, she knew this wasn't a blip in their relationship. Like five years ago, he'd simply walked away from her. Every time she glanced at her silent phone, every time she peered out the window, hoping to see his Mercedes pull in her driveway, she felt the awful ache of reality.

He'd left her once and never looked back.

He had done it again. He might have asked her to leave his apartment, but he'd done the asking and now he was ghosting her.

Saturday morning, she woke knowing she had to get her thoughts off Jack. Her comments at breakfast the day after Christmas hadn't been an accusation but were meant to be the start of a discussion. But that wasn't how he'd taken them, and she couldn't turn back the hands of time.

She forced her thoughts to her interview with the Raise Your Voice board. Not one person on the board had a problem with her until Quincy Fallen had asked about her relationship with Ivy. She'd kept her response brief, then shifted the conversation to her knowledge and experience with Raise Your Voice and most of the members had nodded with approval—

But what if Quincy was a holdout? Could one negative vote ruin her chances of being appointed CEO?

And what would it be like not to be able to tell Jack? To commiserate. To have him remind her there would be other opportunities?

She groaned. She'd circled back to Jack! Why did she want a guy who had no problem leaving her?

And why did it hurt so much that he'd simply told her to leave his apartment? No discussion. No chance for her to think it through and apologize—

Because that's how their last foray into a relationship had ended. With him simply deciding it was over. And never calling her again.

Angry with herself, she grabbed her jacket and mittens, as well as clothes for an overnight stay and called a ride share to take her to her parents' house.

When she finally arrived after lunch, she hoisted her duffel over her shoulder and headed for the front door. It opened before she could reach it and her mom frowned at her.

"What are you doing here?" She eyed the duffel. "Are you planning on doing laundry?"

"No. I thought I could watch a little basketball with Pop and maybe we could play a game tonight."

"Your dad's at Tony's with his friends. But he'll be

back in a few hours." Her mother took the duffel from her shoulder and guided her inside the foyer. "So if this isn't laundry, you must have brought clothes to stay overnight?"

She shrugged.

"You're not going out with Jack tonight?"

She peeked over at her mom. "No." She struggled with tears. She was tired. She was hurt. But more than that, she couldn't escape the feeling that she'd overstepped her boundaries and hurt *him*.

And that was what was really bothering her. She'd missed something. They'd had other discussions of his mother's death and vague discussions about his taking over Step Inside. Not enough for her to know his entire story, but enough that she should have known not to speak until she could do so intelligently.

But she'd pushed ahead.

Because she'd been so sure she was correct about Step Inside.

It hurt that she'd lost him. But she ached over the realization that she could have hurt him.

Avoiding her mom's eyes, she said, "Let's go make cookies or something."

Shaking her head, her mom walked to the kitchen. "Okay. Don't tell me. I'm happy to distract you with cookie making. You're also lucky that the oven is fixed. Your nephews will be here tomorrow afternoon. They like snickerdoodles and chocolate chip. We'll make both."

Relief rippled through her until watching her mom mix batter reminded her of watching Jack cook. She grabbed the recipe and began locating ingredients for her mom to add. That made her feel marginally better.

But when her dad came home, the cookies were cooling and the game was at halftime, the achy, horrible realization that she was alone rolled over her again. Not because she didn't have someone but because *she* hurt Jack.

She was going to have to go to his penthouse and apologize.

Of course, that didn't mean he'd take her back.

But at least she'd have the chance to admit she'd been wrong.

She sucked it up, retrieved her duffel from her old bedroom, called a car and said goodbye to her parents.

She didn't like the idea of carrying her duffel bag into his penthouse, then realized if things went well, it would be good to have clothes for tomorrow morning.

With a deep breath to encourage herself, she walked into the lobby.

Josh, the doorman, stopped her. "Miss Jones."

She smiled. "Yes... Oh, wait! I probably don't have today's elevator code."

He chuckled. "You're also out of dress code."

"Excuse me?"

"It's a party, remember?"

It took a second for that to sink in. When it did, she swore her heart exploded. While she'd been upset for days, worried that she'd overstepped her boundaries and hurt his feelings, he'd been planning a party?

She forced herself to smile at Josh. "You know what? I forgot." She took two steps backward, toward the lobby door. "And I'm not going up in jeans."

Josh laughed. "There's some pretty fancy dresses in that penthouse right now."

She smiled again, but she had to grit her teeth to keep it in place. "I'll bet."

She turned and raced out into the frigid night. The

cloudless sky was inky black. The marshmallow snow had become dirty gray from days of pedestrians walking on it. She picked up her pace and told herself to call a ride share but the humiliation cut too deep.

When would she learn that Jack Adams wasn't ever going to love her?

And why did a realization that should have been common sense hurt so much?

Jack woke the next morning to silence so thick and so total it reminded him of the day after his mother's funeral. He'd lived alone, but he'd stayed in his mother's penthouse that night, simply to make things easier.

But he'd woken to the reality that he was alone. Truly alone. He'd woken to the realization that his selfish desire to spend the night with Autumn might have caused her death. Her cardiologist had told him that her condition had been severe and that his getting her to the hospital sooner *might* have saved her...but his professional opinion was that a few extra minutes probably wouldn't have made a difference.

So he'd woken in her penthouse, knowing she was gone, knowing he was in charge and so tired he wasn't sure he could think.

Today, he didn't have that problem. The party the night before had been filled with executives who were happy to give him their opinions. He had a million possibilities floating around in his head about how to expand Step Inside, and no desire to work toward fulfilling any one of them.

He rolled out of bed, strolling to the kitchen in a navy-blue silk robe that cost more than his mother had made in a year when she was raising him on a waitress's salary.

He made a cup of coffee, and read the *Times*, which had been brought to his penthouse by whoever was manning the lobby desk. He didn't think about Autumn; just as he had after his mom died, he'd blocked her from his thoughts.

But his heart hurt, and his head about exploded from the waterfall of good ideas that had been presented to him the night before…and behind all that was guilt.

Not that his mom had died but that he was living her dream and he didn't appreciate it.

He ran his hands down his face, showered and dressed in jeans, a leather jacket and sunglasses. Without clouds, the sun was a ruthless ball in the sky that didn't provide warmth this frigid Sunday. It only glared down at him.

Arnie awaited at the curb. Holding the back door of the limo, he said, "Good morning, sir."

"No *sir*," Jack growled. "Just Jack…remember?"

"Yes, sir… I mean, Jack."

Jack slid inside. Arnie closed the door. When he was behind the steering wheel, he said, "Where to?"

"New Jersey… The mausoleum."

Arnie caught his gaze in the rearview mirror. He'd been Jack's driver for years. He knew exactly what Jack was talking about. "Okay."

Jack stared out the window as they drove to his mother's resting place. Almost an hour later, they pulled onto the winding road. Trees typically thick with green leaves stood bare and empty.

When they reached the building, Arnie stopped. Jack got out without a word.

He walked into the silent space. Beautifully appointed with murals in the domed ceiling and gold trim, the echoing room spoke of peace and tranquility.

He ambled to the bench closest to his mom's space and sat.

"I haven't been here in a while." The quiet of the room greeted him. No reply. Not even his own imaginings of what his mother might say.

He sat in the silence. Sorrow for her loss and faded memories filled the air. But he couldn't hold them. They all withered away.

Into nothing.

Alone in the cold bleak room, he wondered what he was doing there. There were no answers in the mural. There were no answers in the silence of the room.

He lifted himself from the bench, walked over and touched the gold-plated square that held his mom's name.

He longed for her to be in his life, but he didn't cry. She'd been gone five years. He missed her laugh. He missed her crazy sense of humor. He missed her smart-as-a-whip way of running Step Inside.

But she wasn't here and nothing about the past could be changed—

And life had gone on.

Arnie drove him home and Jack handed him the tickets for the next Knicks game to thank him for working on a Sunday.

Arnie beamed. "Jack! Thank you. You don't have to do this..." He laughed. "You do pay me."

Jack shook his head and walked toward the lobby doors. "Take your son."

As the word *son* spilled out of his mouth, his chest tightened. He always thought of himself as a *son*. But the way the word rippled through him was different this time.

He waved at the doorman as he ambled to the elevator, then rode it up to the penthouse.

The place was as sterile and empty as he remembered. He walked through to the bedroom, into the closet where he hung his jacket, took off his sweater and exchanged it for a T-shirt.

Turning to go, he saw a wink of light and stopped. Sitting on the counter of the closet table was the necklace he'd given to Autumn.

If he closed his eyes, he could feel the soft skin his fingers had grazed as they fastened it around her neck. He could see the look of surprise on her face. He could her the whisper in her voice when she thanked him. He could feel her kiss.

His heart stumbled.

He lowered himself to the bench beside the table.

His mother was gone.

The life she wanted was over.

He'd fulfilled her dream.

But *his* dream had frozen in time.

And Autumn had seen that.

He hadn't gotten mad at her because what she'd suggested was absurd. He'd gotten angry because it wasn't. The time had come for him to move on and he didn't want to see it.

He should have seen it. Having Autumn walk into his life again, bring him joy, should have been a clear sign. The way she'd filled the empty spaces in his soul felt like he'd been waiting for her.

But he was too busy trying to have the future *and* the past—too busy working at something that was wrong for him—to see he'd been waiting for Autumn to somehow come back into his life. She hadn't been Cinderella waiting for the Prince to find her again. He'd been the Prince, working through his grief, straightening out his life. So that when she came back into his life, he'd been ready for her.

The love of his life.

*The love of his life...*

Oh, God. She was the love of his life. The rest of his life. But having dumped her again, he'd blown their second chance.

She'd be crazy to even answer a phone call from him, let alone love him.

# CHAPTER SEVENTEEN

AUTUMN HAD SPENT the Saturday night and most of Sunday crying. She couldn't believe it was possible to fall in love in four weeks, but she had. And losing Jack this time was worse than waking up to find him gone after a one-night stand.

After four weeks together she knew he was wonderful, kind, smart and imaginative. They were meant to be together.

But how could they ever be together? How could Fate possibly believe they were meant to be together when they kept screwing things up?

First, he ghosted her.

Now she'd hurt him.

And he wouldn't talk about it. Everything wrapped up in his past seemed to be off limits.

They were doomed. And she decided it was time she accept that.

Jack Adams might not want her, but someone would.

She was a catch.

She might not have seen that before he'd waltzed back into her life, but she did now. Not just because she had a shot at becoming a CEO—and even if she didn't get it, there were other charities in New York City that could use her expertise—but because she finally realized she wanted a family.

She strode into work on Monday morning so confident she could have fought a tiger. She hung her coat on a hook and tossed her purse into her old metal desk, knowing that if Raise Your Voice didn't want her, she was ready to job hunt.

She would forget about Jack—eventually. She simply had to plow through a few weeks of a broken heart, knowing she'd caused it herself.

But Monday went by without Gerry making an announcement about the new CEO. Still, she calmed herself with the reminder that they had one more day, December thirty-first, to make their decision.

Tuesday, she dressed for work in a somber mood. If they didn't offer her the job that day, she'd be reading the name of the new Raise Your Voice CEO in Thursday's *Times*.

So she walked into the office with her head high, reminding herself there were other charities who needed CEOs. She might not get the job as the CEO for Raise Your Voice, but she would begin her quest for a CEO position somewhere. And she would someday be running a charity.

"Can I see you for a minute?"

Autumn glanced up to see Gerry standing in her doorway. She rose from her seat. "Sure."

He led her down the hall to his office and closed the door behind her. Her heart stopped. He was so somber he could be about to tell her that she didn't get the job.

Motioning for her to take a seat, he walked to his desk chair. "As you've probably guessed, we've made a decision about the CEO position."

Her breath stuttered. This was it. She got the job, or she moved on. It almost didn't matter either way. She'd lost Jack but she planned on getting back out into the dating pool and looking for someone who would really love her. She could lose this position. She would apply for other jobs.

She had found herself as a woman and a worker. She would not lose that.

Gerry said, "Congratulations! You've got the job."

Her mouth fell open. Here she was, ready to start making copies of her new resume, expecting the worst. Getting good news shocked her.

"I'm…"

"Speechless." Gerry laughed. "We would like to announce on January second, so that gives you about twenty-four hours before we need your answer."

She burst out laughing, even as her heart tweaked with longing to call Jack and tell him she'd gotten the job. Maybe to thank him for his help. Probably because she still loved him. He was a great guy. And she wasn't entirely sure how she'd gotten everything wrong, but she had and she had no one to blame but herself for losing him.

Knowing that didn't help. It only made her heart ache. But she pulled herself together and forced herself into the moment.

She might have lost the man she loved, but she'd gained the job she'd been working for forever. She had to get her head back in the game.

Gerry handed a folder across the desk. "This is the full benefit package and the formal written offer." He rose. "I hope you'll accept."

She stood. "You know what? I don't need twenty-four or thirty-six hours. I've wanted this job forever." She reached across the desk to shake his hand. "I'm your new CEO."

"Congratulations!"

She took a breath. "Thanks." But despite her bravado, her chest hollowed out. She was getting what she'd worked for since the day she walked into the Raise Your Voice offices. But she wasn't getting what she wanted.

The only reason she wanted to be a mom was because she wanted Jack's kids. She wanted to raise kids with Jack. To instill in them his sense of humor and drive. And hope they got a thing or two from her too.

Getting the job didn't exactly feel meaningless, but she now knew there was more to life than work, and she wasn't sure what to do about that.

She turned to go but Gerry stopped her. "Oh, I almost forgot." He reached into a desk drawer and handed her two tickets.

"Those are tickets for Audrey Brewbaker's annual New Year's Eve party tonight. I'm not CEO anymore." He smiled. "You are. Because we're not announcing until January second, you can't actually talk Raise Your Voice business. But you can go, look around, figure out who you need to schmooze. You never know when you'll have to replace a board member or need a benefactor to fund a special project."

He laughed and she smiled, looking at the tickets as if they were foreign things. But she'd longed for this challenge, and she was up to it. She simply might need the whole day not just the afternoon to get ready for her first party as newly appointed CEO.

She walked out of Gerry's office, directly into hers, grabbed her purse and coat and headed home, refusing to let herself think about the fact that she'd gotten what she'd always wanted but she wasn't complete. There was a hole in her heart.

Still, she would fix it. Without Jack. He'd rejected her twice. She got the message.

# CHAPTER EIGHTEEN

JACK WALKED INTO the ballroom for Audrey Brewbaker's annual New Year's Eve party, not feeling very much like schmoozing or dancing or even eating dinner. But he'd RSVP'd for two, when he believed he would be taking Autumn. He couldn't back out completely. He would say hello to the hosts, eat dinner and then race home.

After greeting Audrey and her daughter Marlene in the reception line, he walked farther into the ballroom and saw a swatch of red. The same color as the gown Autumn had worn to the Montgomerys' Christmas party.

*She was here?*

Telling himself he was crazy, he edged over to the bar, but he saw the red again and *knew* it was the same gown.

His heart did a flip. But as the bartender poured him a bourbon, he reminded himself that her being here was a long shot. She needed a ticket to get in.

Still, when he turned from the bartender, his bourbon in hand, he couldn't stop himself from scouting for the red again. He found it and saw her, and his stomach fell to the floor, but his brain clicked in. If he genuinely believed Fate had brought her back into his life because he'd been waiting for her and was finally ready, then he had to have the guts to face her.

He worked his way through the crowd that milled around the linen-covered tables and after ten minutes of following her from one group of people to the next, he finally caught up to her.

"Hey."

Obviously recognizing his voice, she turned. "Hey."

"I'd really like five minutes to talk to you."

She smiled...that same smile that she'd given him at Ivy and Sebastian's the night they'd all had dinner together. The fake one.

"That would be fun," she said, not meaning a word of it. "But I'm not really here as a guest." She winced. "Well, I am a guest. But I'm also CEO of Raise Your Voice."

She'd gotten the job! "That's great!"

"Yes. And I know I owe it to you. But I'm also here to make connections." She stepped to the right. "If you'll excuse me."

And just like that, she was gone.

He started after her, but she really was talking with people Jack knew were benefactors for charities. Good business sense kept him from interrupting her or joining her groups, making her nervous on what was—technically—the first day of her new job.

Dinner was served and he tried to find Autumn but couldn't. Audrey Brewbaker's New Year's Eve party was the party of the year in Manhattan. There had to be four hundred people in attendance and lots of women wore red gowns.

After Audrey's thank-you-for-attending comments and wishes for everyone to have a wonderful New Year, the band began to play.

As people ambled onto the dance floor, the crowd thinned, and Jack spotted Autumn. He was not leaving without apologizing or better yet, explaining.

He'd run out on her the first time. Though he had a good excuse, he would not run out on her a second time. He would explain. He would apologize.

He eased through the tables toward hers. Four steps before he reached her, she rose and headed to the right.

Close enough to reach her, he caught her wrist and stopped her. She turned and looked at him.

Everything inside him melted with need. He could see their future. But he didn't deserve it and even if he did he had no idea how to tell her that. He released her wrist but couldn't resist the urge for one final dance.

"Dance with me."

"I don't know—"

"Please. I need to apologize."

The surprised expression on her face confused him. She glanced left then right, then caught his gaze. "I thought I needed to apologize. I was hoping, though, to see you in a more private place."

"No one even cares we're here." He waited a second then said, "Dance with me."

This time when she smiled at him, he saw the real Autumn. He held out his hand and she took it. They reached the dance floor as one song ended, and another began.

"A waltz."

She shook her head. "Looks like the heavens are smiling down on you."

He laughed. "Yeah. I literally get to put my best foot forward."

He took her into his arms and glided them out onto the dance floor. Autumn's heart lurched. Nothing had ever felt so right as dancing with him. She'd never had the feelings for another man that she had for him. To be this close physically and so far away emotionally was a pleasure-pain too intense to describe.

"I just…" He paused. "I need to tell you that I'm sorry. What I was going through on Christmas Day was nothing like either one of us thought. I thought I was feeling guilty that I had forgotten my mom. But the truth is I think Fate was trying to tell me it was time to move on."

She pulled back so she could see his eyes. She hated that he had gone through that. Hated even more that she'd made it worse. "And I'm sorry I said those things about your mom's real plan."

"No. You might have been right." He swung them around the dance floor in a flawless waltz. "It's been five years. I did everything my mom had planned, but I'd gotten bored with it. Cooking for you nudged me to remember how much I loved it."

Surprised, she said only, "Oh."

"And that's not all I want to say to you… What made me realize I needed to move on was how much I missed you."

Their gazes caught and clung. "I missed you too."

"The night we met, I knew I'd found the person I wanted to spend the rest of my life with."

Her heart stuttered.

"Then everything went wrong, and I almost forgot you."

"I thought you had forgotten me."

"I sort of had until I saw you at Ivy and Sebastian's. You came out the door when I was waiting by Sebastian's limo and I couldn't believe it."

Not sure what to say, she only held his gaze.

"I'd hardly thought of you in five years and suddenly there you were. I realized today that Fate hadn't brought you back into my life until I was ready for you…ready to move on. And in the five years we were apart, I chose the three worst women to have a relationship with because I think deep down I knew I was waiting for you."

She blinked up at him. "I'm not sure if that's the craziest thing I've ever heard or the most romantic."

"Make it the most romantic thing you've ever heard because I really believe we're a match. I've never felt about anyone what I feel about you. I don't want to."

Her heart swelled at the romance of it, but she had to be sure they were on the same page. "Now it's my turn. I realized on Christmas Day that I didn't just want to be the CEO for Raise Your Voice. I want to have kids. *Your* kids. I want the whole thing. I don't want to be the second half of the power couple you envisioned. I want more. I want it all. I want the fairytale."

He whirled her around. "Really?"

"Think that through because you will not get a chance to leave me a third time. There will be no charm in your life if you ghost me again."

"How many kids are you thinking?"

The interest in his voice gave her enough courage to say, "How many kids are you thinking…"

He considered that. "One of each I guess."

"Seriously? You saw how much fun Mark and Donnie have. You need two of each so they can be friends."

He laughed. "We do have enough money that we could hire help."

"A nanny? My mother would shoot me if we shut her out."

"Looks like we're going to need a bigger penthouse."

"Or a house in Hunter."

He frowned. "Near your parents?"

"Why not?"

He looked at her for a few seconds, then smiled. "Why not?"

The music stopped but instead of pulling away, they stepped closer and kissed.

Dancers walked by them, couples exiting or entering the floor.

They kept kissing.

When the music began again, he pulled away and they headed for the coatroom. She texted Arnie as he found their coats.

A half hour later, they were kissing their way to the bedroom. When they reached it, he stopped. "Hold on a second."

She frowned. "What?"

He held up one finger. "Just give me a second."

She shook her head, but he returned quickly. "Turn around."

Confused, she only stared at him.

He held up her necklace. "You must have forgotten this the day after Christmas."

She smirked. "Must have."

He laughed, fastened the necklace around her neck and gave her a little nudge that tumbled her to the bed.

"I love you."

She froze. Her eyes filled with tears. "I don't think we've ever said that."

"Well, now that we have, let's not stop."

She smiled. "I love you, too."

# EPILOGUE

THEY WERE MARRIED on Valentine's Day two years later. Believing Ivy and Sebastian had brought them back together, they asked Ivy to be maid of honor and Sebastian to be best man.

They held the wedding in the same venue Sebastian and Ivy had, Parker and Parker. The castle-like building stood tall in the thick February snow, as Autumn raced inside, Ivy holding her long lace train. Her entire dress was lace and her headpiece a tiara that sparkled in her reddish-brown hair.

In the bride's room, her mother fussed, but her dad grinned. He loved the new addition to their family. Not just because Jack had Knicks season tickets but because he was a great guy. They waited in the quiet room with four full-length mirrors and ornate French Provincial furniture until the wedding planner opened the door and announced it was time for Autumn's mom to be seated and for Autumn to position herself to walk up the aisle.

Her parents scurried out, along with the wedding planner and suddenly Ivy and Autumn were alone.

Ivy's eyes pooled with tears. "I'm so happy for you."

"I'm so happy for me too. You don't know how close we came to losing each other twice."

"I've heard the story about the night you met." Ivy winced. "Jack told Sebastian."

"He thinks we're destined to be together."

Ivy straightened the veil beneath the glittering tiara. "I agree."

"Then let's go get me married."

They left the bride's room and headed to the chapel area. Autumn's dad, looking dapper in his black tux, walked her down the aisle.

When it came time to say their vows, Jack took her hands and smiled at her. "Autumn Jones," he said, beginning the vows he had written for the ceremony. "I think Fate saved you for me and I'm grateful. You're smart and funny and you love my cooking. But I think our adventure is just beginning."

Staring into his blue eyes, she whispered, "I do too."

The minister laughed. "Was that your vows?"

She blushed. "No." She swallowed then said, "Jack Adams, you're the strongest, smartest person I know. And I love you in a way I didn't know existed before I met you. We're going to have the best kids ever and the most fun showing them the world."

He nodded slightly, then leaned in and kissed her cheek.

The minister sighed. "It's not time for a kiss."

"I didn't kiss her lips."

A chuckle ran through the crowd.

The minister shook his head. "May I have the rings?"

Ivy and Sebastian stepped forward and the ceremony proceeded normally from there. They ate a rich, delicious supper prepared by Step Inside chefs and then danced the night away.

With their family.

And their friends.

So many wonderful people now populated his life.

Jack took it all in and every once in a while glanced heavenward, knowing his mother would approve.

Especially since he'd resigned as CEO of Step Inside and now devoted himself to creating new dishes and new menus.

Autumn had been right. As soon as he shifted back to the job he loved and settled in with the woman he adored, his life had blossomed.

He didn't think he could be happier...but Autumn's dad had told him to wait till the first time he held his newborn baby. That moment would steal his heart.

He was looking forward to it.

\* \* \* \* \*

# COMING SOON!

We really hope you enjoyed reading this book.
If you're looking for more romance
be sure to head to the shops when
new books are available on

## Thursday 19th December

MILLS & BOON

LET'S TALK

# Romance

For exclusive extracts, competitions
and special offers, find us online:

 MillsandBoon

 @MillsandBoon

 @MillsandBoonUK

 @MillsandBoonUK

Get in touch on 01413 063 232

# MILLS & BOON

## MODERN

# Power and Passion

Prepare to be swept off your feet by sophisticated, sexy and seductive heroes, in some of the world's most glamorous and romantic locations, where power and passion collide.

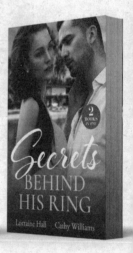

Eight Modern stories published every month, find them all at:

**millsandboon.co.uk**

# MILLS & BOON

## HEROES

*At Your Service*

Experience all the excitement of a
gripping thriller, with an intense romance
at its heart. Resourceful, true-to-life
women and strong, fearless men face
danger and desire – a killer combination!

Eight Heroes stories published every month, find them all at:

**millsandboon.co.uk**

# MILLS & BOON

## MEDICAL

### *Pulse-Racing Passion*

Set your pulse racing with dedicated, delectable doctors in the high-pressure world of medicine, where emotions run high and passion, comfort and love are the best medicine.

# MILLS & BOON

## THE HEART OF ROMANCE

---

## A ROMANCE FOR EVERY READER

---

### MODERN

Prepare to be swept off your feet by sophisticated, sexy and seductive heroes, in some of the world's most glamourous and romantic locations, where power and passion collide.

### HISTORICAL

Escape with historical heroes from time gone by. Whether your passion is for wicked Regency Rakes, muscled Vikings or rugged Highlanders, awaken the romance of the past.

### MEDICAL

Set your pulse racing with dedicated, delectable doctors in the high-pressure world of medicine, where emotions run high and passion, comfort and love are the best medicine.

### *True Love*

Celebrate true love with tender stories of heartfelt romance, from the rush of falling in love to the joy a new baby can bring, and a focus on the emotional heart of a relationship.

### HEROES

The excitement of a gripping thriller, with intense romance at its heart. Resourceful, true-to-life women and strong, fearless men face danger and desire - a killer combination!

From showing up to glowing up, these characters are on the path to leading their best lives and finding romance along the way – with plenty of sizzling spice!

To see which titles are coming soon, please visit

**millsandboon.co.uk/nextmonth**